SAM TIME

History Professor Slips into the Past
and Befriends Ulysses S. Grant

A Novel

Donna Balon

Copyright © 2023 by Donna Balon

All rights reserved. This book or any portion thereof may not be reproduced or used in any manner whatsoever without the express written permission of the publisher except for the use of brief quotations in a book review.

Printed in the United States of America

First Printing, 2023

ISBN: 979-8-9886199-0-1 (Ebook)
ISBN: 979-8-9886199-1-8 (Audio)
ISBN: 979-8-9886199-2-5 (Kindle)
ISBN: 979-8-9886199-3-2 (Paperback)

Publisher
Desert Day Press LLC
Las Vegas, NV

www.SamTimeBook.com

Preface

Although *Sam Time* is a fictional novel, readers are enriched with historical details that have been researched in nonfictional works. This time-travel story follows the life of Ulysses S. Grant; the dates, places, and events closely align with his real life. The fictional scenes and dialogue are interpretive, and many are based on similar anecdotes occurring during Grant's life.

For the centennial chapter, the historic details of the festivities in Fairmount Park, Philadelphia, were obtained from the book *1876 A Centennial Exhibition* (Smithsonian Institution, 1976), Robert C. Post, editor.

The book cover includes a colorized-enhanced image of Major General Ulysses S. Grant (circa 1863, age forty-one). The photographer is Theodore Lilienthal of New Orleans, LA. The Filson Historical Society, Louisville, KY, provided the original image.

Beginnings with Aaron

The newlyweds-to-be were matchmaking. Having confidence their own union was imminent, the bride and the groom, Grace and John, arranged for the maid of honor, Samantha, and the best man, Aaron, to meet. Grace had long hoped her younger sister, Samantha, would partner with John's best friend, Aaron. Now, two weeks before the wedding, the four agreed to spend a day together.

The meeting place was Grounds for Sculpture, fifteen minutes south of Princeton in New Jersey. Their early-morning reservation time would allow them to spend much of the day on the enormous outdoor grounds.

They met in the parking lot on a partly sunny, warm day. The sisters had obviously conferred with each other on what to wear. They both wore comfortable jersey dresses just below the knee with slip-on shoes, and each carried a small crossover handbag. Grace wore a blue round-neck, A-line, short-sleeve dress. Samantha wore a three-quarter-length-sleeve faux-wrap dress in a multicolor flower print. Although not intentionally coordinated, John and

Aaron both wore jeans; small-checked, button-down long-sleeve shirts (untucked); and sneakers.

Samantha greeted her sister with a hug; John and Aaron shook hands.

Grace said, "Aaron, this is my sister, Samantha."

Samantha was slim, five five, with wide hazel eyes and well-proportioned feminine facial features. Her cinnamon-brown wavy hair fell to the middle of her back.

Aaron said, "A pleasure to meet you at last."

"Likewise," Samantha replied.

She had googled Aaron Parker's LinkedIn profile and had seen photos Grace had taken of him. He stood five nine, a runner's build, dark brown hair, deep blue eyes—good-looking.

Grace shared a familial resemblance with her sister, including similar height and size, although Grace had shoulder-length dark brunette hair. Her fiancé, John, was a handsome Black-White biracial man, six feet with the broad shoulders of a former collegiate swimmer.

John said, "Okay, we have reservations at one o'clock for lunch. I'll text you twenty minutes before to give you enough time to get there. It's easy to get lost here."

"Okay," Aaron said, viewing the map placard with Samantha.

"Have you ever been here?" Samantha asked.

"No, first time. And you?" Aaron asked.

"First time for me too."

They studied the map for several minutes.

"So, it shows we are here," Samantha said, pointing at the red dot on the map.

"We should start this way." Aaron motioned with his hand to the right.

Sam Time

Samantha looked around. "Where are Grace and John?"

"I don't see them either," Aaron answered.

"My own sister has left me with a stranger."

Aaron laughed.

"They're trying too hard," Samantha said. "I guess we're just stuck with each other for a few hours."

"Doesn't seem like a bad thing."

"Aren't *you* a charmer?"

They walked side by side down a path into the park.

"We do come prescreened by Grace and John," Samantha said.

"Yes, ever since after John finished law school and met Grace, I've been hearing about you," Aaron said.

"And they told us about our love lives or lack thereof."

"Well, what's your version?" Aaron asked.

Samantha put one hand on her forehead. "Let's not go there. I would prefer not to talk about my failed relationships. I tried the dating apps. I know many people who found their mates that way. The apps don't work—for me."

"I guess Grace told you about me and my past girlfriends," Aaron said.

"I know that, like John, you're from Southern California, 'SoCal.' And with girlfriends, you're Mister In-N-Out Burger."

Aaron laughed. "Wow. I can't believe you said that!"

"Listen, you give me an opening for a layup, I'm going to take it. No one is spared."

They walked and there was a long pause in the conversation.

"Okay, I'll start over. Hello, I'm Samantha Hunter. Call me Sam. Grace and I are Jersey girls. Grew up in Atlantic Highlands. Like Grace, I went to Rutgers in New Brunswick. I studied history then got my master's. I teach at the university, part-time history professor. It's really hard to get full-time. You need a doctorate, so I'll probably do that when it's economical.

"You're an accountant; I'm sure Grace has told you I am debt-free. Student loans were paid off through a work-study program.

"Grace and I shared an apartment, and we bought furniture and small appliances together. When she moved in with John, I told her to take everything. Now I'm a boarder. One of my sorority sisters, Deanna, has a house—it was her parents'—in Atlantic Highlands. I'm helping her pay the bills. And I'm saving, hopefully for a deposit on a house someday. So debt-free and savings account in my plus column.

"Your turn," Samantha said playfully. "Give me your best elevator pitch."

"Went to Penn, where I met John. We were roommates. He came from SoCal too, so that was a nice connection. I graduated with a degree in economics. Passed the CPA exam. Work at a CPA firm in Philly. But you knew all that."

"Yes I did. But I wanted to hear you say it. And we're both runners. I do five miles every other day. Then I lift weights on off days. Do crunches."

"Same here, at least five, sometimes eight miles, a few times a week. Exercises too."

They walked to another park area and Samantha said, "I thought those sculptures were real people."

"Yes. They're so lifelike. Amazing."

They leisurely wandered the grounds. Samantha spotted a porch swing, hung by a tree branch, and sat down. Her phone made a ding sound. "Grace sent me a text." She read it out loud: *"How's it going?"*

She looked up at Aaron. "It's only been an hour."

"John sent me the same text."

"Come sit down," she said.

Aaron sat comfortably distant from Samantha.

"Let's mess with them," Samantha suggested while lifting herself a little closer to Aaron.

Aaron looked at her incredulously.

"I'll send a text to Grace saying I somehow lost you, and I haven't seen you for twenty minutes." Samantha began typing the text and laughing. "Come closer to see."

Aaron moved toward Samantha in the center of the swing.

She said, "Okay, now you send a text to John saying the same. No. Don't say twenty minutes. It sounds too contrived. Say fifteen minutes. Come on, it's just a little fun. If we're caught, we may have to pay for everyone's lunch."

Aaron was shaking his head, but he sent the text to John anyway.

Samantha looked at her phone, "Grace sent me another text. She gave me your phone number. That's good."

Aaron said, "John sent me your phone number. Now what?"

"I'm not sure. I didn't think this all the way through."

Aaron said, "John sent another text: *Are you guys messing with us? This sounds like Sam. And her little tricks. Come clean or you're paying for lunch.*"

They both laughed.

"John is such a law-and-order guy," Samantha said. "Okay, let's take a selfie. Come in."

Aaron leaned close to her for the picture, and she snapped a photo.

"I like it. See?" She said, showing Aaron the photo.

She typed the text while saying, "Now, sending photo with message: *Busted!*"

After putting her phone in her handbag, she said, "Now we won't hear from them until lunchtime. Wasn't that fun? Grace says this park has areas that replicate impressionist paintings. There's even a Monet lily pond. We should find it."

Aaron said, "Grace never told me about your spunk."

"Spunky. That's a good description of me. But I'm also serious. Serious about my work. My studies."

"What was your master's in?"

"Well, my bachelor's degree was in history. For that, I took courses in everything—world history. Subsequent degrees, you need more focus. My master's was in U.S. history. It's a natural choice. To be a full professor, I need a doctorate. I'm leaning toward the Civil War period and Reconstruction. Sorry. Am I boring you?"

"No. Not at all. What do you like about history?"

"It gives perspective. Popular sentiment is that it's not relevant. Of course I disagree. When I teach, I try in every lecture to relate the history we're discussing with the present. Compare and contrast.

"Oh, look at that sculpture on the hill. It's Monet's woman holding a parasol."

"Looks so real."

Samantha asked, "Do you have hobbies?"

"I run and read the news. I do collect coins."

"Coins. Both art and history. Interesting."

"I like the U.S. precious metal coins. Liberty quarters. Half dollars. Silver dollars."

Samantha said, "My father has a collection. Passed down through a few generations. I never thought about it, but I should ask him about the collection. Maybe it could be a muse for my doctoral dissertation. You've given me an idea."

"Glad to help."

"This bamboo pathway is beautiful. Would you take my picture?" Samantha handed Aaron her cellphone.

He snapped a few shots. "I want to take one with my cellphone."

"Oh." Samantha smiled and posed.

Someone walked by and said, "Do you want me to take the two of you?"

Samantha turned to Aaron for affirmation. "Okay. Here, take my phone and press the white dot."

Aaron moved next to Samantha. But he didn't put his arm around her. She was also unsure of any touching. So they stiffly stood shoulder to shoulder.

"Thank you." Samantha took her cellphone back. "Good shots. See? Do you want one?"

"Yes. Send it to me."

"Okay, you should have it." Samantha was looking down at her phone, then glanced up, and Aaron was staring at her.

Aaron's phone made a ding sound. "Yes, got it."

After a few hours walking the grounds, they met Grace and John for lunch. Samantha motioned for Grace to sit next to her and whispered, "Tell me if I get anything in my teeth."

The waiter handed them the menus and Samantha said, "Aaron, are you going to have a burger?"

Shaking his head, he replied, "I guess not if I want you to stop with that joke."

Grace smiled at John and raised her eyebrows as if to say, "It's looking good."

They ordered their entrées, and Samantha took pleasure in watching her date with his best friend. Aaron was relaxed with John; together they were witty and entertaining.

After the meal, John said he needed to return home early to do some legal work. Aaron had come with Grace and John; now they were going to drive home early.

Samantha said, "John, you're such bad liar. Your ruse is so obvious." She shook her head, then took advantage of the lull in conversation to compose a limerick:

> *A man named John practiced law,*
> *So smart people were in awe,*
> *So honest was he,*
> *So good to a tee,*
> *His wont to lie his one flaw.*

They all laughed.

She turned to Aaron. "This is their plan. Make up an excuse that John has to work, so you and I will stay here longer. And then, I'll drive you to the station so you can catch a train back to Philly."

Aaron said, "Sounds like a good plan to me."

AFTER LUNCH Samantha and Aaron lingered on the Monet bridge and meandered the sculpture grounds. Then Samantha drove Aaron to the train station.

"I'll wait with you," Samantha said and parked the car.

"You don't have to."

"I want to."

Walking from the car to the platform, Samantha said, "My

parents remember the days when you could go into Newark Airport and go to the gate without a ticket to see someone board a flight."

They laughed.

"And you could wave to them when they climbed the stairs to the plane—then watch the plane take off."

They climbed the stairs to the platform. "We can still do that with trains," she said.

They reached the platform, and Samantha sat down on a bench. She crossed her legs, sat straight with her hands on her lap. The flare of the dress skirt fell nicely. Aaron sat next to her.

"So watching someone take a train can be a moment, sentimental." She thought, Romantic. She glanced at Aaron then looked straight ahead. "Do you think Grace and John are right? It's probably an unfair question after one day together. Do you think we could be like them?"

"I'd like to see you again."

"I'd like that."

"Next Saturday?"

"Sure."

"Why don't you come to Philly? We can walk around. Have lunch. There's plenty to do."

"I like to do plenty," Samantha joked and Aaron smiled.

"They did plan a wonderful day. The Grounds for Sculpture was a green canvas, a perfect way to meet someone for the first time," Samantha said.

"I had a good time. The day went by quickly."

A train appeared in the distance.

"That's my train."

They stood as the train pulled into the station.

"You can call me during the week. Evening is good for me," Samantha said.

"Sure. To talk about particulars for Saturday."

Their introduction was unremarkable, and Samantha wanted their parting to end well. She said, "There's a custom here on the Princeton platform that kissing brings safe travel. No other touching required. Only kissing. The longer, the safer."

Aaron grinned at her playful instruction.

They moved closer and kissed on the lips, several sensual kisses. Then they locked eyes but said nothing. Aaron stepped away and boarded the train. Samantha watched the train pull out of the station until it disappeared from view. After the train left, she made the lonely walk to her car and the even lonelier drive home.

AARON CALLED during the week and they made plans for Saturday. Samantha would arrive by train at noon. The return trains back were not as frequent, and Samantha didn't know how long she would stay. Aaron blurted, "Listen, you can stay at my place, if you don't want to travel back at night."

"Oh." Samantha was taken aback. "Thank you for the offer. It may be too soon. You seem really nice. It's just all the guys before you. Usually, things like that haven't gone well. I'd like to wait and get better acquainted."

"I understand."

She tried to lighten the conversation. "I'm really looking forward to it. Last Saturday was great. I'll go for great again. And you don't have to plan a whole itinerary. I've been to Philly many times. I've seen the bell, Independence Hall. I'm coming to be with you."

"Sounds good. See you at noon on Saturday."

Sam Time

Saturday at noon Aaron called Samantha's cellphone. She said, "Hi, the train is pulling into the station now."

"I'm standing by this statute the *Angel of the Resurrection*. It's at the entrance. You can't miss it."

"I have another idea. I'll text you."

She texted: *See you in the north waiting room off the main concourse. The west wall by The Spirit of Transportation. Got it?*

Aaron texted: *Got it.*

When Samantha arrived at the spot, Aaron was already there. They were both wearing jeans. Samantha wore an olive-green long-sleeve V-neck top, a black blazer with a light blue scarf, and black flat lace-up shoes. Aaron wore a burgundy crewneck sweater over a T-shirt and black sneakers.

She said, "It's amazing. Isn't it?"

"Have you ever seen it?"

"No. But I googled the station and found this."

The bas-relief consumed the wall, thirty feet long, with carvings of raised figures in a rectangle picture-like frame.

Samantha illustrated, "An immigrant to America, Karl Bitter, created this piece and completed it in 1895. From left to right you can see the evolution of transportation. On the far right, a figurine is holding an airship, portending air travel. Impressive."

"I never knew it was here."

"That's what I thought. Most people coming here would probably say that. It's lost history."

She stared, admiring the work of art, and then she turned to Aaron. "Good to see you."

"Same here. Lunch?"

"Yes, and this can be your choice. I won't interfere."

They laughed.

Samantha had been excited and nervous about the day. But after a few minutes, she was comfortable and sensed Aaron felt the same. Conversation flowed easily.

At lunch, they sat across from each other, getting another good look. She kept her long bangs out of her face with her apt French braiding from her side part to the opposite ear, where she pinned and tucked the braid end behind her ear. The rest of her wavy hair fell naturally.

They talked more than they ate. After a leisurely lunch, Aaron said, "What to do next? I thought maybe we'd go to the Philadelphia Museum. Walk up the steps shown in the *Rocky* movie."

Samantha smiled, assuming Aaron had done this before: meet a woman at the train station's angel statue, then go the *Rocky* steps. "Maybe another time, when we're in our running clothes, we could do the *Rocky* steps. But I have another idea."

"Why am I not surprised?"

"Are you up for something different?"

"I'm game."

Samantha said, "There's another movie location I'd like to go to. You may like it too. I've already saved it on my phone." She looked at her phone. "It's a twenty-minute walk from here."

When they arrived at St. Augustine Church, Samantha said, "The movie *The Sixth Sense* was filmed in this church. Are you okay going into a church?"

"Can we?"

"There's one way to find out."

She pulled on the handle of the red wooden tri-panel door and it opened. "Voilà." They entered the church. "As long as there's not a mass, churches in cities are usually empty, other than a few homeless people. We'll be quiet and whisper. I'll put money in the donation box. Let's sit."

She slid onto the last pew, and Aaron sat next to her.

Whispering, she explained, "The ceiling frescoes were painted in 1844. Other parts of the church date back to 1848. Where we're sitting is original, all of these pews and the balcony. It's like going back in time. What do you think?"

"I like seeing you enjoy it. Do you belong to a church?"

"My father isn't anything. My mother is Catholic. Grace and I were baptized, did First Communion and confirmation. But that was it. My mother goes to church every week, but Grace and I don't even go on Christmas and Easter. My mother is thrilled Grace is getting married in a church. How about you?"

"No. My grandparents were Protestant, but it ended with them."

"Some well-preserved churches hold history. Some like this one. It's pleasant to sit and imagine being in the past."

She looked around, then closed her eyes. When she opened them, Aaron was gazing at her. She whispered, "It's nice to be comfortable with someone in silence. Calvin Coolidge, Silent Cal, would spend hours with a friend without talking."

"I call that sleeping."

They laughed.

Samantha said, "There's a funny story about Coolidge when he was president. A woman who sat next to Coolidge at a White House dinner said, 'I have a bet with a friend that I can get you to say more than two words to me,' to which the president replied, 'You lose.'"

"I never heard that."

She placed her hand on his. "I appreciate your suggestions to show me the city." She paused to avoid saying "but"—although it was implied. "I'm a history professor. When I travel, I want to explore the past. The *Rocky* steps are twentieth century. This church is older; the history is deeper."

She took a five-dollar bill out of her purse. "Ready to go back to the twenty-first century?"

Samantha slipped the bill in the donation box. They opened the doors, and the sun was bright.

"Back to the present," Samantha said.

"What next?"

"Meander, find a park bench."

The day went by quickly. Later, while walking down a park path, Aaron took his phone out of his pocket and glanced at it. "It's six o'clock. What time is your train?"

Samantha stopped. Aaron walked a few steps before noticing his date was no longer next to him. He turned around. "What's the matter?"

"You made an offer, and I said it was too soon. Now I don't want to leave. I don't want to go home. I'm having so much fun. Why stop?"

"Do you want dinner?"

"I'm not hungry."

Aaron said nothing and waited for Samantha to say what she wanted. "I don't even have a toothbrush and nothing to change into."

"I buy toothbrushes in packs. I have several new ones. You can choose your own color. And you don't need to change. I can lend you a T-shirt."

"And I don't like my bare feet touching the floor."

Sam Time

"I'll give you socks."

"Okay," Samantha said, smiling.

For the first time, he took her hand, and they walked to his apartment.

His place was a sizable second-floor loft in a renovated building with stores on the first floor. It had an industrial look, brick walls, and glossy hardwood floors. The shelves, end tables, and a coffee table were black metal. The sofa and chairs were eclectic. The kitchen was small with new appliances and barstools at the counter. To her relief, the bathroom was new, and the whole place was clean.

"Do you want anything to drink?"

"Water is fine." Samantha took off her blazer and scarf and hung them on a coatrack. Then she sat down on the sofa and took off her shoes. Her thin socks were tight around her feet. She took them off and threw them on the floor. "May I have those socks now?"

He walked to the far end of the room and returned with a pair of white crew socks. "Are these okay?"

"Yes. Thanks."

Aaron placed two glasses of water on the glass-top coffee table.

"Nice place. How long have you lived here?"

"Three years."

Samantha thought, We don't want to talk. Why are we even trying to have a conversation?

She moved over to be next to Aaron. They embraced and kissed.

"I'd like to see your bedroom," she said.

They stood and he held her hand as they walked past a room divider where the bed was.

"I'm on the pill."

"Thanks for telling me. What side do you want?"

"This side is good." She walked to one side of the bed, turned her back to Aaron, unzipped her jeans, and took them off. After looking for a spot to lay her jeans, she laid them flat on an oversized leather chair facing the foot of the bed. Aaron followed suit and took off his jeans. Then, with perfect aim, he threw them over the bed onto the chair on top of Samantha's.

Samantha laughed. "Well that was symbolic."

Partially clothed, she unfolded the blanket and sheet, and she slipped under the covers. Aaron did the same. They both moved to the center of the mattress.

Samantha whispered, "Let's play."

Soon after, their remaining clothes were lost between the sheets.

THE NEXT MORNING, they awoke and lay in bed, kissing and talking.

Aaron's feet touched hers. "Are you still wearing the socks?"

"Yes. I like my feet warm."

"You wore them all night?"

"They're my 'cat feet.' When I'm wearing ankle socks on bare legs."

"Do you want coffee?" Aaron asked while dressing in a T-shirt and gym shorts.

"Sure. May I have a T-shirt and gym shorts?"

"Check the first and second drawer. Take what you want."

Samantha slipped on a T-shirt and loose-fitting gym shorts. In the kitchen, she sat on a barstool, swinging her legs. After Aaron finished making the coffee, he pulled a stool next to Samantha and sat. They chatted, enjoying being close. When they finished their coffee, Samantha looked around and noticed a fedora hat on a shelf.

Sam Time

"What's this?"

In her stocking feet, Samantha slid across the glossy hardwood floor over to the shelf.

"Oh, it was a joke present. An office party gift."

"Sounds like an interesting story."

"I discovered some accounting irregularity, and they teased me about being Dick Tracy."

"Accounting humor. Sounds like an oxymoron. Do you ever wear it?"

"No."

He watched as she hung her head down so her hair fell to the floor. Then she twisted her long hair with one hand, making a makeshift bun on the top of her head. She stood, took the fedora from the shelf, put it on her head, and then tucked her hair under the hat.

"Oh, it's big," she said, giggling. The hat covered most of her ears and forehead. Aaron watched Samantha walking, then sliding on the floor to a rack of coats and jackets. She rifled through them, pulled out a brown leather bomber jacket, and put it on over her T-shirt. She flipped up the collar, covering her neck and obscuring part of her face. The sleeves covered her hands, so she put them in the jacket pockets.

"There's something Grace and John didn't tell you about me," Samantha said, gliding to an open space of the loft. "I have a little skill I learned from my sorority sisters. You have to practice. And I need socked feet, my cat feet."

Samantha slid backward across the floor moonwalking to one end of the room. Then she turned on the ball of one foot and moonwalked to where she began, this time swaying her arms, adding rhythm. Then she pivoted again and looked up at Aaron. The rim of the hat covered her eyes, so she held her head back to see him.

"It's not hard once you get the hang of it." She made another pass. She turned around, started back, and bumped into Aaron.

She said, "I didn't see you there. With this hat on, I can only see the floor. Do you want to learn?"

He scooped her up with both of his arms. The hat fell to the floor, and her hair fell down. Aaron carried her to the bed and placed her down on the mattress. Samantha giggled. "I guess you liked it."

He kissed her on the lips, and she wiggled out of the jacket. He shoved it off the bed onto the floor.

They made love—again. Samantha was over the moon.

That afternoon, they walked hand in hand to the train station. Aaron asked, "Did you have a good time?"

"I think my body spoke for me."

Aaron's eyes widened. "I can't believe the things you say."

"Well, get used to it. I don't have to ask you; I see the signs and you enjoyed yourself."

They stopped and viewed the departures board. While walking to track eight, Samantha said, "You collect coins, I like to make moments, making memories. I try not to over-orchestrate things. But the way you departed at the Princeton train station was romantic. It's not only what you do, it's how you do it."

The train was in the station and passengers were boarding.

Aaron teased Samantha and said, "And what if I don't want to play your little games?"

She kissed him on the lips. "You lose."

She walked to a train door, looked back at Aaron and smiled, then stepped aboard.

THAT WEEK, Samantha and Aaron talked at length every night on the phone. Grace and John's wedding was the coming weekend, so there was last-minute planning.

Friday was the rehearsal dinner; Samantha introduced Aaron to her parents. When Samantha and her mother were alone, she said, "He seems nice, Sam. But don't rush into it."

"I know," Samantha said. Yes, she was rushing it.

Despite the thirty-plus guests at the dinner, Samantha and Aaron spent the evening as if they were alone. Samantha neglected her maid-of-honor duties: greeting the out-of-town guests and helping Grace. But Samantha was enthralled with Aaron. Miss Manners would have disapproved.

THE OVERCAST DAY did not dampen the joy of the bride and groom, who exchanged vows in a church wedding. At the reception, Samantha and Aaron sat next to each other during the meal. They gave short but loving tributes to the bride and groom.

Afterward Samantha said, "There are many people here I want to speak with. I'm sorry to have to leave you alone."

Aaron said, "I'm fine. Go ahead. Have fun."

She kissed him on the lips.

Occasionally glancing back and smiling at Aaron, Samantha gracefully crisscrossed the room. She was wearing a dusty rose-colored gown, which softly flared from the midhip with a strapless bodice. It was topped with an above-the-elbow-length chiffon wrap that split in the back. Her hair was side-parted with French braids around the sides, tendrils at her temples, and a generous loopy bun at the nape of her neck.

When she finished making the rounds, Samantha stood at the edge of the dance floor watching everyone. Aaron came from behind her and put his hand on her back. "May I have this dance?"

She smiled. The band was playing a slow song.

Aaron wrapped his arms around Samantha's waist, and she put her arms behind his neck. They shuffled their feet in little steps and swayed to the slow rhythm. Samantha noticed her mother watching them.

Samantha said, "I'm sorry I left you for so long."

"No worries. I enjoyed watching you, in my own silent movie, not knowing what was being said—or caring."

She opened her mouth to say something but she stopped. Nothing she could say would match his comment.

As he stared at her, Samantha's eyes looked into his, then down and up again. Then Aaron said, "We should blend our lives."

Samantha's eyes widened. "We met only two weeks ago."

"Move in with me." He emphasized his desire with a tug pulling Samantha closer to him. "The few days you're on campus, you can take the train from Philly to New Brunswick."

"You thought this through." Samantha watched as the staff set up the three-tier cake on the head table. "Well, the move would be easy. I have only a few suitcases of clothes. What will I do with my car?"

"You can sell it. We need only one car in the city."

Samantha put her forehead against his and she whispered, "I'm thinking."

Sam Time

Aaron looked at her and said, "We're good together. Old enough to know. We want the same things. And yes, it's only been two weeks. But I don't want to just talk with you on the phone. I want you to be with me. I want Sam time."

It rang in her head: *Sam time.* If he wanted to charm her, this was the way to do it.

"Move in and after some time, we take the next step."

Samantha knew "the next step" meant marriage. "What would Grace and John say? They'd come back from their honeymoon, and we're living together."

"They'd be happy for us. Come to Philly. Say yes."

"I need to think about it."

When the song ended, they stopped moving their feet but stayed attached. After a few seconds, Samantha snapped out of her trance. "I see my mother by herself. I haven't spoken with her all night."

Aaron squeezed Samantha's hands before she walked toward her mother.

"Hey, Mom. It's been a lovely day."

An announcement was made that the bride and groom would cut the cake. Samantha and her mother watched and clapped with everyone. Then Grace and John danced to an upbeat song in the center of the parquet floor.

Samantha said to her mother, "I'm so happy for them."

"I see you and Aaron are very close."

"He asked me to move in with him."

Her mother gasped and placed her fingers over her mouth. "That's too soon. You don't know even him."

"It's been a short time, but it feels as if I've known him longer."

"Has he told you he loves you?"

"Not yet."

"I don't want either of my daughters getting hurt. I know Grace will be okay."

"Mom, I'm in my late twenties. The clock is ticking."

"I'm not going to tell you what to do. But the beginning may only be physical attraction. Then once you get to know him, he may not be a compatible partner."

"I know. But this feels right. Not like the others. Grace and John think he's great." There was a long pause, and then Samantha said, "Well, don't be surprised if I tell you to update your Christmas card list for my new address."

Samantha walked to the table where Aaron was sitting and said, "The band is so loud. Let's find someplace quiet."

"Good idea."

He took her hand and they went outside.

She pointed to the gazebo in a grassy area. "Let's go over there."

The air was warm, thick and humid. Samantha lifted her gown while walking on the grass. They climbed several steps into the gazebo.

She said, "It's anticlimactic. Made solely for photo ops. But it is quiet. What do we do now?" She wrapped her arms around Aaron. "Do we dance and think of our own music? Maybe we should—"

Whatever Samantha was going to say next was interrupted by the sound of raindrops falling on the roof of the gazebo. Then came a downpour. They laughed.

"We're stranded. What can we do?" Samantha asked.

"Call someone. Tell them to bring an umbrella."

"One, my cellphone is in my hand clutch on the table, and two, umbrellas don't help when it's raining this hard."

"I have my cellphone." Aaron pulled it out of his breast pocket. "I'll call John."

"It's his wedding. He's not going to answer."

"I can try." Aaron waited. "You're right. He's not picking up." He slipped his cellphone back into his breast pocket. "I guess we wait until it lets up."

"You don't know New Jersey. We could be waiting for days."

The downpour wet the gazebo on all sides, so they huddled in its center.

Samantha said, "We'll wait until the rain slows down. I'll take my shoes off, lift my gown, and we can make a dash for it. We're going to get soaked."

They laughed.

She said, "We're missing the bride throwing the bouquet and the garter thing. You know that's intended for us. And we're not going to be there. Grace will say, 'Where's Sam?' She's going to think I orchestrated this."

"It sounds like something you would do."

"It does. And Grace knows I don't like the bride throwing the bouquet and the garter thing. It's too predictable. At our wedding, we're not doing that, the bouquet and garter bit," she said flipping her hand for emphasis.

She caught herself and covered her face with her hands. "Oh my God. I'm so embarrassed. I can't believe I said that!"

"You're not sure if you want to move in with me, but you're planning our wedding?" Aaron smiled, now knowing Samantha was thinking yes to moving in with him.

"Let's rewind and pretend I never said that. I don't want to scare you away by jumping way ahead."

Aaron wrapped his arms around Samantha and kissed her. "I'm not scared."

The rain slowed. "This is the best we can hope for." Samantha took off her shoes and lifted her gown. She looked at Aaron.

He said, "I don't care if I get wet."

"Ready?"

They ran in the steady rain, splashing through the wet grass.

Once inside, they laughed. Samantha said, "I'm wilted. You look okay. The black tux doesn't show how wet you are. I'm going to the ladies' room. Maybe there's a hand dryer in there."

Aaron kissed her on the lips. "I'll see you inside."

Samantha dried herself with paper towels, but her wet gown clung to her. She came back into the reception room and spotted Grace.

"Sam, where were you? I wanted to throw my bouquet to you."

"Aaron and I walked outside to the gazebo and got caught in the rain. I want to hug you but I'm wet. I'm so happy for you and John."

"I see you and Aaron are getting along nicely."

"I'm falling for him. I think it's mutual."

"John and I have been wishing this for you and Aaron for a long time."

"It's happening so quickly. Maybe too quickly. That's what Mom says."

"Go for it, Sam. Don't hesitate. Mom means well, but your big sister knows."

Someone else was now demanding Grace's attention and she turned away. Samantha stood watching everyone hug and say goodbye to the newlyweds while absorbing her sister's advice.

Samantha then turned around looking for Aaron, not knowing he was only an arm's length away.

Samantha laughed. "Oh, there you are!"

Aaron put his arm around her, and she leaned against him as they walked.

Samantha said, "Take me home. I have packing to do. Yes, I'm going to Philly."

TWO MONTHS after Samantha moved in with Aaron, they lay in bed snuggling. She said, "I don't have classes tomorrow, so I may sleep later."

"Okay, I'll be quiet so I won't wake you."

"You know, Aaron, we skipped a few steps when I moved here and I'm very happy."

"So am I."

"But it's been two months and neither one of us has said those three magic words. And I'm not going to be the first. Just saying."

They fell asleep.

The next morning, Samantha awoke past her normal time. Aaron had already left. On this cool and rainy day, the loft was drafty. She dressed in black leggings with a pair of Aaron's knit crew socks and slipped on Aaron's knit fisherman sweater over a T-shirt.

She made coffee and read the news online. While sipping coffee, she looked out the window. The panes were foggy, but on one window, Aaron had traced two hearts and written the words "I love you" with his finger.

Samantha took a picture of the inscribed window and sent it to Aaron with a text message: *Love you too.*

Thereafter they exchanged this sentiment daily.

Six months after they were married, Grace and John moved from Philadelphia to Austin, Texas. John, having grown up in Southern California, wanted to live in a warmer climate. He accepted at job offer at an Austin law firm. Grace was promoted to director of human resources at a regional company.

Samantha cried for days, having enjoyed spending time with Grace while they both lived in Philadelphia. Save for a couple of years, the sisters had always lived close by. Aaron consoled Samantha saying they too would eventually move to Austin.

Both Aaron and John had enjoyed living on the East Coast during their college years and after starting their careers. They were also blessed having met two Jersey girls who were their soulmates. Like John's, Aaron's SoCal roots were persuasive in his desire to return to a warmer climate.

Once Grace and John were settled in their new home, they urged Samantha and Aaron to join them. Aaron was hired by a CPA firm, and Samantha accepted a position as a part-time professor of history at the University of Texas at Austin. Moreover, they bought a house around the corner from Grace and John.

Samantha and Aaron celebrated their first-date anniversary at an Austin restaurant. The happy couple agreed to wait another year before becoming engaged. On their second anniversary, they went to a jewelry store to select an engagement ring and wedding bands.

One weekend Aaron suggested they take a drive to Georgetown, a town thirty miles north of Austin. While holding hands, they walked the downtown streets and came upon the Grace Heritage Center, a former Episcopal church built in 1881. They stood in front of the narrow white wood-frame church building with a steeply pitched roof and a bell tower at the front entrance that rose above the roof's apex.

Samantha was intrigued. "Let's go inside. I want to see the interior."

They wandered into the former church. The interior was white with the original wooden pews. The windows were a lancet architecture, narrow width with arched, pointed tops. The building was so small, a posted sign at the entrance limited occupancy to fifty people.

In the middle of the nave, Aaron knelt on one knee.

Unsuspecting, Samantha said, "Did you plan all this?"

"Yes. I've been trying to act casually, but I had to rent this place for a short window of time. Now will you marry me?"

Her answer was never in doubt. The wedding would be in a year.

Samantha took an eighteen-month leave to work on her doctorate. Two university history professors planned on retiring in a few years. Samantha's strategy was to earn a doctorate for a full-time professorship.

EARLY ON A WEEKDAY morning, Aaron left for an in-office company meeting. When he returned before noon, Samantha was in the kitchen. Her hair was styled in a single, centered, back-of-the-head French braid. She was wearing one of Aaron's white T-shirts, black leggings, and slip-on shoes. "How was the meeting?"

"I need to talk with you about a big job I'll be involved in."

"Okay. Do you want tea or something?"

"Tea is fine. Whatever flavor you're having," Aaron replied.

He sat in a chair at the table. Sam leaned her back against the counter, listening to Aaron's news.

"I've been assigned as manager on a job for a Denver company, which is going public. There's a lot of work before the initial public offering. I'll be there during the weekdays with a team. Leaving Monday morning, or Sunday night, and returning Friday night. The assignment will take about nine months."

As Aaron talked about the details of his new out-of-state assignment, Samantha's breathing deepened. She folded her arms against her chest, her eyebrows furrowed and lips pursed. When he was finished speaking, he waited for her reply.

She glared at him, took a deep breath, and said, "I don't like you anymore."

Aaron was stunned.

"How could you do this to me? You know I don't like being alone!"

"Actually, I didn't."

"Well, I don't." She walked out of the kitchen into the living room and paced. "You're the one who said you didn't want to just talk with me on the phone, so I should come to Philly. I moved in with you after two weeks. Now we're going to go back to phone calls during the week. We're regressing! You wanted Sam time. What happened to Sam time?"

Samantha's reaction was fierce, and he tried to calm her. "It's not permanent. It's for nine months—maybe. I'll be home on weekends."

"What about working from home? Grace and John do two days a week. You're doing that often. Why now, five days—out of state?"

"The company has a subsidiary, which is a defense contractor. Employees can't work from home because of security clearances. And contractors, like our accounting firm, must be physically on the premises. Also, I'm the manager; staff can cycle in and out, but I'll have to be there. The firm is renting a condo where I'll stay."

Sam Time

"Well, like I said, I don't like you anymore." She folded her arms on her chest while pacing.

"You don't mean that. Go for a run."

"I already did."

"Well, go shopping. Get something that will make you feel good."

Samantha sat down at the table and held her forehead in the palms of her hands. "Why do men think shopping is the cure for a woman's problem? Besides, you have enough clothes for both of us."

"You're making my point." He took a sip of tea. "Maybe it's time to get a dog or a cat."

"We can't," she said.

"Why not? It doesn't matter to me which. I like them both."

"Dad is allergic to cats. And Mom is allergic to everything. We never had pets growing up. Good thing the neighbors did. Plenty of dogs to become attached to."

"But your parents come here only a couple of times a year."

"I like that we can spend quality time with them, because they're states away. If we have pets, they won't be able to enter our house, even if they stay with Grace and John."

He said softly, "Sam, it was an idea. I'm trying to help."

Samantha sat up, took deep breaths. "You know, I want to get my mother's bridal gown redesigned for me. Grace told me about this dressmaker who's supposed to be really good. I'll go now."

As she walked out of the kitchen, Aaron said, "You don't like me anymore, but you're getting the bridal gown ready for our wedding."

Samantha yelled back, "Oh, stop making sense!"

A few minutes later, she returned wearing jeans, a red V-neck T-shirt, black blazer, and slip-on shoes. She carried her tote bag in one hand and the bridal gown bag in the other. Aaron stood and hugged her. Samantha didn't drop the bags she was holding and kept her arms at her sides, protesting their soon-to-change circumstances. But she laid her head on Aaron's chest and enjoyed being hugged.

Aaron put his hands on her forearms. "This is good for my career. I'll get a nice bonus for this work. This is good for us. I don't want to be away from you either."

Samantha nodded and left.

Samantha was driving when Grace called. "Hey, Sam. I have some time in between calls. Can you talk?"

"Yes, I'm driving. Did Aaron call you?" Samantha asked.

"Yes, he's concerned about you."

"Did you hear? He's deserting me."

"It's not desertion. He'll be home on the weekends."

"This has happened before. You know I don't like being alone."

"Yes, and I told Aaron what happened to us."

Samantha said, "You mean when you and John agreed to live together? You left me all alone in a two-bedroom apartment!"

"Yes. I told him. He didn't know the full story. That you were delighted when John and I got serious, but when we agreed to live together, you were upset because you were losing me as a roommate. I know you like company, never lived on your own, and don't want to. You were so upset that you gave me all the furniture. But I told Aaron it worked out. You moved in with Deanna. She's like a sister to you. I love Deanna too.

"Sam, I never told you this, but your reaction to me leaving—leaving 'the nest'—caught me off guard. You're so put together, and

Sam Time

I didn't expect your reaction. But it passed; it didn't last. You found a solution."

Samantha remained silent.

Grace asked, "Sam, are you still there?"

"I'm here."

"Remember when John and I left Philly for Austin, you cried for days?"

"But I had Aaron."

"Yes, you pulled yourself together quickly."

"What am I going to do now? I'm so disappointed at his news. But I could tell he was shocked at my reaction. I threw a tantrum. It was ugly. I'm regretting it."

"Sam, I have time between video calls. Let's go to lunch."

"I'm not hungry."

"What about coffee? Or ice cream? Let's go out for ice cream."

"Ice cream for lunch. Okay. I'd like that. I don't mind Aaron calling you. I feel loved. It warms my heart you both care so much."

"When do you want to go?"

"Well, I'm on my way to that dressmaker's shop you told me about. Mary Sanchez. I'm taking Mom's wedding gown and redesigning it for me. I may be an hour."

"No problem. Text me when you're on your way home and come pick me up."

Several women were busily sewing and repairing garments in the dressmaker's shop. A woman introduced herself as Mary Sanchez and showed Samantha into the dressing room. Samantha tried on her mother's bridal gown and explained the desired alterations to transform the gown.

Mary asked about the wedding party. Always-thrifty Samantha and her accountant fiancé were keen on a small, affordable wedding. John would be Aaron's best man, and Grace would be Samantha's matron of honor.

The dressmaker offered suggestions for a customized bridesmaid's gown, pointing to three cotton fabric rolls with color choices in light green, pink and powder blue. Samantha contemplated which floral print and color she liked best. She noticed labels on the fabric rolls: "Mfg. 1882." Mary explained she had purchased the material from a seller who recently discovered the hundred-plus-year-old, well-preserved fabric.

As a student of history, Samantha loved the idea of making a gown in a Victorian-era style with fabric from that period. Perhaps Aaron's suggestion to shop for clothes had inspired Samantha to order a custom bridesmaid gown with this gorgeous floral fabric.

Samantha chose the light green fabric and discussed with Mary the gown design while paging through pattern books. Because the sisters were similar in build, Samantha would act as the model for fittings once Mary sewed, then tailored the gown.

After leaving the dressmaker's shop, Samantha picked up Grace. From the waist up, Grace was professional: button-down blouse and a navy blazer. Below the waist, she wore black leggings and ballet shoes.

At their favorite ice cream shop, Grace ordered a scoop of rocky road, and Samantha ordered a scoop of chocolate mint chip. They sat at a table on the sidewalk.

While Grace engaged in cheery conservation to lift her sister's mood, Samantha looked down at her paper cup, dug the plastic spoon into her ice cream, and ate her comfort food.

Grace said, "You know, I got a year-end bonus, so I treated myself to some new clothes. My closet is very full, so you can come by, see what you like of my older clothes, and take what you want."

"Why do you and Aaron think a new wardrobe is going to make me feel better?" Samantha shook her head.

Grace didn't say anything.

"I'm sorry I snapped. That's so generous of you. Of course, I love your taste in clothes and would be happy with your hand-me-downs. Lucky for me, you're a clothes horse. All these years, I've gotten free beautiful clothes."

Then Grace leaned in and lowered her voice as if she was telling her sister a secret. "You know, John told me about Aaron's dating before he met you. And I saw it too. He would cycle through relationships quickly. Not many steadies. Nothing too long. With you, Aaron is a changed man. John said he's never seen Aaron like this. And I've seen a change in him."

Samantha had heard this before and concentrated on eating her ice cream.

"I know you get lonely, but you and Aaron are solid. You can both handle this," Grace said.

Once her cup was empty, Samantha looked up and leaned her left elbow on the arm of the chair, shifting her weight to one side. "I know my reaction and my loneliness is on the extreme side of the spectrum. But that doesn't mean I'm wrong about having concerns."

Grace leaned over the table. "Concerns about Aaron? I just told you. He's crazy in love with you."

"When a couple is apart—distance-wise—because of work or whatever, the relationship stagnates. It can't move forward. And that's not good."

Grace ate the last spoonful of her ice cream, listening to Samantha, and sat up straight.

"Aaron and I are great together. But being apart is at least unhealthy, at worst, dangerous."

"Sam, he's coming home every weekend. He's not going to stray."

"I'm not talking about him."

"Sam, what are you saying? You're in love with Aaron."

"That's not what I mean. You're taking this the wrong way. I don't want anyone but Aaron. But being apart means I have to learn to live without him. And that's the contradiction. Five days a week, I have to pretend I have my own life, then two days, he's back. It's not a switch I can easily turn on and off.

"When he goes on this job, his career is advancing and, yes, it's convenient for me to work on my dissertation, which is nowhere. I haven't even started. So we can both concentrate on work. But relationship-wise, for nine months we'll be stuck, on hold. I hate that. Because it's the best part of my life, and it's going to be suspended."

Grace said, "You'll learn how to cope. You'll find something to fill the void. And John and I are around the corner."

Samantha gathered their cups, spoons, and napkins and threw them into a trash can. "You have to get back. Thanks for listening."

"Sure. You're still my little sister."

AFTER DROPPING OFF Grace, Samantha returned home and Aaron came out of the den to the kitchen, where Samantha placed her tote bag on the counter.

Aaron hugged Samantha and said, "Don't be mad at me."

"I'm not mad at you. I'm upset with your news."

Sam Time

Aaron tried to soothe her. "It will go by fast. It's going to be all right."

Samantha put her hands on his chest and pushed abruptly away from Aaron, stunning him. "It will go by fast! Time is constant. It doesn't accelerate."

"Sam, it's an expression, meaning it's going to be okay."

"That is the worst movie line, the worst script line ever: 'It's going to be okay!'"

Aaron stood frozen.

"You don't know if it's going to be okay. I don't know. Don't give me platitudes!"

Aaron said, "I don't know what to say."

She yelled, "Then say nothing. Remember Silent Cal? Say nothing, if you have nothing to say. And never give me platitudes!"

"Sam, chill."

"Chill! Chill!" She yelled louder and stomped one foot. "Do you even know who you're marrying? There is nothing chill about me!" She paced, knowing she was unhinged. She lowered her voice, held up her index finger and said, "And don't you dare ask me."

"Don't ask you what?"

"If I have my period."

"I was going to ask you what flavor of ice cream you had. You should never have it again."

Samantha chuckled. "That's what you should do. Disarm me with humor. You do it so well."

She hugged Aaron and he kissed her on the forehead. With her inside voice, she said, "I should come with instructions: How to Get Along with Sam: disarm with humor, hugs and kisses, and default to silence."

"That's my Sam."

They were still embracing and Samantha said, "I appreciate you and Grace caring. Rationally, I understand your work situation. Emotionally, I'm going to let the days roll by and see what happens." She shrugged her shoulders. "Thank you for trying to make me feel better. Sorry I yelled."

She broke away from his embrace, held his hands, and said firmly, "But I meant everything I said."

"I know. This assignment starts next month."

Samantha frowned and said, "Well, this loneliness thing I have, it's up to me to find my way through it."

SAMANTHA'S PLAYFULNESS was zapped out of her. She was, however, affectionate and loving to Aaron. On the Monday morning he left, they hugged and kissed before the car service arrived. Wearing his T-shirt from the night before, black leggings, and slip-on shoes, Samantha followed him out to the car. As he opened the door, she placed her hand on the middle of his back. She closed the car door and stood in the driveway until the car turned the corner out of sight.

She came back into the house, closed her eyes, and put her hands around her waist, hugging the T-shirt of Aaron's she was wearing. Then she changed into her sportswear and went for a run.

Soon after she returned from running, she received a text from Mary the dressmaker saying the gown was ready for a fitting. Samantha showered and changed, then went to the dressmaker's shop.

To Samantha's surprise, Mary and her seamstresses had sewn the bridesmaid's light green floral print gown. Samantha had instructed Mary to make alterations on the bridal gown before fabricating the bridesmaid's gown. Mary was nonchalant about the mistake and urged Samantha to try on the gown. As she stood in front of the full-length, trifold mirror looking at the perfect-fitting gown from all angles, Samantha fell in love. She paid for the gown and took it home.

THAT EVENING she tried on the gown again, roaming around the house. Her phone rang; Grace was calling. "Hi, Sam."

"Hi. It's day one. I went to the dressmaker's shop for a fitting of Mom's redesigned bridal gown. But you know the dressmaker Mary, who you told me about? She made this bridesmaid's gown instead. The first time I went to her shop was that day when I was upset with Aaron's news. Maybe I didn't communicate properly what I wanted. Anyway, the gown is beautiful. And now I am rethinking the redesign of the bridal gown."

"If you're happy, it doesn't matter in what order things are done."

"I think you'll like it. It's cotton. A light green print with scrolls of vines with white and gold flowers. Here, I'll take a picture and text it to you."

After she texted the photo to Grace, Samantha continued describing the gown. "The style is Victorian. See the mini buttons—there's ten—down the front with looped buttonholes. It's fitted at the waist with mini pleats on the skirt waist. See the full skirt? It looks like two pieces: a jacket and a skirt, but it's really a one-piece gown."

Grace said, "I see it. Very pretty."

"Can you see this faux jacket with its sloped shoulder seams and peplum? The peplum is fabric that's attached to the waist and falls to the midhip. Like a flounce with a curved hem. You can't see the back, but the fabric is longer, like a bustle.

"Mary took some liberties. She fabricated bell sleeves, which widen at the cuffs. And each cuff has several one-inch horizontal pleats. She reversed the fabric for these pleats, the ruffle, the covered buttons, and the buttonhole loops. There's also a ruffle around the crew neckline and down the front, covering the buttonhole loops. The fabric's reverse side is pretty too. It's a nice contrast. Can you see the reversed fabric?

"I can. Very nice."

"When designing the gown, we spoke about the ease of putting it on and taking it off. So I selected a style with buttons in the front and a pleat at the waistline. But it still takes a while to slip on. At the shop, Mary helped me to get into it. Tonight it took me a while to put it on."

Samantha looked at the gown in the mirror as she was talking, "I'm also amazed how quickly this gown was made. Mary has a few women working there. Maybe they all pitched in sewing it. They are great seamstresses. The gown is completely lined, and the skirt has a sewn-in petticoat."

"Is it comfortable?"

"That's why I'm wearing it. Sitting, moving around. Cotton doesn't have any give. The fabric weight is heavier and sturdier than a thin poplin. Oh, and I had her sew in deep pockets on the side seams, so you can carry tissues and other necessities without needing a handbag."

Grace said, "You thought of everything."

Samantha received a notification on her phone. "Aaron's calling."

Grace said quickly, "Okay, I'll call tomorrow."

"Bye." Samantha hung up with Grace and picked up Aaron's

call. "Hi, sweetie."

"How are you doing, Sam?"

"Oh, fine. How was your day?"

"Okay. Lots to do. Meetings."

"I was just on the phone with Grace. I picked up her bridesmaid gown today. I'm wearing it now. It's this Victorian-style gown. And I'm not making any progress on my dissertation; maybe this will give me some inspiration. Anything to give me a start."

"I have confidence in you. Anyway, it's been a long day. I wanted to say hi. A group of us are going out to dinner now. Call you tomorrow night. Love you, Sam."

"Love you too."

After Samantha put down the phone, she stood in front of the bathroom mirror, fussing with different hairstyles for her wedding day. Using her skills in French braiding, she fashioned a crown braid: two side-by-side braids around the head like a crown.

Feeling Victorian, she wore the gown while paging through a history book. She lounged on the sofa with the book propped up. Still wearing her shoes on her always-cold feet, she draped her grandmother's cream-colored crocheted afghan over her shoulders.

Later that night, her eyes tired, and she turned off the light on the end table.

She thought, I'll close my eyes for moment, then go to bed.

The book fell against the back cushion. An hour later, Samantha was still lying on the sofa, now in a deep sleep—unaware of the confluence of unknowns that would seemingly transport her back in time.

Donna Balon

Northern California

During the night, Samantha had a vivid dream. She was in a rural town wearing her Victorian-style dress. The weather was cool so she wrapped the crocheted afghan around her shoulders. And her sockless feet were cold in her slip-on shoes.

The few men she saw were in worn, soiled work clothes and walked with purpose. The so-called roadways were not paved but dirt paths. No cars or trucks, but horses and carts. A few wooden one-story buildings scattered here and there.

This must be a dream in which the clock has been turned back, Samantha thought. But where am I?

She strolled, aware she had not seen any other women. Pulling the afghan around herself snugly, she walked with her head tilted down to avoid catching the eye of any man in whatever this place was, glancing up often to learn more of her surroundings.

Then two women hurried toward her, each carrying a wooden bucket of water. Their cotton dresses hung to their ankles, with full skirts gathered at the waist of fitted bodices. Plain white cotton bonnets covered their heads, and shawls were wrapped around their shoulders. They looked at Samantha disapprovingly. Her dress was too fancy for this rural town. Moreover, she wasn't wearing a bonnet or hat; a bare head was a means of solicitation by prostitutes. She hugged her body with the afghan, which served as a shawl to hide her uncorseted torso.

The dream seemed authentic. Despite her uneasiness, she thought, Enjoy the dream. If I don't like it, I'll wake myself up.

Around a corner, she spotted a few men in uniform. Soldiers. Maybe the army. This might be a small town next to an army fort, Samantha guessed. Still, not a good place for a woman.

Samantha approached a horse stable and heard a man say, "Lieutenant Grant." Another said, "Ulysses."

She snapped her head around.

Oh my God, Samantha thought. Grant was promoted to captain in the middle of the decade, so if he's a lieutenant, it's 1850-ish. And this must be northern California.

The two men approached Grant, and Samantha watched. She no longer cared about keeping her unbonneted head down. This was her dream, and she wanted at least a glimpse of Grant. He was wearing an army uniform: an above-the-knee-length navy coat, with a stand-up collar closed by a single row of brass buttons down the center front; baggy pants; square-toed boots with a one-inch heel; and a black felt slouch hat with a wide brim.

The three men spoke for a few minutes and then the other two left, leaving Grant and the horse he was tending.

Samantha hesitated and recalled what she had learned of American history. Although the United States had separated from its mother country, the former colony still followed many of

Britain's customs. Named after Queen Victoria, who reigned from 1837 to 1901, this period is called the Victorian era—with social rules: many dos and even more don'ts.

But Samantha wanted to have fun. So she approached Grant while thinking about all the customs she should abide by.

At age thirty and unmarried, Samantha was an old maid. Without a hat or a bonnet she could be mistaken for a prostitute, and there were plenty of those women around any town adjacent to an army fort.

But this was Samantha's dream, and she could be bold. She stepped forward until she was several feet from Grant and stopped. "Lieutenant Grant," she said softly.

He turned around. His light blue eyes were his most striking feature. Chestnut-brown hair, mustache, and beard. Straight nose. Square jaw. Wide-at-the-temples facial bone structure. About five eight in height. Slim beneath the soldier's coat. This was Ulysses S. Grant. In his early thirties. Good-looking.

He glanced at Samantha and then turned around to tend to his horse.

He's a married man, and he sees an unknown woman. What are the protocols?

Her dream. Her rules.

Samantha persisted, using what she thought was common phraseology for this era. "Lieutenant Grant, I am Miss Samantha. I hear you are an expert horseman. I would be most pleased in taking lessons under your tutelage."

His back still facing her, he made no reply.

She thought quickly of a scheme. "My brothers are in town on business. It would be most helpful to our family business, if I could learn how to ride."

"I am a soldier with duties at the fort."

He speaks.

"I understand, Lieutenant Grant. But surely you have leave."

While keeping a distance of several feet, she stepped to his side so she could see his profile. "I understand you will not transact with a lady, but I will return with one of my brothers. He will pay you compensation."

"Others can teach you."

"But I hear you are the best. A quarter dollar for a day's riding lesson. We can meet you here tomorrow, at this hour or the next day or the next. Oh, I would like to ride astride, not sidesaddle."

Although riding sidesaddle was more conventional for women, riding astride was becoming more common in the West.

Grant didn't reply, but he didn't say no, either.

"Thank you, Lieutenant Grant, for considering our offer. My brother and I will return."

That was fun, thought Samantha. I'll play along as if this dream is real. So, what's next? I need riding clothes. And I need money. I'll worry about that later. Riding clothes first.

Close by there was a petite woman in a worn apron, a faded tan dress, and a plain white bonnet.

"Good day," Samantha said.

"Good day," the woman replied, then turned away.

"I'm Samantha Hunter." The woman seemed suspicious because Samantha wasn't wearing a bonnet. Knowing this, Samantha said, "My family settled here a few days ago. And I lost my bonnet!"

Satisfied with Samantha's explanation that she wasn't a harlot, the woman turned to Samantha. "Alice."

"A pleasure to meet you, Alice. I will sew myself a simple new bonnet. But I lack expert sewing skills. And I need riding clothes. I will be taking riding lessons. I need a split skirt. A woman's riding habit." Samantha knew the nomenclature for a complete woman's "costume" for horseback riding. "Do you know where—"

Before Samantha finished her sentence, Alice said, "Yes. I get. I get." Walking into the house, she waved for Samantha to follow.

The small one-room home with a fireplace smelled of stale air. The ceiling was barely six feet, and two small windows did not provide much light, giving a dreariness to the space. It was sparsely furnished: a table with four chairs, a bed, a sideboard, and a trifold dressing screen. And the wide-planked wooden floor creaked with every step.

Alice walked to the back corner and returned, placing the clothes on the table. Her eyes welled with tears. "Edith, my daughter." Alice murmured something Samantha could barely understand.

Samantha thought: Alice is probably a Chinese immigrant who had arrived with her husband and daughter during the early years of the gold rush. Alice is her adopted American name, and English is her second language. I understand only a few words, but I gather the clothes were worn by Alice's daughter Edith, who had died of consumption (tuberculosis) last year.

"I am sorry to hear of your dear daughter. May I see if these fit?"

Alice showed Samantha the screen to stand behind for dressing and undressing.

Samantha emerged wearing a white cotton chemise under a brown waist jacket, with a stand-up collar, closed by a dozen small buttons down the center front from the neckline to the waist hem. Pairs of darts on the left and right front and back shaped the jacket's waistline. A short peplum adorned the center back jacket hem. The brown split skirt gathered at the waistband and looked like a woman's dress skirt with a full hem but was split into wide culottes so a rider could comfortably straddle her horse's back. A suede brimmed hat with a chinstrap was topped on her head.

Samantha couldn't see herself. There weren't any full-length mirrors. But the garments felt ill fitting. The sleeves of the chemise and the jacket were too short by several inches, as was the hem of the split skirt. The jacket was snug, and the skirt waistband was too tight.

Alice tugged at the sleeves of the jacket and chemise, then the skirt waistband and the skirt hem. She nodded, indicating there was enough fabric in the sleeve and the skirt hems to lengthen, and extra fabric in the waistband for a roomier fit.

"I fix," she said.

Samantha said, "I would like to buy these clothes with the alterations. What is the cost?"

Alice held up four fingers.

"Four dollars. I will return with four silver dollars. I come a distance to get to the stable. I would prefer wearing my dress to walk through town and to the general store. May I leave the clothes here and dress in them before I ride? Are you here most of the day, so I may enter?"

Alice nodded yes to both questions.

Samantha went behind the screen to change back into her dress. Afterward she came around the screen and folded the riding clothes on the table with the hat on top. "Alice, in a few days, I will return with four dollars. And with this lovely habit, I can learn to ride. You are so kind."

Samantha walked out the door and toward the area where she had arrived. Time to wake up. How could she do that? She landed here while sleeping, so she should mimic her sleeping position. Samantha found an isolated spot, closed her eyes, placed her hands at her sides, and took a deep breath.

It worked. She was at home on the sofa. Grabbing her cellphone, she checked the time: 1:21 a.m.

The dream was exceptional. It was self-directed and realistic, not broken up in pieces or disjointed.

She took off the gown, dressed in one of Aaron's T-shirts, and went to sleep in her bed—dreaming of tomorrow night's adventure.

Sam Time

First Ride

Tuesday morning Samantha awoke, made coffee, and ate yogurt. Then she went into her home office, searching through her history books for answers about the context of last night's dream.

She had arrived in the newly settled bay town of Eureka, California, which was adjacent to Fort Humboldt. The region had been settled by Native Americans. But when gold was discovered in the area—*eureka* means "I found it"—skirmishes between the natives and the gold pioneers ensued, so the army established a fort to keep the peace.

Lieutenant Grant arrived at Fort Humboldt in the beginning of 1854. Lack of sufficient finances prevented Grant from bringing his family.

This dream, a seemingly once-in-a-lifetime experience, was enabled by her dress—more specifically, the 1882 fabric. But why would she be visiting 1854?

Regardless of this mystery, Samantha wondered if she could experience another consecutive dream building on the first: I'll fall asleep again wearing the gown and the crocheted afghan as a shawl over my shoulders. Then I need money and a few other things.

On their first date, Aaron had said he was a coin collector. Soon after, Samantha called her father about coins that had been passed down in his family for generations. Mr. Hunter adored his daughters and spoiled them with anything they wanted. So when Samantha called saying she was interested in his coin collection, he searched for it. The Hunters, however, had moved from New Jersey to Florida. Once in the new home, Mr. Hunter took a while to unpack and find the box with the coin collection. After Samantha and Aaron had moved to Austin, Samantha's father located the collection and shipped it to her. Aaron sifted through the coins, looking for the rare and valuable ones, which were few. He stored away the remaining coins.

Later in the morning, Samantha retrieved the remaining coin collection. She smiled when she opened the box. Aaron had organized and labeled the coins according to type and years.

She reached for the coins labeled "1850s." There were many Liberty Seated half dollars and silver-dollar coins. The coins could be used to pay for the riding lessons and clothes.

Then she shifted through her bottom dresser drawer and found her mini change purse. The palm-sized ivory cotton lace drawstring purse had been gifted to Samantha as a child by her grandmother. Suitable for holding coins, this purse, like the crocheted afghan, was befitting as a mid-nineteenth-century woman's accessory.

At nighttime Samantha made a mental checklist: hair styled in a single, centered, back-of-the-head French braid, for a better fit while on horseback wearing a brimmed hat; wide cream headband knitted by Grandma for a head covering; thin ankle socks to keep her feet warm; old pair of leather lace-up ankle boots; mini drawstring change purse with money; afghan wrapped around her shoulders; history book on the nightstand opened to the same page as last night.

She put on her gown, stuffed her deep pockets with her boots, headband, and change purse, then climbed into bed and fell asleep.

THE MAGIC CONTINUED. Samantha arrived in the same spot as in her first dream. The sun was overhead, so she guessed it was around noon. She took out her headband and put it on her head, covering her ears and braid tail. Then she pulled her ankle boots out of her pockets, put them on her feet, and laced them up.

Now she needed to exchange her half dollars and dollar coins for smaller change. The small rural town didn't have a bank or even a post office. There was, however, a makeshift general store where Samantha exchanged her coins for half dimes—the term "nickel" was not yet in use—dimes and quarters.

Then she walked toward the stable and saw Grant was there. Now she needed to find a brother. She spotted a man who was unloading a wagon. "Would you be of my assistance?"

"Heading out. Need to leave soon," the stranger said.

"Only a few minutes of your time would be required. I would like to take riding lessons. But I need a gentleman to arrange the transaction. If you would vouch for me, I will pay with a dime."

"Got to go."

Samantha countered, "A quarter dollar for five minutes saying you agree to the transaction."

He reluctantly agreed.

"What is your name?"

"Joseph."

Samantha held his arm. "Joseph, I am going to say you are my brother. Then you say you agree—" She stopped herself. "No, do not say anything. I will do the talking." They walked toward Grant.

"Good day, Lieutenant Grant," Samantha began.

"Good day."

"It's Miss Samantha. This is my brother Joseph, who is here to approve my horse riding lessons under your tutelage."

The men didn't say anything. At least Grant wasn't objecting.

Samantha whispered to Joseph, "Shake his hand."

The men shook hands.

Samantha looked at Grant and opened her mouth then closed it. She wanted to say, "I need a few minutes to change." But was this twenty-first-century lingo? So she said, "I shall return." She turned around, closed her eyes, and made fists. She thought, That's wrong; don't embarrass yourself.

She walked Joseph back to his wagon and gave him a quarter. Samantha was happy he was leaving town so her ruse would not be discovered.

Then she hustled to Alice's house and knocked on the door. Alice opened it and they greeted each other good day. Samantha placed four silver-dollar coins on the table, took the clothes that were on the table, and stepped behind the dressing screen.

She emerged. "What do you think?"

Although Samantha couldn't see herself, the clothes fit better. The skirt waistband was a more generous fit, and the skirt hem now fell to her ankles. Several darts were let out in the jacket waist, which was no longer tight. And the sleeve hems on the chemise and jacket were lengthened.

Sam Time

She hoped her lace-up ankle boots wouldn't give her away. A pair of shoes during this era were identical; there was no left and right. Samantha thought her old black ankle boots were so worn, the machine stitching wouldn't be noticeable and perhaps neither would the left and rightness of the pair.

As Samantha turned around, Alice nodded and Samantha smiled. Now game on. Samantha walked outside to the stable.

"Lieutenant Grant, I am ready for a lesson."

Without making eye contact, she remained several feet away because she was nervous. The dream felt real.

Grant went back into the stable and returned holding the lead rope of a horse wearing a halter. He said, "See that house over there?" She turned and saw a wood-frame building about fifty feet down the dirt road. "Walk the horse down to that house, turn around, and come back. Stay on the left side of the horse."

"What's the horse's name?" Samantha asked.

"Beckley. See the way I'm holding this rope?"

Samantha nodded.

"It's called a lead rope. Hold the rope with your right hand close to his nose, with some slack, and your left holds the extra rope like this." He held the extra rope in the palm of his left hand. "Don't wrap the rope around your hand. If the horse takes off, you could break a bone. You are not wearing gloves. That's good. Better to learn the feel of holding the reins."

He gave the rope to Samantha, and she held it as instructed.

"Walk so your shoulder and his neck are aligned."

She protested, "I want to ride the horse!"

He smirked. "You need to gain the trust of a horse and lead him. Taking a stroll with the horse helps establish yourself as the leader. When you get in the saddle and take the reins, the horse will know you're the leader."

Samantha blushed. Grant watched Samantha hand-walk the horse down the road.

"Good Beckley," Samantha said often. She turned around and led the horse back to the stable, approaching Grant.

"Have you ever ridden a horse?"

Samantha thought quickly. "Only sidesaddle. I had poor balance and never mastered it. Maybe the saddle wasn't a good one. How do I pet him?"

"Stand at his side and stroke his neck. Long strokes."

"Good Beckley." She stroked the horse's neck.

"Walk with him again. This time, stop at intervals. Train him to stop with you and start again. And pet him when he obeys."

She hand-walked the horse down the road, stopping, starting, and petting. Beckley complied. "Good Beckley," Samantha said while stroking his neck.

When Samantha arrived back at the stable, Grant was standing next to his horse. Then he bridled and saddled both horses.

"Before riding, check that the bridle and the saddle fit the horse well. Not taut or too tight," he said putting his hand against the horse's skin and underneath the girth. But Samantha wasn't looking at the fit or the girth or the horse. She was looking at Grant. This was not the fifty-something, puffy-cheeked president on the fifty-dollar bill. This was soldier Grant, prime-of-his-life, fit and handsome.

Grant handed her the reins in her right hand. "Put that hand with the reins on the pommel. Your left hand on my shoulder."

He lowered his right hand, indicating Samantha should put her left foot in his hand so he could lift her up. With her right hand in position, Samantha lifted her split skirt, then put her left hand on Grant's right shoulder, and her left foot on Grant's hand.

"Push off with your right foot and spring up." He lifted her left foot up. Samantha rose up and swung her right leg over the horse. Grant strode to his horse, and Samantha watched Grant mounting his horse with ease.

They rode slowly on flat ground into the country. The beach was in the distance, but Samantha wasn't enjoying the scenery because, as the horse walked, Grant's instructions replayed over in Samantha's head: Point your toes slightly out and heels down, side calves against the side of the horse. Slack in the reins, hands up, gentle tap of the heels to start the horse walking. Lower your hands, no slack in the reins while walking. Hold the reins in a straight line from the horse's mouth to your hands and forearms. Light in the saddle. Straighten your posture. Close the right rein and the right leg, open the left rein to turn the horse to the left. Stay vertical; don't lean into the turn. Pet the horse. Close the left rein and left leg; open the right rein to turn the horse to the right. Keep your right and left hands on right and left sides; never cross your arms. Pet the horse. Say "Good Beckley." Read his ears. Bear down in the saddle, squeeze your thighs slightly against the horse, and lightly pull the reins to halt. Pet the horse. Say "Good Beckley."

After some time and distance, Grant said they should take a break to relax and allow for Samantha to dismount and mount again. Grant dismounted, showing Samantha how to do it. Then he assisted Samantha's dismount. They hand-walked their horses for a while.

They were in a wooded area. As Grant tied the horse reins to a tree, Samantha sat on a felled log. Then Grant sat two arms' lengths away on the same log.

Samantha thought, No chatting. Say nothing, unless he engages in conversation. He didn't.

The silence was pleasant. She looked up at the evergreen trees that were at least a hundred feet high. She glanced often at him, then wondered, Why is he doing this? He was bored out of his mind. He loved horses and riding. He needed the money.

After a brief rest, Grant stood and untied the horses. He assisted Samantha in mounting, then mounted his horse. Samantha said "Good Beckley" often. Otherwise, the trip back was silent.

Upon arriving at the stable, they dismounted and Samantha said, "I will return in a few minutes with your compensation."

Grant nodded.

Samantha walked to Alice's house, changed into her dress and headband. Alice was home and motioned for Samantha to stay and have some tea.

"I must pay for my riding lessons, and then I will return."

Wrapping her shawl around her shoulders, she went back to the stable and took out a quarter to pay Grant. He was busy grooming the horses. Samantha walked toward him and held up the quarter.

He said, "There's a shallow shelf to the right of the door. Please leave it there."

"Thank you, Lieutenant Grant. I appreciate today's lesson. I would like more practice."

"In a few days."

"Good day, Lieutenant Grant."

"Good day, Miss Samantha."

Grant watched as Samantha approached Beckley and stroked

his neck. "Good Beckley. We will meet again in a few days. Good day, Beckley."

Samantha glanced at Grant, who made a tight-lipped smile. She placed the quarter on the shallow shelf, then walked out of the stable and returned to Alice's house.

Two small cups were on the table. Samantha sat and sipped the hot tea. "My family arrived last week. Have you lived here long?"

Samantha didn't understand Alice's entire answer, but she did glean that Alice's husband was in San Francisco on business for several months. Like Samantha, Alice was lonely and wanted company.

Remnants of fabric cut in squares were stacked on the table. Alice was making an afghan-sized quilt. Samantha watched Alice hand-stitch fabric pieces together.

Samantha's grandmother quilted, and had taught Grace and Samantha. "May I?"

Alice handed Samantha several square pieces of fabric, a needle and thread. Although the light was dim, Samantha could see well enough. Together, the two lonely women hand-sewed in silence.

An hour later Samantha bid Alice good day, then walked to the place where she had arrived. No one was around. Did she remember how to return?

She said to herself: Close your eyes, palms on your sides, and a deep breath.

She was back in her bed, a few minutes past midnight.

More Practice

Wednesday morning Samantha awoke tired and sore in her thighs, butt, core, and forearms. If she was only dreaming, why did her body ache as if she had actually ridden a horse for a couple of hours? Best if she did not make any dream traveling plans tonight. Let her muscles relax a day.

Thursday night she repeated the same routine she had done the night she dream-traveled last. Samantha arrived in Eureka early afternoon on another pleasant day. Alice wasn't home, but the house door was not secured, so Samantha entered and changed into her riding clothes.

Grant brought Beckley outside of the stable. Then Samantha took Beckley's lead rope and hand-walked the horse down the road and back, stopping, petting, and talking to him. She returned to the stable; Grant assisted her in mounting.

"Do you remember what you learned?" Grant asked.

"Yes. But I need practice."

Sam Time

On their way out of town, she was struck by a foul smell: manure from several pigpens. She knew from her history courses that pigs were an inexpensive source of meat, and the pens were situated on the outskirts of town to avoid the stench permeating the residential areas.

About halfway during their trip, Grant stopped again, dismounted, spotted Samantha on her dismount, and then tied the horses to a tree. Grant sat down on a felled log.

The forest was thick and Samantha wandered, looking up at the huge evergreen trees. She then sat on the ground not far from Grant and asked, "Is there poison ivy here?"

He shook his head. Samantha took off her hat and put it on the ground behind her. She lay down on her back and rested her head on her hat, which flattened as she stared at the treetops against the blue sky. "They are so beautiful. What a stunning perspective."

She was entranced with the view, but she did notice Grant had stood and walked away. She relaxed on the ground, legs stretched out for a while. She thought, Aaron would appreciate this too.

"Oh my God." She scrambled to her feet and covered her mouth with her hand. This was 1854. What was she doing in a near-missionary position with a married man next to her?

She picked up her crushed hat, punching the inside with her fist to reshape it. Then she slapped it with her hand to remove the soil and leaves. After placing the hat on her head, she secured the chinstrap in place. Then she gripped her split skirt and shook it to remove any soil.

She walked within a few feet of Grant, her arms at her sides and her hands in fists. "Please forgive me. I am a proper lady. I meant no disrespect."

Samantha paced. "When I was a young girl, I would lie on the ground looking at the treetops. I forgot where I was. That I was not alone. Please do not tell my brothers. If they find out, I will not be allowed to ride anymore."

This wasn't an act. Samantha regretted she had made Grant feel uncomfortable and embarrassed herself by carelessly acting as she would in her own present day. With a few deep breaths, she tried to compose herself. She tugged on the front brim of her hat so her eyes were obscured.

Then she stood on the left side of the horse ready to mount, and Grant lifted her into the saddle. They rode back, as they came, in silence.

When they returned to the stable, he dismounted and walked over to Samantha and instructed her, "Both feet out of the stirrups, left hand holding the reins, right hand on the front of the saddle. Lean forward, swing your right leg over the horse's back, and land away from the horse."

Samantha did as instructed and dismounted the first time without Grant spotting her.

"Good," he said.

Without looking at him, Samantha said, "I will be back in a few minutes."

When Samantha returned to the house, Alice was home hand-sewing fabric pieces for the quilt. She had set on the table a stack of fabric pieces where Samantha sat last time. She nodded. After changing into her dress, she said, "I will return."

Samantha walked back to the stable and placed a quarter on the shallow shelf, then said to Grant, "I regret my actions. I meant no disrespect and hope—"

"I will see you in a few days," he said.

"Thank you. Good day, Lieutenant Grant."

"Good day, Miss Samantha."

"Good day, Beckley," Samantha said, petting the horse's neck.

Samantha returned to Alice's house. The two women hand-sewed in silence until Samantha finished sewing her stack of square fabric pieces.

Then she went to her landing spot, struck the magic pose, and was back in her bed. She undressed, slipped on one of Aaron's T-shirts and a pair of crew socks. Then she walked into the kitchen, opened the refrigerator, grabbed a bottle of sparkling water, and gulped it down. After a trip to the bathroom, she climbed into bed and fell asleep.

FRIDAY MORNING she awoke, still sore in the thighs, butt, core, and forearms.

Aaron returned home that evening. Samantha told him she was adjusting well to being home alone, because she was doing something called "immersive research." Instead of looking for a doctoral thesis using a top-down approach, she was using a bottom-up approach: exploring daily life in the mid-nineteenth century to discover issues, which might develop into a dissertation. She made no mention of her night adventures, because they seemed to be actual experiences—not dreams.

THE FOLLOWING WEEK Samantha dream-traveled twice. In planning, Samantha bought a half dozen white cotton handkerchiefs. They were a necessity because tissues had not been invented. At night, she prepared as usual, adding a new handkerchief in her dress pocket; then she fell asleep. Once in Eureka, she went to Alice's house, changed, and met Grant at the stable.

Feeling bold, she said, "I want to mount like you do. I would like to try."

Grant said, "First, lower the left stirrup. Once you are in the saddle, you can rebuckle the leather, so the left stirrup is the same height as the right."

Samantha unbuckled the leather to lower the stirrup. Then she put her left foot in the stirrup, grabbed the pommel with her left hand, and placed her right hand on the back of the saddle. Mentally she counted: One, two, three. She pushed off with her right foot, lifted herself, then her right leg over the horse. Then she readjusted the left stirrup length and straightened her back, sitting up in the saddle and grinning, proud to have mounted in one try.

Grant mounted and they rode side by side out of town at a walking pace. She said, "You must be bored at this slow pace."

"This is your lesson. You need to be comfortable in the saddle at a walking gait. Horses are herd animals. If your horse is following mine, Beckley will feel at ease. But horses spook easily, and you need to know how to handle a horse, especially when you are alone."

After riding for a while, they halted and Grant viewed the area. "See those two trees there?" He motioned with his head. Samantha looked over at two trees standing about six feet apart.

Grant said, "Walk Beckley between those two trees. See if that makes him nervous, and I will tell you what to do. I will stay here."

In her head, she recited the instructions for a left turn: Close the right rein and the right leg; open the left rein. Stay vertical.

Then she walked Beckley toward the trees. He stopped.

Grant said, "Be patient. He doesn't like that narrow path

between the trees. Give him time. Now slowly put slack in the reins so he can lower his neck. That will calm him."

Samantha did as instructed, and Beckley lowered his head toward the ground.

"Pet him. Now walk him through with your aids."

Samantha thought: Slack in the reins, hands up, gentle tap of the heels to start walking. Lower your hands, no slack in the reins while walking.

Beckley walked through the trail between the trees. "Good Beckley." She petted the horse.

There were other "spooky" encounters (a large rock and a few wild turkeys) giving Samantha practice in controlling her horse. During the break, there was much horse talk, and the return trip was at a slightly faster pace.

After the lesson, Samantha changed, returned to the stable, and placed a quarter on the shelf. Then she said good day to Beckley and came outside through the stable door, where she found Grant cleaning some brushes.

Samantha was self-conscious that her so-called brothers were never around. So this time she looked in the distance and spotted a well-dressed man. She waved and smiled at the man who waved back. "There's my brother."

Grant looked up and saw a man waving at Samantha.

Turning to Grant, she said, "The lessons are much appreciated. Good day, Lieutenant." Then she walked briskly toward the smiling man.

Samantha knew a woman waving to a man was improper and provocative. This was a newly settled rural area, however, and perhaps certain customs would be disregarded.

When she was several feet from the stranger she said, "Oh, I'm so embarrassed. I thought you were my brother." She looked back, and Grant had already turned around and was walking back into the stable.

"That's okay, ma'am."

Why wouldn't a man standing alone wave at a pretty young woman waving at him? Samantha's trick worked, and she would use it often.

For a month Samantha had night-traveled to Eureka. Rides twice or three times during the weekdays when Aaron was working in Denver.

One day she arrived in Eureka and another man was talking with Grant. Samantha recognized the man; he was the storekeeper who exchanged Samantha's coins.

As the men talked, Samantha approached Beckley, petting his neck, then taking hold of the reins, leading him out of the stable. She heard the storekeeper say, "I wanted to let you know it was delivered two months ago. In case there's a need for it."

"Good day, Lieutenant."

"Good day, Stanley."

As Stanley was leaving, Samantha said, "Good day."

"Good day," Stanley said to Samantha.

Then Grant told her to hand-walk Beckley with his bridle and saddle to the nearby greensward.

"What are we doing today?" she asked.

"All will be revealed. I will meet you."

Samantha hand-walked Beckley down the road. "What is he up to, Beckley? Did he tell you?"

Sam Time

Samantha and Beckley arrived at the open field, and Grant rode up on his horse. "I think you're ready for a lesson in trotting and cantering."

Samantha clasped her hands together against her chest and raised her shoulders in an "oh goody" reaction.

"Watch the horse's legs. This is Yukon." Grant changed horses often, and Samantha had not seen this horse. He rode the horse in a large circle as Samantha watched.

"The walk is a four-beat gait. One foot down at a time. Can you see it?"

"Yes."

Grant accelerated the horse to a trot. "The trot is two beats. A front leg and the opposite back leg. Notice the difference from the walk?"

"I do."

Samantha grinned watching Grant riding his horse in a canter, a three-beat gait. Grant was tone-deaf and found music grating. While courting his future wife, Grant stood off to the side at balls while she danced with other men. But on horseback, he had perfect rhythm. Horse and rider were synchronized.

He rode to Samantha and Beckley. "Can you see the difference in gaits?"

"Yes, I can."

"When you're riding the horse, you will feel it. And on certain surfaces, you will hear it."

"I am ready to learn."

"That is what we are here for. It's your lesson."

Samantha mounted and learned the trot and canter.

After months Samantha no longer believed she was dreaming but traveling back in time. And the light green dress fabric was key to the experience.

She thought, The dressmaker Mary showed me two other fabric rolls—one in pink and the other in powder blue—also manufactured in 1882. Could I travel back to the past with dresses made from these other fabric rolls? My guess is yes.

Samantha returned to Mary's shop and ordered a pink dress and a powder-blue dress, which were similar to the original light-green dress. The new dresses, however, would have self-piped edging, rather than ruffles. And the faux jacket peplum on each dress would be different. The peplum hem edge of the pink dress formed a right angle on the left and right front and a right-angle edge at the center back. The entire peplum hem of the powder-blue dress was a straight edge parallel with the floor resting at midhip.

The expense of ordering two other dresses concerned Samantha but she rationalized the purchase. Time traveling was extraordinary. Her sister, Grace, as the matron of honor, would have the choice of selecting the color and floral print she preferred.

Samantha also sought evidence—proof—that she was time traveling. Twice she went to bed with her cellphone in her pocket. Both times, she slept through the night. She concluded the time-travel gods didn't approve of this twenty-first-century gadget.

If she couldn't use a digital device when traveling in the past, could she use a nanny cam in the bedroom to record what happened on the nights she traveled?

Samantha bought an inexpensive nanny cam at an appliance store and set up the device focused on the bed. She adjusted the dimmer light low so she could fall asleep. That night she prepared as usual. This time, however, she went to Eureka, stayed for ten minutes, and then returned to the present.

Back at home, she watched the nanny cam recording. The dimmer light wasn't illuminated enough to record anything other than darkness.

She tried again the next night, increasing the dimmer light to medium. She fell asleep, arrived in Eureka, stayed for five minutes, and returned. The camera recording was like the first: it was too dark to see anything. The third night she tried sleeping with the lights on, which only made for a sleepless night.

Perhaps there were cameras with nighttime recording functionality, but Samantha was too frugal, and she gave up on the nanny cam. The next morning she tossed it in the kitchen trash and put the trash bag out for garbage pickup that day.

NOTWITHSTANDING THE LACK of digital proof of her time traveling, Samantha remained convinced that what she was experiencing was real. Not long after, Mary texted Samantha to say that the pink and powder-blue gowns were ready. They were as gorgeous as the first.

She time traveled to northern California wearing the new pink dress, and then two nights later, the powder-blue dress. Both dresses were as magical as the original. Samantha continued her evening time travel rotating the dresses she wore.

Now she had to fabricate a story to Grace about why her frugal sister ordered three customized gowns. The first time Samantha went to Mary's shop was the day Aaron told her he would be working out of state for nine months. Samantha told her sister that in her distress, she accidentally ordered three gowns instead of one.

After several months and much practice, Samantha was now comfortable in the saddle: walking, trotting, and cantering. On some days, Grant picked up the pace and added graded terrains. On flat terrain, they rode at a trotting pace or a canter.

When she'd first started the lessons, Samantha's horse had followed Grant's, but now they often rode side by side. At least once a week, Samantha rode her horse a mile before Grant followed from behind; the objective of this exercise was to train Samantha to handle the horse on her own.

Her interactions with Grant were friendly. They talked often of academic subjects. Samantha asked many questions about the Mexican-American War, West Point, and military life. Grant found Samantha curious and knowledgeable about topics typically discussed by men. That Samantha did not confine her conversations to home and family was a trait uncommon in most women. Many subjects, however, were verboten, nothing too personal.

One sunny day Samantha asked, "Can we go to the beach?"

"Will you ever have occasion for your family business to ride on the beach?"

"No." She blushed. "We do not have to tell my brothers."

"I do not know if Beckley has ever been on the beach. He'll follow my horse, but if we get close to the water, it could still spook him. Or he may canter—fast. And you could lose your balance. Walking on the sand will quickly tire the horses."

"I apologize for asking," she said.

"There is a narrow strip that will get us close to the beach."

Samantha was charmed Grant wanted to please her. So their course for the day was arranged to accommodate Samantha's request.

Sam Time

The sun was bright and the beach desolate when they arrived. Samantha had an urge and felt the need to ask for permission. "I would like to dip my feet in the water. Is there enough time?"

Undressing in public was scandalous—even merely shoes and socks. Undressing in front of a man, especially a married man: a no-no.

But Samantha persisted gently. "You could turn around and not look. Spend time with the horses. I want only a few minutes."

"The water is cold."

"I know. I will only be a few minutes."

Samantha walked away from Grant and the horses to the shoreline. She sat on the sand with her back toward him. She took off her ankle boots and socks, then lifted her split skirt hem a few inches, exposing her ankles.

She stepped in the swash so her feet would get wet but quickly retreated to the dry sand because the water was indeed cold. After waiting a few seconds, she stepped toward the water again, and the swash lapped over her feet. She took off her hat and held her head back. The sun shone on her face, and she held her arms out to her sides, soaking in the warmth of the sun. The split skirt hem puddled in the saltwater.

She thought, This is not a dream. I smell the salt air and hear the waves crash. I feel the cold water on my feet and feel the warmth of the sun on my face. This doesn't happen in a dream. This is real.

Her eyes took time to adjust so she could see again. She turned around. Grant had walked with the horses closer to the shoreline and was watching her.

She shouted, "You were right. It is cold." She was flattered he was staring at her.

Samantha thought, Well, well, guess you're not such a prude after all. Nothing wrong with looking, Lieutenant.

She had promised a few minutes, so she snapped out of the moment, put on her hat, walked onto dry sand, sat down, and dried her feet with her handkerchief. Then she put on her socks and ankle boots. After she mounted, they rode back in silence. The next morning at home, Samantha discovered sand in her socks.

A FEW WEEKS LATER, feeling confident, Samantha arrived at the stable to see Grant standing holding the lead rope of a new horse that was wearing a halter.

He said, "This is your horse today."

She was surprised. "Where's Beckley?"

"He was sold."

"No!" She screamed. The horse's head jerked up and its eyes widened. Grant's light-blue eyes shot her a look of disapproval. This was unacceptable, unladylike behavior. Samantha could throw a tantrum in front of Aaron, but not Grant. One day he would be general of the U.S. Army. He would not tolerate immature conduct.

She untied her handkerchief from around her neck and covered her mouth with it. After breathing deeply through her nose, she lowered the handkerchief and said, "But we trained him!"

"He belonged to someone else. And the owner sold him."

"I was not expecting this," she said sternly. Then she turned around and walked a few steps away. Samantha had thought she was coping well with the loneliness of Aaron being away. Being with Grant, quietly hand-sewing a quilt with Alice, and riding Beckley filled the void. She loved Beckley. Now he was gone. That feeling of loss overcame her.

Sam Time

She took a few deep breaths. Best to compose herself quickly. She walked back to Grant. "I apologize for my outburst. What's the horse's name?"

"Elsie."

"Elsie," she said, petting her neck. She turned around to Grant. "Do horses have good memories?"

"Yes."

"Well. She does look like a nice horse. You would not give me one that was not suitable. I'll take for her a walk."

Grant handed the lead rope to Samantha, and she hand-walked the horse down the road to the wooden house and back. When they arrived back to the stable, Grant's horse, Yukon, was already bridled and saddled.

Samantha said, "I need more time for groundwork. I see you are ready to mount. I should spend the first hour with Elsie walking. We'll go to that greensward, and she can eat some grass. Why don't you go ahead and come back in an hour?"

He nodded. "Eugene can help you saddle the horse when you're ready." Samantha looked over at a small man in the stable.

Samantha hand-walked Elsie down the road. When she heard the trot of Grant's horse behind her, she looked up. Grant lifted his hat as he rode by.

She said to Elsie, "He's such a show-off."

As they walked to the field, Samantha talked to Elsie as if she were a person. Elsie ate grass, and then Samantha walked her back to the stable. Eugene helped Samantha bridle and saddle the horse, and Samantha was ready when Grant returned. They rode for an hour, Samantha riding comfortably on Elsie.

After they returned, Samantha changed, and she strode back

to the stable. "Elsie," she said. Petting the horse's neck, Samantha spoke loud enough for Grant to hear, "I apologize, Elsie. I want to be good friends. We did have a nice day together. Good day."

She turned with a smirk on her face and looked at Grant. Everything she said to Elsie, Samantha intended for him as well.

"Good day, Lieutenant."

"Good day, Samantha."

Before returning to the present, Samantha spent some time with Alice. All the square quilt pieces were hand-sewn together, and they were now quilt-stitching the afghan-sized bedcover.

THE ULTIMATE TEST of Samantha's newly learned riding abilities was a new route that would be most challenging. They had ridden on slopes before, but Grant warned her this hill, which was thick with trees, was steeper and longer.

"Do you remember what I told you about riding on hills?"

Samantha nodded.

"Keep straight and remember how to shift your weight. Elsie has done this hill before, and you are light. Follow me and go slowly. We will zigzag up."

They slowly ascended the hill. Although she was nervous, Samantha concentrated and was pleased when they arrived at the summit.

Grant instructed, "Descending is harder. Elsie may want to go fast. Pace her at a walk, and stop her if she is going too fast. Then start again at a slow pace. We will zigzag down."

Samantha adjusted her hat and nodded.

Soon after they started down the hill, Samantha lost sight of Grant, who, despite his warnings to her, aptly steered his horse quickly down the hill. She paced Elsie slowly and thought, I could dismount and hand-walk this horse faster down this hill.

She wasn't enjoying the ride, but it was a good experience. Then she saw the sun glistening on a river at the foot of the hill. She arrived at the bottom without incident and was relieved.

Grant said, "We are going to cross."

Samantha had expected they would have a pleasant ride along the river and then take a break. "This river? No."

"You can do it. It looks more intimating than it is. We do this all the time."

"We? You mean the army?"

"It is not that deep. Your feet will get wet. Elsie will make it."

"It must be twenty, thirty feet wide," Samantha shouted.

"It is wide, but the current is not strong. You can do it. You cannot go back. You do not want to climb that hill again."

Samantha protested. "No!"

"Follow me. Your horse will follow my horse."

"What if I fall off?"

"Can you swim?"

"Yes, but the water is probably very cold."

Grant agreed, "It is cold. But it is not that deep. I know; we were here recently."

"You are in the army!"

"You can do it."

"What if I fall?" Samantha asked.

"I will get you and the horse. I will."

Samantha thought, Saved by Ulysses S. Grant. Mouth-to-mouth by Ulysses S. Grant.

"Okay," she said.

She was afraid, but Elsie did navigate the water well. The horse's legs were submerged, but the water barely touched her stomach. Samantha's feet did get wet. So far, so good. Halfway across the river, however, Samantha realized that mouth-to-mouth resuscitation didn't come into practice in the United States until the middle of the twentieth century.

They arrived on the other side of the river and Samantha said, "I am not talking to you."

About a mile later, Grant said they should take their break. They sat down on a felled log. Samantha stretched her legs out. She was still pouting, not saying anything.

Grant threw small pebbles at her feet. She thought he was trying to break her mood. She looked at him, and he seemed to be in good spirits. Why? Then it dawned on her.

"You got a letter?"

He nodded. Grant wrote frequently to his wife, but she didn't often reply in kind, despite his pleas for letters.

What could Samantha say? Was asking any questions about a private letter between him and his wife too personal? Probably.

She said, "It is always nice to hear from family."

He didn't reply but asked the question Samantha had been expecting. "What business does your family operate here?"

"Gold mining, like everyone else. We have a few claims."

"Most miners arrived years ago, when gold was first discovered. Why did your family settle here only recently?" Grant asked.

"We now know what was not obvious before we made the journey: We should have arrived among the forty-niners." The term forty-niners referred to the people who flocked to California in 1849 in search of gold, which was discovered in northern California a year earlier. The gold prospects were depleted by 1855. "We will not make a fortune. But I am glad to have seen this part of the country."

"How was the journey here?"

Samantha knew the history. Crossing the country, overland, from east to west was a six-month arduous trek. A quicker, but more expensive, route also existed: people and goods traveled from the East Coast by steamship south, around Cape Horn in South America, and then headed north. The shortest route was crossing the Isthmus of Panama, but it was typically jammed with miners and tradesmen.

She paused then said, "Long. We came by steamer, around Cape Horn. Took us six weeks. I was seasick for most of the trip. And you?"

"Our ship was crammed. Much seasickness. We crossed through the isthmus. Took the railroad to its terminus. Then there was a cholera outbreak. I was glad I had not taken my family. My firstborn would not have survived. What was left of the Fourth Infantry came by steamer, to San Francisco. Eventually I came here."

Although Samantha wanted to know more, Grant stood and took the horses' reins, ending the conversation. When they returned to the stable, Samantha went to Alice's house, changed into her clothes, and walked back to the stable to say good day to Elsie and leave a quarter on the shelf.

Grant was outside and she approached him. Samantha was contrite. "It was a challenging ride today. I appreciate your patience with me. Despite what I said, I still would like more lessons."

"In a few days."

Samantha smiled. Then she looked in the distance and spotted a man standing alone. He was in work clothes but clean. Samantha waved and he waved back. Grant turned to look.

"Good day, Lieutenant Grant."

"Good day, Samantha."

When she was several feet from the man, Samantha apologized for mistaking him for someone else. He was delighted to see her close up. She turned around and Grant was gone. Then she quickly passed the man.

Samantha had told Grant she had four brothers. If she continued to wave at pretend brothers, would Grant ever suspect a ruse? She quickly dismissed this concern; nearly every man sported a brimmed hat, beard, and mustache. At a distance they looked alike.

She found a solitary spot, closed her eyes, palms at her sides, and took a deep breath—she was back in her bed, a few minutes after 2:00 a.m.

Sam Time

Show-off

The two couples, Grace and John, and Samantha and Aaron, spent a weekend at a luxury resort. John had successfully resolved a case with a major client at the law firm and was rewarded with two suites for a two-night weekend at the resort. Along with golf, tennis, and a pool, the resort offered horseback riding excursions. The four agreed on booking the last.

The two couples assembled at the stable in a group of a dozen people. Everyone was given black equestrian helmets. An instructor explained that two groups would be formed: novices and intermediate. Novices would be given a brief lesson on handling a horse before leisurely riding around a quarter-mile track several times. Eventually, they would enter the grounds for a short loop on the scenic trail. The intermediate group would ride the long, scenic trail. Another instructor asked for intermediate riders to move to the right and novice riders to the left. Samantha moved to the right while the others in her party, along with everyone else, moved left. She was standing alone.

Grace motioned with her hand for Samantha to move to their side, thinking she had heard incorrectly. But Samantha stayed where she was.

Grace said, "Sam, you never rode a horse."

"You don't know everything about me," Samantha replied.

"Intermediate? When did you learn how to ride?"

"Oh, a long time ago."

Ken, the instructor assigned to the intermediate excursion, approached Samantha. Aaron, Grace, and John watched incredulously as Samantha explained her experience to Ken. He walked away and returned with a medium-sized horse.

"What's his name?" Samantha asked.

"Gleason."

"May I hand-walk him down and back?" she said, tilting her head in the direction where she would go. "I'd like to get to know him."

"Sure," Ken said.

Samantha glanced back and heard Aaron say to Grace and John, "What is she doing?"

"Beats me," Grace replied.

Although the novice group was pairing with their horses, Samantha's companions were distracted and continued to watch Samantha hand-walking her horse.

When she returned to the stable, she checked the fit of the girth and said to Ken, "We're ready."

The stable had mounting blocks, which were plastic portable steps. Samantha donned the helmet, walked up the mounting block steps, put her left foot into the stirrup, swung her right leg over the horse, and slid into the saddle. She took hold of the reins and waited for Ken to mount his horse.

Sam Time

She looked down at her companions. John took out his cellphone and snapped photos. Samantha smiled and posed for the shots. Then he switched his cellphone to video mode to record Samantha's newly discovered talent.

Grace turned to Aaron, "Did you know about this?"

"No. It's news to me."

Samantha was the only intermediate rider. Ken wanted to observe how she could handle a horse, so they rode side by side around a one-quarter track near the stable.

Ken asked Samantha to steer the horse right and left.

"Do you want me to trot halfway, then canter?"

"Show me what you can do," Ken replied.

Samantha showed her riding proficiency. As she and the instructor trotted past the novices, on their way to the scenic trail, Aaron shouted to her, "Who are you?"

"I'll be fine. You have fun," Samantha countered.

Two hours later, when Samantha and Ken exited the scenic trail, the novice group had reassembled at the stable and dismounted from their horses.

She asked Ken, "Can I do a canter once around the quarter-mile trail?"

"Go for it. Then meet me in front of the stable."

Samantha could not resist showing off. She steered her horse onto the track in a trot and transitioned to a canter. The novice group applauded as John recorded the scene on his cellphone.

Exiting the track, Samantha trotted her horse to the stable. She halted the horse in front of everyone. In one fluid move, she took both feet out of the stirrups, swung her right leg over the horse's back, and stuck a two-footed landing like an Olympic gymnast.

She removed her helmet and thanked Ken. Aaron walked up to Samantha, picked her up, and twirled her around, saying, "I love you" for all to hear. Then he whispered in her ear, "Let's skip lunch and go right back to the room."

With his arm around her waist he said, "You surprise me." Samantha grinned, pleased with herself.

"We're skipping lunch and heading back to the room. Let's go out for an early dinner," Aaron said to Grace and John, who agreed.

After Samantha and Aaron were refreshed and had lounged in the room for a few hours, they walked the grounds in a retail area. There was an antique store in which Aaron found a coin set he liked.

He said, "It's expensive. You're so good at saving. I can't justify spending money on this. It's a hobby. And we have the wedding coming up."

To his surprise, Samantha asked, "If there wasn't a Sam, would you buy it?"

"Yes."

"You know our finances. We're doing fine. Right? This is your one splurge. I don't want to be a spoiler."

"That's so sweet, when I know you're so frugal. You're okay with it?"

"Yes. I want to see you happy."

Samantha replied, "It's such a nice weekend, this purchase will be a fond memory. But I must admit, my motive is not pure. Despite my penny-pinching ways, I think somewhere, someday, I will want my own splurge, and you'll have to say yes because I agreed to this."

She kissed him on the lips, and he bought the coin set.

As they walked back to the room, Samantha asked, "What if you went back in time. Say, to the early 1850s. What coins from that time are the most valuable now, and how would you know?"

"There are websites that list the values. Generally, the more pristine condition, the more valuable. And rare. A coin is rare if few were minted in a certain year. When we get back to the room, I'll show you a website."

Once they returned to the room, Aaron placed his purchase in the room safe; then he opened his laptop and connected to a website showing U.S. coins no longer minted and their estimated value. Then Aaron received a work-related phone call. While he took the call on the balcony, Samantha searched the website for coins dated 1854 and prior. If the opportunity arose when she time traveled, she would find rare coins to bring back to the present.

LATER THEY TEXTED Grace and John to meet for dinner at the resort restaurant. After they'd been seated and had ordered, Grace said, "So Sam, where did you learn how to ride like that?"

"As I said, it was a long time ago."

"Where, with whom?"

"I am not going to talk about past relationships. Aaron and I are engaged, and I don't want to talk about it."

Grace pressed her sister, "So it was a long time ago, but you rode that horse with such confidence."

Samantha had to concede something, "Okay, when I found out we were going to this resort, and we agreed on the horseback riding excursion, I went to a stable to brush up. Twice."

Anxious about Grace asking anymore questions, Samantha said, "Let's play our pun game. Horse puns. You start, Aaron."

They went around the table each taking turns; the objective of the game was to see how long they could go.

Aaron: *He was in a stable relationship and would not horse around.*

Samantha: *Stop making hay of her abilities.*

John: *Aaron should pony up some money for the drinks.*

Grace: *After the wedding she would be unbridled with the matron-of-honor duties.*

Aaron: *Samantha would take the reins of the family.*

Samantha: *Someone would need to bring out the cavalry to stop her from marrying Aaron.*

John: *His long office hours make Aaron the workhorse of the household.*

Grace: *Samantha was making good strides on her doctorate.*

Aaron: *He would jockey not to wash dishes this weekend.*

Samantha: *Aaron was a stud.*

John: *They wouldn't be waiting furlong for their drinks.*

Grace: *There were hurdles in raising a good family.*

They had made three rounds of cringe-worthy puns. It wasn't a record for them, but they toasted once the drinks were served.

Samantha and Aaron strolled the resort grounds at dusk. They were a touchy couple, often holding hands, walking arm in arm, sitting on a sofa watching television snuggling together, and spooning in bed. This weekend was like a mini prelude honeymoon, and they couldn't keep their hands off each other.

Samantha found good fortune. She was engaged to Aaron and able to visit the past. The two delightfully merged this weekend. She was naïve to think it would always be this way.

Sam Time

Samantha Stumbles

The weather in Eureka was warm, and the horseback riding with Grant had been enjoyable. They returned to the stable, and Samantha headed toward Alice's home. Before changing back into her dress, she walked to the back of the house and ventured where she had never been: the privy, the outhouse.

On longer riding days during their breaks, Samantha would excuse herself and walk away for a private moment. Or she would comfortably wait until returning to her Austin home for a bathroom stop. But not today.

The privy was as nasty as expected. Pieces of newspaper, which were nailed to the inside wall, served as toilet paper.

She stepped out of the outhouse and let the wooden door slam shut behind her. After taking a few steps down the narrow dirt path toward the front of the house, she heard a fluttering in the trees. She saw a bird's nest. For a closer view, she stepped off the path.

Inattention to her feet was her downfall. Samantha's right foot caught under an exposed tree root. Instinctively, she put her arms out to break her fall, then landed stomach down on thick brush. Her left hand landed on something sharp and hurt badly. As she pulled herself up, her left hand was stuck. So she turned it, and the pain was even more pronounced. Now on all fours, she looked to see what was causing the sharp pain. There was blood.

Propping herself on her knees, she could now see something had pierced through the palm to the top of her hand, where the bones of the thumb and forefinger meet. She blew on the blood and touched gently with her right-hand fingers. It was a fishhook.

She stood and hustled to the stable, where she showed Grant her injury. She was distressed but she wasn't crying. "I think it's a fishhook. Can you pull it out? I will look away."

He held her wrist, staring pensively at her hand. "This is not like a nail or a bullet. This is lodged near a vein next to those two bones. I see the barb sticking out of the top of your hand and the fishhook eye protruding from your palm. It's not a straight pull. It will come out, but . . ."

"But it will hurt," Samantha said. Grant's silence meant yes.

Still holding her wrist, he walked Samantha to Alice's house. "First, let's wash it with alcohol."

Samantha thought of her options. Go home to Austin. But I need my dress. I will have difficulty slipping my hand through the sleeve. The hook would get stuck in the dress lining. Blood would stain the fabric. I could try ripping the sleeve off the dress at the shoulder seam. But the machine-sewn stitches would be hard to pull out using only one hand. That won't work. I can't go home yet. Stay here. This is not life threatening. Although it will hurt badly.

She said, "I made it worse as I rose. I turned my hand and pulled. Or pulled and turned. How clumsy of me. Can you take care of this?"

Grant nodded.

Once at Alice's house, he knocked on the door. Alice answered. Samantha's hand was throbbing, and she didn't hear what Grant said to Alice. But Alice left while Grant and Samantha went inside.

He sat her down on a chair next to the table. She laid her arm on the tabletop.

Maybe this was a dream. Samantha was appeasing herself. After spending months convincing herself she was actually time traveling, now she wanted to believe differently. She wanted this to be a dream—a nightmare.

The settlers who moved out West were hardy, self-sufficient people. Samantha was a mere visitor, used to and dependent on twenty-first-century modern medicine. So if this wasn't a dream—real—she needed to embody her Victorian character and muster some pioneer spirit.

Alice returned and Grant asked, "Alice, would you get a washbasin and alcohol?" She nodded. Samantha always had difficulty understanding Alice. But she did hear, "He has it. He's coming."

Alice brought over the washbasin and alcohol, placing them on the table. Grant picked up Samantha's wrist, placed it over the basin, and poured the alcohol on her injury. She moved her feet back and forth, gritting her teeth to distract from the pain.

Alice cleared the tabletop of the few bowls that were on it. Then she motioned for Samantha to stand. Alice said something, then repeated, "On table."

"Lie on the table?" Samantha asked.

Alice nodded.

There was no refined way to do this. Samantha slid butt first onto the table and lay down, faceup. Her feet protruded beyond the table's short end.

Staring at the ceiling beams, Samantha heard a knock on the door, the squeak of the door opening, and heavy boot steps on the wooden floor planks. Samantha turned her head to see a man's silhouette. She blinked and recognized the man. Stanley from the general store.

Deep breaths, she thought. Why is Stanley here? Why did Grant summon Stanley?

The last thing she remembered was a cloth placed over her nose and mouth.

SAMANTHA WAS DAZED, waking in and out of sleep—having been drugged. She was no longer on the table but on the bed against the opposite wall. One of the men asked Alice to get something.

Samantha wondered if this was all a dream. The song "White Rabbit" played in Samantha's head. This was so weird. Going back in time. But it seemed so real. She was embarrassed. Could she snap out of this dream? Samantha slipped back into sleep.

She awoke feeling groggy. She looked down at her throbbing hand, which was wrapped with her handkerchief.

Grant was literally talking war stories—about the Mexican-American War. Samantha would have normally listened with interest, but she was still recovering. No one noticed when she tried to lift her head. She took deep breaths to relax.

After some time, Samantha sat up slowly, dangling her legs off the side of the bed. She held her head with her good hand.

Sam Time

Samantha stood slowly. "Where is my dress?" Where it always was, on the chair behind the dressing screen. She went behind the screen, changed out of her riding clothes and into her dress.

When she emerged from behind the screen, Alice rested her hand on the back of the empty chair. Samantha shuffled to the table and sat in the chair. Then Alice placed a mug in front of Samantha. She picked up the mug, then took a sip. It was broth. She was thirsty and wanted to gulp it down, but that wouldn't have been ladylike.

"This is so kind of you, Alice." Samantha sipped the broth.

Grant said, "We removed the hook. There are two pieces of tree bark, oak, on each side of the wound to stop the bleeding. Don't remove the dressing until morning; then clean the wound."

"I am grateful for your kindness," Samantha said.

A clear small bottle was in the center of the table. She leaned over to read its inscription: "Chloroform. 4 fluid ounces. Mfg. Boston, Mass. For anesthetic use."

She said, "This is the magic potion. It has come a long way, like many of us."

Stanley said, "Got it two months ago."

"It looks full."

Stanley said, "Only one teaspoon for a dosage. Last month, a man had a tooth pulled. Used it on him. You're the second person."

Samantha thought, The first woman, a test case. Six teaspoons in a fluid ounce, four ounces in a bottle makes a mere twenty-four doses. "It says 'anesthetic.' This is for surgeries. Amputations. Why use your limited supply on me?"

"The lieutenant asked," said Stanley. Then Samantha remembered when she saw Stanley talking with Grant at the stable. Stanley was spreading the word about this anesthetic, which was replacing the highly flammable ether.

Samantha said to Grant, "I appreciate your kind consideration." He wanted to spare her the indignity of biting on a stick or stuffing her mouth with a handkerchief to muffle her screams.

Alice said, "You ask me?"

Samantha shook her head.

"You ask me?" Alice said again.

Samantha didn't understand but forced a smile and shook her head.

Grant said, "We heard people under this anesthetic can become talkative. You were incoherent."

She straightened her back, thinking, What did I say? Did I say I was from the twenty-first century?

Stanley interrupted her thoughts. "Something about rabbits and mushrooms."

Samantha closed her eyes. "Was I singing?"

"You could say that," Stanley said while he and Grant snickered.

She blushed with embarrassment, now realizing that when she was lying on the bed still groggy, she was actually singing the "White Rabbit" song.

"I must go." She reached for her mini drawstring change purse in her dress pocket, placed it on the table, and took out three quarters. She slid a coin to each person. "For the lessons. For the chloroform. For the alcohol and the broth. I am grateful for your kindness given my clumsiness. I need to return to our lodgings. My brothers will be worried." She put on her headband.

"I should return to the store," Stanley said.

Everyone stood to leave and bid one another good day. Once

outside, Samantha inhaled the fresh air. Stanley left in one direction, and Grant walked in the other direction back to the stable.

Then Samantha thought, The departure, make it count.

"Lieutenant," she called out, and Grant turned around.

Walking toward him, she said, "I am not sure when I will return. My hand must heal before I hold the reins again."

She stopped at an arm's distance from Grant. "My oldest brother agreed to my riding lessons because it is beneficial. But he said if anything should happen, he would no longer allow me to ride." She couldn't look Grant in the eye because she was lying. Bowing her head, she said, "They have enough worries with the business, they don't need me getting into trouble. I can be persuasive, but it may take some time before I return."

Then she looked at Grant and he nodded.

They locked eyes. "I will miss Elsie." She meant, I will miss you. She punctuated her sentiment. "She is a fine companion."

Did he understand her implication? His penetrating stare said yes.

After a few seconds, she said, "Good day, Ulysses."

"Good day, Samantha."

Walking to her landing spot, she repressed any urge to ponder her feelings for Grant. He was kind, patient, and of good moral character. He was handsome, and she knew who he would become. If she was honest with herself, she was infatuated with him.

Finding an isolated place, she closed her eyes, placed her palms at her sides, and took a deep breath—at last she was back in her bed. Tired, she pulled off her headband and flung it on the floor. She unlaced her boots and pushed them off the bed. Then she fell asleep without taking off her dress.

Donna Balon

Travel Delays

Early in the morning, Samantha awoke thinking it was strange she was still wearing her dress. She rolled on her back to undo the mini buttons down the front bodice. Lifting her hands to unbutton the dress, she said out loud, "Oh my God." Her left hand was wrapped in her handkerchief.

She thought, This wasn't a dream, a nightmare. It actually happened. Proof I've been time traveling. But this is getting out of hand. No time for puns—this is serious. And did I really inhale chloroform? What am I going to say to Aaron? To Grace?

She sat up and unwrapped her hand. There was no tree bark; perhaps it had fallen out. She didn't see any swelling or fresh blood. The bleeding had stopped. The wound was pink—not red—and the pain had subsided.

When was the last time she had a tetanus shot? She couldn't remember and needed to go to an urgent care clinic to get a jab. She took off her dress, slipped on a T-shirt and jeans, and drove to a 24-7 clinic, which was a block from the university. The clinic and the university were partners in an agreement allowing students and staff nominal co-payments for medical services.

She arrived so early, only a few homeless people were sitting or sleeping in the clinic's waiting room. Was Samantha as adrift as these unfortunate people?

Samantha checked in, took the clipboard with a bunch of forms, and signed without reading any of them, except the HIPAA form. She signed this form, leaving blank the space for the names of people who could access the details of this visit. Typically, she would fill in Aaron's or Grace's name, but she didn't want either to know about this doctor's visit.

A nurse took Samantha down a long white corridor and pointed at the exit doors down the long hallway.

"After your exam, walk out those doors to the parking lot. We don't mind the homeless occupying seats when we're not busy, but it's safer for you to leave by that exit, so no one follows you to your car."

"Okay. Thank you."

In the exam room, Samantha told the doctor she was hiking on a wooded trail with friends when she fell, and her hand landed on a fishhook. A nurse cleaned the wound, gave Samantha a tetanus shot, and took two vials of blood.

The doctor said the wound looked fine. "Does it hurt?"

"A little."

"We have strict protocols for prescribing antibiotics and pain medication. Your body is healing itself. But in the next day or two, if your hand swells, gets red, hurts more than it does now, or if you have a fever, come back, and we'll prescribe medication."

Samantha asked, "But why did you take vials of blood?"

"It's part of our Wellness Program with the university. When you checked in, reception handed you a packet of forms explaining the program," the doctor said, knowing many patients don't read the forms.

"And I say this to everyone I see. Hydrate. Drink liquids. And when was the last time you ate?"

Her sense of time was mixed up. Should she count the broth she drank? "Ah, let me see. I don't remember."

As she was leaving the exam room, the doctor added, "Get something to eat."

The words rang: Get something to eat. This triggered her memory of the closing refrain of the "White Rabbit" song. As she walked down the long hallway, the song played in her head. And it looped in the back of her mind during the drive home. Samantha wondered, Am I crazy?

AFTER SHE ARRIVED HOME, Samantha toasted a whole wheat English muffin, spread it with peanut butter, and poured a glass of orange juice. Sitting at the kitchen counter with her meal, she opened her laptop and searched the Internet for "chloroform." There were alarming articles that chloroform was no longer used because it could cause cancer, among other nasty side effects, with long-term exposure or taken in large doses. She felt reassured the one dose would not be harmful. Then she promptly deleted her "chloroform" searches from the Google history.

A COUPLE DAYS LATER, the doctor called with the results of her blood work. Everything looked normal, except the toxicology screening showed a positive result for a controlled substance (chloroform), which was not normal. The doctor gave her a referral to see a therapist.

When Samantha protested, the doctor said she had signed a consent form agreeing to consultation with a therapist for any drug use. Failure to attend two therapy sessions was against the university/clinic agreement. Samantha would have to pay the full price of the visit, the tetanus shot, and bloodwork if she didn't attend two therapy sessions.

She inferred this policy was a way of dealing with student and faculty addictions. Although she wasn't using drugs, she couldn't say what actually happened. Reluctantly, she made an appointment with a staff therapist.

Perhaps this could be helpful. She wouldn't reveal everything—she would be considered crazy—but she would reveal "sleeping problems." Her main objective, however, was to act normal and upbeat, to avoid triggering any more compulsory appointments.

AT THE END OF THE WEEK, Samantha returned to the clinic. She had been assigned a therapist with an unpronounceable last name. Dr. Nancy Something. Apparently, even the administrators at the clinic didn't know how to pronounce it, because they all referred to the therapist as Dr. Nancy.

The therapist was a petite, light-haired, fair-skinned woman. She looked and sounded as if she came from a Scandinavian country. Her accent was so thick, Samantha could not understand a third of what the therapist was saying. Regardless, Samantha planned on answering no to most of the questions.

Samantha was nervous throughout the fifty-minute appointment. Dr. Nancy looked at the forms Samantha had completed. "Your parents are alive. Do you interact with them much?"

"My parents live in Florida. They still work. Three of my grandparents are still alive, so my parents live there to stay close to the grands. My parents come here at least once a year; we fly out there for the holidays; we talk every week."

"You're single."

"Engaged. We live together. My fiancé is out of town on business. Away for the workweek, home on the weekend. But it's hard, you know, compressing a relationship into two days. But that's temporary. His assignment should be finished before the wedding."

"How do you feel about this?"

"I miss him. But I'm working on my doctoral dissertation, so I'm filling my time with that. When he's not there, I don't sleep as well."

"What do you mean by 'don't sleep well'?"

"I fall asleep okay. But I have dreams. They seem long, vivid, and intense. Real."

"You said 'dreams' not 'nightmares.'"

"Generally dreams, but an occasional nightmare."

"How do you feel when you wake up?"

"Tired. Like I haven't slept, having this long-running dream for several hours on some nights."

"When did these dreams begin?"

"Recently."

"Since your fiancé has been away."

"Yes. That's about right."

"They found a controlled substance in your toxicology screen. Can you tell me about that?"

"It surprised me too. Listen, I eat well. Exercise. I run five miles every other day. I try to get a good night's sleep. I drink occasionally, one or two drinks on the weekend. I don't smoke pot or use other recreational drugs." Samantha didn't make eye contact and squirmed in her seat.

Dr. Nancy glared as if to say, "Methinks thou dost protest too much."

Samantha noticed and stopped talking.

"Tox screens don't lie," the doctor said.

"Well, I don't know how it got there," Samantha snapped.

"Sleeping problems can be caused by stress. Sleep apnea. I am asked about sleepwalking, but that's rare in adults. I'll confer with our psychiatrist and recommend an MRI of the brain, which will serve as a baseline. We'll discuss the results in your next session."

Samantha tried to contain herself. This was overreaching.

"I don't understand the need for an MRI. A baseline for what?"

"You're complaining about sleep problems, your tox screen was positive, and you have new stress factors in your life. Have you heard about our Wellness Program?"

She stared and didn't answer. She hated this doctor.

Samantha returned home and went out for a five-mile run.

SAMANTHA WAS DELIGHTED when Aaron returned home on Friday night, and she said nothing about the drama during the week. And she hid her black-and-blue hand injury using makeup concealer.

Late Sunday afternoon, they walked to a nearby supermarket for a few items. There was a panhandler outside, and Samantha reached into her purse and gave him a five-dollar bill.

The thin disheveled man said thank you. Then he shouted,

"You're the pretty lady from the clinic!"

Samantha shook her head.

"I don't forget a pretty woman. I saw you at the clinic. You drive a silver car, a Honda." The man then recalled the complete license plate number! He pointed to his head. "Got a good memory."

Samantha replied, "Have a nice day."

Aaron asked, "Why were you at the clinic? Are you okay?"

She grabbed Aaron's hand and led him into the store.

Samantha had to come clean. "Yes. I was there," she said, looking for an empty aisle where they could talk privately. "I didn't want to bother you with it."

"We're engaged. Why would you not tell me about this?"

"You're right." They walked deep into the store. Aisle nine, frozen foods, was empty. Samantha was now holding on to Aaron's arm, pulling him down the middle of the aisle. She turned toward Aaron and showed him her left hand, gently wiping the concealer off her skin.

"You put makeup on it? What happened?"

"I was running, tripped, and fell. My hand landed on this fishhook. It punctured my skin."

"When was this?"

"Tuesday."

"Tuesday? All this time and you said nothing?"

"I was embarrassed and didn't want to talk about it. Didn't want to relive the experience." She didn't want to lie to Aaron.

"But this is me, your fiancé. Why didn't you tell me about this?"

A man came down the aisle with his cart. Lowering her voice, Samantha said, "You were in that big meeting on Tuesday. Remember? I wasn't going to bother you with this."

Aaron whispered, "But what about the rest of the week?"

"Excuse me," said the man with the cart.

Samantha and Aaron shuffled farther down the aisle.

"I know, but after I went to the clinic and took care of it, I thought I would tell you when you came home. And then, I was so happy to see you, and we were having such a good time, I didn't want to drag down the weekend with this story."

Aaron did a double take of the man and said to Samantha, "Do you see him loading his cart with TV dinners?"

Samantha snickered. "Yes. I guess he lives alone. Listen, when something ugly happens, I want to forget it. Pretend it didn't happen. Bury it."

"I learned this from a stranger."

"It's kinda funny. But I'm telling you now. It hurt. I felt clumsy and stupid. I didn't want you to see me that way."

"How would you feel if I cut my hand, went to urgent care, and didn't tell you?"

"I agree. I would be baffled. Aaron, I love you. Don't read anything more into this than I had a bad week and don't want to discuss it. Okay?"

He hugged her. "I'm sorry to hear you had a bad week, and I wasn't there to make it better."

Samantha said, "You're so warm, and this aisle is so cold."

Aaron looked into a freezer. "Do you want ice cream?"

"Yes, but will it survive the walk home?"

"It's hard as a rock now. Should be just right when we get home. What flavor?"

Samantha said, "Chocolate mint chip."

"White or green?"

"Green."

They left the store and Aaron put his arm around Samantha's waist. She tried to charm her way out of her predicament with a limerick:

> *There was a woman who loved ice cream,*
> *She found her true love who was a dream,*
> *He was mad she did not tell,*
> *Of her gashed hand when she fell,*
> *Trust in her would take time to redeem.*

Aaron smiled and kissed her on the forehead.

She said, "It's not my best, but it's my way of saying I'm sorry. I was unhinged when this fishhook thing happened. But I managed. Now you're here and I want to focus on us."

"Well, I'm glad you're okay. Do Grace and John still have a key to our house? And we have one of theirs?"

"Yes, to both."

The couples had thought they should share their house keys in case of an emergency.

As they were walking home, they ran into their next-door neighbors, George and Marion. "Hot out today," Samantha said.

"If you want, you can use our pool anytime. We no longer use it in our advanced age," Marion said.

Samantha replied, "We may take you up on that."

George said, "The code to the gate lock is the reverse of our house number. Stop by anytime."

Once they were in the house Samantha said, "Did you hear that? They said we could use their pool anytime. Would you like to go for a dip and swim sometime?"

Aaron was spooning the ice cream into bowls. "Yes. Sounds like fun."

THE NEXT WEEK Samantha went for an MRI. She lay down faceup on the table. The technician told her to relax as the machine slid her into its confining tube.

She tried to ease her anxiousness with the pun game. I have gotten myself in a tight spot, she thought.

That was all she had. But then she composed a limerick.

There was a therapist named Nancy,
The patients of whom did not fancy,
Her accent was thick,
Made all people sick,
And every diagnosis chancy.

SAMANTHA RETURNED to Dr. Nancy's office a week later for the second consultation. This time Samantha planned to be composed. She had replayed the first visit over in her head many times, and she thought her body language betrayed her.

She often watched reruns of the *Law & Order: Criminal Intent* series. The climax of every episode was the interrogation scene, in which the accused typically presented a "tell." It's a poker term: when a player manifests some type of behavior—such as an eye twitch—revealing a latent emotion to the other players.

In the first consultation, when Samantha protested the results of the toxicology report, she lost eye contact and moved around in her chair, revealing to Dr. Nancy that Samantha wasn't telling the truth. This time Samantha would sit still, place her hands on her lap and keep them there to project confidence and honesty.

Samantha was relieved the MRI showed no abnormalities. She tried to be upbeat. Of course she said she had been sleeping better, enjoying being with her fiancé on weekends, working on her dissertation, and talking often with her parents and sister.

When Dr. Nancy was speaking, Samantha became fatigued trying to understand what the doctor was saying with her thick accent. Samantha's mind wandered off, thinking about her next time travel. Samantha nodded gently, pretending to listen. After fifty minutes, Dr. Nancy said any further consultation was at Samantha's discretion.

Samantha thought, Good. I'll pretend this whole episode never happened.

Sam Time

A Confidant

The following Thursday evening, a university professor hosted a party, which Samantha attended. She wore a black sequined tunic top borrowed from Grace to dress up her black leggings and black ballerina shoes with a small black crossover handbag. Over a hundred professors and adjuncts mingled at a contemporary mansion, with an infinity pool and a view of the city lights.

Samantha enjoyed hors d'oeuvres and an elaborate spread of food while talking with colleagues. Even Dr. Nancy was there—Samantha avoided her.

"Hey, Sam." A fellow adjunct professor tapped Samantha on the shoulder.

"Hi, Olivia. So good to see you."

"How are you?"

"I'm well. Planning the wedding. Aaron is away on business during the week. I'm working on my doctorate. How are you?"

"Better, since I saw you last. After my parents died, I was a mess. But I met with Philip Hastings for therapy sessions. He was great."

"Professor Hastings?" Samantha asked.

"Yes. He's antisocial. Maybe on the lower end of the Asperger's spectrum. But he approached me when he heard both my parents died within months of each other."

"Really?"

"Yes, he's licensed, so he can meet with patients. And he didn't charge me, because we met on campus. I think he liked the challenge of my case."

"Case?"

"Yes. There's some pretty weird stuff in my family. He wasn't judgmental. Methodical. He was so helpful. He's here. I just saw him. Anyway, Sam. Good to see you. I need the ladies' room."

"Nice to see you too, Olivia."

Samantha opened the sliding glass doors and stepped onto the patio. There, by the firepit, she spotted Professor Philip Hastings, who was sitting by himself on the half-moon, shaped sofa. Philip was a well-respected, tenured professor in the philosophy department who also had a doctorate in psychology, with an undergraduate degree in theology. He was a thinker and a loner, who enjoyed listening more than talking. Samantha knew Philip causally and liked him for his intelligence.

And tonight he was staring at the flames in the firepit while smoking a joint. Olivia said Philip was instrumental in a dark time in her life. If there was someone Samantha could talk with about her nighttime adventures, Philip was her guy.

Samantha walked to the firepit, where Philip was seated, and said, "May I join you? It's Samantha Hunter. I'm an associate professor of history, although I'm taking a year and a half off to work on my doctorate."

She sat down before he could say no.

"Yes, I know who you are. I met your fiancé at the last of these soirees. Aaron, right?"

"Good memory. He's away on business. He'll be back tomorrow night."

"Would you like some?" Philip offered Samantha the joint.

"Oh. No, thank you."

Tall and thin, Philip had a Woodstock look. He wore jeans, a T-shirt, and flip-flops year-round. He parted his shag-styled gray hair in the middle and wore rimless glasses.

Samantha was timid. "There's something I would like to discuss with you. Something that would need your pledge of confidentiality. It's not illegal. I have an unusual situation. I cannot even speak to Aaron about it. Are you game?"

"I've heard much. There's not anything that would shock me."

"This is literally out of this world. I need your utmost confidence."

"I give you my word."

"There are certain nights, under certain conditions, I have extremely vivid dreams, so real I think they're not dreams but genuine experiences. For example, in this experience, I've learned how to ride a horse. And the next morning, I'm sore in my thighs and butt. I've never ridden a horse before. So I keep having these dream experiences and practice more horseback riding. And I go out with Aaron and another couple for a horseback riding excursion, and I'm an intermediate rider."

Samantha stopped, waiting for a reaction from Philip. He asked, "Is there more?"

"A lot more. One time, I'm walking on this dirt path, and I step into this wooded area to see what I think is a bird's nest. I'm looking up and my foot gets caught under an exposed tree root and I fall. My hands break the fall, but a fishhook pierces the skin right near the bones of my thumb and index finger. The next morning I wake up. And I have this injury. Here, see?"

It was after dusk and dark, so Samantha held her phone with the camera light on over her hand.

"Philip, I haven't even got to the interesting part."

He stared at her. "Go on. I'm listening."

"I swear I'm being transported to a different place and time. It sounds so strange, even to hear myself say it. Do I have your interest?"

After thinking for a few seconds, he asked, "Why don't you stop by my office tomorrow? Let's talk some more."

They exchanged phone numbers and a time to meet.

SAMANTHA HAD NEVER been to Philip's office and was curious to see his chaise lounge, the type of sofa used decades ago, on which patients lie during sessions with a psychologist. Faculty knew that Philip would sleep on the lounge if he worked into the night. She noticed a folded afghan on the foot of the sofa, before taking a seat in front of his desk.

He leaned back in his chair, while Samantha recited what she told him the night before, assuming that, since he'd been smoking weed, he may not have remembered what she said. Philip closed his eyes and scratched his eyebrows, "There's many ways to look at this. Many ways. But first I want to understand what you think, what you believe."

He cleared his throat and then said, "So you disappear. And where do you go for these horseback riding lessons?"

"The year is 1854."

He had no reaction and stared at her. "Go on. I'm listening."

"Aaron and I are getting married next year. I went to this dressmaker, and she had this lovely fabric labeled 'manufactured 1882.' So she made this gown out of this fabric. I tried it on, it fit, and I took it home. That night, I fell asleep wearing this gown and voilà. I'm in a rural town in northern California. And frankly, I don't understand why I would be going back to 1854 with fabric manufactured in 1882. This has been happening for over a few months, a few times a week. During the workweek, Aaron is in Denver on business."

Philip listened, then looked up at the ceiling. "Go on."

"There's something else that occurred to me. I can smell during these experiences. Like, when I'm horseback riding, I pass by these pigpens, which stink. And in my dreams, I have never had a sense of smell. I searched on the Internet, and found a reliable report saying it's rare for people to dream of smells."

Philip stared at her.

"You're not convinced." Disappointed, she said, "You said there are many ways to analyze this. I believe this is real."

Philip shifted in this chair, revealing an obvious tell for a psychologist who recognized signals and tells in others. "Analysis takes time."

"Analysis—as a philosopher or psychologist?"

"Fair question."

Samantha said, "I want Philip the philosopher right now. Any psychologist would say I'm crazy. But what I need is a philosopher. What is happening and why? Can you do that?"

Philip replied, "Yes, under one condition."

"What?"

"That you come back, and we talk about the other ways to analyze this. Looking at the psychological angle."

"Okay. That's fair. You should know when I injured my hand, I went to the clinic. And they did blood work, and the results showed a controlled substance in my bloodstream because I was drugged with chloroform in 1854."

Philip's eyes widened.

Samantha said, "I told you there's a lot more. So, the clinic said because of this finding—they thought it was substance abuse—I needed counseling. I had two sessions with Dr. Nancy."

"She's good."

"I wasn't comfortable with her. And I didn't tell her any of this. We talked only of sleep problems and my fiancé being away on business. She conferred with another doctor to order an MRI. So I got an MRI. That seemed extreme."

Philip asked, "Did you read all the papers you signed at the clinic?"

"No. I didn't know the clinic and the university had this Wellness Program. That's why they took vials of blood. The good news: I'm healthy. The bad news: they found a controlled substance in the tox screen, which started all of this."

Philip said, "Well there was another form you signed, saying your reports could be used in research—anonymously of course. I don't know what Dr. Nancy is working on, but she may be partnering with another professor, or a physician, and they ordered you a baseline MRI. Some studies look at sleep disorders with functional MRIs. I'm guessing that's one reason Dr. Nancy ordered an MRI. They may be collecting metadata for a national study. But there's no harm."

Samantha didn't know what a functional MRI was and didn't want to know. Her attorney brother-in-law, John, urged her to always read forms before signing. Now she wished she had done so.

She said, "I have the results and will send everything to you. But the results were normal, other than the controlled substance."

"Okay. Let's entertain the possibility your experiences are true."

"It's time travel." Then she explained how she came and went and how she prepared every night. "I don't know the why. Why is this happening? Why me?"

Philip said, "'Why' is the smallest word with the biggest mystery."

He rocked back in this chair. "I wouldn't say it's a waste of time pondering any 'why' question because, if so, I've wasted much of my time. And I don't want to believe that. But what I have concluded is we (humans here on earth) will never grasp the answer. It is not possible. Probably by design. If there is something after, when we're no longer here . . . Perhaps death is absolute knowledge, and that's when we will have all the answers. But that's a whole different topic."

He paused then said, "It's futile to try to understand the ways of the universe. Why things happen or why they don't."

Samantha said, "Right now I'm having fun—except for the hand injury—like I'm visiting, on a vacation. But I don't want to do something to disturb history."

Philip said, "Have you heard of the butterfly effect?"

She shook her head.

"It's a theory of the interdependence of things. That the flap of a butterfly's wings on one continent could ultimately cause a tornado on another continent."

"Oh, so that's like the *Back to the Future* movie. Marty goes back in time, meets his parents. Events change, and when he returns to the present, his parents have a better life."

She paused then said, "Do you think the butterfly effect would apply to my time travel?"

"I have actually thought about the concept of time travel. Though I never talked about it with anyone. It's popular culture in movies and novels. Sometimes the plot allows a time traveler to change the past, and therefore change the future, like the movie you mentioned.

"I have two theories about time travel: One, if—and it's a huge if—if time travel is possible, the past is fixed, and the universe would not allow anyone or anything to alter the timeline. Or two, changes can be made, but we can't be aware of them because that's the only timeline we know. So it's this second theory that's interesting.

"For this discussion, I'll enter your world, in which you say you are going into the past. My view is you can affect the qualitative aspects of life. You say you're horseback riding. Well, if you're riding with someone, the person you're with would have been doing something else, like reading a book rather than being with you. But it's not going to affect any significant outcomes. So the universe is allowing you into this one period of time, but otherwise, the timeline remains the same, because you've only affected the qualitative aspects. And we here in the present don't know—actually can't know—the timeline has changed.

"But let's say in 1854 a young boy swimming in a river drowns. Then you enter the past, see the boy, and save him. You think you're doing what's right, but you're changing history. What if the boy grows into a man who is a serial killer and murders many people?

That's chaos. The timeline changes with respect to this boy, and your actions change the lives of many. I believe the universe will ultimately rebalance history so the present looks exactly as it does now, but the intervening years would be chaotic. The possibility exists, however, that history would never rebalance if the change was significant enough."

Samantha thought, Well, this is cheery news. "I'm being careful."

Philip said, "If you traveled to 1865, you wouldn't want to go to the White House and tell Lincoln not to go to Ford's Theatre."

"Of course not."

"You should be vigilant and avoid even the smallest act that could change outcomes. That's why I find the butterfly effect fascinating. Because in the extreme, even one flap of a butterfly's wings could cause chaos. Even if it's intervening chaos. Acting in even small ways to change history—that could have huge impacts."

"This is not comforting," Samantha said and her eyes widened. She took a deep breath and thought, No wonder he's a loner.

"My theory is, you're allowed to do this time traveling, because you won't make waves or even ripples. You fit in because you know history. You know how to act."

Then Philip paused and asked, "Do you have any proof you temporarily leave the present and slip into the past?"

"I tried bringing my cellphone, but when I put it in my dress pocket, I fell asleep and woke up the next morning. I tried twice."

"Okay, that reinforces the theory that the cellphone was inconsistent with the period of time you're visiting. Like I said, the universe won't allow it."

"Then I tried using a nanny cam in the bedroom to capture my disappearing and reappearing. But that didn't work either. Maybe

I bought a cheap camera, because it was too dark to see even with a dimmer light on. And I wasn't able to sleep with the lights on or sleep deeply enough for the magic to happen." She stopped then said, "I sound crazy when I say it out loud."

Philip looked down on Samantha's left hand. "What about your engagement ring? Does that raise any suspicion during your travels?"

"I take my engagement ring off when I'm home. I keep it in a crystal container for safekeeping, so it doesn't end up in the plumbing. So I don't wear my ring during these trips."

Samantha paused. "What? You're thinking this has some meaning? I take off my ring and assume another identity?"

"I'm taking it all in."

"What I'm experiencing is not *Groundhog Day*. For example, I can't go back and relive my first landing in northern California. Time is advancing. I don't know if that's relevant. But I sense there are rules in this time travel."

She paused then said, "This started when I was lonely because my fiancé was away."

"If this was a case of loneliness, you'd know what to do" was Philip's curt reply.

She didn't take offense because it was his honest assessment. Philip liked the tough cases. Loneliness? That was too easy. Buy a self-help book, join a club, or adopt a pet.

"While visiting the past, I met this lady. She's Chinese and doesn't know much English, and the words she does know are difficult for me to understand. But we're hand-sewing a rustic quilt. Her husband is away; my fiancé is away. And we sit in silence but together. Creating something. It's comforting. I think it's helping with my loneliness."

She covered her face with her hands, "You think I'm making up little fictitious friends."

"I think you believe it."

"Well, I haven't traveled since my hand injury. But recently I've been feeling confident about returning. I would like to redeem myself after that embarrassing fall. I'll go back to the past soon. So I will probably have more stories to tell you the next time we meet."

"And when we do meet, we need to explore other possibilities."

"You mean that I'm making this up and I'm crazy."

"I would not use that term. Now, because you've told me, I feel a responsibility to look at all possibilities with your welfare in mind."

"It does feel good to at least talk with someone. With you. Would you please keep this between us?"

"Of course. Let's meet in a few weeks. Text me."

Donna Balon

Back in the Saddle

After several weeks, Samantha's hand healed well enough so she could comfortably hold the horse's reins. She prepared as usual and returned to the year 1854 on an overcast day. Grant was not at the stable, so Samantha went to Alice's house, where she sat at the table with her friend, quilt-stitching the hodgepodge of fabric remnants of the afghan.

Samantha thanked Alice again for providing her house, bed, broth, and alcohol when Samantha injured her hand. Alice smiled, a closed-mouth smile. Dental hygiene was poor in the nineteenth century, and Samantha had the best teeth and gums in Eureka. She always tied her handkerchief around her neck. Should she feel the urge for a wide, toothy grin or a hearty laugh, she could use her handkerchief to hide her straight, white teeth and healthy pink gums.

Later Samantha walked to the stable. To her delight, Grant was there, cleaning the saddles. She straightened her back for good posture, looking poised. "Lieutenant Grant."

Grant turned and offered a closed-mouth smile. Samantha had never seen Grant's teeth, because his lips covered them when he spoke. She was sure, however, if she ever did, they would be his least attractive feature. Later in life, he would wear dentures.

He walked over, took hold of her wrist, inspected her hand, and nodded.

Samantha said, "I appreciate your coming to my aid. It was so clumsy of me."

Grant put his hand on her shoulder—an unusual display of affection, especially from a married man. She expected him to say something like, "It's okay." Samantha was charmed.

Instead he said, "Elsie was sold."

Her mouth dropped open, and she closed her eyes. Then, like a good Victorian woman, she took her handkerchief and covered her mouth, suppressing her urge to scream.

Samantha thought, Here I go again. Another loss. Despite the friendships I've made, it still hits me hard. I loved Elsie. Deep breaths. Deep breaths.

Grant lifted his hand from her shoulder. "Yukon was sold too."

Samantha shook her head in disbelief.

"There are a couple of horses we can use today."

Samantha returned to Alice's house, dressed into her riding clothes, and walked back to the stable to see Grant holding a lead rope of a large horse. Given the size of the horse, Samantha guessed the horse was his. But Grant handed the rope to her. She had grown self-assured in riding, but when she saw this horse, she questioned whether she was overconfident.

She knew animals could sense fear, so she petted the horse's neck in long strokes. "What's his name?"

"Thunder," he said, smirking. Was he teasing her?

She asked, "Is that his name?"

"That's what I call him."

She led Thunder down the road to the wooden house and back. He complied with her commands and she said often, "Good Thunder."

Grant's horse was as large. He bridled and saddled both horses and Samantha said, "I will need help mounting him. Like you first taught me." He assisted her mount.

Being higher in the saddle, Samantha focused on riding—not the route. Grant led the way, diverting from the typical path into a densely wooded area.

Samantha concentrated on riding her new mount and steering her horse through the labyrinth of enormously tall trees. After a while she took note of their surroundings. She looked over her left and then her right shoulder to see behind her: trees everywhere. And through the thick covered canopy of branches above, she could see the sky was gray.

Gently applying pressure with her calves against her horse's sides, she signaled for Thunder to accelerate the pace. She aptly steered him so she was now alongside Grant and his horse. He halted his horse and she halted hers. Samantha said, "Without the sun, I have lost all sense of direction."

Knowing her concern and in his teasing manner, he said nothing. But his smirk was revealing: yes, he knew where they were; no, they weren't lost.

She pressed anyway, "I begged my oldest brother to allow me to ride again. I must return at the regular hour. If I don't, he will not give me another chance."

Sam Time

Grant nodded and started his horse; Samantha and Thunder followed.

Rain fell without warning. Then a downpour.

Grant slowed his horse, allowing Samantha to pull alongside. He said, "There's a place for shelter. We can wait there until the storm passes." Looking forward at the flat terrain ahead, he motioned with his head. "We can dismount there, then walk a short distance with the horses."

Samantha nodded and followed Grant. They halted their horses and Grant dismounted. Samantha attempted to dismount swinging her right leg over the horse. Her left foot slipped through the wet stirrup, catching her ankle. She was gripping the pommel with her right hand, and her right leg was still over the horse. Her hat fell on the wet ground.

"Ah," Samantha shouted, struggling. Her left leg now was through the stirrup up to her knee. She didn't scream for help. But she needed to be rescued, again.

Her grip was weakening, and her hand was slipping off the pommel. She panicked and thought, I returned to 1854 to redeem myself. If I can't hold on, I'll be hanging upside down with my leg stuck in the stirrup. This would be even more embarrassing than the last time I was here.

Then Grant came from behind and wrapped his arms around her. "Turn and put your arms around my neck." Samantha did so happily.

Grant took one hand to release Samantha's leg from the stirrup. After her foot was free, while holding her torso with one arm, he put his other arm under her legs.

She said, "My hat."

"I'll come back to get it."

The rain still heavy, she could hear the sloshing of Grant's boots on the wet ground. While he carried her, she laid her head on his chest and could hear his heart beating.

They were in this vast wilderness. The remoteness made Samantha feel as if the rules of civilization didn't apply. She was enamored.

She could hear her mother's voice. "I trust you. I don't trust the situation."

Samantha had convictions. A list of don'ts, I-would-never-do-that rules. Sleeping with a married man was on the list. She was a good girl. Solid. In love with Aaron.

But lifelong morals could be erased in this tempting moment.

This was time travel. She was on vacation!

Besides, what happens in the past stays in the past!

He stopped and placed her feet on the ground next to a small wooden shed. "The army owns this. Uses it for training and drills."

The inside was dark and empty. Samantha thought, This is creepy and smells as if animals use it more than the army. She asked, "Are they going to shoot at us?"

"It is safe."

She had complete confidence in him.

Grant left to retrieve her hat and then the horses and tied their reins to a tree. He pulled out from his saddle pouch a thin blanket the size of a small tablecloth and placed it on the wide-planked floor. "Something to sit on." She sat down, shivering because her clothes were wet. He handed Samantha's hat to her.

Grant sat on the blanket to her left, took off his hat, and placed it down by his left side. Then he lay down on his back.

"Let's wait an hour. See if it stops raining. If you get cold, stay close to stay warm."

Then the faithfully married Grant turned over on his left side and fell asleep. Samantha was even more attracted to him.

She placed her hat to her right and lay down on her left side, snuggling close to Grant's back, feeling his warmth. She thought, I'm lying next to Ulysses S. Grant.

Not long after, the rain stopped and they returned to the stable. Samantha came back to Alice's house, but she couldn't find her dress. She left the house, walked to the stable, and told Grant she would pay him next time, to which he seemed indifferent.

Samantha found Alice and told her the dress was not in the place where she always left it. They went inside the house. Alice didn't know what had happened to the dress and sat down at the table unconcerned about Samantha's plight.

Maybe I don't need my dress to return to the present, Samantha thought. I'll give it a try.

She ran outside on the slushy ground to the back of the house, closed her eyes, placed her hands at her sides, and took a deep breath. And she was still in 1854. Panic overcame her.

She ran back into the house, sobbing to Alice. "Where's my dress? I need my dress."

Alice thought, then shook her head.

"What?"

Samantha heard "Peyton girl." Samantha could glean that Alice bartered something, exchanged maybe food, for something this Peyton family had that she wanted. Perhaps, a Peyton girl had sought refuge inside the house during the downpour.

"Please take me to them. Where is their house?"

As they walked, Samantha cried at the thought of never seeing Aaron again. Only two hours ago, she was charmed by this unspoiled area. Now she could see only its flaws. It was cold and boring, with shacks for houses, little potable water, no medical care. Samantha's present day was lush with choices, cellphones, streaming, spandex, and same-day delivery. Being stuck here would be unbearable.

About a quarter mile down the road, Alice knocked on the Peyton house door. Mrs. Peyton and her three daughters were home. In Alice's garbled way, she explained a dress in her house had disappeared. Samantha looked at the girls for tells. The median-height sister hung her head down.

Samantha said to the girl, "I know it was raining, you came inside, and you saw a pretty dress. I need it back now."

Turning to the mother, she said, "One of the girls wanted to play and try on the dress. There is no harm."

She looked at the middle sister, "Would you return it? I need it back now."

The girl walked behind a screen dividing the room. She returned with a flour sack, from which she pulled out the dress and gave it to Samantha.

"What's your name?" Samantha asked.

"Emily."

"Good day, Emily."

She turned to the mother, "Good day, Mrs. Peyton." She smiled at the sisters. "Good day."

Alice stayed behind and Samantha ran along the muddy road with the dress back to Alice's house. To hell with 1854 rules and what women couldn't do; Samantha ran as fast as she could. The first woman settler to do a nine-minute-mile pace.

Sam Time

Once inside the house, Samantha took a rag to clean her shoes and changed into her dress. Then she assumed the magic pose—and she was back in her bed at 2:33 a.m.

Samantha undressed, gulped down a glass of water, and slipped on Aaron's T-shirt and a pair of crew socks. She went back to bed thinking, That was scary.

Donna Balon

Making Friends and Plans

After a few days, Samantha's fear of traveling to the past dissipated. Loneliness returned as Aaron was still away on business, and she desired to travel to Eureka to see her new companions. Before her next trip, however, she called a friend and former Rutgers University colleague Sarah, who knew all things Victorian, having thoroughly studied this era.

Samantha talked about her dissertation then smoothly segued to the topic of women's fashion. Sarah was a fountain of knowledge and cautioned against over-relying on Internet articles, which often glossed over nuances.

Contrary to popular present-day perception, gloves were not essential. In cold weather, women wore gloves outside for warmth and for protection when working—if they could afford a pair. This was consistent with Samantha's observation in rural Eureka: women were too poor to own gloves. In urban areas, affluent women wore daytime gloves for fashion while displaying their elevated station. Evening gloves were ubiquitous for all women attending a ball, theater, or the like. Unlike gloves, however, a hat and proper undergarments were a necessity.

With this information, soon after the call, Samantha styled her hair in a double-braided crown and went to the dressmaker's shop. Mary suggested a braided halo hat, a decorative detail mirroring her braided hair, made with the dress fabric. The "hat" would resemble a wreath or halo, which would rest on top of Samantha's double-braided hair crown. It would attach to her hair with pins secured by a thin ribbon sewn to the hat's interior.

Mary also suggested reversing the dress fabric: the green dress would have a coordinating white-on-green braided halo hat; the powder-blue dress a white-on-blue hat; and the pink dress, white-on-pink. Samantha loved the concept and ordered three hats, one for each dress.

As to proper undergarments, a corset a was necessity. Every woman in Eureka wore one. Not the tight-fitting style creating a disproportional tiny waist, but a fashionable undergarment providing bust support—like the brassiere—and a desirable hourglass shape. Samantha's lined dresses provided modesty. With her firm core and sports bra, the dresses fit comfortably, but her figure lacked the feminine curvy silhouette of a corset-wearing lady.

She searched the Internet and bought a corset that replicated a Victorian style. A white cotton sleeveless chemise was typically worn under a corset, but Samantha chose not to wear one under hers. She did, however, purchase a couple pairs of pantalets to cover her bottom. A week later the undergarments were delivered.

The white satin corset was bust-covering with crisscrossing back laces, which threaded through two dozen metal grommets along the spine. The center front busk opened and closed with clasps. Thin vertical metal stays, strategically spaced for support and hidden between two layers of fabric, created the corset's hourglass shape.

The pantalets were made of white lightweight opaque cotton fabric. The leg hems were calf-length and adorned with eyelet lace. Gentle gathers along the waistband edge allowed for a loose fit around the hips, and a single center back button held the waistband in place. In true vintage fashion, each leg top was a separate open panel; that is, there was no center crotch seam. This crotchless design allowed for convenient squatting and elimination over a chamber pot.

Samantha slipped on the pantalets. Then she stood in front of the bathroom mirror putting on the corset. With the center front closed, Samantha adjusted and readjusted the back laces, then tied the back bow for a snug fit. She threw on a T-shirt over the corset and sat at her desk researching while acclimating to the fit of her new undergarments. Later that day, she stood in front of the bathroom mirror, untying the back bow, and then tugging on the back laces to loosen the corset before opening the front clasps to remove it. She practiced this on-adjusting and off-adjusting routine the next day, becoming accustomed to the mechanics and fit of the corset.

After several days, Samantha felt adept at corset dressing and undressing. She looked at herself in a full-length mirror wearing the snug-fitting corset and pantalets. Samantha felt feminine and more comfortable than she had imagined wearing these Victorian-style undergarments.

She thought, Aaron will like this too. I'll surprise him and wear this when he returns home this weekend.

Sam Time

When the new braided halo hats were ready, Samantha prepared to time travel again. Wearing her new corset and pantalets, she put on her pink dress with the matching braided halo hat, which fit nicely over her double-braided hair crown. By 8:00 p.m., feeling tired, Samantha turned off the lamp on the end table and fell asleep on the sofa.

She arrived in Eureka on a sunny day, early in the afternoon. Instead of horseback riding, she paid a visit to the Peyton house. The three sisters were there and loved Samantha's double-braided hair crown and her new braided halo hat. Samantha asked Mrs. Peyton for her approval to teach the girls how to braid their hair like hers. Beth, Emily, and Molly were excited their mother agreed to the lesson.

They went onto the front porch, where there were two chairs. Samantha asked for a comb, pins, and string or ribbons. She discerned the family hair hygiene looked clean and safe—that is, no lice.

There were seven members of the Peyton family: father, mother, two boys, and the three girls. Although the children were taught how to read and write, the instruction for braiding hair was best taught by watching and memorizing.

Samantha said, "Let's begin with the youngest, Molly, so the two older girls can watch and remember the steps."

The girls watched with interest and recited the steps. Samantha then styled Beth's hair. Having learned the steps, Beth then styled Emily's hair. Samantha also showed them the difference between French and Dutch braids. The girls were delighted.

Molly asked, "Do you have a beau?"

"Yes, I do. His name is Aaron. He is like—do you know the story *A Christmas Carol* by Charles Dickens?"

They said yes.

"My beau Aaron is like Bob Cratchit, a counting clerk."

The girls laughed.

Samantha asked, "Do any of you have a beau?"

The girls giggled and shook their heads.

"Do you go to any balls and dances?"

Beth, the oldest, said, "I do not have a dress for a ball. Emily and Molly are too young."

"Do your older brothers know boys who they could introduce to you? There are soldiers from other parts of the country here at Fort Humboldt. Perhaps a soldier would like to take a lovely young lady as his wife back home with him."

Samantha knew these girls were destined to live in this isolated place unless they married.

Mrs. Peyton was making bread, a weekly chore, and Samantha offered to help knead the dough, something her mother had taught her. In a corner of the room was a wooden washstand topped with a cream-ceramic washbasin with matching pitcher and a dish filled with soap shavings. The water was cold, and this cleaning ritual was novel for Samantha.

A small elliptical-shaped mirror hung above the washstand. She looked at herself in the mirror and thought, I'm doing it. Living the Victorian life. Part of the community. A never-before experience. Although I miss Aaron, I am not lonely.

As they were kneading dough, the oven was baking other loaves. The Peyton home oven was like ones in colonial times, a brick hole at the side of the fireplace with a steel cover that was kept closed while baking. Mrs. Peyton took the loaves out of the oven. They smelled good. Once the bread cooled, Mrs. Peyton pulled off a piece and gave it to Samantha with tea.

After a couple of hours at the Peyton house, Samantha said she had to leave and would be stopping by the stable. Mrs. Peyton wrapped a loaf of bread in a cotton towel and asked Samantha to give it to Alice.

Samantha walked by the makeshift general store and remembered her plan to search for rare, valuable coins. When she entered the wood-frame building, she expected to see Stanley, but he wasn't there. The store clerk said, "Good day."

"Good day," Samantha replied while her eyes adjusted to the dark interior of this hole-in-the-wall, one-room shop.

"I have a quarter that I would like to exchange for small change." Samantha held up a quarter while speaking. The clerk said nothing.

"May I have four half dimes for two dimes?" she asked. If he was a store clerk, he should know math, Samantha thought. But he said nothing.

She set a half dime on the counter, pausing to recall the correct term for pennies. Then she remembered: cents. During this era, a one-cent coin was the size of the quarter, what Aaron would call a "large cent." Then Samantha said, "Cents? For a half dime?"

The clerk took a cloth bag and poured the large cents on the counter. Samantha sifted through the coins, searching for the shiniest coins in perfect condition. She selected five of the newest-looking large cents and slid the half dime across the counter. "Good day," she said, dropping the five coins in her mini drawstring change purse.

The bright sun temporarily blinded Samantha when she opened the store door and walked out onto the dirt road. Once her eyes adjusted, she noticed trees and bushes had leaves; it was late spring. She knew from the history books that Grant would leave Fort Humboldt before summer. Best to start saying goodbye.

Once at Alice's house, Samantha placed the Peytons' bread on the table. Then Alice pointed to the quilt on the bed.

"It's lovely." Samantha passed her hand over the top. Although it wasn't a work of art, the quilt was functional and showed their collected efforts. This would have been a perfect time for a selfie—of Samantha, Alice, and the quilt. But Samantha settled for the pleasant mental image.

"I will be leaving soon. Taking a steamer home, far away."

Alice walked to the back of the room, returning and handing Samantha her riding clothes. Samantha embraced the clothes, giving them a hug. "I love this riding habit. But I do not have much space in my traveling trunk, and I cannot take everything home with me. I will make myself a new habit after I return home. Perhaps someone else will use these." She handed the clothes back to Alice, who hugged them.

"I hope to stop by again before we leave. Thank you, Alice, for everything."

Alice nodded, her eyes tearing. Samantha pursed her lips tightly to keep from crying.

Then Samantha walked to the stable where Grant had just returned from a ride.

"Good day, Miss Samantha."

"Good day, Lieutenant Grant. How was your ride? No one slowing you down."

"I always like to ride. Nice to have company."

Samantha smiled, hearing his compliment. "I was at the Peyton house making bread. But I owe you this for our last lesson." She handed him a quarter.

"My commission should be in soon. Promotion to captain."

"Good news. Well deserved. I—my family—appreciates your time teaching me how to ride. With your promotion to captain, I understand, we understand, riding lessons may not be possible. But I will call again. Before we leave."

"Where are you going?"

"Back home to New Jersey. Maybe we will do business in New York City. We have mined out our claims here. And we are tired and homesick. Before we leave, I will stop by the stable to say good day one final time."

Grant nodded.

"Good day, Lieutenant Grant."

"Good day, Miss Samantha."

Samantha found an isolated spot and disappeared from Eureka, reappearing on her sofa. She looked at the clock: 10:07 p.m. Time travel did not sync with the present. Although time in the past seemed to run several hours, time in the present would lapse only a couple of hours.

She sat up on the sofa undoing the mini buttons on the front dress bodice. The doorbell rang and startled her. Too scared to open the door at night, she shuffled quickly to a front window without flipping on any light switches. The front of her dress gaped as she peered out the window to see who was outside.

Grace and John were standing at the front door. Samantha turned on some inside lights to signal she was home. Then she scurried into the bedroom, quickly removed her dress, and flung it in the back of her walk-in closet. Not having enough time to remove her corset and pantalets, she threw on a plush white terry cloth bathrobe and tied the waist belt. Then she hurried to the front door.

She opened the door, breathless. "Hello there. What's up? Is everything okay?"

John said, "That's what we were going to ask you."

"Come in."

John explained, "Aaron called and said you had agreed to talk tonight, and he hadn't heard from you."

"Oh my God. I fell asleep on the sofa. It was early. Let me call him." She walked to the kitchen, picked up her cellphone, and dialed Aaron: "Hi, sweetie, it's me."

Aaron answered, "Oh good. What happened? We agreed to talk tonight."

"I fell asleep on the sofa. I don't know the exact time but maybe eight-ish."

"You weren't answering my texts. And after your hand injury, I was concerned. So I called Grace and John. They offered to stop by our house."

"I feel so loved." Samantha put her arm around Grace. "And now that Grace is here, I'm going to try to convince John to let her stay the night."

Grace moved to put her arm around Samantha's waist. Samantha slinked away so her sister could not feel her corset.

Aaron said, "Sam, I'd like to speak with John."

"He wants to speak with you." After she handed her phone to John, Samantha said to Grace, "Now that you're here, let's sleep in the guest room. The two twin beds in that room are rarely used. Only when Mom and Dad are here and when Deanna visits."

Sam Time

Grace replied, "Well, I do want to tell you about our DNA ancestry results. And I'm building a family tree. So fascinating researching the past."

Although Samantha was listening to Grace, she was glancing over at John. Why did Aaron want to speak with him? Self-conscious from having lied to her fiancé about her hand injury, she imagined what he was saying, "Sam had this bizarre story where she injured her hand, went to the urgent care clinic, and never told me."

She heard John saying, "Don't worry. It's okay. It's okay. No problem."

John handed the phone back to Samantha. Aaron said, "Hey, I apologized to John. I overreacted."

Samantha walked out of the room so Grace and John couldn't hear. "Sweetie, it's okay. Also, after my hand injury and the way I told you about it, I understand your concern. This was my doing. Really."

"Well, I'm relieved you're okay."

"I think I've convinced Grace to stay with me tonight."

"Okay, love you, Sam."

"Love you too." Samantha hung up and walked toward Grace and John. "Sorry, guys. So sorry to disturb your night."

"We were up anyway and you're family," John said.

"But this is my gain. Grace, you can stay?"

"Yes, I can swing it. I don't have any video meetings until midmorning."

"Good. We can have waffles. You know, Mom gave us a Belgian waffle maker as a housewarming gift. And she gave me her recipe. I've been practicing, and I think my waffles are as good as hers."

"I love waffles."

Samantha asked John, "Can you come over in the morning for waffles? Maybe eight?"

"I'll text Grace. I'll stop by, at least, for coffee."

John hugged and kissed Grace goodbye. Samantha hugged John and he left.

Grace said, "I love your hair. The double crown braids. I also like the fabric braided crown."

Samantha touched her head, having forgotten that she was still wearing the braided halo hat. "Oh, before I fell asleep, I was trying this on. What do you think?"

"I love it."

"Mary Sanchez, the dressmaker, made this. This was a sample. I'm thinking of having a white one made, and then I would attach a bridal veil. I'll show you." Samantha unpinned the braided halo hat, took it off her head, and showed Grace where the veil would be attached.

Grace said, "I think that would be lovely."

Samantha fake laughed. "So this evening I was fussing and experimenting. Then I got tired and fell asleep on the sofa."

She changed the subject. "Come on into our bedroom. I'll give you one of my nightgowns. I never wear them. I always wear one of Aaron's T-shirts instead."

As Grace slipped on the nightgown, Samantha excused herself and went into the bathroom. She stuck her head out of the bathroom door and said, "There's herbal tea in the drawer by the microwave. Take what you want. I'll have what you're having. The cups are in the upper cabinet by the coffee machine. Give me a few minutes."

Samantha closed the bathroom door. She removed her corset and pantalets. Then she slipped on one of Aaron's T-shirts and a pair of his crew socks, then threw on the terry cloth bathrobe, before placing her nineteenth-century undergarments in a drawer.

She walked into the kitchen. "So tell me about the DNA results and our ancestry."

Grace answered, "The DNA was nothing unexpected. We're of European descent. A mixture of many countries. But what's interesting is the family tree."

Samantha asked, "Did you find anything about that one ancestor who disappeared?"

"You mean Peter Hunter, Dad's great-great-grandfather. The story is he went to Virginia City, Nevada, to mine for silver. He was there for a while and sent money back to the family in Lancaster, Pennsylvania. Then the packages of money stopped, and they never heard from him again. He didn't return home. No one knows what happened to him."

Samantha said, "How devastating, not knowing what happened. What was Peter's wife's name?"

"Isabelle."

"And kids?"

"Six kids. Two girls, four boys. Let me think. Nora, Claire, Alan, Oliver, Thomas, Randal."

Samantha thought about it, then said, "Rearranged, the first letters of the children's names spell 'CONTRA.'"

"I didn't think of it that way."

"It's a way of remembering the names."

Then Grace added, "Oh, and Dad said his coin collection includes the coins Peter sent home while he mined in Nevada. He said coin collecting wasn't common in the nineteenth century, but Peter had a stash even before he went to Nevada. You have Peter's entire collection."

"I'm amazed generations kept, and didn't spend, the coins."

Grace said, "Dad talked about that. Peter's boys, Alan and Oliver, were old enough and working on the farm. So the family had income. Dad also said the family used some coins for expenses and saved the rest. Peter's plan was to return home after a couple of years and perhaps use the saved coins to start a business."

Grace paused, then said, "How did Dad put it? Oh, now I remember. The family wouldn't spend the coins from Peter's collection—even during the Depression—because it was a vestige of Peter. And, in reverence, every generation passed down the coins. Then Dad got them. Now you have them."

"I didn't know of this dramatic story attached to them."

"You still have them?"

"Of course," Samantha replied, but this was only partially true. She had been using some coins for her time travel.

Grace finished her story and noticed Samantha was staring at her teacup in deep thought. "Sam, what is it?"

Samantha didn't answer because she was thinking: Could this be another piece to the time-traveling puzzle? Or am I squandering these precious coins for my own purposes?

"Sam, are you with me?"

"What?"

"What is it, Sam? You look so pensive."

Thinking quickly, she said, "I told you I've been doing immersive research."

"Yes, what is that, anyway?"

"It's my own terminology to describe how I'm building a foundation for my dissertation. I tried reading white papers and other academic works. But since Aaron left on this Denver assignment, I've been looking into people's daily life during the mid-nineteenth century. It's like a change of scenery, and it's spurring ideas."

"And this story of Peter and the coins? How does that fit?" Grace asked.

"Something popped into my head as you were telling me the story. But do you really want to hear about my evolving thesis? Now that's something that will put you to sleep."

Grace laughed.

Samantha said, "I'm glad you told me the story."

They finished their teas and then went into the guest room with the two twin beds. Samantha switched on the dimmer light to a low setting.

"Which bed do you want, Grace?"

"It doesn't matter to me. I'll sleep here."

They climbed into bed and Samantha said, "Grace, you should come back soon to select your matron of honor dress. I told you I had three made in different colors and slightly different styles."

"Dress? Why are you calling it a dress? It's a gown."

"Gown." Samantha needed to use the correct nomenclature for the period of time to which she was referring.

Grace said, "I want to come back and try them on when I have the proper undergarments. Besides, this evening I feel bloated."

The sisters laughed and said good night. Samantha turned off the dimmer light, and Grace fell asleep.

When Samantha was sure Grace was asleep, Samantha quietly slid out of bed and grabbed Grace's handbag from the top of the bureau. Samantha tiptoed out of the room, went into the master bathroom. Then she shut and locked the door.

She searched Grace's handbag for her keys and found the key to Aaron and Samantha's house. She removed the key from the key ring, went into the kitchen, and fished through the junk drawer to find the handheld tool used for sharpening knives.

The house key locked and unlocked all the exterior doors. Samantha tested the key to open the back door, and it worked. Passing quietly by the guest room, she checked that Grace was sound asleep. Then Samantha returned to the master bathroom, shutting and locking the door. With the tool sharpener, she filed down the teeth of the key. Then she walked out of the bathroom to the back door and tested the key, and it no longer worked.

She put the key back on the key ring and dropped it back into Grace's handbag. Tiptoeing back into the guest room, she placed the handbag on the bureau top, where Grace had left it.

Samantha climbed into bed and lay on her back. She was lucky tonight, having returned to the present in time to answer the door, showing Grace and John nothing was amiss. But if they had knocked, and Samantha hadn't answered, they would have used the house key to enter, only to discover she wasn't there.

The back outdoor landscaping lights cast a glow, so the room was not completely dark. Samantha stared at the spinning ceiling fan and thought about the time-travel rules as she understood them. In her experience, no one could ever see her disappearing or reappearing. But she could enter a room, then disappear while she was alone in the room. An observer who watched Samantha enter a room would be perplexed if the observer then went into the room, and she was no longer there.

It would be strange—eerie even—if Grace, John, or Aaron entered the house, walked into the bedroom and closet looking for

Samantha, and couldn't find her, only minutes later to see Samantha walking out of the bedroom that had just been searched. She couldn't risk that. So to slow down Grace and John while Aaron was away, making the key inoperable would allow Samantha time to reappear without confusion.

What if, however, Aaron returned home when Samantha wasn't there because she was time traveling? She needed a plan. Staring at the rotating ceiling fan, she spun a scheme. Time traveling was getting complicated.

Donna Balon

Soldier Blanket

In preparing for the night's journey, Samantha slipped on her light-green dress and stuffed her pockets as usual. But she couldn't find her mini drawstring change purse, with the five 1853 coins from the Eureka general store. Then she remembered the purse was in the pocket of the pink dress, which she'd stashed away quickly when Grace and John made their surprise visit. She dug into the pocket of the pink dress and grabbed the change purse.

Once at her desk, she turned on the light and poured the contents of the purse onto her desktop. Then she separated the five large cent coins from the rest of the change.

The patina on the five large cent coins had darkened slightly, presumably because over 160 years had passed. She picked up her cellphone and turned on the magnifying app for a better view. The 1853 coins were in good condition. Satisfied, Samantha stacked the five coins in a corner of the desk drawer and continued preparing for the night's travel.

As she planned on saying goodbye to Grant and not staying

long, she didn't fuss with a double-braided hair crown or the braided halo hat. Instead, she styled her hair in a single, centered, back-of-the-head French braid and stuffed her knitted headband in her pocket. She placed her cream afghan around her shoulders, climbed into bed, and fell asleep.

SAMANTHA ARRIVED in Eureka early evening, before dusk. She couldn't find Grant, so she assumed he was at the tavern. Not good.

Taverns were places for men—not ladies—and only women with questionable reputations would frequent one. So she would not dare enter. Standing in front of the porch step to the tavern, Samantha approached a presumably sober man. "Please find Lieutenant Grant and tell him Samantha is here outside waiting for him."

Having little confidence any one man would pass along her message, she asked two other men who were entering the tavern. The third man said, "You mean Captain Grant. Just got his promotion."

She waited, pacing the length of the building. Then Grant, in his soldier's uniform, fell out the door onto the porch. Samantha raced to help him up. He was too heavy for her to handle, but she did provide support leading him down the step of the tavern onto the ground.

His breath smelled of whiskey, and he could stand only with Samantha as his crutch. His knees wobbled as he took a step and another, then tumbled onto the dirt ground with Samantha. His hat flew off his head, then rolled on its rim in spiraling circles before landing brim side up several feet away.

Dusty but not hurt, Samantha stood while Grant seemed

content staying on the ground. She took hold of his left arm, pulling with all her body weight to get him to stand. He jerked his arm toward him, causing Samantha to fall spread-eagle on top of Grant, who was now lying flat on his back.

"Oh no," she said, slapping his chest and scrambling to stand, her legs straddling his body. He grabbed her hand and pulled her down again. Now she was sitting on his stomach. This tug and pull continued several times. People were gathering and staring at the Grant-Samantha spectacle.

Samantha changed tactics. While sitting on him, she bent down close to his face. "Get up and I will bring you something to drink."

It worked. He turned on all fours, lifting his legs then his body, and with help from Samantha, he stood.

While supporting him with her arm around his waist, she looked for a place to sit. Down the side of the dirt road was a rustic park bench. Dragging Grant a few feet, she gingerly bent down to pick up his hat with her free hand. In a zigzag route, they stumbled together and then both plopped down on the bench.

"Sit! Stay! While I get something for you to drink." He leaned back, appearing settled. She threw his hat down next to him. He picked up his hat and placed it on his head. Samantha tossed her shawl on the bench and lifted herself to stand. But she couldn't. Her braid was caught on something, and it hurt.

She turned her head. Grant was holding the tail of her single back braid.

"Hey, let go!" she said.

He smirked and held tightly on to her braid tail.

"Ha ha, that's very funny. Now let go."

It wasn't happening. So she stretched her neck so her face was nose to nose with Grant's. She smelled the whiskey on his breath. "You do not want me to leave. But I will return. With a drink for you."

He let go. She stood, took her braid tail, moved it to the front, and tucked it into the neckline of her dress. Then she walked down the dirt road looking for someone to help her. She spotted Alice.

"Oh, Alice. The captain needs our help. I need some broth. Two large mugs of broth." Samantha reached into her deep side pockets fishing for her mini drawstring change purse. "Here, Alice. A half dime for two mugs of broth." Alice took the coin and walked back to her house.

Samantha turned around. A crowd of men were congregating in the road, so she couldn't see the bench or Grant. She poked her head to the left, then to the right to see past the group, but the crowd had grown.

She lifted the sides of her dress, shaking off the dust. Alice returned quickly, carefully carrying two mugs three-quarters full of broth.

"You are so kind, Alice. I will take one." Samantha smelled the mug and took a small sip. Yes, it was broth. "Captain is on this bench. Follow me please."

They walked past the crowd toward the bench. It was empty!

Where was he? Samantha gasped and twirled to one side, then the other, holding the mug shoulder height, not spilling any of the contents.

She then heard the thunder of hooves and looked up. Grant was riding a horse at a galloping speed down the street past the cheering crowd.

Samantha turned to Alice. "Here. Hold this." Samantha placed the mug in Alice's free hand. "Please wait here. I'll return with the captain."

Walking quickly toward the crowd, Samantha thought: He's drunk; he's riding fast; he could fall off and be injured. How can I get him off that horse before something bad happens?

Her thoughts were interrupted by the sound of the horse's hooves at galloping speed. Grant was making a second pass around the town.

"Whose horse is that?" Samantha asked everyone she passed. A few pointed in the same direction. There was an old, small, thin, hunched man wearing tattered clothes, muddy boots, and a floppy-brimmed hat. She recognized Eugene from the stable.

"Eugene, is that your horse?"

"Wild, he is."

Grant had a way with horses, taming wild ones. This was a dare. To ride this wild horse for how long and for what prize Samantha didn't know, but this could end badly if she didn't stop it soon. Grant rode a third loop around town, accelerating the horse's speed. The crowd was as excited as Samantha was worried.

"Get him down! Take back your horse!" Eugene ignored her. She dug into her dress pockets, found her mini drawstring change purse, and took out a dime.

"Here. A dime to get the captain off the horse when he comes down the road again."

Eugene took the dime and agreed. He walked into the middle of the road, took a white handkerchief from his pocket, and waved both of his arms over his head with the white handkerchief in one hand. The crowd jeered, seeing this was coming to an end.

Grant came thundering down the street again, past Eugene,

before eventually slowing down. He turned the horse around and rode a trot in a fitting finale. The crowd cheered and Eugene took his horse by the reins. Grant dismounted, then stumbled to his knees. A man grabbed Grant's arm, helping him stand. Samantha was relieved. But she gasped when the crowd rewarded Grant with a stein of beer, which he chugged instantly.

Pushing her way through the unruly men with the worst body odor, Samantha grabbed Grant's elbow. With theater she said, "Okay, Captain. Time to go home!"

The men howled; Grant had lassoed a lass. Samantha played along, pulling him toward the bench. Once they were a block away from everyone and alone, Samantha turned to Grant. "Open your mouth."

He was drunk and thought this was a game, so he complied. Samantha stuck her index and middle finger far down his throat. In a few seconds, Grant vomited the beer he'd just drunk.

Samantha didn't move out of the way fast enough. Vomit splashed on her dress. But Grant was her first concern. She'd worry about the dress later. She pulled her handkerchief from her pocket and wiped the vomit off her fingers.

"Whadda youd fora?" He slurred his words, pulled away angrily, forcefully from Samantha.

As he strode away, she ran behind him and placed her hands on his shoulders. With all the femininity she could muster, she whispered in his ear, "I am sorry. So sorry. Please forgive me." This soothed him. She said in a sweet voice, "Come here. Have something to drink."

They were now close to roadside bench where Alice was still dutifully standing, holding the two mugs of broth. Speaking as if she was dealing with a petulant child, Samantha said, "Captain, Alice is here. She has been so kind to bring you something good to drink." Grant sat down on the bench, and Samantha handed him the mug.

He took a few gulps. "Thisth iznt—"

"No, but it's good. Isn't it?"

He was tired and didn't argue. And drank.

After he finished the first mug, Samantha sat next to him, took the first mug from him, and handed him the second. He turned his head away. "No."

Samantha insisted. "Drink. You will feel better." She handed Alice the first empty mug and mouthed, "Thank you."

When Grant finished the second mug, he handed it to Samantha. Then he stood.

"What?" Samantha asked, "Where are you going?"

"I gotta, I gotta . . ." and he walked along the side of the road toward some bushes. Okay, Samantha thought, he needs to relieve himself.

She turned to Alice and handed her the second mug. "You are so kind to help. The captain thanks you. Good evening, Alice." Alice made a tight-lipped smile and walked away.

Samantha picked up her shawl from the bench and laid it over her shoulders. Grant returned, took off his hat, and hung it on the corner of the bench back. Then he plopped down.

The hat was his tell. Samantha realized Grant would signal his actions with his hat. When they'd first walked to the bench, she'd slapped the hat down on the bench seat. In defiance, he'd picked it up and put it back on his head. Now he was submissive and rested his hat on the bench back.

Samantha said, "Come, lie down. Here." She tapped her lap. He reclined, stretching his legs on the bench and lying faceup with his head in her lap.

He closed his eyes and Samantha said, "Rest now, Captain." He was asleep in a few minutes.

Although Grant was now safe, night was falling, and loud cantankerous men were roaming the street. At times they were close to the bench and Samantha was scared. But she wanted to stay with Grant, lest he awake and go back into the tavern. She thought, Stay still, like a statue.

A sheriff, or someone like a sheriff, came on horseback through town after the tavern closed and shooed the last of the drunken men off the dirt road. Samantha stayed still, and the sheriff didn't bother her or Grant.

The night was cool, but Samantha was warmed by her soldier blanket. The few lanterns cast enough light for her to see the contours of Grant's face. She petted his thick hair, placed her other hand on his chest, feeling it rising and falling with the deep breaths of his slumber.

"O Captain! my Captain," Samantha whispered.

She opened her mouth in a lionlike yawn. Her head fell to her chest and she fell asleep.

SAMANTHA AWOKE to blackness. Total blackness. She could not see anything, even when opening her eyes as wide as possible.

After a few seconds to get her bearings, she realized she had not yet returned to the present. Grant was sleeping soundly, his head still on her lap. This gave her consolation. If she did panic, she would wake him. But she didn't want to bother him. He needed to sleep off his drunkenness.

Everyone was asleep. Every candle and lantern extinguished.

Then she looked up and gasped. The sky was clear. The stars and planets were shining, twinkling. A shooting star. And another. The Milky Way was visible, a strip of variegating white haze with crackles like river tributaries against the dark sky with shades of blues and purples.

"Awesome," Samantha whispered. She had never seen the sky like this. Pure. Unspoiled by twenty-first-century light pollution.

"Thank you," she said, speaking to the universe. "Thank you."

Samantha stared at the sky for a while. Then she whispered to Grant, who was in a deep sleep, "I have to go. Be good. Stay safe." She kissed his forehead and slid off the bench.

She heard him adjust to his side with his arms underneath his head to serve as a pillow. Years of being in the army had taught him to improvise for sleep comfort.

Samantha walked away, and in the blackness, she closed her eyes, placed her palms against her thighs, and took a deep breath—leaving the past.

THE NEXT MORNING, Samantha awoke feeling tired, which was typical after a time-traveling night. Soon after, Grace arrived to try on the matron of honor gowns, while Samantha lingered over coffee at the kitchen counter, recalling last night's events.

Samantha snapped out of her daze when Grace walked into the kitchen wearing the light-green dress from last night. "Why does this one smell like vomit?"

Sam Time

When Aaron returned home for the weekend, Samantha told him a tale of newly discovered coins.

"Remember when my father shipped his coin collection to me?"

"Yes, it was shortly after we moved here."

"Do you remember we looked at the coins on my desk? And you sorted out the ones you wanted for your collection?"

"Yes."

"Well, some must have fallen behind the desk. I found them the other day when I was cleaning." Her story of the recently discovered 1853 pennies would have sounded strange if she found only coins from the same year. So Samantha mixed the five 1853 large cent coins, which she'd picked up in her time travel, with a handful of coins from her father's collection.

"Put them on my desk, and I'll check them out later," Aaron said.

A few hours later, Aaron had sorted through the coins Samantha had presumably just discovered. He isolated the five 1853 large cent coins. "These are in great condition. Since they're so old, it's rare to see pennies like these. They may fetch a significant price at auction."

"Like what?" Samantha asked.

"A thousand dollars for each."

"Well, remember what we agreed, when you first went through Dad's collection. We should ask if he wants the coins or the money from the sale of them. I'm sure he'll say no. But Grace should get half of anything."

"There'll be taxes to pay. But of course, Grace will get her share."

Samantha correctly predicted her father's reaction and Grace's entitlement for one half of the proceeds. Ultimately, Aaron sold the 1853 five large cent coins in an eBay auction for $8,000.

Donna Balon

On Campus

Samantha returned for a second meeting with Philip. Unsure how much she would reveal to him, she let him start this session. "So have you had any more nighttime adventures?"

"Yes. Generally good, except one time I was afraid I wasn't coming back. Once I'm there, I change into riding clothes. And this young girl saw my dress, liked it, wanted to try it on, and took it. I tried leaving the past while wearing the riding clothes, but it didn't work. I was so scared. But I found this young girl, and she gave me back my dress, and I came back."

"So you need your dress to come and go. It's a condition of your time travel. You don't think you would find another way back?"

"Perhaps. But I don't want to test it. It's fascinating being there, but I want only to visit."

"Okay, let's explore other possibilities. It's a big leap to say you disappear from your bed, but it's another huge leap to say you're slipping into the past. That's fanciful."

Samantha countered, "So I disappear from my bedroom, and

you're saying I could be in my living room, inhaling chloroform and piercing myself with a fishhook."

"Something like that," Philip replied.

"But I have other evidence. I feel sore after riding, especially when I first started."

"Your brain is convincing you that your muscles are sore."

"But I never rode a horse before, and now I'm at an intermediate level."

"You may have learned to horseback ride earlier in your life and your brain is repressing the memory. Because of some traumatic event."

"Philip, even my sister said I never learned to ride."

"You may have never told her, because you're repressing the memory for some reason."

Samantha folded her arms in disgust and took a deep breath.

Philip read her body language. "Samantha, if you want someone to agree with you, you could walk on the street and find many who would. But you came to me for critical thinking. This is what I do. What I like to do, and I am very interested in your case."

"So now I'm a case."

"Yes, you came to me for clinical and psychological analysis. Don't fight me. I'm here to listen. But you need to understand how I work. Put yourself in my position. What if Aaron told you what you're telling me?"

"It would scare me. I would have concerns about our future together, which is the reason I've haven't told him or my sister—and won't ever tell them. You're the only one who knows my secret."

"My point is, why would I not have the same concerns as your family members?"

Samantha squirmed in her chair. "You're right. I can't disagree."

After a pause she said, "I've been holding back something. And it's no doubt relevant to your analysis. I've been returning to the past because I met someone."

"You made friends with this woman."

"Yes, Alice. But there's someone else." She closed her eyes, hesitating to say something so strange. "I'm working on my dissertation, so I'm researching the Civil War and people around that time. And the first time I arrived in 1854, I met Ulysses S. Grant."

She couldn't look at Philip because it sounded so absurd, "He taught me how to horseback ride. And we're friends. Friendly."

Philip clasped his hands, elbows on the desk. "So while your fiancé is away, and you're researching for a dissertation, you're having these nighttime adventures with someone else. Someone who resembles your fiancé?"

"No. They both have dark brown hair. Aaron's eyes are a darker blue, he's an inch taller. They don't look alike. But you're saying it's some substitution pathology?"

"There's a few pathologies that fit."

She hated hearing this. "So what? I'm sleepwalking? I have a split personality?"

"Or a combination of pathologies. The pathologies could be something like empty-nest syndrome combined with sleep deprivation or another parasomnia. Those are the least severe. Up the scale are a host of other possibilities, including adjustment or personality disorders. A psychosis. There's borderline personality disorder manifesting in a fear of abandonment and being alone."

"My MRI didn't show anything abnormal."

Sam Time

"I reviewed the reports you sent me. And yes, your MRI was normal. No tumors, which could cause neurological disorders. How is everything else in your life?"

"Well, as I said, I don't like that my fiancé is away on business during the week and I miss him. Philip, my life is normal other than when I fall asleep while wearing one of those dresses."

"Do you have seizures?"

"No."

After a pause, Samantha said, "I do feel better speaking with you. And if I'm reading you correctly, besides your interest in my weird case, you don't want me spiraling out of control and jumping off a bridge.

"I'm not sure you and I will ever agree on what's happening. I'm okay with that. Because this is so strange. But I'll admit, it's good to talk. So, can we meet regularly and talk? You can make your diagnosis. At least I can speak with someone."

Philip said, "So long as you're functioning normally in your daily activities, and there's no escalation, we can continue to meet and talk."

Samantha thought, No escalation? Escalation in what?

She didn't want to know.

"In strict confidence," Samantha demanded.

"Yes. Everything is private."

Samantha didn't know if she would ever tell Philip about the five 1853 pennies she brought back from northern California. This was solid evidence her time travel was real, but she was uncomfortable about discussing it for a few reasons. She believed Philip would be dismissive of the coin story, saying she merely discovered the coins in her father's collection. Moreover, she felt guilty about profiting from her time travels. Even though Grace received one-half of the money from the sale of the coins, Samantha still felt it was greedy, unfair. She assuaged her guilt believing that if Aaron time traveled, collecting coins would be his main objective. Perhaps, if she had the nerve or felt a need, she would tell Philip in another session. But not now.

When she was leaving, Samantha said, "Well the good news about my nighttime adventures—as you refer to them—is that I may have a doctoral thesis. My conversations with Grant have spurred ideas. So I'm meeting with my doctoral advisor in ten minutes. Wish me luck."

Samantha left Philip's office, walked to another building on campus, and entered the office of her doctoral advisor. She sat and began her pitch. "The title is 'How to Keep the Republic: The Elements for Dissention and Analysis of Maintaining the Union While Marking the Milestone Anniversaries of the U.S.A.'"

She glanced at the advisor and continued, "So Benjamin Franklin famously said, 'A republic, if you can keep it.' To determine the level of dissention and likelihood of a fracture in the union, one can look at certain factors, or elements, for any period of time in our country's history. My analysis would concentrate on fifty-year intervals beginning with 1826; then the centennial, 1876; 1926; and the bicentennial, 1976."

Still no reaction from the advisor.

"So the factors or elements are structural execution (the founding documents, federalism, state actors and agencies and the execution of their mandates); economics; demographics, which includes immigration and ethnicities; innovation; and culture, which encompasses subsets of family, religion, journalism, and social media. There are also externalities: foreign powers and force majeure. I'm not sure that's an exhaustive list. But I'm calling them the most popular elements for disunity."

The advisor was now taking notes.

"In addition to that list of elements are relativism and presentism. Relativism being the opportunities of citizens to make choices or not, and whether those choices would be any better elsewhere. For example, in the nineteenth century, the western frontier was an option for dissatisfied citizens east of the Mississippi. Or relocation out of the country. Many times throughout our history, the general sentiment has been that it's better here than elsewhere, so we stay and our country, the Republic, remains intact.

"Presentism is a relatively new concept. It's defined as, if I may, the hubris of viewing past history through a current-day lens.

"My fiancé is an accountant, so he's influenced me into thinking more mathematically. So I will weigh these factors to determine which are more significant to tip the balance of disunity in one direction or the other.

"The dissertation would focus specifically on fifty-year intervals, those milestone anniversaries. I will discuss 1826, when this young country was fragile but unified, and why, based on the factors I enumerated. The focus of my research, however, would be on 1876, 1926, and 1976, and the influence of journalism during these times. Resources are available for these periods.

"The country's centennial in 1876 will be a substantial section. Followed by the Civil War, when the Republic was the closest to the precipice of failing, this centennial celebrated the country's innovations. Also at this time, the railroads accommodated a westward movement; commerce was growing, sustaining the Union despite the incompletion of Reconstruction.

"My analysis would rely substantially on journalistic resources. I went back and searched national newspapers a few years before and after July 4th of these milestone years. I compared the article length and the word usage. It's my own mini algorithm. Based on the positive word usage, the anniversaries appear to lift the unity shortly before and for some time thereafter, despite other factors pulling in the opposite direction: disunity."

The advisor's interest piqued, especially at the last mention. Samantha had a developing dissertation.

Sam Time

Summer 1854
New York City

Samantha's days and evenings were filled with research and writing. She often lunched with Grace and spoke at length on the phone with Aaron every weekday. But there remained a void, an emptiness. Loneliness—especially at night.

She had spent money for three dresses, hats, and undergarments. Why not flip through the history book and take another journey, advancing in time to someplace new?

Samantha surmised her time travel was connected to Grant. When Grant left northern California, he made the long journey by steamship around South America to New York City. Would the time-travel gods allow her to travel to the East Coast in 1854?

New York was the biggest populated American city, with more structure than the rural town of Eureka, California. Even though she was a history professor and had studied the mid-nineteenth century, time traveling to a major city was intimidating.

Despite her concerns, Samantha dressed in her corset and pantalets. Then she styled her hair in the double-braided crown with the braided halo hat and put on her powder-blue dress. She chose a pair of old black lace-up shoes and stuffed them in the dress pockets with her mini drawstring change purse and handkerchief. No shawl tonight because she opened the history book hoping to arrive in the summertime. She was prepared for a new journey—and fell asleep.

THE TIME-TRAVEL GODS had always placed Samantha's arrivals outdoors. To her surprise, she landed inside a building, in a coatroom where the door was open. She took her shoes out of her pockets, slipped them on, and laced them. Then she walked out of the coatroom into what appeared to be a small hotel lobby. Taking a deep breath, she opened the front door and stepped outside onto a wooden sidewalk.

There were many brick four- and five-story buildings side by side, similar in width with three windows on every floor. Carriages and buggies drawn by horses on the cobblestone street. Men walking the streets. Fewer women.

Samantha spotted an abandoned newspaper on a bench. She picked up the paper: New York City, Monday, August 14, 1854. The time and place were as expected, but how would she find Grant?

She felt uncomfortable, looking like a lost bumpkin. And the longer she stood on the sidewalk, the more she would be suspected of being a streetwalker. Not knowing what to do, she stared the newspaper, pretending to read.

"Samantha?"

She recognized the voice and looked up. The time-travel gods had done it. Captain Grant was standing in front of her. Nervous, excited, and relieved, she said, "Captain Grant, what a wonderful surprise."

"What are you doing here?"

"I am with two of my brothers. They insisted I repose and wait until they returned. But I was bored. I ought not to be out alone. But I am a country girl, and I want to explore the city. And you? How long are you staying?"

"Until I find a way home." What he didn't say was that he had arrived in New York penniless, having unknowingly entrusted his money to a swindler. An army buddy had helped Grant get a hotel room. Now Grant, in his early thirties, was waiting for money from his father.

His appearance conveyed despair. He was still wearing his soldier coat, which was unbuttoned and dirty; his hair and beard were longer. His face looked wistful and he was disheveled. If he took his coat off, he would probably have smelled of body odor.

"Would you be so kind as to show me the city?"

She was making a proposal to spend an afternoon with a married man on a city street. But only they would know. What else would he be doing? Drinking or sitting in small, hot room reading a book on this humid day?

Samantha turned and took a step forward. Then another and another, hoping Grant would join her.

He hustled from behind and walked next to her on the carriage side of the street. Samantha smiled and slipped the newspaper in her deep pocket. They walked in silence.

Samantha saw a park across the street. "It would be nice to sit on a bench. I have a newspaper. We can read it."

Crossing the street was a free-for-all. Men scampered across often, with confidence they could dodge the slow-moving horse traffic, peddler pushcarts, and piles of horse manure. Custom dictated ladies be escorted by a gentleman when crossing the road. So Samantha took Grant's elbow, and they crossed without incident.

They spotted a park bench. She sat a foot from the center, and Grant sat an arm's length away. She took the newspaper out of her pocket and placed it on her lap.

"So you resigned from the army."

"How do you know?"

"Resignations are printed in the *Herald* under Army Intelligence. 'On July 31, Capt. Ulysses S. Grant, 4th Infantry.'"

"Now I can go home to my family and become a farmer."

Samantha said, "We cannot do that. We don't have land."

"My wife's father has land and gave some to Julia."

"George Washington and Thomas Jefferson were farmers. You will be in good company."

Grant asked, "What business is your family doing here?"

Samantha hadn't prepared for this question. She scanned the newspaper for an idea. "Import-export." Although it sounded good, she had no clue what it was.

"In what?"

She skimmed the news headlines. "Nonperishables."

Then she looked down at her dress. "Fabric. Primarily clothing fabric. Mostly from Europe. England."

There was a pause and she said, "Acquaintances call me Sam."

He shook his head. Samantha looked at him in disappointment. And he noticed. Was she not his friend?

Sam Time

He explained, "In the army, soldiers called me Sam."

Samantha tilted her head as if to say, "I don't understand the connection."

He said, "U.S. Grant. Uncle Sam."

Samantha thought, How did I miss that? Huh. Sam time. A play on words. Being with Grant was Sam time.

"Have you read the newspaper today?"

He shook his head.

"Here. Take your time. If you see anything interesting, please read it to me."

Grant took the paper and scanned it, telling Samantha about the different articles, reading a few to her.

She concentrated on listening to Grant's recognizably deep and masculine, but not a standout you-should-be-on-radio voice. He was raised in the Midwest, and the army had taken him out West. She did not detect any strong regional accent. His cadence when reading was steady, pleasant, and soothing to Samantha's ear. Like his demeanor, his voice fit him; it was modest.

Although she enjoyed being with Grant, the day was hot and muggy. How she yearned for a large tumbler of water she could gulp down. Here, people sipped tea in tiny teacups. Grant was a true soldier and would bear the heat and not complain while wearing his soldier coat.

She watched the surreal display of people walking in the park. No single women. They were paired with a man or a matron, an older woman. Upper-class ladies wore wrist-length ivory kid gloves. Every woman wore a hat or a bonnet while gliding along the park gravel in their skirt dresses made full by layers of petticoats. Many women looked comfortable wearing white and cream linen dresses.

Samantha was envious; although she loved her dress, the medium-weight cotton fabric was hot. She dabbed her face and neck with her handkerchief to absorb the beads of sweat.

The gentlemen wore hats, some brim hats like Grant's, but many men were in top hats. The men's "costume" (the term for "suit") was mostly dark fabrics (black and navy), but men also sported tans and lighter linen frock coats and pants. It was, however, the "waistcoat" (the vest) that displayed character, as a tie does in the present. Waistcoats varied in colors and patterned fabrics (such as stripes and plaids) over a white linen shirt and a black bow tie.

And everyone—at least in this part of the city—behaved with refined manners. They were strolling in the park, all at the same pace, speaking softly.

Women laughed into their ever-present white handkerchiefs. And they didn't wear any makeup. (Those who did wear makeup were not ladies, they were prostitutes.)

Present-day Samantha wore lipstick and eyeliner. But since she was home, working on her doctorate, she didn't wear any makeup.

A few passersby did sneer at the disparity between Samantha, an attractive woman in a lovely dress, sitting with a scruffy man, as if to say, "You can do better than him."

Samantha knew what they didn't: her untidy friend would one day be president of the United States.

When he stopped reading out loud, Samantha peeked at the newspaper to see what Grant was silently reading: Wanted.

He glanced self-consciously, having noticed Samantha peering at him reading the want ads. Then he said, "Some positions for women, if you are looking."

"You do know I help with our business. Counts."

Sam Time

"You seem to have a lot of idle time," he countered.

She snatched the paper from his hands. She scanned through the want ads.

> *Domestic work by a respectable Protestant Woman*
> *Middle-aged seamstress wanted*
> *A respectable English girl as chambermaid*
> *A situation to take care of children by a German girl*

She breathed deeply, then rolled up the newspaper. Being playful, she pretended it was a telescope and held it up over one eye. "I can see far in the distance."

Grant was not amused.

"So far that I can see the future," she said. Be careful, she thought; Philip said even the smallest acts or words could change history. So she was vague. "I see you are successful." She smiled at Grant, then looked back into the hole of the rolled paper and said, "Very successful—eventually."

"What? Do I strike gold?"

"Everything is fading now. I cannot see anything anymore." She laid the rolled newspaper on her lap.

She looked straight ahead and said, "We ought not to waste the present, because we are wishing for the future. Enjoy the day as it is given to us."

"I have not seen my family in two years. I have never seen my youngest son."

Samantha had no reply. They sat in silence.

While she enjoyed watching the well-dressed people strolling in the park, she sensed Grant's thoughts were far away. She felt the urge to express her emotions. "Well, I will save this paper, because I want to remember this day." She tucked the newspaper in her pocket.

She didn't look over to see his reaction. For sure he'd heard her. But what he thought, she didn't know. But she meant it, and she was glad she'd said it.

Samantha had wanted to discuss with Grant topics relating to her developing dissertation. But her friend was in no mood for discourse.

They sat quietly and comfortably for a long time. Then she said, "Let's take a stroll. I see buggies and horses over there." He liked horses; maybe this would snap him out of his funk.

When they approached the spot with the buggies and horses, Samantha said, "Let's rent a buggy and go for a ride. It costs a dollar."

He hesitated because he didn't have any money. But Samantha did. She reached into her pocket for her mini drawstring change purse, taking out a silver dollar. "It would be splendid to go for a ride. You can be my driver. I ride alone on country roads and do not know these streets. Would you be so kind? You can choose the horse and buggy you like." She took his hand and placed the coin in his palm and then mouthed the word "please."

Grant liked the horse drawing an open-air buggy with a bench seat for two. Samantha feared slipping and falling when climbing into the buggy. This establishment, however, set a crate on the ground. Grant held her right hand as she stepped on the crate, grabbed onto a rail, placed her foot onto the long step, and climbed into the buggy and onto the seat. Grant then walked to the driver's side, climbed in easily, sat, and took the reins.

Sam Time

The ride began at a pleasant fast-walking-horse pace. Then another driver pulled alongside their buggy. Samantha missed the communication between Grant and the other driver. Then both buggies took off racing. Grant was energized.

Samantha was scared. No helmets. No safety belts. She bobbed around on the seat. There was nothing to hold on to, so she grabbed the hem of Grant's coat, not sure whether he noticed.

She had already injured her hand. What would she say if she flew off this buggy, cracked her head open, and needed a dozen stitches that would leave a permanent visible scar in her hairline?

When was this going to end? When Grant overtook the other buggy and won.

The race ended on the outskirts of the city: dirt road, a few scattered buildings. Hilly country.

The losing driver was slow to move next to Grant's buggy and claim defeat, because a wheel spoke was cracked. Grant jumped out of the driver's seat onto the dirt road to inspect the disabled wheel. Samantha stayed seated. If she precariously jumped off the buggy, her skirt could catch on something, causing her to stumble onto the ground. Not an image she wanted Grant to see.

Samantha waited patiently, observing the men and listening to the conversation to her right. She smelled a stinking odor that made her gag. She looked to the front, and the horse was defecating. Flies swarmed. Samantha thought, This never happens in the movies.

She turned to the right, and Grant was still talking with the competing driver. She pulled out her handkerchief from her pocket. Having endured enough, Samantha yelled, "Ulysses!" while holding the handkerchief with one hand over her nose and mouth and using the other hand to swat away the flies.

Samantha slid to the side of the seat. Grant walked over. Samantha stood, stretched out her arms, and put her hands on Grant's shoulders, while he put his hands under her elbows, lifting her out of the buggy.

She walked to the other side of the road, wanting to cross her arms under her chest. No, undignified in this era. Put her fists on her hips? That too, not proper for a lady. So Samantha paced and stewed.

Grant offered to take the man back to the city. Samantha thought, Three's a crowd. But the driver knew how to ride a horse bareback, which would be faster. So the driver took his horse to return to the city and left the disabled buggy on the side of the road.

Grant crossed the road to Samantha. "A wheel spoke cracked."

"Of course something was going to break at that speed!" Samantha snapped.

"Are you cross?" Grant was taken aback.

She looked him in the eyes, saying firmly, "I could never be cross with you."

Samantha paced. "I was scared out of my mind."

After taking a few deep breaths to compose herself, Samantha said, "At least one of us was amused. Your mood has lightened. That pleases me." She nodded her head once, signaling "Ready to go."

Grant climbed into the driver's seat and turned the buggy around to head back into the city. He dismounted, strode to the other side, and assisted Samantha into the buggy to ride shotgun.

During the leisurely ride back into the city, Samantha asked, "Why do you like horses?"

Grant shook his head.

She asked, "What?"

"You amaze me. No one asks the questions you do."

"I think most people see the utility of a horse. Work. Transportation. But you enjoy them. Why? What is it about horses?"

"They are magnificent creatures. The faster they go, the more magnificent," he said, grinning, holding the reins of the horse drawing the buggy.

Samantha laughed. "You certainly have a way with them. You like them and they like you. How is that?"

He gave a slight shrug and didn't answer.

"You are a mystery," Samantha said.

"I am a mystery? You are the one who seems to fall from the sky."

Samantha shuddered at the accuracy of Grant's observation.

He said, "New York is a large, populated city. But we met on the street. How is that possible?"

"It is a mystery to me too. I cannot explain it," she said.

"Strange coincidence."

"I call it a happy coincidence. And you spotted me. I did not notice you. You are"—she thought about how to say it—"you are unpruned."

She looked over at him and he smiled. Then he touched his long beard. "I will trim it before I go home."

"I think you like horses more than people."

"Well, I have known horses smarter and more loyal than people."

She let the conversation lapse.

Once they had returned to city center, the street was cobblestone. She had a renewed appreciation for twentieth-century vehicle suspension and shock absorbers. For a smooth ride, some carriages had suspension systems, but this buggy had none. So passengers felt every bump and rattle, especially on cobblestones. Samantha's teeth involuntarily knocked together.

She took in the passing sights. The city was impressively large and developed: blocks and blocks of mostly brick buildings, church steeples poking out here and there.

But the movement in the city fascinated her: the carriages, wagons, buggies, the horses, and the people. Commerce was happening on a Monday afternoon. Wagons and pushcarts filled with goods on large, tenuous spoke wheels maneuvered to avoid the mangy roaming dogs, cats, and pigs.

Then she closed her eyes to hear the sounds of 1854 New York. Horses neighing. The clomping of horses' hooves. The rattle of spoke wheels on the cobblestones. The hum of people talking. She opened her eyes and glanced at Grant, who was still happily steering the horse through the stop-and-go city traffic.

It then occurred to Samantha: she had failed as a history professor. She didn't ask to see the Croton Aqueduct or Trinity Church. She didn't even know the name of the street they were on. Rather than exploring for nuances in history, she embodied the character she was playing, Miss Samantha. So focused on her companion, she forgot who she was in her own present day. She sighed and thought, The day was well spent.

Grant returned the buggy and Samantha was tired. Grant walked her to her hotel.

"The day was enjoyable. The buggy ride was memorable," Samantha said with restrained emotion. But she thought of Shakespeare's words, "Parting is such sweet sorrow."

"Good day, Miss Samantha."

"Good day, Captain Grant."

Sam Time

Samantha opened the door to the hotel, then felt an urge to look back at Grant. He was heading toward the tavern across the street.

"No," she said out loud. Fortunately, the road was clear of horse and carriage traffic, so she ran—very unladylike—out onto the porch, down the step, and across the street toward Grant.

When she was close enough for him to hear, she said, "Ulysses, no!"

He turned around.

"No!"

"Just one drink."

"It is never only one. Mrs. Grant would not want you to go."

"She is not here. She will never know." He turned around and continued walking toward the tavern.

Samantha shouted, "And she will not write either."

Grant stopped without turning around. And Samantha ran in front of him.

"Women know women." Even over a century and a half apart.

"She is raising two young children. Maintaining a household. She dearly misses her husband."

Grant's face was stoic, but his eyes filled with tears.

"And she will not write to the husband who frequents taverns," Samantha said sternly.

The truth hurt.

She softened her voice. "I regret to say it. And to intrude on a family matter. But women, we are alike. And I am on her side. Do not go. Go back to your hotel. Write her a letter. That's what she wants."

Samantha stood uncomfortably and waited for Grant to absorb her words. "It will be easier when you are home. Less temptation. You will be with your family. They love you and need you—sober."

She took and squeezed his hand, softly saying, "You will feel better in the morning. Get a good night's sleep."

He squeezed her hand before letting go and walked to his hotel.

Searching for an isolated spot to disappear, Samantha stepped toward the side of the hotel, but the side alleys were strewn with garbage and stench. She thought, So that's why I landed inside a building.

She walked into the hotel, looked around, and tiptoed around a corner next to the stairs, where no one was. She needed only a few solitary seconds. She placed her hands on her stomach, closed her eyes, and took a deep breath. And she was back in bed in her home at 3:14 a.m.

THE NEXT MORNING Samantha awoke, went into the kitchen, and made coffee. As it brewed, she remembered the newspaper in her dress pocket. She backtracked into the bedroom and retrieved the newspaper from the deep pocket of her dress. Reentering the kitchen, where the light was bright, she unrolled the newspaper on the counter.

"Damn!"

Over 150 years had passed since the newspaper was published, and the print had completely faded. It was a brittle blank paper in beige patina. Samantha sighed and threw it in the recycle bin.

Sam Time

April 1861
Galena, Illinois

Samantha's 1854 trip to New York was exceptional. Could she learn and experience more by following Grant's life? She was still wrestling with the "how" and the "what" of time travel—Philip said trying to solve the "why" mystery was futile. And she could stop anytime, but Aaron was still away on business during the weekdays and would be for several months.

So one night she dressed and organized as usual, except this time, she didn't flip through the history book designating where and when.

Samantha thought, I'll go to sleep in my dress with my shawl around my shoulders and see where the time-travel gods take me.

The initial landing at a new location would be uncomfortable. Where would she find herself? What would the year be? The month? And what would she be looking for?

Trust the time-travel gods, she thought. And she fell asleep.

As with her arrival in New York, she landed inside a building without anyone noticing. She walked to the front door, opened it, and stepped onto an uncovered porch. Next door was a brick building with an affixed white painted sign; its black lettering read "St. Louis State Bank." She was in Missouri during the heyday of the steamboat. Commerce was flourishing, and the Mississippi River was jammed with at least a hundred steamers. Like New York City, the St. Louis city center was lined with brick buildings, four and five stories high.

Samantha pulled her shawl around her torso to cover herself for modesty. This was a market. Many men were selling wares and produce. Fortunately, most were too busy to notice Samantha standing on the sidewalk.

Across the street, despite the distance, she recognized the light-blue eyes of Grant. He was wearing the same clothes she had last seen him wearing: his old navy soldier coat, brimmed hat with the vest, and white shirt with the small black tie. His baggy pants, however, were tucked into his knee-high boots. Everything looked aged, including his face. He was selling cords of wood. She was embarrassed for him.

She didn't approach and speak with him, because she knew the conversation would be short and predictably uncomfortable. She would make an excuse why she was here passing through on family business. He would then say a drought had devastated farming, and he was selling wood to feed his family. Even though he would show no shame in providing for his family, she didn't want him to know she saw him in this humiliated state.

She turned around and went back into the building in which she had arrived, struck the magic pose—and returned to her bed.

Sam Time

Samantha looked at the clock; it was just before midnight. She rolled out of bed, went to the bathroom, and then walked into the kitchen to drink some water. She climbed back into bed thinking it was still early, and perhaps, another time-travel trip was possible. In less than an hour, she fell back to sleep.

WHEN SHE RETURNED to consciousness, Samantha was in another busy city on a cooler but pleasant sunny day. She was now accustomed to inside arrivals. She walked outside the building she was in, around to the main street, found a general store, and went inside. The newspaper on the counter showed she had arrived in Galena, Illinois, April 25, 1861.

From her research, Samantha knew Galena is situated in the northwest corner of Illinois along the Galena River near the Mississippi River. In this era, mining of lead ore made the town a hub of commerce and politics. Nine Civil War generals would hail from Galena, Grant being the town's most famous resident.

The newspaper was reporting that civil war was imminent. On April 12, 1861, the precursor to the Confederate army attacked Fort Sumter, located on a small man-made island built to protect Charleston, South Carolina. The U.S. Army surrendered the next day. Less than a week later, the newly inaugurated President Lincoln issued a call for volunteer soldiers.

Two other women were in the store. The store clerk was helping one woman while a Black woman waited. Samantha perused the shelves. Perhaps there was something she could take back with her. Another woman entered the store. The clerk ignored the Black woman, who had been waiting, and helped the woman who had just entered. Samantha picked up the newspaper to buy it and waited.

After the clerk was finished helping the woman at the counter, he motioned to Samantha that he could help her.

Samantha said referring to the Black woman, "She was here before me."

The clerk motioned with his hand for Samantha to come forward. She threw down the newspaper and walked out. Once outside, she peered through the window. The clerk was finally helping the Black woman only after everyone else had left.

A few minutes later, the Black woman left the store with her purchase. Samantha nodded and smiled at the woman, who returned a nod.

Shuffling in small steps, Samantha turned around, saying to herself, What am I looking for?

It wasn't hard. Across the street was a three-story brick building with three long windows on the second and third floors. A sign above the door, spanning the width of the building read "Grant & Perkins."

Samantha crossed the street and opened the door. Grant was inside.

"Good day, Captain Grant."

At age thirty-eight, he was still handsome. His beard and mustache were cut short, and his clothes were tidy. He was still wearing his navy soldier coat, vest, baggy pants, and white shirt with a small black tie. His hat was on the counter.

Seven years had passed since Grant had last seen Samantha in New York City. He was surprised. "Good day, Miss Samantha. What brings you to our fair city?"

"We are passing through. For the night. I saw the sign and thought by chance I would see an old acquaintance."

Sam Time

He said, "How is the riding?"

"It has been helpful to our family business. Do you work here?"

"Not any longer. My father owns this store. I am recruiting now."

"Recruiting for war?"

"Yes, we are doing well with signing recruits."

"Remember our discussions about our young nation. That which binds us or not."

Grant looked at her. "How prophetic."

Their conversation continued, and Samantha asked Grant about the details of recent developments. What newspapers was he reading? What were other written sources? Her keen memory, which could formulate rhymes easily, was also apt at memorizing information and resources for her dissertation research.

They spoke for a while until the store door opened. Two young boys, a girl, and a toddler ran in. Samantha said, "Oh, they must be yours. They are carbon copies"—she caught herself. "They look like you."

Grant beamed. The little girl, Nellie, age five, ran to her father and clung to the hem of his coat. The oldest son, Fred, age ten, and Ulysses Jr., age eight, were handsome like their father. The youngest, Jesse, was three and shared a likeness with his father.

The rambunctious boys ran around the store. Samantha said, "I must be going. Good day, Captain Grant."

She turned around, and the little toddler ran into Samantha's dress and fell down. "Are you all right, little man?"

Apparently so. The toddler scampered up and continuing running. Grant smiled and said, "Good day, Miss Samantha."

Samantha opened the door and left the store to find crowds of people gathered on the sidewalks. She tried to find a clearing but people were everywhere, cheering the new recruits who were marching to the train station. Wearing blue uniforms recently sewn by the town's tailors and women, over a hundred young men were on their way to their first camp for what they expected to be a three-month military service. The entire town had come out to bid them goodbye. Balconies were jammed with people, women waving white handkerchiefs, men swinging their hats.

But Samantha knew what they didn't. The war would endure for four years, and many of these men wouldn't return home or would be maimed for life.

She found an isolated spot in a building to disappear. And she reappeared in her bed.

After getting her bearings, Samantha slid out of bed and hurried to her home office, sat in the desk chair, and opened her laptop. She typed out all she could remember Grant had referenced: news articles, names, town meetings, and dates, which could be rich material for her dissertation. She finished at 1:14 a.m.

Sam Time

March 1862
Fort Henry

Making progress on her dissertation, Samantha routinely spent most of her days working in the library or at her desk. She couldn't resist, however, the urge to time travel. Flipping through her history book, she looked for the next date and place to visit Grant.

She turned the page to February 1862. Brigadier General Grant had commanded the Union army to victory at Fort Donelson along the Tennessee and Kentucky border. Grant gained national recognition and praise from President Lincoln.

Shortly thereafter, Henry Halleck, Major General in the regular army, accused Grant of insubordination for failure to send daily reports to the army headquarters in Washington. In fact, a telegraph spy prevented Grant's reports from reaching Halleck. Until the matter was resolved, for a couple of weeks Halleck sidelined Grant, and he languished on a ship on the Tennessee River near Fort Henry.

In Grant's isolation, Samantha anticipated a short visit would be mutually agreeable. But planning the trip was complicated, because it was winter, and Samantha needed to dress warm. Her medium-weight cotton dress would not provide enough comfort. Thin long johns, thicker socks, and the cream headband were a must but not enough.

Women wore cloaks in cold weather, and Samantha contemplated how to fashion one. Her grandmother had gifted her a thin white woolen blanket, which could be used as fabric for a simply constructed cloak. But she expected this to be quick one-off visit in a cold region and didn't want to cut up the blanket. Instead, she would double- or triple-fold the blanket around her shoulders, even though it would be an untraditional style.

In final preparation that night, she flipped through her history book looking for March 1862, then paper-clipped the pages so the book would remain open. Samantha styled her hair with a single, centered, back-of-the-head French braid. Then she stuffed her lace-up shoes and headband in her pockets.

She climbed into bed and fell asleep. During the middle of the night, she was transported back in time.

SHE ARRIVED OUTSIDE the ship in which Grant was under house arrest. After she slipped on her headband, pulled out her shoes, and double-tied the laces, she introduced herself to the ship's watchman and asked to see Grant.

Less than a year had passed since Samantha had seen Grant. Under overcast skies, she embarked on the otherwise empty ship and Grant greeted her.

"Good day, General."

Sam Time

"Good day, Miss Samantha."

The knee-length navy frock coat of his soldier uniform denoted his rank: In a double-breasted style, sixteen brass buttons in two vertical rows of eight buttons were grouped in four pairs. And the insignia on the shoulders displayed the single silver center star of a brigadier general.

Black velvet topped the coat collar and sleeve cuffs with three small functional brass buttons. Baggy pants were held up by suspenders covered by a vest over a white shirt. A short, thin black ribbon was tied in a bow under the shirt collar. His black brimmed hat was made of felt with a gold cord at the center base.

Since his victory at Fort Donelson, he'd taken up the habit of cigar smoking. This soldier, who could endure long periods without water and food, smoked constantly throughout the day. The etiquette of the time frowned on smoking when someone came to call. "To call" meant "to visit" in the Victorian era. Even though Grant wasn't smoking in Samantha's presence, the cigar smell was pungent.

They walked on the main deck to the side of the ship. Samantha sat on a bench, and Grant sat on her left.

Grant was irritable, having been unjustly taken out of action. After the Fort Donelson victory, Grant's intention was to continue to pressure the Rebel army. While he remained idle on the docked ship, the enemy had time to regroup. This setback was also reminiscent of others in his life.

Samantha had hoped merely visiting and listening could be cathartic, but now she wasn't sure. She was freezing and said only, "Your staff will vouch for you. They know the reports were sent. Surely this will resolve soon."

After he was finished venting, he said, "It is kind of you to call."

Samantha broadly interpreted this to mean "How are you?"

She replied, "Family business has been strained with England because of the war. And on the way here, there was an incident, and my cloak was ruined. When I heard you were here, and we were passing through—it was providence."

Although Grant's eyes were fixed on her, she wasn't sure he was listening. She kept her head still; only her eyes moved to look into his and then down at his right hand, which was on his knee. She could feel his stare. What if she put her hand on his? Would he pull away? She stared back at him and did it: she put her hand on top of his. And he fanned his fingers to grasp hers. They held hands—for a long time.

Then Samantha whispered, "I have to go." She lifted her hand away from his.

They stood and she looked in the distance. Was there any man to whom she could wave? She waved anyway and a disheveled man reciprocated.

Embarrassed, Samantha said, "That's one of our workers, William. He will take me back."

Grant walked her to the plank to disembark.

"Good day, General."

"Good day, Samantha."

When Samantha was a short distance from this pretend worker, she turned around to see Grant had retreated inside the ship. She approached the man. "I have mistaken you for my brother. Please accept my apologies."

The man moved toward her, not letting her pass. So it was true: a woman waving to a strange man could be construed as solicitation.

Sam Time

This was one horny-looking man. Samantha was scared. What could be worse than rape? To her left were four men around a campfire. Gang rape.

She lifted the front of her skirt and darted away, making a wide berth past the man, running as fast as she could. But she wasn't used to running on irregular surfaces. The dirt road inclined slightly, and the hard washboard dirt road made running arduous. She tried to keep her blanket from falling off her shoulders. With the adrenalin pumping, she wasn't cold anymore.

Glancing back quickly, she saw a few men were running after her. Even fit men, however, needed endurance to run as Samantha could. Good that she'd double-tied her shoelaces.

Her lead from the men was increasing. Then Samantha's foot caught a rut in the road, and she fell on her left hip. Although it hurt, she scrambled to her feet and ran. Glancing back again, she saw someone riding a horse. The other men fell back with confidence the horse rider would catch Samantha. True, she couldn't outrun a horse.

But maybe the horse was the solution. She slowed her pace and looked over her shoulder to see how far behind the horse and rider were. When they were ten horse lengths away, Samantha dropped the front of her skirt. She slowed to a jog, then a fast walk because if she ran she would trip on the hem of her dress. Then she took the white blanket on her back and held it up by its lengthwise edge as high as she could, stretching her arms up and out. She hung the entire blanket behind her trying to confuse the horse and make it look as if the horse would ride into a white wall.

It worked. The sound of the horse hooves stopped. Samantha stopped too. The rider mishandled his mount, causing the horse to rear, lifting its front legs and standing on its hind legs. Samantha, still holding the blanket high, heard the thud of the rider falling off the horse. She slowly turned around. The rider lay on the ground, stunned. Maybe the wind was knocked out of him. Perhaps he'd broken a bone or two.

Samantha lowered the blanket, and the horse galloped past her. She gathered the blanket and ran into the woods before the fallen rider could get up and notice in which direction she'd fled.

She looked behind her and she was alone. In case someone was around, she hid behind a thick tree, assumed the magic pose, and disappeared—back into her bed.

Samantha shook as she undressed and slipped on Aaron's T-shirt and a pair of crew socks. She went into the kitchen and gulped down a large tumbler of water. After climbing into bed, she lay awake for hours.

THE NEXT MORNING, she awoke with a bruise on her hip the color and size of a small eggplant. When Aaron returned home, Samantha said she fell running, which was true.

Sam Time

Summer 1863
Vicksburg, Mississippi

The following week, Philip texted Samantha asking how she was. Samantha replied that, if he was available, she would like to talk. They arranged a time, and Samantha went to his office. She summarized her recent travels.

"The last time I was here, I mentioned my dissertation was taking shape, in part because of my time traveling and the conversations I've been having with Grant. When I met him in New York City, he wasn't in the mood for academic talk, but in Galena, Illinois, we had this insightful conversation. He's unwittingly helping me with my dissertation. He reads the papers, knows people. I'm getting direction from him. Focus. Where to look. These resources are out there, but they're voluminous. It sounds so crazy. But it's working. Time traveling. Meeting Grant and my studies.

"But then I saw him at Fort Henry. He was in a foul mood and I felt awkward. And then having a bunch of horny men running after me was hellacious." She explained what had happened in detail, hoping Philip would believe her stories were real.

He asked, "How did you know the blanket would work?"

"I didn't. It popped into my head. When I was in northern California, Grant taught me how to handle a nervous horse. And he told me the ways and things that could spook a horse. Maybe the idea germinated from that conversation. So when this man was chasing me on this horse, I could hear the horse's hooves. And I heard when the horse stopped. If I had heard the rider dismounting, I would have started running again."

"Can you really outrun a man?"

"Listen, men are strong but not necessarily fit for running. Besides, many in that era were cigar smokers, and they're wearing boots, which are difficult to run in. Now, I was wearing a long dress and shoes, which are not made for running. Thank God, I'd double-tied my shoelaces. And I was also carrying a blanket. Yet I was confident I could still outrun the horny bastards."

Philip listened, stroking his chin.

"So it's been a week since I time traveled. I was so scared when I returned home, I thought, I'm never going back. But now I think the time-travel gods have my back."

"What do you mean?"

"Well, this is the second time—the first, when the Peyton girl took my dress—that I thought I would never return. Now I'm thinking the universe will, maybe should, always bring me home. Perhaps there will be other scary moments, and I wouldn't stand around not doing anything, saying, 'The travel gods will take me back.' Despite those two scary moments, I returned."

"So what's next?" Philip asked.

"There's Vicksburg. A Union victory in the summer of 1863. Whereas Gettysburg was a major victory in the eastern theater, Vicksburg was a major victory in the western theater."

Philip said, "Supposedly, I have an ancestor who went AWOL in Vicksburg and never returned home."

"Fascinating."

"I think it's a burden. My ancestors were racist Southerners."

"So tell me about this relative and Vicksburg."

"The story was Henry Sparks, a guy with seven kids, enlisted in the Confederate army only to flee during the Vicksburg battle."

"How did they know that's what happened?"

"I don't know. I never paid attention because they were racist."

"But that's the family legend?" Samantha asked.

"Yes."

"I could go back to see if I can find out anything about him. Henry Sparks. How old and from where?"

"About thirty and from Richmond," Philip said.

"I'll also need the names of his seven children and wife. This way I'll know if I have the right guy."

"I'll text you the names. I need to look at my family tree."

Philip thought and added, "Should you come across this guy, say this: 'Half mile down a gravel road.'"

"Half mile down a gravel road," Samantha repeated. "Okay. What is it?"

"I'm going to leave it at that."

"Well, tonight I'm off to Vicksburg, summer of 1863."

SAMANTHA PREPARED that night, hoping the time-travel gods would take her to a day and place when and where it was safe. As usual, she opened her history book to 1863 and paper-clipped the page to lie flat.

She dressed in her Victorian undergarments and styled her hair in a double-braided crown. For this trip she chose the green dress with the matching braided halo hat and the afghan that served as a shawl. During the night, Samantha fell into a deep sleep.

SAMANTHA AWOKE NEAR a wood-frame house. She approached a soldier standing guard. "Soldier, is this Vicksburg Union headquarters?"

"Yes, ma'am."

"I would like to see General Grant for only a few minutes. Miss Samantha Hunter is calling."

The soldier turned around and entered the house. Not too long after, Grant came outside. He took the cigar stub from his mouth, threw it on the ground, and stepped on it with the ball of his boot. Then he picked up the extinguished stub and threw it in a bucket used for that purpose.

Over a year had tolled since they had last seen each other, but his uniform had changed, as had his rank. His double-breasted frock coat sported eighteen brass buttons in two vertical rows of nine buttons, grouped in a trio of threes. And the insignia on the coat displayed the two silver stars of a major general.

As Grant walked toward her, Samantha had the urge to smile. But she caught herself. She wasn't looking at a page in history. She was inside it. This was real. She tried closing her mouth tightly, knowing many were watching. But Major General Grant had stopped the important work he was doing to see her. She tilted her head to the side so no one could see the smirk on her face as she stared at Grant.

Sam Time

If Grant was pleased to see Samantha, his stolid expression did not reveal it. As he approached her, his eyes alternated, looking at the ground and then at Samantha.

"Good day, Miss Samantha."

The cigar smell was pungent.

"Good day, General. I appreciate you taking time to see me. I need only a few minutes. I am a Yankee, but I have a Southern friend. This family friend may be a prisoner here. His name is Henry Sparks from Richmond, Virginia. Age thirty."

"I will have someone check. How are you?"

"I am well, thank you. If he is here, may I see him?"

"With conditions," Grant said as he walked away.

"Of course."

Grant was businesslike and Samantha understood. He was in the middle of a major military campaign. There wasn't any time for diversions. Also Mrs. Grant was in the camp and now standing on the porch when Grant walked back to the house.

Samantha wished she knew how to lip-read. But Samantha imagined what they were saying:

"How do you know her?"

"Her family had business out West."

"What does she want?"

"She asked about a Rebel prisoner. Wants to see him."

"Why couldn't she ask another officer?"

He didn't answer, but he reassured her by kissing her on the cheek and said, "You know you have my heart."

Grant then walked with his wife into the house.

Samantha waited until another soldier came out of the house, introducing himself as Lieutenant Carter. He said there was a prisoner named Henry Sparks. The lieutenant would escort Samantha, but he had strict instructions from the general: Samantha was restricted from entering the fort or garrison and could only meet with the prisoner outside. Also, the lieutenant must return with Samantha in two hours. She understood and agreed.

The garrison holding prisoners was a mile down the road. As they walked on the dirt path, she asked, "What would the general do if you didn't return me after two hours?"

"I do not want to say, ma'am."

Samantha asked, "How is life as a soldier?"

He didn't reply. She understood his uneasiness and said, "My young nephews are in the army. I have heard their stories. I do not judge."

After a few minutes, she asked in a whisper, "What is it like?"

"Most days are boring. Drills and more drills. When it rains, there is little we can do. Rainy days at camp are the most depressing. If it lasts several days, the mood of the soldiers is gloomy. The days drag on.

"Marching, when we are moving from one camp to another location, is invigorating. But we never know when we will get orders to move out. If a regiment moves by rail, they use boxcars, not the passenger cars."

They were now walking in step. She waited a minute, then asked, "And the food?"

"Hardtack, coffee, bacon for the soldiers. Sometimes rice and beans. Officers may get potatoes, biscuits, butter, and cooked ham."

Samantha knew hardtack was a stiff biscuit, so tough that this tasteless unleavened bread needed to be dipped in coffee to soften before eating.

Lieutenant Carter elaborated. "We have camped in regions where there are berries or corn. Unfortunately, that does not happen often."

To draw more conversation, Samantha said, "My nephews write how they miss home."

"Everyone gets homesickness."

Samantha asked, "And other sickness?"

"Soldiers get sick if the food is not cooked and the water not boiled. There's also malarial fever."

Then Lieutenant Carter spoke without prompting, "One time we marched to a camp, pitched our tents, but we were ordered not to build any campfires at night, because we were so close to the enemy. The campfires would have given away our position. That night was freezing cold; no one slept, because we were moving around to stay warm. At daybreak, we were allowed to build small fires to cook breakfast.

"Hot days are bad too. One time, many soldiers wearing buttoned jackets developed heatstroke."

"And the battles?" Samantha asked.

"A battle is like a thunderstorm. You hear the thunder, the wind picks up before the deluge. In war, you hear the cannon fire and the deafening sound of gunfire. The ground actually shakes. Dreadful.

"On sunny days, you can see flashes of sunlight reflecting off the metal on the Rebel guns and bayonets. You cannot see anything because of all the smoke. But the commander gives the order to fire. A soldier fires his gun not knowing if he will hit anything. Aim low, they say. Aim low and shoot. You smell burning gunpowder. And hear the bullets zipping by. A zip, zip sound. And when they strike a soldier, you hear the thud. The wounded screaming.

"And as horrific as war is—I hate to admit this—when we are fighting, a demon possesses me. I want to kill. I want to kill many Rebels. The more I kill, the more intensely gratifying it is."

His strides were longer, and Samantha kept up with his pace. But he stopped talking. Then he said, "I should not have said that."

"It is I who asked. I do not judge you. A soldier is trained to do what you say. And I will not repeat it to anyone. Have you seen General Grant in the field?"

"Yes, in the chaos I described, he comes through on his galloping horse, his staff riding behind him. Branch limbs from trees are falling from gunfire, and he rides unflinchingly."

After a mile, Lieutenant Carter met with another Union soldier and asked to see the prisoner. Samantha was escorted to an open field with piles of cut wood. There was also a wooden wagon cart propped on logs.

Samantha expected to see an ambulatory prisoner. Instead, the prisoner was carried out on a stretcher by two Union soldiers. They laid the stretcher straddling the sides of the wagon, which was low enough for Samantha to stand next to it and speak with the prisoner. Lieutenant Carter stood next to her. The severely wounded man's clothes were soaked in blood.

She asked, "What is your name, soldier?"

He struggled to say "Henry Sparks."

"Where do you live?"

He took a while to say "Richmond, Virginia."

"Do you have a wife?"

"Theresa."

"Any children?"

"Henry Jr., Thomas, James, Luke, Margaret, Esther, and

Sam Time

Susanna," he said, taking a breath or two before he said every name.

It's him, she thought, putting her hand on her chest.

Her heart was pounding. "Have you deserted?"

He replied but she didn't understand and looked to Lieutenant Carter to interpret. "He said his two friends, family men, did desert and went out West. But Henry continued to fight until he was wounded."

Henry's eyes didn't focus. He stared straight up at the sky, as if he was blind.

Whispering, he said, "Who are you?"

Samantha replied, "Who do you want me to be?"

After taking a deep breath, he said, "Theresa. My wife, Theresa."

She said, "Henry, I am here, your Theresa."

He cried. She motioned to Lieutenant Carter, asking if she could hold his hand. He nodded.

Samantha held his hand. "Henry, half mile down a gravel road. Half mile down a gravel road."

She would barely understand what he was saying, but Lieutenant Carter repeated what Henry said:

> *Half mile down a gravel road,*
> *A clear creek in back flowed,*
> *Wood swing under old oak tree,*
> *Porch creaking steps number three,*
> *Two-story white house fits nine,*
> *Round kitchen table made of pine,*
> *Thought all sunny days would last,*
> *Now memories in the past.*

While holding his hand, Samantha asked Henry to repeat the poem, so she could remember it. Eight lines; the rhyming words: road/flowed, tree/three, nine/pine, and last/past. She turned to Lieutenant Carter to help her understand the words.

"We have seven children," Samantha said.

Henry closed his eyes and tears came down the side of his face, "Seven children. Three died of measles: Thomas, James, and Esther."

Now Samantha was crying.

Henry said, "Fits nine. Now memories in the past."

She understood and cried harder.

He gasped for breath. "The measles outbreak was three months after you died of consumption."

Samantha straightened her back, glanced at Lieutenant Carter. She was impersonating a dead woman.

He said, "Theresa."

Samantha said, "Yes, Henry."

"I will be with you soon."

She had started this; she was going to finish it. "It is beautiful here. No war. No disease. Thomas, James, and Esther are here with me. You can let go."

A tear rolled down Lieutenant Carter's cheek. Henry took his last breath. His hand fell limp in Samantha's. After placing his hand on the stretcher, she took several steps backward. She had never seen anyone die.

Henry's eyes were frozen open. Lieutenant Carter placed his hand over Henry's face to close his eyes. The lieutenant turned around to Samantha. "We should get back," she whispered. Then she pulled her handkerchief from her dress pocket and dabbed her eyes.

They walked in silence for a half mile, and then Samantha said,

Sam Time

"Henry's family thought he deserted. How can that be?"

"He said two of his friends deserted. Not only did they desert the army, they deserted their families and went out West. If a soldier is not on the wounded list, sick from disease, dead or prisoner list, desertion would be a possibility, especially if his friends deserted."

"And the injured or prisoner lists?"

"We do our best, which is better than the graycoats, but the lists may not include everyone."

"I appreciate you telling me this," she said.

When they were almost at headquarters, Samantha said, "Would you relay to General Grant my gratitude for this visit? Also two hours has not passed. I would be grateful if you would walk me back to my lodging."

Grant was on the porch conferring with other officers. Lieutenant Carter relayed Samantha's message, and Grant agreed for the lieutenant to escort her back to her lodging.

Several soldiers were milling around outside, one leaning on the building, another sitting on the porch steps, a couple roaming the grounds. She had wrapped her shawl so the two ends crossed over her left shoulder—an attempt at modesty around the soldiers who were staring at her with thoughts below the waist.

As she walked away from headquarters, she glanced back at Grant. He had been looking down at papers but lifted his head for a glimpse of Samantha.

Lieutenant Carter escorted Samantha to her landing place. After he walked away, she found an isolated place outside, assumed the magic pose, and returned home to her bed in Austin.

Before undressing, she took her laptop and quickly typed the Sparks family eight-line poem, recalling the rhyming words: road/

flowed, tree/three, nine/pine, last/past. She recalled other details: half mile, gravel, clear creek, wood swing, old oak tree, porch steps, two-story house, round kitchen table, sunny day, and memories. And she typed the poem, printed it, and put the paper in her tote bag.

She undressed, slipped on one of Aaron's T-shirts and a pair of crew socks, drank some water, climbed into bed, and fell asleep.

THE NEXT MORNING she texted Philip: *Do you have time today?*

He did and they arranged a time to meet in his office.

When Samantha arrived in Philip's office, she took from her tote bag the paper with poem and handed it to Philip. She sat down watching him read it. Philip finished, then looked up at the ceiling. Then he stood and paced his office with his hands in his jeans pockets.

Samantha wanted Philip to speak first, but that wasn't going to happen. So she said, "What does the critical thinker think?"

"Interesting."

"What do you mean?" She stumped him. He was speechless. "Philip, what do you mean by 'interesting'?"

He was still pacing and refused to answer. So she said, "Okay, I'll give you some background. Henry Sparks, age thirty, living in Richmond, Virginia, was a wounded prisoner of the Union army at Vicksburg, having fought in the battle on the Rebel side. I saw him. He was on a stretcher barely holding on to life. But I asked about his family, and he said his wife was Theresa, and they had seven children."

She took a few moments to think. Except for Henry, all the names were biblical, which was a helpful reference. "Henry Jr.,

Thomas, James, Luke, Margaret, Esther, and Susanna. So I knew I had the right guy. Agreed?"

"Agreed."

"His two friends deserted—the term they used, not AWOL. And apparently these friends went out West, deserting their families as well. Even though Henry's name was on the Union list in Vicksburg, he wasn't listed as a wounded prisoner in the Rebel records. Some type of error. So the assumption was he deserted with his friends. Questions?"

He shook his head.

"I recited the first line of the poem, which I didn't know was a poem. And Henry recited the entire poem three times so I could remember it. Now, I did have trouble understanding his accent, because his breathing was labored. The Union soldier who was with me helped interpret what Henry was saying."

She waited for Philip to say something. He didn't, so she continued, "After he recited the poem three times, he said—" she stopped to remember the names. The first letter of each name spelled "JET." There were two boys and a girl. "James, Esther, and Thomas died of the measles, which was the reason the poem ends solemnly."

Samantha rested her elbows on his desk and opened her hands up, showing Philip she was done, and it was time for Philip to react. He stared at her, saying nothing, so she prompted him. "Is this your family story? Does it line up?"

"Yes."

"Thank you. What do you think?"

"He was a racist, fought with racists."

"Oh, Philip, there was no hatred in his final moments. He was a dying man stripped of everything. It was so sad, even the Union soldier had tears in his eyes. I've never watched anyone take their last breath."

Samantha became introspective. "You know, I've been wondering, why me? What's the purpose? Now this is uncovering a family mystery. As if Henry were talking from the grave, saying he wanted his honor back. That he wasn't a scoundrel who deserted from the army and never returned home. Instead, he fought, was wounded, and died."

She thought for a few seconds then added, "It's not as if you can tell your family this and correct the family history. But. But, you could start a new trend. Tell the existing generations, based on new research, this might have happened."

At this point, she was conversing with herself. She hoped Philip was amused. But he was hard to read. Then she realized. "You don't care. This was not about solving a family mystery."

He didn't disagree.

"This was a test. You were testing me. You told me the names of the kids only to prove Henry's identity. But the poem. That I came back with the poem is the clearest evidence I am going back in time. How else would I know a rudimentary poem composed by some Sparks family member? And you didn't even tell me it was a poem. You probably never told anyone or never wrote it down. Only family members knew this poem."

"You're right."

Samantha threw her hands up. "Thank you, Philip. Finally!"

Her jubilation was temporary. "Okay, you say, 'You're right.' What does that mean?"

Philip was still silent. Mr. Critical Thinker wasn't going to be easily convinced.

She blurted, "You Socratic psychologists drive me crazy! You never answer a question. Fine, I'll figure it out."

After only a few seconds, she said, "I got it. I'm right that you were testing me. But the question is, did I pass? Do you believe that I'm traveling back in time, or am I crazy?"

Philip said, "I would like to believe you. Even with this. I'll even call it 'evidence.' But I just can't say, 'You're time traveling.'"

"I should not be surprised. But does this mean, at least, you don't think I'm crazy?"

He didn't answer.

"You still think my experiences are pathological and not authentic," she sighed. "Well, I have to go. See you in a few."

Despite Philip's pessimism about her time travel, Samantha felt buoyed when she left his office. She walked to the cafeteria, bought juice, and sat down with a few friends. They teased her about having a bachelorette party at a nightclub, which featured male strippers on Wednesday nights.

"Come on, Sam. Have a last fling before your nuptials," they said.

She knew they were looking for an excuse to go to the nightclub. But they planted something in Samantha's mind: one last fling.

Donna Balon

Late Spring 1864
Mechanicsville, Virginia

Samantha skimmed through her history book for the where and when of her next time travel. During the Civil War, Julia Grant lodged often at the Union headquarters. And the war was raging, so choices were limited.

No time or place seemed appropriate, especially Cold Harbor, the place of a brutal battle lost by the Union. After General Robert E. Lee's troops pounded the Union's, Grant's critics were emboldened, and Grant lost favor with some supporters—save for Lincoln. The battle was fought near Mechanicsville just northeast of Richmond, Virginia, lasting over two weeks in the late spring of 1864.

Paper-clipping the pages of the history book, Samantha chanced perhaps this would be her next destination. She expected the weather to be warm in Virginia, so she chose the pink dress and slip-on shoes. Because this was near a war zone, she didn't wear

Sam Time

the matching braided halo hat, and she styled her hair in a single, centered, back-of-the-head French braid. She fell asleep that night.

SAMANTHA AWOKE STANDING on a covered porch of a one-story white wood-frame house. She knocked on the door. After a few taps, when no one answered, she opened the unlocked door.

"Hello. Is anyone home?" she called out, expecting someone would be home during the daytime. But no one answered.

Stepping a few feet into the house, she looked around for clues. Where was she? A clock on the mantel displayed the time: 10:55. To the right was an oak desk, topped with a pile of letters. She walked to the desk, sifted through the letters, and flipped a few over. The delivery address read Stephen Ellerson, Mechanicsville, Virginia.

She pulled and jiggled open the sticky top desk drawer, took out a blank piece of writing paper and a fountain pen. Then she wrote:

> Dear General Grant,
> I arrived in Mechanicsville today. Your company at Ellerson house would be appreciated should you be available.
> Respectfully your obedient servant,
> Miss Samantha Hunter

Looking at the Ellerson letters, she tried to deconstruct how they were folded and sealed, so she could do the same for hers. But they were too complicated to replicate. Instead, she folded her letter in thirds, like a present-day business letter, then folded it in thirds lengthwise. She rummaged through the desk drawers for a wicked wax stick and sealing stamp to no avail. But she found string and secured the letter closed as if she were wrapping a package.

Walking out onto the porch, she then strode to the center of the dirt road and looked around. The town was deserted since the recent battle. In the distance, she spotted a group of Union soldiers. Raising and waving both of her arms, she caught their attention. When they approached, she asked if they would deliver her letter to General Grant. A soldier dismounted and walked to Samantha. She recognized him and said, "Lieutenant Carter? It's Miss Samantha. We met in Vicksburg."

He acted as if he had never seen her. "How can I be of service, Miss Samantha?"

"Would you give this to General Grant?" She handed him the letter. He nodded, mounted his horse, and rode away.

Samantha walked back to the house, sat on a porch chair, and waited. Her eyes were fixed on the bend in the road about a quarter mile from the house. Soon after she heard the clock strike noon, she saw a soldier on a large galloping horse. As they came closer, she recognized Grant. She stood as he ably slowed the horse to a canter, then transitioned to a trot when approaching the house. He lifted his hat when he passed by and trotted the horse to the back of the home. Despite the warm weather, Grant wore his soldier coat buttoned, the respectful etiquette when making a call.

There was war, disease, pain, and death surrounding them. Homes and lives destroyed. The general commanded a brutal losing battle that had killed and wounded thousands. Some called him the Butcher. But when Grant rode past her on his horse, Samantha could compartmentalize and ignore everything around her—and her twenty-first-century life for this moment.

Sam Time

She thought, Now this is what happens in the movies.

As she walked around the house, Samantha knew that, in his depression after the Cold Harbor battle, Grant was seeking an escape. He tied his horse to a tree behind the house.

A year had passed since Samantha had seen Grant. As she approached him, she noticed the insignia on the shoulders of his coat displayed the three silver stars of a lieutenant general.

"Good day, Miss Samantha."

"Good day, General."

Grant said, "What are you doing here?"

Samantha had planned an answer. "Collecting my niece. She married a Southerner who is in the Rebel army. She is with child and has a toddler. We thought two of us needed to make the journey to take her and her daughter back home to New Jersey."

"Travel is dangerous."

"I know. But it is also dangerous to leave my young niece in the South. We do not know what will become of her husband. But if she is back home with us, she and her children will be safe."

The explanation was plausible.

Samantha knew that during the war civilians needed a government-issued passport to travel the railroad in the Confederate states. "My brother got passes for us to ride the train. Then we rode horses to get here faster. I am glad I learned to ride. I made myself a split skirt. Then we paid for a buggy. When we arrived here, we saw this empty house. I changed out of my riding clothes. My brother went to find my niece and her daughter. We thought I should stay here, so no one else comes by with the same purpose."

Grant said, "All the residents have fled. No one will return to town until they hear it is safe."

"I see. Well, if we do stay, we will leave a quarter dollar on the table for the night's lodging."

Samantha said, "How about you? Is it not unwise for you to ride without your staff?"

"They are here. In town. They know where I am."

"I did not see them," she replied.

"I have a faster horse," he said, smiling.

Samantha smiled realizing Grant had probably challenged his staff. Who could make it to town first? It was no surprise who won.

They were still standing by the horse. "He is a beauty. What's his name?" Samantha said of the huge chestnut horse.

"Cincinnati."

Samantha wanted to know how the horse got this name, but this was not a day for many questions.

"May I?" She asked for permission to pet the horse. This was Grant's favorite, and only he would mount the horse with two exceptions—President Lincoln being one of them.

She petted the horse with long strokes on the horse's neck. "I am still learning how to enjoy horses like you do."

The horse turned his head toward her.

"He likes you," Grant said.

Samantha smiled and thought, The horse is taking his cue from you. Then she stepped back.

Grant said, "He is the finest horse. Good temperament on and off the battlefield."

Samantha spoke softly, "How is the war going?"

Grant looked away, shaking his head as if to say, "Not good."

Samantha surmised Grant was ruminating on war strategy. She said, "It is helpful to set something aside for a while, take a break, and when you return to the matter, you will see it in a fresh way."

Was she giving him modern self-help advice?

"You met Lincoln. What is Lincoln like?"

"Tall." They laughed at his self-deprecating comment. Lincoln, at six four, was at least seven inches taller than Grant.

Grant said, "He listens."

Samantha recalled what Lincoln had said of Grant: "He fights." She probed to hear more. "You have much in common."

"You mean two men from the Midwest with few successes until their older years?"

Well, yes. But their lives were inspirational because of their hard times in their early years.

"He promoted you to your rightful position. So I like him."

"We share the same views. We're abolitionists. Agree on the way forward for our nation."

"Amen," Samantha said.

"His wife, though. She's unpredictable."

Samantha agreed. "I have heard the rumors." She changed the subject. "I sent the letter with some concern. Your soldiers. Do they think I am a spy? A Rebel spy?"

Grant jerked his head back and scrunched his face. "No."

"Well, for the record, I am not."

He shook his head again. Then he asked, "And your family? Your nephews?"

"The family is well, considering." As to her fake nephews, she could create and kill them within seconds, conjuring a story of young men dying in a Civil War battle. "My nephews—" She paused, looking at the sun dappling through the trees, and said, "The day is beautiful. I will defer my grief until the evening."

She was acting the role of Miss Samantha and felt the gravity of what she had just said. They stopped talking, comfortable in silence. During the long lull in the conversation, she heard rippling water.

"Is that a creek?"

"Yes, not far down the path."

Grant led the way down the narrow dirt path. Approaching the creek, Samantha saw the sun glistening on the water. She walked off the trail, turned around. "I want to dip my feet in it. Perhaps it is not too cold."

Samantha had done this before, when she and Grant rode their horses to the beach in northern California. She recalled that day, Grant took pleasure in watching her. She could do so again without offending his sensibilities.

As Samantha removed her shoes, lifted her dress, and dipped her feet in the shallow bank of the creek, Grant stood on the trail, his eyes fixed on her.

"The water is cold but it feels good."

Facing toward the sun, Samantha stretched out her arms. The warmth of sun was convincingly real. She closed her eyes, savoring the moment. Her dress hem puddled in the water. "The sun feels so good, and the breeze is even warm."

She opened her eyes, and Grant was staring at her. She stepped out of the water, stomped her feet on wild grass to shake off the water, and slipped on her shoes. Looking up at Grant, she smiled as he stared at her.

Then he took off his hat, letting it fall onto a nearby rock.

That was his tell.

Samantha gazed at Grant, then walked toward him, stopping when they were face-to-face. He placed his arms around her waist, and she lifted her arms around his neck. They kissed. Although Samantha was elated, she could smell only cigar, taste cigar.

He tightened his arms to lift her, but she whispered, "Wait." She stepped away, grasped with her hand the bottom front of her skirt and petticoat and lifted them up. She looked at Grant and nodded. He lifted her, and in unison, she wrapped her legs around his waist.

Their movements were in slow motion. They kissed and then stopped, touched foreheads, and kissed again. Samantha ran her fingers through his thick hair. More kisses on her cheek. Cigar kisses. They did this again and again.

Then they stopped and she whispered, "I am barren."

She wasn't barren; she was on the pill. But this was her way of saying she couldn't get pregnant.

He looked at the house and then at Samantha. She nodded gently, dropped her legs to the ground, picked up Grant's hat, and placed it on her head. It sunk, covering her forehead and ears.

Once inside the house, Grant strode to the bedroom and Samantha followed. The room appeared large because only two wooden chairs and a bed, with a smaller-than-double-sized mattress, occupied the space.

Grant took off his coat and laid it on the foot of the bed. He sat on a chair and removed his boots.

After slipping off her shoes, Samantha took off Grant's hat and then her dress and put them on the chair. Still wearing her corset and pantalets, she pulled the string on the base of her braid, unbraided the tail, and then combed her hair with her fingers, letting her thick wavy hair flow freely.

Grant undressed, leaving on only his long white cotton shirt. Samantha took Grant's soldier coat from the bed and slipped it on.

Grant's coat was oversized for her. The sleeve cuffs covered her hands so only her fingers were showing. The length fell to her shins.

She folded the left front over the right, so the coat entirely covered her. She pointed her toes and slid her feet across the floor in long, strutting steps as if she were modeling the coat. She made an abrupt runway turn and walked back the same way. She lifted the collar, so most of her face was hidden. And she slid across the floor again. After another quick turn, she let the front of the coat fall open, exposing her corset and pantalets.

She patted the inside breast pocket. Oh goody, Samantha thought. From the pocket, she pulled out a fresh cigar, put it in her mouth and pretended to smoke it. Then she took the cigar out of her mouth and ran her fingers up and down it. Maybe she did like cigars after all.

Although she intended other metaphorical cigar acts, Grant stepped toward her, opened the coat, and placed his arms around her waist. She let the coat and the cigar fall to the floor. He scooped her up and laid her gently on the mattress.

After taking off his shirt, he lay on his side facing the center of the mattress. She turned to face him. He stretched his arm over her back. With one hand, he yanked on the center tail of the back bow to untie the laces of her corset. They stared at each other as his fingers loosened the pairs of crisscrossed laces along her spine. Her corset fell loose, and she turned on her back. With both hands he unclasped the front. She slightly lifted her torso and pushed the corset off the bed onto the floor.

He lay next to her. Kissing her on the mouth. Touching her body.

What did this 1860s man know about satisfying a woman?

Sam Time

Enough. There were no known stories of Grant being with any woman other than his wife. Presumably, however, soldiers who frequented brothels had told stories from which Grant had learned.

He knew how to satisfy her. He knew to be patient.

Samantha was aware Grant had been in theater for a while, living in a tent. Weeks may have passed since he had bathed. Perhaps he freshened up with something akin to a sponge bath. Although he wasn't shower fresh, his svelte and muscular body was sensual and excited Samantha.

Then Grant moved on top of her and inside her easily.

The floor creaked. The bed squeaked.

Afterward he remained on top. She could feel his full weight because the thin feather mattress on the wooden box frame had no give. He kissed her on the mouth, on her cheek and forehead, and ran his fingers through her hair. Then he turned onto his back and fell asleep.

She pulled the sheet and blanket to cover both of them and lay on her side staring at Grant. Adoring him.

She sat up in bed and looked at him, studying his face so she would never forget this moment. He was now forty-two. His left eyebrow was slightly lower than his right. Smooth skin. His straight nose and thin lips disappeared under his thick mustache and beard. So handsome.

Reaching to the floor, she picked up her corset and put it on. When he stirred and woke up, Samantha lay back down, pretending she too had been sleeping. Then she rolled onto her side, facing Grant.

He rolled over to face her, then stroked her hair and kissed her on the forehead. "I have to go."

"Of course."

Grant sat up as Samantha slid out of bed. He dressed in his underclothing, then white shirt, pants, and suspenders. She slipped on her dress and shoes.

As he pulled on his boots, he said, "I love my wife."

"Of course you do."

He lifted his shirt collar and put his black silk tie around the back of his neck. "I love my children."

"Of course you do. Here, I'll do it." She shuffled to Grant, tied a bow, and flipped down his shirt collar. His light-blue eyes penetrated her.

His vest lay on the chair. She picked it up and helped Grant into it. Coming around in front of him, she tugged on the vest and said, "Nothing has changed."

She buttoned a few of the small, domed brass buttons and looked up at Grant. "You're still a loving husband and father."

When she finished buttoning the last few, she fixed her eyes on his. "*Nothing* has changed. You're still the man you have always been."

Then she picked up the cigar off the floor, then Grant's coat, which she shook gently to remove any dust. She slipped the cigar back into the inside breast pocket, then helped Grant into the coat. Standing in front him, her fists holding the front lapels, she tugged them toward her. "Never tell her."

They locked eyes.

She tugged on the lapels again. "Never tell her."

In silence, she placed the right top of the coat down against his chest and buttoned all the inside buttons. Grant never took his eyes off her.

Then she placed the left top of the coat against his chest. "You are—" She stopped, inspecting the outside brass buttons; each was embossed with a spread eagle.

She buttoned the outside coat buttons and continued, "Unconditional Surrender—"

She paused, smoothed the coat fabric, and said, "Grant."

After tugging the sleeve cuffs so the coat looked crisp, she pulled her hands off him and took two steps back. She turned around, picked up his hat from the chair, and faced Grant. He walked toward her and placed his hands under her jaw, kissing her on the lips, then on her cheek and forehead. She handed him his hat, and he placed it on his head.

She said in soft voice, "Godspeed."

Then she stepped aside to let him pass. Alone in the bedroom, she listened to the sound of Grant's boots on the wood-plank floor as he walked down the hallway and out the front door.

Samantha had a passion for arrivals and departures. She ran to the front room, opened the door, and stepped out onto the porch. Grant had arrived so gallantly, she wanted to be there for his departure.

He had gone to the back of the house to retrieve his horse. After a few minutes, he rode his horse slowly past the front porch. He then turned the trotting horse, making a wide circle in front of the house. Grant looked down the street, the opposite direction from whence he'd come. When he passed by Samantha, he raised his hat, and she rested her right hand on her heart. Once past the house, Grant put his hat back on his head and rode the horse in a canter toward the bend in the road.

Still looking at Grant riding his horse out of town, Samantha stepped off the porch onto the road. She was startled by the thundering sound of horses' hooves coming from the other direction. Two riders were on galloping horses. Union soldiers. Officers. Grant's staff. The two riders flew past Samantha, and she walked out onto the dirt road, watching as the two men converged with Grant. And when the three horses aligned—all were galloping—the race was on back to the Union headquarters.

The three riders and their horses turned, following the bend in the road, disappearing from view. Samantha thought, This time travel is the best vacation ever.

She went back into the house, placed a quarter on the table, and hustled to the bedroom.

At the side where she had lain, she straightened the sheet and blanket. Then she moved to the side of the bed where Grant had been. The pillow was still indented from the impression of his head. She finished straightening the bedding; then she climbed onto the mattress, putting her face into his pillow to smell his scent. Cigar and perspiration. She smiled, then turned over to lie on her back. Samantha closed her eyes, laid her hands on her body, and breathed deep—leaving the past instantly—arriving safely in her own bed.

Sam Time

Confession

That weekend Aaron's cellphone rang, and he left the room to talk privately. Business calls were sporadic throughout any weekend, so this was not unusual. When he returned, he appeared distraught and said, "Sam, we need to talk."

He took her by the hand and sat down on the sofa. They held hands facing each other. "I just got a call from a woman I met about two years ago."

"We've been going out for over two years."

"I know. I know. So it was probably two and a half years ago that I met this woman," he said. "I was away on business. About two months after we started dating." Aaron was looking down at their hands. "She was a consultant working at the client's office. We were at a bar. We did shots. I had too much drink, and we went back to her apartment. I didn't sleep there. I went back to my hotel. But we were intimate."

"Two months, Aaron. We were a couple then. Exclusive. That was when you wrote 'I love you' on the window."

They were still holding hands despite the news.

Aaron said, "I know. It was stupid. It never happened again. With her or with anyone else. That night I forgot us. And I slipped back into my old ways. But the next morning, I called you and we talked. You were your normal bubbly self. You're the whole package. I knew when we met, you were the one. And after that drunken night, I knew I would never cheat on you again."

"So why now? Why are you telling me this now? Why is she calling? Why does she have your phone number?"

"She has my phone number because of work. I never deleted it. But I swear, I have not spoken to her since." Aaron tightened his lips together before he could say, "She called because she's tested positive for HIV."

Samantha snapped her hands from Aaron's. She sat up straight. Horror consumed her.

Aaron looked her in the eye. "Listen. She's being extra cautious. She thinks she got it from her current partner in the last nine months. It takes about six months before you have antibodies to test positive. She says she was okay two years ago. She just wants to make sure everyone she has been with gets tested."

Samantha grew hysterical. "AIDS. You may have AIDS? I may have AIDS?"

"She's says no. Based on her timeline. No. She called to say, 'Don't let this happen to you.'"

"You didn't wear a condom?"

"She said she was on the pill. Like you."

"You trusted a stranger?"

"She worked at the client's office."

Samantha covered her mouth with her hand, stood, and ran

into the bedroom. Aaron didn't hear her say, "Oh my God. What have I done?"

She fell facedown on the bed, sobbing as if it hurt. Aaron ran after her. She turned onto her side, and Aaron sat behind her back, stroking her arm.

"I am so, so sorry, honey. Please forgive me," Aaron said, crying.

Samantha wailed.

Did she have AIDS? What did Philip say? That the past could change. Was this the butterfly effect? One act creating chaos. Had she changed history? Was she a carrier of a disease first known in the 1980s that she pulled into 1864 because she was a carrier? Would whole generations be eliminated because of her? What did Philip say? History would eventually rebalance to the present day as we know it but intervening years would be chaotic for many. Did she pass it on to Grant? Would he give it to his wife? There were no drugs then. They would die horrible, painful deaths. Doctors who treated them would come in contact with their blood and pass it on to others. These thoughts were unbearable.

Samantha sobbed. Aaron had never seen her like this. It pained him. Then his phone rang. "I forgot. I promised John I would help him move some furniture out of their spare room. I'll tell him I can't do it now."

"No, go," Samantha said. She could call Philip if Aaron left the house. She was in such distress, perhaps speaking with Philip would calm her.

"I'm not leaving you like this. After what I've done."

"Aaron, go. Grace is excited about finally using that room."

"You sure?"

She squeezed his hands. "Go. I'll be fine. I'll stay right here."

Aaron hugged her. "I'm so sorry."

"I know."

"I'll be back soon." He left the bedroom, and Samantha heard the front door open and close. She rolled off the bed and hustled into the kitchen to retrieve her cellphone. Breaking down crying again, she walked back to the bedroom.

As she scrolled through her contacts, she thought, if I call Philip, I'll have to tell him I slept with Grant. I can't do that.

She paced back and forth saying out loud, "Oh my God, oh my God. What have I done?"

Her breaths were rapid; she felt light-headed; her hands shook and she dropped the phone. Realizing she was hyperventilating, she dropped to her knees, then slumped down. She fell back, lying on the carpeted floor, and passed out.

When Samantha regained consciousness, Aaron was crouched on his knees next to her. He had set two pillows under her feet to raise her legs, and she was lying flat on her back. "Sam, take deep breaths."

She blinked, opened her eyes, and whispered, "I think I fainted."

"Deep breaths, Sam. I thought of something. I had a physical at work a few months ago. Nothing came up."

Still drowsy, she whispered, "Do they always test for it?"

"I think so," Aaron replied.

"Because when I hurt my hand, they took some blood."

She hadn't told Aaron the clinic took two blood vials when she injured her hand. Still groggy, she closed her eyes.

She opened her eyes again. "Did you have a blood test recently?"

"Yes. Everything was fine."

"I had a blood test when I injured my hand."

"Yes, you just said that."

She sat up and Aaron said, "Slowly. Take it slow. Let me get you some water."

Placing her hands on the carpet to steady herself, gaining composure, she thought about her recent blood test. If they found the chloroform, they would likely have tested for HIV.

Aaron returned with a tumbler of water. Samantha drank some then said, "Let's get tested. Let's go to the clinic now."

They stood, Aaron holding Samantha. She hugged Aaron. "It's a shock. It's the disease. I want to have children. I want to have a long life with you."

He held her. "I'm so sorry, honey. It will never happen again."

"Let's go now to the clinic." Samantha was feeling better. "But you'll have to say you're my husband so you can get the university co-pay discount." They both laughed through their tears.

"Here's your phone. It was on the carpet. Also we'll tell the doctor about your fainting spell to make sure you're okay."

A CLINIC DOCTOR saw them together. After reviewing the records on a computer, the doctor said to Samantha, "You were in here a few months ago. Your blood test for HIV was negative." Aaron squeezed Samantha's hand.

The doctor continued, "We'll take a vial of blood from each of you. They say it takes a few days, but we typically know the next day. We call if it's positive. But if you want to pick up the test results, sign a form at the front desk, and we'll give it to you. We have technicians who come in at night. The results are usually done early morning and certified by a doctor. Everything should be ready by ten o'clock tomorrow."

The doctor paused then said, "I'm not supposed to say this. But the test kits at the drugstore are pretty reliable." After she checked Samantha's eyes, she said, "Everything looks okay. Since you passed out after hearing shocking news, the fainting episode is likely isolated. If you have another fainting spell, come back and we'll order some tests."

After they left the clinic, they bought two test kits at a drugstore. When they returned home, they read the instructions and swabbed their mouths. Then waited for twenty minutes.

Negative. Negative.

They cried and hugged. Then they went for a run to relieve the day's stress.

THE NEXT MORNING they drove to the clinic to get their results, which were available. Both were negative. They walked out of the clinic holding hands and hugged in the parking lot.

After returning home, they sat on the sofa together. Holding Samantha's hand, Aaron said, "You know I love you and would not do anything to hurt you. What happened will never, never happen again."

Samantha said, "Everyone makes mistakes. I'm glad you were honest with me. It means a lot. And it was difficult for you to do."

And Aaron didn't even distort the truth. But Samantha had not been honest with Aaron. Her affair with Grant was last week.

"You know, I have not asked you this woman's name or what she looks like. It doesn't matter. I'm just so grateful we're okay. And we'll have healthy children and a long life together."

Aaron hugged and kissed her.

"Is she going to be all right?" Samantha asked.

"She said she's being treated. She sounded well. I don't know more."

"Well, for us, life goes on."

THAT NIGHT, Samantha dressed for bed in one of Aaron's T-shirts and a pair of his crew socks. Aaron wore a T-shirt and loose gym shorts. They climbed into bed and turned on their sides, facing each other, touching feet.

"I'm sorry," Aaron said, stroking her hair.

"I know. I'm so happy we're healthy."

Samantha took a deep breath and said, "Did you ever play the board game Monopoly?"

"Sure. Why?"

"I liked the iron piece."

Aaron said, "I always liked the top hat."

"That's very gender-biased of us."

They laughed.

Samantha said, "So you roll the dice, move your piece, and land on a certain space. Then pick a card. And one card is a get-out-of-jail-free card. A onetime pass."

She stared at Aaron. He understand why she was bringing this up. "So I used my one get-out-of-jail-free card."

"Yup."

"I don't need to roll the dice. I don't need another card. I'm not playing games. I want you and only you."

Samantha turned over on her other side, spooning with Aaron. She closed her eyes and said, "Love you."

"Love you too, Sam. I'm responsible for the mess I created, so I didn't want to bring this up earlier. But when you were on the floor coming to, you said something about two therapy sessions and an MRI."

She opened her eyes and her body stiffened. "I did?"

"Yes. Is it true?"

"Yes," Samantha admitted. "What did I say?"

She feared she blurted out she was time traveling.

"I said I had a blood test for a physical at work. Then you said you had one too, when you injured your hand. Then you closed your eyes and murmured, 'With therapy sessions with a clinic doctor and an MRI.' Then you opened your eyes and asked me about my blood test and repeated you had one too. I'm guessing you don't remember everything you said."

Samantha turned around to face Aaron. "I did have two therapy sessions with this judgmental Dr. Nancy. Then she ordered an MRI."

"Why? Are you okay? Why didn't you tell me?"

"Yes. I'm fine. Everything's fine. The MRI was normal. It was just stupid."

Samantha sat up, switched on the light, and placed her hands on Aaron's chest. This gave her time to think—of an excuse. A good excuse. "I saw Professor Philip Hastings at the university. He was sitting outside, and I stopped by and spoke with him."

"I remember him. Brilliant guy."

"He remembers you too. Anyway, he was smoking a joint, and he offered it to me. I smoked some with him. Then I drove home under the influence. I was so high, I don't even remember getting home. That's one reason I didn't tell you."

Aaron laid his hands on top of hers.

"So then, the next day, I was out running and fell on this stupid fishhook. I went to the clinic and signed a bunch of forms. The university has an agreement with the clinic: they have this Wellness Program, so they took some blood. A few days later, they called and said the tox screen showed a controlled substance."

He said, "Pot? It's been decriminalized."

"Aaron, here in Texas, weed is allowed for certain medical use. It's still considered a controlled substance. Anyway, the university is concerned about drug and alcohol addiction, so that's why I had two therapy sessions. If I didn't go, I would have had to pay full price for the visit, the tetanus shot, and everything."

"It still doesn't make sense they would ding you for cannabis."

Of course it doesn't make sense, Samantha thought, because I'm making it up on the fly. If you really knew what happened, you'd be the one passing out.

Instead she said, "And John has cautioned us to read documents before we sign them. So there wouldn't have been any blood draws, therapy sessions, or the MRI, if I had not signed certain forms."

"But an MRI? That sounds extreme."

"I told Dr. Nancy I was not sleeping well since you were away. Apparently, that triggered a test for sleep pathologies. One form I signed, which I didn't read, allowed testing for research. Metadata collection. This Dr. Nancy is collaborating with another professor."

"Why didn't you tell me this, Sam?"

She replied, "This was all my own doing. I'm looking at this objectively, and it's not a pretty picture. I didn't want you to know I was so irresponsible."

"Sam, no one is perfect. See how I messed up our weekend? I'm ashamed at what I did."

In a moment of honesty, Samantha said, "There are times I think of Mister In-N-Out Burger."

Aaron furrowed his eyebrows as if to say, "What?" He squeezed her hands to reassure her. "Sam, we moved out here together, bought a house. We're engaged. I'm not that guy anymore. You changed me."

"I believe that too. But if I messed up, badly—"

She took a deep breath and said, "Aaron, I heard the stories. That's why it took me so long to meet you. Grace and John would talk about how great you were and said we would be compatible. But I heard, 'He's going out with Judy.' A couple of months later, 'He's going out with Iris.' The stories were repeated often enough, I told Grace, 'Why would I want to go out with someone who doesn't stick around?'"

Aaron sat up. "Sam, I knew my own proclivities. That's why it took me so long to date you. John is like a brother to me, and Grace is great, a good friend. But if I dated you, and it didn't work out, Grace would be miffed at me. And John. I didn't want to lose his friendship. I saw your pictures. You were so cute. And if you were anything like your sister, I would be hitting the jackpot. I didn't think I was ready for a serious relationship. But when Grace and John's wedding was around the corner . . . Well, you know the rest. Sam, being a committed couple is new to me."

"Me too."

"You're better at relationships. I see Grace and John. They're synchronized. A couple, but yet with their own identities. They found a balance. I want to strike the right balance."

"I'm sorry I didn't tell you everything about my hand accident."

"I'm sorry for what I did and scaring you this weekend. I don't want to hurt you ever."

They kissed and hugged. She turned off the light and they lay spooning. While Aaron fell asleep, Samantha remained awake. She had mixed so many lies with the truth—such deceit. She thought of a line from the Sir Walter Scott poem, "Oh, what a tangled web we weave..."

How did time travel work? She suspected Philip would say the answers to these questions are not knowable. But she would never tell Philip about this HIV scare. And even the thought of passing a wretched disease, such as AIDS, to Grant and his wife, his countrymen, was chilling.

The night, however, had ended well. Aaron promised he would be faithful to her. Samantha resolved she was going to be faithful to him—no matter the time.

Donna Balon

Mourning in D.C.

After several hours researching and summarizing her findings, Samantha took a break and went for a run. When she returned to her desk, satisfied she had accomplished much in one day, she grabbed her history book.

She paged through the book and stopped at 1865. On April 14, while watching the play *Our American Cousin* at Ford's Theatre, Abraham Lincoln was shot by John Wilkes Booth. The president died the next morning.

Samantha wanted to experience this period of American history. That evening, she prepared as usual and fell asleep.

The time-travel gods placed Samantha in Washington, D.C., outside a government building. A sign by the War Department dated April 20, 1865, was posted on the building: "$100,000 Reward! The murderer of our late beloved President, Abraham Lincoln, is still at large." The reward was $50,000 for Booth and $25,000 for each of his two accomplices.

Sam Time

People were quiet and wearing black. Samantha felt self-conscious wrapped in her cream shawl and pink-flowered dress.

She guessed Grant's office was in this building, so she opened the door and ascended the staircase. The hallway was empty. Follow the cigar smell, she thought. The door to Grant's office was open, and she stopped at its threshold.

Not even a year had passed since Samantha had last seen Grant. He was no longer wearing a soldier's uniform. He was sitting at his desk, but wasn't smoking, and was wearing civilian clothing: a dark frock coat and pants; vest with a pocket watch, over a white shirt with a thin bow tie. His top hat was on a chair.

He didn't stand and walk over to greet Samantha, which was common courtesy when someone made a call. Instead, he remained seated.

"General Grant, my condolences."

She felt awkward entering his office.

"We were supposed to go to the theater with the president. He practically begged me. But we wanted to go home. We did not want to endure Mary's company. I wanted to see my children."

As he spoke, he wasn't making eye contact. "Had I been there, maybe Booth could have been stopped."

"Do not burden yourself with actions or inactions."

"I feel guilty about it. About everything."

Samantha understood what he meant by "everything." She said firmly, "Do not conflate the two."

He looked up when she said "conflate." She stood in front of his desk and leaned over, placing her hands shoulder apart on the desk top.

"You never retrace your steps. Do not do that now. Booth was determined; if not at the theater, he would have tried another time." Then Samantha stood straight.

Grant sat back in his chair, glaring at her. "You usually call at my lowest. When despair governs me. And temptations are the hardest to suppress. This has been the saddest week. And here you are again."

"You may have noticed, you are a popular man. You attract crowds, making it difficult for me to call. And then you were fighting a war. I tried to find gaps, when I would interfere the least, and coordinate with our family business."

Samantha paused then bent down again, even lower to get closer to his face. "And leave what happened in the past."

"I love my wife."

"Of course you do. It was war. War. You were in the thick of it. And you and I—happened. War. A good reason to seek comfort."

Grant looked up at her and said, "What's your excuse? You breeze in and out. You show little sadness or worry. I bore the weight of war! You—nothing!"

He was right. She was a traveler—and it showed—far detached from the pain and suffering of the Civil War. To her, it was history. But it was his life, his countrymen, his burden.

His question wasn't rhetorical. He snapped, "What is your excuse?"

She wanted to say, "It's the I-Went-Back-in-Time-and-Met-an-American-Icon Exception." That many women from her present-day would desire to travel in time and spend an evening with an American hero, Thomas Jefferson or Alexander Hamilton. Samantha would not care if Aaron went back in time for an evening with an American woman icon. Jackie Kennedy—go for it!

Sam Time

But she couldn't say, "My excuse? You're Ulysses S. Grant!"

Instead she said, "I have no excuse. But my actions of one day are not the whole of me."

"And I know nothing about you."

"Because you never ask!" This was true. Samantha entered his world, and it was all about his world. This was convenient for her. Until now.

"I had a suitor. Actually two. But my oldest brother did not approve of either. Because little sister runs the family business, pays the bills, collects the money, directs her brothers where we will go and what we will do. There was no room for a suitor. So now you know my story. It does not change anything."

He was looking down at his desk when Samantha added, "Your heart has never been unfaithful. Living with guilt is useless."

Samantha believed Grant felt guilty because their interlude was so passionate. But saying this would not have been helpful.

Grant said, "You should leave."

He didn't greet her, and he wasn't going to walk her out, the respectable way to begin and end a call. She was crushed.

"And do not return!"

Another affront, he was throwing her out of his office. This was bad. Banished by an American icon.

She shuffled shamefully to the doorway. Then she stopped at its threshold and turned around. "Are those your orders?"

Walking back to his desk, she said, "General Grant is giving me orders?"

Pausing, she mustered more nerve. "I am not one of your soldiers. Get off your high horse, General."

After she said it, she cringed. Worst pun never.

But she became bolder. "You were never a general to me. You are a dear acquaintance I met along the way. Someone to speak with for intellectual enjoyment in this difficult and boring existence. Saying that and treating me like this are offensive."

She was on a roll. "This is the general who will be conciliatory to the South and who favors pardoning Robert E. Lee. But me, you toss *me* aside!

"I hide behind my brothers like a good little woman, supporting four families, twelve children. And you know what people call me? Old maid! And I come here to Washington, everyone is in mourning clothes wearing black and looking at me with disgust. Well, I do not have a black dress. Because my young nieces and nephews have more needs than I."

Samantha had roughly conceived her story should Grant ever ask, but even she was surprised at her spontaneous embellishments.

"Now, you, my fond acquaintance, are tossing me out like a—"

She stopped and couldn't say the word "whore." Samantha wanted to stay strong, but she cried thinking of that word.

Grant said, "I would never call you anything shameful."

"But you are treating me shamefully! You say, 'Be gone.' What is the implication?"

She could tell he was listening, although he was looking down. "You would not have spent time with me, if you did not respect me. And I believe you still do. It was one moment. You rode to that house. You found me. It was mutual. So do not say I am only to blame because you are the man, you are the general, and I am only a woman, I have no standing in—anything."

Her lips were shaking. "We, men and women, were created to be like this. We both succumbed to the temptation. But it does not

Sam Time

undo who we are or will be. It is our secret."

It then occurred to her. Did he tell anyone? His wife?

She asked, "Is it still our secret?"

He gently nodded.

Relieved, she put her hand on her chest. "So it remains hidden. On my honor, my family's honor, I vow it will not happen again."

She was sounding like her mother, a churchgoing woman, like Grant, a churchgoing man. So Samantha channeled her mother. "What about redemption? Go and sin no more. Ask for forgiveness, and we will be forgiven."

She walked to the door. "Your grief is speaking. Time will heal you."

Samantha paused then said, "My condolences." She added, her voice cracking, "He was my president too."

She crossed over the threshold into the hallway. Grant reached for a cigar and lit it.

That didn't go well. A dressing-down by an American hero. Samantha was losing her much-admired friend. She walked slowly down the hallway. He said many things she had never considered. She needed to think. She wanted to disappear, literally. But if she did, she would be doing exactly what Grant was accusing her of, breezing in and out.

She descended the stairs. The tragic news of Lincoln's assassination hung over the city. She should stroll the streets. See the people and feel compassion. Samantha was so deep in thought she didn't hear the boot footsteps behind her.

"Samantha." She turned around. It was Grant. "Please forgive me. I cannot carry the burden of you being cross with me."

"I could never be cross with you. We can disagree, we can argue.

But never be cross." Samantha was immensely relieved.

"Do not be me angry with me. Please forgive me. It has been the saddest week. Do call again." Grant took both of her hands, holding them firmly.

Samantha said, "You gave me much to think about. I will. I want only to be a fond acquaintance. I am not angry with you. Never."

She wanted to hug him. But this was 1865, and hugging a married man would not be proper.

He looked her in the eyes, paused, and kissed both her hands. Then he turned around and ascended the staircase to his office.

Samantha left the office building and roamed on the sidewalks. The streets were quiet, despite the crowds of people who had lingered in the city after the funeral procession. People were somber.

While strolling through the city, she had this feeling, this sixth sense, she should return home. So she entered another building, found an isolated nook, struck the pose—and reappeared in her bed.

Sam Time

Busted

Samantha returned from the past, lying in bed during the middle of the night. She stretched as she slid out of bed and then turned on the light and took off her dress, corset, and pantalets. She opened Aaron's top drawer, took out a T-shirt, and slipped it on over her head. As she walked to the bathroom, she took off her braided halo hat and unpinned her crown braids. In front of the bathroom mirror, she restyled her hair into a single, centered, back-of-the-head French braid.

She picked up the dress, which she had put on the bed, and headed toward the walk-in closet. Then she opened the closet door, flipped on the light switch, and said, "Oh my God."

Aaron's suitcase was in the center of the closet. He had come home while Samantha traveled to the past.

She quickly hung the dress in the back of the closet, slipped on a pair of shorts and shoes. Then she looked at her cellphone. Aaron had sent several texts saying his plans had changed, and he would be flying home this evening rather than tomorrow.

The house was dark, and his car was gone. Apparently, he was out looking for Samantha. In a way this was good. If she had reappeared while he was in the house, it would have been difficult to explain.

She called his cellphone. "It's me."

"Where have you been? It's one o'clock in the morning. We've been worried sick." Aaron was panicked.

"I'm home. I'm here now. Everything is okay. Come home—I'll explain."

Samantha heard Aaron say, "It's Sam."

She asked, "Where are you?"

"Grace and John's. Grace has been crying."

"Put her on the phone."

Grace cried. "You scared us. What happened?"

"Oh, sweetie, I'm so sorry. But I'm back home. Everything's okay. I need to talk with Aaron. But I'll call you in the morning. Come over; I'll make waffles."

Grace sniffled. "Okay. Love you."

"Love you too."

Aaron took the phone. "I'm coming right home."

In less than five minutes, Aaron pulled his car into the garage. Samantha was waiting for him by the house door. They embraced, not letting go for a while.

Samantha whispered in Aaron's ear, now breaking down and crying, "I'm sorry I scared you and everyone."

Aaron didn't say anything because he was crying. A few minutes later he said, "I didn't know what to think. Maybe there was an emergency because all your things are here. Or maybe you up and left because of what I did."

"Aaron, I forgave you. It's done. In the past," Samantha said, referring to Aaron's one-night stand early in their relationship.

He took a few deep breaths. "Where were you? Your phone is here. Your car is here. The doors are locked. It's as if you disappeared."

"That's right," Samantha would have said if she were telling the truth. But she couldn't. And wouldn't.

"I did go out, locked the house. And yes, I mistakenly left my cellphone at home." They held hands walking into the house to the bedroom. She took a T-shirt and shorts out of his dresser drawer. "Here, put these on," she said, and then she threw sneakers next to his feet. Samantha went into the walk-in closet and took out a large canvas tote bag.

Samantha still hadn't said where she had been. Aaron deserved an immediate answer, but he was composing himself and dressed as she directed.

"Come. I'll retrace my steps with you. I took a key and locked the front door." She took his hand and led him outside the house. She tucked the key in a zippered compartment in the canvas tote bag. Talking softly, Samantha said, "Remember that day, when the homeless man ratted me out?"

Aaron shook his head as if to say, "So what does that have to do with anything?"

Samantha asked, "Remember on the way home, we ran into George and Marion?"

She led him to their neighbors' backyard gate and entered the four-digit code on the keypad. The gate opened.

"Well, they said we could use their pool anytime and gave us the code to the gate."

"But it's 1:30 in the morning," Aaron said in a firm whisper.

"I've been here other times of the day. I met the pool guy, Mateo. But sometimes—" She stopped talking so Aaron could take in the ambiance of the backyard pool setting. Bistro lights were strung along the frame of the patio, giving enough light to see the irregular-shaped pool.

"Sometimes, I come at night. If I can't sleep. Tonight, I lay on this recliner and dozed off."

Aaron said, "People are sleeping. What if they see or hear us?"

"I've spoken with them about night swims. And they can't see. Look, the shrubs and the trees are blocking the view from the house. This is very private. Besides, George is hard of hearing. And did you ever see the thick lenses of Marion's glasses?"

Samantha pulled two floating lounge chairs from the open shed. "Mateo blew these up last week. Come."

She walked to the pool steps, took off her shoes, placed the floats into the pool and slid onto one. "You'll get a little wet, but I have two beach towels in that canvas bag. Come sit on this one."

Aaron slid onto a float.

She said, "These even have cup holders for drinks. We should bring some next time."

Samantha held on to the arm of Aaron's floating chair so they glided over the water together. She whispered, "You can never say I'm boring."

Aaron was resting his head on the float, looking up at the sky, still stunned, and said nothing. The night was still except for the water lapping against the sides of the pool.

She whispered, "I wanted this to be a surprise. I'm sorry it turned out this way. But this is serene." To lighten the mood she said, "I have a sinking feeling your confidence in me is drowning."

"That's not going to work tonight," Aaron replied.
Samantha persisted.

> *There once was a woman who disappeared,*
> *All worried the truth would be as they feared,*
> *Later when she was found,*
> *The excuse was not sound,*
> *Her reputation was forever smeared.*

Aaron cracked a little smile. Samantha let go of his float and walked her hands along the pool's edge, making her way to the steps.

She slid off the float and took off her T-shirt, then threw it on the concrete surrounding the pool. After taking off her shorts and underwear, she threw them next to her shirt. Then she stretched her arms out in front of her and plunged underwater.

Samantha resurfaced, swam to Aaron, and hung on to his float. "The water's nice if you want to take a swim. But of course you don't want to get your clothes wet. Why don't you join me?"

She dragged his float to the steps so he could undress. He placed his clothes on top of Samantha's. And they made love in the pool's shallow end.

THE NEXT MORNING Samantha made waffles. Grace and John came over and shared their happy news: Grace was three months pregnant. Samantha hugged Grace, and Aaron hugged John.

Grace said, "Sam, I'm sorry I will not fit into any of the gowns the dressmaker made for your wedding. I'll be in my final trimester."

"I don't care about that. It will be fun shopping for a nice bridesmaid gown for you." Samantha thought, Besides, I'm wearing those dresses often.

"Well, I was thinking. You know my friend Tina?" Grace asked.

"Yes."

"She's plus-sized and was in this wedding. I'll find a picture of her on my phone in her bridesmaid's dress."

Grace scrolled through the photos on her phone. "Here."

Samantha took Grace's phone. "Very pretty. She looks great. I like the dress and the color."

"Tina will give me the gown. I'll have it resized for me. It makes sense. A pregnant matron of honor. I'll never wear it again."

"I love the idea."

"Okay, I'll text Mary Sanchez and make an appointment."

On a serious note, Samantha apologized for lounging at the neighbors' pool the night before without taking her phone or telling anyone. It was a lie.

It had been Samantha's contingency plan. She did actually use the neighbors' pool often. But not last night when Aaron came home early.

The plan had worked. This one time. She would need another scheme, however, if she wanted to continue to time travel. Even then, her credibility would be strained with every bizarre disappearance.

Sam Time

A New Plan

Weeks had passed when Samantha arrived in Philip's office to ask for a favor. She began, however, summarizing her recent travels, and Aaron's unexpected early return. She hadn't finished, when Philip blurted, "Is there any way to get Grant's DNA?"

The question surprised Samantha. "Why do you ask?"

"Because it could prove you're actually meeting him."

Samantha pushed back. "Is that so? My trip to Vicksburg, where I found your ancestor and confirmed a family poem, wasn't enough? And Grant's DNA would be the ultimate evidence? I'm incredulous."

"It's worth a try."

"So now you want accumulating evidence that I'm slipping into the past. Then you'll be persuaded? I've given much evidence, all of which you have dismissed. And frankly, I'm no longer interested in convincing you."

"So you can't somehow get DNA?"

The answer was yes, she had Grant's DNA. Monica Lewinsky kept the blue dress, Samantha kept her unwashed pantalets from the time she and Grant were intimate. She had purchased two pairs and was now only wearing and washing the other one.

Philip stared at her. She refused to say anything, but she moved in her chair. It was a revealing tell.

"You're having an affair."

"No!" She protested, but she squirmed again in her chair.

Philip stared and Samantha relented. "It was only once. It won't happen again."

"If you sleep with someone other than your committed partner, it's an affair."

"It's not an affair. The guy's been dead for well over a century."

"Wait. You can't have it both ways. You say, 'It's real. I've met the real Grant.' Then you say, 'He's dead.'"

"Well, he's dead when I return to the present."

"But your entire existence is in the present. It's infidelity."

He was right of course, and Samantha knew it. Without looking at Philip, she said softly, "It was one time. We're back to being friends. It won't happen again." She didn't explain why. Then she added, "I didn't tell you because, besides it being personal, I didn't want you to go all Freud on me."

"So let's get back to the DNA."

"Yes, I have his DNA. But a DNA test is expensive."

"I could get funding."

"How? A GoFundMe campaign? I don't think so."

Philip mused, "There's got to be a way."

"Maybe there is, but not without revealing my identity."

"We would keep it anonymous."

"That won't work. With all the social media out there, someone is bound to attribute it to me. I would become a public figure. Half of the people will think I have a divine connection, and the other half will think I'm a wacko. Life would never be the same. What I want more than anything else in the world is a quiet family life with Aaron. If this became public, I wouldn't blame him if it was too much for him to handle. The time travel is temporary, but my future life with Aaron is something I don't want to risk."

Philip pressed Samantha. "We could make sure none of this is ever attributed to you."

"I don't believe it. Listen, I know I could make this all go away. I could get rid of the dresses, or stop wearing them, and never time travel again. It has been amazing, and I could stop anytime. But Aaron's still away on business. And I think the time travel is following Grant's life; it's going to end when Grant dies. So Philip, no to the DNA. I have to protect my future with my fiancé."

"Okay."

"Am I making sense? Very sane of me, isn't it?" Samantha thought this may elicit a smile or laugh from Philip. But he was a serious guy, or, more specifically, he lacked a sense of humor.

"I'm protecting what is dear to me. From the start I said I wanted our sessions to be confidential. I'm assuming you are not taking notes, not speaking with anyone, and there's no audio or video recording. Nothing that can be discovered."

"That's correct. I do consider this a case, but it's off the books."

"Thank you. I also don't want to hear there's a journal publication about 'A history professor at the University of Texas, who believes she time travels.' So, no publication ever."

"No publications."

"We have an understanding."

Neither said anything during a long pause. Samantha was uneasy about changing the topic, but the silence was even more uncomfortable, so she blurted, "I need a new launching place. It's convenient to fall asleep in my own bed and return there. But after Aaron came home early and I wasn't home, I need to find another spot. Someplace where I could bring my dress, shawl, and everything, and launch from there. A hotel would work. But that would be expensive."

She stopped to see Philip's reaction. He said, "You could use this office. The sofa is comfortable. I haven't been working late recently. So I'll give you a key."

"Isn't that against any rules?"

"Probably. But so is smoking weed. And I do that all the time." He opened a desk drawer, took out a spare key, and slid it across the table. "Here."

"Thank you. I don't expect to be doing this often. Only on the days when I suspect Aaron or Grace may check up on me. My cover story will be that I'm researching, working on my dissertation, and stayed late on campus. But I won't stay all night."

Philip added, "It's safe here. There's security. On your way out, speak to the people at the security desk and get their number. The exterior doors lock after nine o'clock, so no one can enter the building. You can get out but not without setting off the alarm. Call security when you're leaving so they can let you out without activating the alarm. Then they'll escort to your car. Also, you can get to this building from the library's south door by the stairs."

Samantha mouthed "thank you" and took the key. She had a new contingency plan.

Sam Time

April 1873
Central City, Colorado

Samantha spent the day in the library. Aaron called while she was driving home in the evening. To her delight, he was always keen on knowing Samantha's progress on her research, and she happily explained her recent findings. Their conversation continued when she came home. She plopped on the sofa while laughing at Aaron's musings of his day.

After they said goodbye, she hung up. The house was quiet. Too quiet. The rooms felt large and empty. She knew this feeling. Loneliness. She imagined Philip would say, "You know what to do."

She walked into her home office, placed her laptop on the desk, sat in the chair, and then reached for her history book. Time to visit her famous friend.

"Where to now?" she said out loud, flipping through the book, past Lincoln's assassination in 1865. Vice President Andrew Johnson became president and promoted Grant to General of the

Army of the United States. Grant's popularity remained so strong, the Republican Party nominated him for president in 1868. He won the election, and in 1869 Grant took the oath of office at the age of forty-six. He was nominated again and won a second presidential term.

In preparing for her nighttime traveling, Samantha chanced launching from home rather than Philip's office. That night, however, she texted Aaron and Grace to make sure they wouldn't be looking for her. Wearing her corset, pantalets, the light green dress, and matching braided halo hat, she flipped through her history book and paper-clipped a page for time-travel destination. Then she climbed into bed and fell asleep.

THE TIME-TRAVEL GODS placed Samantha in a small room with a round wooden table and chairs, suitable for playing cards. Coasters on the table were inscribed, "Teller House, Central City, Colorado." From her research, she knew of the establishment, a redbrick four-story hotel on a city corner in Central City, in a booming gold-mining town, less than thirty miles west of Denver.

Samantha stepped out of the room, walked down the hallway, then into the hotel lobby. A man, who was leaning on the wall, was reading a newspaper. Samantha squinted to read: "April" and "1873." Before she saw the date, the man turned the page. She said, "News the president is arriving today?"

"Yes, with Mrs. Grant," the man replied.

"How exciting," Samantha said.

Someone called out, "Carter." She turned around and recognized Lieutenant Carter, who had escorted her in Vicksburg, Mississippi, and delivered her letter to Grant in Mechanicsville, Virginia.

She approached him and said, "Lieutenant Carter."

He stood erect and said, "Captain Carter."

Realizing he had been promoted, she said, "Captain Carter, Miss Samantha. We met in Vicksburg and Mechanicsville."

"How may I be of assistance to you?" Captain Carter said, as if he didn't recognize her.

"I request to see the president. He would very much like to know I am here. It would be most kind of you to let him know at once."

The captain appeared to have more pressing matters, but he left the room, returning a few minutes later to escort Samantha to a second-floor room where the presidential staff were assembling. Based on the murmurings of the staff, Samantha gathered the Grants had just arrived. Julia retired to her guest chambers for a repose after the long journey. Whatever the president's plans had been, once word arrived Samantha was calling, Grant scuttled his original arrangements.

Eight years had passed since Samantha had last seen Grant. Now that he was president, much had changed. In appearance, he'd gained at least thirty pounds, looking like a grandpa figure at age fifty-one, with a round belly, puffy cheeks, graying hair, and strips of white in his beard at his chin. In personality, he was more talkative and had become a politician, wielding power in an administration many people said was corrupt. The presidency had spoiled him. His light-blue eyes, however, remained seductive and he oozed charm. Many wanted to be in his company.

The large second-floor room in the Teller House had two chairs arranged for conversation. The public space was palatable for Grant and Samantha to converse without suspicion. Other tables and chairs were in the far opposite end of the room, where president's staff were working.

Grant wore the classic man's uniform: a dark frock coat and pants, a vest over a white shirt with a thin bow tie. A pocket watch was attached to his vest.

"Good day, Miss Samantha."

"Good day, Mr. President."

Samantha sat down.

"Many years have passed since I saw you last," Grant began. He sat down and crossed his legs.

The last time they met was a week after Lincoln was assassinated. For certain, the president remembered their contentious conversation. But she didn't want to recall this visit. Assuming he didn't either, she said, "I have tried but could not get a message to you, since you've been president. Everyone desires your company. One time, when I was in Washington, I gave a lad a nickel to make his way through the crowd to deliver my message to you."

Samantha paused, realizing she had just said "nickel" rather than "half dime." She quickly remembered Aaron had said that, shortly after the Civil War, nickels were circulated, and the term "half dime" was no longer used. So the nomenclature she was using was correct.

She continued, "I watched the lad walk half the distance. But he gave up and ran off with the nickel. I tried the same with another lad with the same result."

Grant laughed. "You should give me your address. I will have Julia send you an invitation to a White House banquet."

Samantha didn't have an address. Moreover, she wanted to say, "If I accepted such an invitation, I would be condoning the extravagant spending at which I am appalled." Instead she said, "You are so kind. But I do not have a fancy dress to meet the standards of such occasions."

He didn't comment, as if he'd read her mind and knew her true meaning. Samantha was silent, letting her words linger, not retracting or softening the jab.

Then she said, "Besides, I do not want to have only five minutes with you and spend the rest of the time making casual talk with people who do not interest me. I fancy you feel the same about the White House banquets."

"Small talk bores me, and I am not good at it. But I have to do these things and keep everyone happy."

"I am pleased to hear you have appointed women as U.S. postmistresses."

"The war made many widows. I was glad to make the appointments for the widows of soldiers so they could support themselves and their children."

"I hear the town made a silver walkway for you."

The silver miners in Central City had laid twenty-six silver ingots on the ground, making a sidewalk so Grant wouldn't dirty his boots. This silver ingot stunt coincided with the politics of backing the U.S. dollar in gold and silver or not. Grant had not made a decision on the issue and didn't want to favor the gold-and-silver proponents by walking on the precious metal. Instead, he used the permanent sidewalk.

He shook his head in disgust. "I refused to walk on it. I have not decided that issue."

"Oh, the miners were clever. Ingenious self-promotion for the mining industry."

"Did your brothers have anything to do with it?"

"No, no. But you have to admit it is funny." Samantha laughed.

No, he didn't.

Samantha wouldn't stop. "Ah. The burdens of the presidency. You have to be serious. Cannot have any fun. I say, one day, you will laugh about this. A silver sidewalk. For you. It means they like you. Does everything have to be political?"

He kept shaking his head as if to say, "Please stop already."

She pressed on. "Look at it this way. Right now, this town is booming. Someday the silver plumes will be exhausted. Miners will move to a faraway town. So let them have their fun. This may be the only time they have a voice and people are listening. Let them have their day."

Still nothing from Grant.

"I'm sure Mrs. Grant wanted to walk on it?"

Grant chuckled.

Samantha said, "Well, if it was me, I would have danced on it."

They shared a laugh.

Most of the time when Grant and Samantha had been together, they were active. Outside, horseback riding, walking. And when they weren't, they were sitting on a park bench, comfortable in silence. This meeting demanded conversation because others were in the room. This wouldn't be difficult; Samantha had memorized a list of questions for her doctoral research.

"In three years, we will be celebrating our nation's centennial birthday," she started, and Grant poured out information on the planning of the celebrations. Then they segued to their ongoing topic of national unity. She steered the discussion to public sentiment. Grant talked of news articles in state and local papers,

Sam Time

while Samantha made mental notes. His knowledge was critical to her research.

A while later he said, "We are going on a carriage ride. You should join us. James will be your escort."

Samantha replied, "That would be lovely." She was self-conscious, however, of her ability to get in and out of a coach. Grant didn't know she had never been in one.

There was a stir in the front of the room at the four tall windows with a street view. Samantha and Grant walked to the far window to see what was causing the commotion. They stood shoulder to shoulder.

An elaborate stagecoach had just pulled in front of the building. "That's Henry Teller's coach. He owns this hotel," Grant said. Teller was a rich man who would become one of Colorado's first U.S. senators.

"I have not seen a stagecoach so ornate." Samantha had seen coaches when she was in New York City but nothing like this one, with its gold-painted decorative designs covering all of the side surfaces. "Look at all the trunks on top and in the back."

There were four horses for this stagecoach. "Of course, you are looking at the horses," she said, making a quick glance at Grant. She smiled and did a double take. Grant was staring at her with his mesmerizing blue eyes. She felt his stare and was enjoying it.

"How is Cincinnati?" She cringed after she asked the question. She had met the horse once on *that* day.

He answered without the slightest hint of recalling Samantha's introduction to Cincinnati. "He is well. The finest horse. Boarded at the White House stables."

Looking out the window, Samantha said, "That coach is so high." It stood at least two feet off the ground. "I am amazed how people can get in and out without slipping onto the dirt." It was a strange comment: men and women ascended and descended coaches regularly and were apt at it. She was, however, projecting her uneasiness of climbing in and out of coaches while wearing a long dress.

Grant's eyes were still stuck on Samantha as if he was not paying attention to what she was saying. She glanced over her shoulder at Grant's staff. They too were preoccupied with the activity outside and did not notice Grant and Samantha standing together. She put her hand on his chest. Even carrying the extra weight, he was still a handsome man, and being this close, he radiated charm. "I'm so glad you made time to see me." And with emphasis she said, "Mr. President."

"May I say, the years look good on you."

She smiled self-consciously, still focused on watching how Victorian women managed descending from a high coach without falling. The coach driver placed a crate on the ground as a step for passengers to use when climbing out of the coach. A well-groomed man stepped ably out of the coach.

Grant glanced down. "That's Henry Teller."

"Of course, he's here to see you."

"Later, for dinner. We have the carriage ride first."

"Someone else is coming out." Samantha looked up at Grant. He was still staring at her. She blushed, basking in Grant's attention.

A lady, assisted by the driver, climbed out of the coach and onto the crate. When she put one foot on the ground, she lost her footing, nearly falling before being propped up by the driver.

Sam Time

Samantha thought, I've never stepped out of a coach. That could be me. Even worse, I could spill on the ground.

Then another lady descended the coach with erect posture, chin held high, balanced with one hand holding the hand of the driver, stepping onto the crate, then the ground with grace and ease. Samantha watched intently, hoping she could be as graceful when she joined the Grants for their carriage ride.

Once the coach pulled away, everyone inside turned away from the windows. Julia entered the room. Grant introduced Samantha to Mrs. Grant and said, "Samantha will join us, with James, on our carriage ride."

Forcing a smile, Samantha asked Julia, "How was your journey to Central City?"

"Very well, thank you" was Julia's curt reply, indicating she was not keen on Samantha joining their excursion.

As a student of history, Samantha studied the presidents and first ladies. She admired Abigail Adams for her intelligence and Eleanor Roosevelt for her charitable works. Samantha, however, was not a fan of Mrs. Grant.

Julia Dent Grant was raised in the antebellum South, and Samantha perceived her as spoiled and entitled. Julia loved being First Lady—the term was not in use yet—holding many banquets and spending public money extravagantly. She desperately wanted her husband to run for a third—and unprecedented—presidential term, despite Grant's desire to be free from his tumultuous political life, which came with frequent assassination threats.

As a matter of appearance, Julia was not confident in her looks. Even when she was young, she didn't consider herself pretty and was self-conscious about her crossed eyes. She stood five two, and the dresses of the era, tightly gathered at the waist with puffy hems, did not flatter her. At age forty-seven, having indulged in multicourse meals at the White House, she looked matronly.

Should Samantha feel awkward in the company of Grant's wife? Julia had first seen Samantha in Vicksburg. Grant had snapped to attention when hearing Samantha's name and tended to her request immediately.

Samantha assuaged any discomfort, thinking, So he stared at me. Well, I'm not some witch who cast a spell on Grant. He can admire another woman. He's president. He'll be sleeping with his wife tonight and remain faithful to her. Why should I feel uncomfortable when Grant appears at ease?

When the open-air carriage arrived, Samantha was not sure of the protocols for getting in and out. So she waited until James prompted her to enter, after Julia. The driver had placed a crate on the ground as a step for climbing into the carriage. James held Samantha's hand to steady her into the coach. Grant, then James, followed. How would it work descending from the coach? In reverse order, Samantha surmised.

Once in the carriage, Grant and Julia faced forward; James and Samantha faced the rear, which Samantha hated. But the president and his wife were entitled to the choice spots.

Julia was as inquisitive as Samantha was evasive. She enjoyed seeing the sights, especially the false-front buildings, and wanted to avoid answering questions. Because the ride was noisy (and bumpy), the conversation (interrogation) was only possible when the carriage was stopped in traffic.

"What did you say your surname was?"

Sam Time

Samantha didn't, intentionally. "Hunter." She didn't see the harm in revealing her real name.

"So your brothers are in the mining business?"

"That is one of our family businesses."

Where was she from? Where did she live now? Samantha was lying so often, she feared there would be a test at the end of the ride and she would fail.

Samantha attempted light conversation with James, but he was keen on talking with Grant. So she changed tactics.

"My three older brothers were schooled at home by Pa. I insisted on learning with my youngest brother. Math, reading, writing, history, and geography. Of course I learned to cook, sew, and needlepoint. We read the classics. William Shakespeare:

What's in a name? That which we call a rose,
By any other name would smell as sweet.

"We read poetry. Emerson." While looking out the window, she quoted Emerson with the dramatic cadence:

Give all to love;
Obey thy heart;
Friends, kindred, days,
Estate, good-fame,
Plans, credit and the Muse,—
Nothing refuse.

Take that, Mrs. Grant. I can recite poetry, like you can, Samantha thought. Her tactic worked. Julia was silent the remainder of the ride.

People on the street waved to the president and he waved back. Then James said, "There's a Hunter wagon. Is that one of your family's?"

On the side of the road was a worn, dusty, uncovered wagon, presumably used for mining, with a "Hunter" sign nailed to its back panel.

Samantha was surprised and had to think quickly. If this was the family's business asset, it appeared pathetic, giving the impression the operations weren't going well. She couldn't say there were many Hunters, and the wagon wasn't from the family business. It would have sounded implausible.

"What is that doing here?" was the best she could come up with on the fly.

"Stop," James said to the driver.

Samantha had been waving at strange men, saying they were her brothers and getting away with the ruse. This would be more challenging. She noticed a man in dirty clothes standing by the wagon. He looked like a miner in his forties.

"Why is it here? Maybe I can help. James, your assistance would be appreciated."

Her anxiousness grew: How to descend from this carriage without falling on my face? Wouldn't Julia like to see that?

James was seated next to the door. He hustled out, grabbed the crate from the back of the carriage, and placed it on the ground. Samantha grabbed both of his hands and stepped on the crate, then onto the ground without incident.

She walked toward the man, knowing all her companions were watching. Fortunately, the wagon was far enough away, so her conversation with this stranger would not be heard.

"Is your name Hunter?"

"Yes, ma'am."

"Where are you from?"

"Lancaster, Pennsylvania."

Interesting, Samantha thought. My ancestors are from there. "I too have family in Lancaster. May I ask your name?"

"Peter Hunter."

Samantha stammered, "I think I know your family. Do you have a wife? Children?

"My wife is Isabelle. My oldest is Alan. Then there's Claire, Nora, Oliver, Thomas, and the little one is Randal."

Samantha felt faint. She grabbed the wheel of the wagon to support herself. Breathe deep breaths, she said to herself.

She was seeing a ghost. This man was her great-great-great-grandfather, confirmed by the names of his wife and children, the first letters of which spelled "CONTRA."

Catching her breath, she said, "I know your family. I want to, I need to speak with you. Perhaps I can deliver a message to your family when I return to Pennsylvania. I would like us to talk. Do you have time?"

"Yes ma'am. Like to see folks from the hometown. How may I address you?"

She opened her mouth, then stopped. Saying "Samantha Hunter" would have sounded strange. Instead, she used Aaron's surname and said, "Samantha Parker."

Because she held on to the wagon wheel, her palms were soiled with dirt, and probably horse manure. She motioned to Peter, showing him her dirty hands. He scrounged for a rag, handing her the least-soiled rag he had.

"Please wait here. I will return shortly," she said to Peter.

"Yes, Miss Parker," Peter said.

She walked to the carriage, wiping her hands with the rag. James was still standing by the door waiting for Samantha to return. Having garnered the attention of the crowd, the president and Julia were preoccupied with well-wishers.

Samantha said to James, "Please accept my apologies. I have a family matter. And please give my regards to the president and Mrs. Grant. Good day, James."

"Good day, Samantha."

Samantha walked to Peter. "Would you like something to eat? I know the hotelier who runs that establishment over there." She was used to lying.

When they entered the hotel restaurant, Samantha negotiated two meals for fifteen cents and asked for a washbasin. The host showed her to an oak sideboard topped with a ceramic bowl, pitcher, and a dish with soap shavings to wash her hands.

A mirror encased in a rectangular oak frame with rounded corners hung above the sideboard. Samantha leaned closer for a better view of her reflection.

She thought, I look tired. I guess this nighttime traveling and lack of sleep are showing on my face.

After towel-drying her hands, she met Peter and they sat down at a table. Today's lunch was pork and beans with coffee or tea.

Samantha recalled Grace's explanation of the Hunter family story, as it had been passed down through the generations: Peter left Pennsylvania to mine precious metals out West but he never returned home.

"Peter, when did you leave Lancaster?"

Sam Time

"About two years ago."

"Your family told me that you were in Virginia City, Nevada."

"I was, these past two years. But I was heading back home when I stopped in Central City. Thought I'd mine some more. Gold this time. Go back by the end of the year."

She was eager to know more, but when the hostess served lunch, the conversation stopped. Peter scarfed down his plate of food. Samantha offered her plate to Peter, and he obliged as she sipped tea. After Peter was finished eating, Samantha asked, "Do you write to Isabelle?"

"Don't write much. Send packages. Send as much money I can that I earn here, after I pay living expenses. I send all of the packages, packages of coins, to Alan, my oldest son. Good, smart lad. He's thirteen now. I tell him take one-half, pay the family expenses. Take the other half, save it."

Tears streaming down her cheek, she pulled her handkerchief from her pocket to dab her eyes. Alan was Samantha's great-great-grandfather. He saved the coins and passed them down to the next generation, and ultimately they passed down to Samantha's father. And now Samantha was using those coins in time traveling. Some coins were in her pocket.

"Miss Parker, did I say anything to upset you?" Peter was uncomfortable seeing Samantha cry.

"No. I heard the same story as you're telling me now." Samantha put the handkerchief over her mouth and closed her eyes.

"May I do anything for you?" Peter asked.

Samantha shook her head. After a few deep breaths to compose herself, she asked, "What will do you now?"

"Have a job with the Lode Mining Company. Goin' to the South

Fork gold mine. Save a little. Then go back home for Christmas."

Samantha knew he never returned home. What happened?

"It was a pleasure meeting you, Peter. I will bring word to your family that you are well."

He replied in kind. Once outside, Samantha watched Peter ride away. She waved goodbye with tears in her eyes.

Then she returned inside the hotel, found an isolated nook, and struck the magic pose, which transported her instantly back to her bed. For convenience, she had placed her laptop on the nightstand. She grabbed it and typed all she could remember from her conversation with Grant. The notes would spur new research for her dissertation. Then she got up, changed, and returned to bed, wondering about Peter's fate before falling asleep.

THE NEXT DAY Samantha couldn't stop thinking about Peter Hunter. She surmised his family thought he was still in Virginia City, Nevada. So when he didn't return home, they didn't know to make inquiries in another mining town.

She searched the Internet for Denver newspapers archived in 1873. Peter Hunter said he was going to mine gold in South Fork with the Lode Mining Company. Using advanced searches, she discovered a newspaper article that explained her ancestor's fate.

Denver, Colorado – June 4, 1873. On Tuesday morning, an explosion in the South Fork gold mine killed nineteen workers, most of whom worked for the Lode Mining Company. The cause of the explosion is under investigation.

The miners killed included "Peter Hunter of Lancaster, Pennsylvania."

Samantha's heart raced. She downloaded the article and called her father, explaining that, while researching for her dissertation, she had discovered this article. Samantha's family was always proud of her studies, but this time she had solved a family mystery.

The coins Peter earned mining out West led Samantha to the discovery. She had been wondering why she was able to time travel. And now she had seen two ghosts: Philip's ancestor and Peter Hunter. She wasn't changing history, these weren't monumental discoveries, but the personal fates of these two men were now known.

Samantha thought, Perhaps, there's another ghost out there for me to discover. A trilogy.

Donna Balon

1876 Centennial Celebration Philadelphia

The 1876 Centennial Celebration was a key part of Samantha's dissertation. After the Civil War ended in 1865, the country remained fractured. The hundredth anniversary was unifying and showed the world the country was an industrial power, gaining on Britain's dominance. Philadelphia was the center of the celebration, where a large exhibition displayed innovations of the Industrial Revolution.

From her research, Samantha learned the Centennial Exhibition opened in May 1876, several weeks prior to the Fourth of July. The president and his wife attended the opening ceremony, hosting the emperor and empress from Brazil.

In this large public setting, with hordes of people attracted to Grant like a magnet, meeting him would be tricky. And liberating the president from his guests might not be possible.

Samantha also cringed at the thought of another encounter

with Julia. Surely the president's wife noticed Samantha's out-of-style dress with its sloped shoulder seams, bell-shaped sleeve hems, and domed skirt.

So vested was Samantha in her time-travel adventures, she spared no expense. She brought her powder-blue dress back to the dressmaker's shop for alterations to better resemble women's fashion in the later nineteenth century. After several weeks, the restyled dress was finished.

At home, Samantha stood in front of a full-length mirror admiring her altered dress. The sleeve caps were set-in, on-the-shoulder seams. The width of the sleeves were slender. Some fabric and pleats were removed around the stomach reducing the volume for a flatter skirt front, while the skirt back remained full. More fabric was added to the back peplum in cascading folds for a bustle-like look.

Having spoken with Aaron and Grace in the evening, Samantha felt confident in traveling from home. With her history book opened to her desired destination and date, she climbed into bed and fell asleep.

AT A MAGICAL TIME during the night, Samantha vanished from her bed and time traveled to Fairmount Park, where the exhibition was located.

Samantha had become reliant on the stealth concierge service of the time-travel gods. Not only would they transport her back in time over a hundred years in *Star Trek*–like fashion, on arrival, the travel-concierge gods would place her exactly where she was supposed to be. And this exhibition was huge, even by today's standards. The footprint of the main building was over twenty acres.

There were other large halls (machinery, agriculture, and arts) and over two dozen other exhibition buildings.

At least one or two senior staff always traveled with Grant, typically staying close to a telegraph to pass messages to him of happenings throughout the country. Samantha entered the main building and looked for the telegraph room, which wasn't difficult to locate. She was pleased to find a familiar face.

Samantha smiled and said, "Captain Carter. Miss Samantha. We met in Central City, Mechanicsville, and Vicksburg. We're practically friends."

"Miss Samantha, how may I be of assistance to you?" was the captain's curt reply.

Samantha thought, Does he not recognize me? Why the formality?

Her smile dropped and she stiffened. "I request to see the president. Please pass my message to him."

The captain must have remembered Samantha, because he promptly left to deliver her message. Samantha followed him out the door and then watched as he walked into the crowded exhibit hall. She waited.

Then Captain Carter came back into view, clearing a path through the crowd for the president, who was wearing a top hat and his classic dark frock coat and pants, a vest (with an attached pocket watch), and a thin dark bow tie over a white shirt.

Samantha said, "Thank you, Captain Carter—once again."

Captain Carter nodded and walked away.

Three years had passed since their last meeting. Grant took Samantha's arm and showed her into the telegraph room. He signaled for everyone else to leave. The door was left slightly ajar.

He said, "You rescued me. The emperor is dallying at every exhibit. This is interminable."

She laughed. "Well, I'm glad I could be of help. I wanted to say good day. Good day, Mr. President."

"Good day, Samantha." He was noticeably happy.

Standing face-to-face, they stood closer than unmarried friends should. Being so close without touching was seductive.

"I wanted only a few minutes. I know you do not have much time. But I wanted to see this exhibit, and I thought it would be nice to see my old acquaintance too."

"My pleasure."

"Is your family well?" she asked.

"Yes, yes. And yours?" the president asked.

Samantha nodded and smiled.

He said, "How do you like the exhibit? I wanted this. Show the world. Celebrate the nation!"

The conversation was secondary. Mutual adoration kept Samantha smiling and Grant entranced. She shuffled her feet a few inches closer to him. She wasn't sure he noticed, but he didn't step back either.

She replied, "It is wonderful. Even more, it is wonderful to see you. I appreciate you giving me a few minutes of your time."

Without prompting, Grant gushed with information that could be helpful in Samantha's research. She nodded while committing to memory everything he said.

Then she leaned in closer and said, "Happy centennial, Mr. President."

She wanted to hug him. She wanted to kiss him on the cheek.

"Mr. President!" Captain Carter interrupted. In unison, the

president and Samantha turned to look from where the sound was coming. "Mr. President," Captain Carter interrupted.

"Good day, Mr. President."

"Good day, Miss Samantha." He lifted his top hat.

Grant motioned for Samantha to leave first, and he opened the door for her. She smiled back at him.

Samantha left the main building to go to the Women's Pavilion, where no one frowned that she was an unescorted woman. The camaraderie among the exhibitors was inspiring. And the inventions were things Samantha could never design or create using twenty-first-century know-how. There was a woman who sold to the government her patent of a three-color pyrotechnic night signal used during the Civil War. Another woman operated the controls of a steam engine, running six looms and a printing press. Samantha lingered, conversing with the women exhibitors and feeling no physical or temporal distance between her and them.

After leaving the Women's Pavilion, Samantha took a buggy ride to a place she had been before. On her second date with Aaron, they'd sat in St. Augustine Church. Samantha wanted to see the church in its earlier years.

How charming it was to see the slender two-story brick building with its front, center steeple. She stood admiring it. The redbrick exterior walls were fresher without the hundred years of clinging soot and grime.

Samantha went inside and sat where she and Aaron had sat. The ceiling frescoes were brighter, and the altar was original. Despite magically being in 1876, she could think only about Aaron and when she was here with him. Time traveling helped Samantha cope with the loneliness while he was away. Sitting in the church only made her long for him even more. If she couldn't live in the moment, best she leave.

The center city was crowded. People were everywhere and Samantha was having difficulty finding an isolated place to disappear. Then she spotted a street poster that read, "Magician and the Disappearing Woman." Samantha thought, This is too good to pass up.

The magician was already onstage extolling his powers to make his lady assistant disappear and presumably reappear. A crowd had gathered around the stage.

Samantha made her way through the crowd and climbed three steps onto the stage. "Oh, Mr. Magician," she said loudly and theatrically, "please make me disappear, so I can go home to Kansas."

The magician was flabbergasted. Only his assistant knew the trick of the false panel in the narrow wooden box that stood six feet high.

"I don't have money for a train ticket. And this would be so much faster." The crowd laughed as Samantha continued her theatrics.

"I miss my mama and papa, and I do not want to ever leave Kansas again. There's no place like home in Kansas."

The magician didn't know how to handle this. Samantha stepped toward him and said in his ear, "I know how to do this." She turned toward the crowd and said loudly, "If you are a real magician, you will make me disappear and send me home to Kansas." She stepped into the box. He reluctantly closed the door.

"Abracadabra," he said, while waving his wand over the box door.

Then he opened the door, and Samantha was still there. The crowd booed.

Samantha tried not to move her lips, "Give me ten seconds!" She hadn't had enough time to get situated, and she needed to make sure the hem of her full dress skirt was entirely inside the box.

The magician closed the door and said, "Apparently, it takes longer to get to Kansas than I thought."

The crowd laughed.

Samantha closed her eyes, placed her palms at her sides, and took a deep breath. Poof, she was home in her bed.

Back in Philadelphia, the magician said the magic word, "Abracadabra." He opened the door, and the box was empty. Samantha was gone. He noticed, however, the secret panel had not been engaged. So he pushed on the panel, and the false back of the box swung open so the crowd could see the other side of the street.

The crowd applauded. They thought he was a genius—so did he.

Sam Time

Summer 1877
London

Feeling confident about time traveling, Samantha thought, Where next? Opening her history, she flipped through to 1877. "London," she said out loud. "That sounds like fun."

For the first time, she would launch her time travel from Philip's office. In preparation, she carefully folded her power blue dress, using tissue paper to prevent wrinkles, and put it inside an extra-large beach tote bag with a zipper closure. She styled her hair in the double-braided crown, took her braided halo hat, and placed it inside the tote bag with the history book earmarked to the desired time and destination. Samantha had spoken with Aaron and Grace earlier and sent a quick text to each. All was well.

She drove to the university and walked through the library to Philip's office. Once inside his office, she put on her dress and hat, then lay on the chaise lounge, and pulled Philip's afghan over her for warmth. Then she fell asleep.

SAMANTHA ARRIVED in an empty vestibule of some building. The door to the inside was open, and she could hear voices with British accents. She opened the front door and walked down the brick steps. The day was overcast. Looking up, down, and across the street, she whispered, "Time-travel gods, help me here."

Then a coach, topped with many trunks, pulled in front of the hotel across the street. The coach door opened and a few people exited, then Grant and his wife. Fortunately, Julia and their son entered the hotel as Grant chatted with the coach driver.

Grant's second presidential term ended in March 1877. Thereafter he and his wife toured parts of the United States and then embarked on a world tour beginning in England.

Samantha stopped a young boy. "I will give you a coin, if you give a message to that man."

Grant always wore the same uniform: dark frock coat and pants, a vest over a white shirt with a thin black bow tie and a top hat.

"The man in the dark costume with the dark beard with white streaks on his chin. Tell him Sam is here. Go and I will give you this coin when you return." She held up a nickel. The boy didn't care his reward was not a British coin.

She said again, "Tell him Sam is here." She kept the message short because she assumed the lad thought she talked funny with her American accent.

The boy crossed the street, tugged at the hem of Grant's frock coat, and presumably passed along Samantha's message. Grant said something to the boy, who ran back to Samantha. The boy said, "Trafalgar Square." The boy didn't give a time, but Samantha assumed it was soon. She handed the boy the nickel and he ran off.

London was the big league. The purveyor of Victorian rules and protocols. Samantha was comfortable, however, she could fit in. Having time traveled extensively, to large U.S. cities such as New York City, Philadelphia, and Washington, D.C., she learned that—except for the upper classes—life was actually more relaxed than twenty-first century perceptions would suggest. Nevertheless, she didn't want to stand on the sidewalk looking like a bumpkin. So she stopped a man to ask for directions to Trafalgar Square. Fortunately, it was only a couple blocks away. She endured a few disapproving glances as she strolled unaccompanied by a man.

Not long after her arrival to the square, Grant followed and greeted her, "Good day, Miss Samantha."

"Good day, General Grant."

"What brings you to London?" Grant asked.

"Not business. My aunt and I are here on holiday. We arrived yesterday. I slipped away while she was reposing."

They wandered, chatting as did others. The fashions and refined manners—of many, but not all—amused Samantha. She blended in as if she belonged in the nineteenth century. But the former U.S. president?

She asked, "Are you not concerned you will attract attention?"

"We arrived not even an hour ago. People do not yet know we are here. When the newspapers publish we have arrived and where we are going, there will by crowds of people. But for now, I am just another gentleman in a top hat with a beard. If they are not looking, there is nothing to see. And if they do recognize me, they do not know what my wife looks like.

"During the war, Edwin Stanton, secretary of war in the Lincoln administration, thought he would recognize me. We had not met. When he came into the railcar I was in, he walked over to my physician and shook his hand saying, 'How do you do, General Grant?' I guess he expected someone taller."

Samantha laughed, taking her handkerchief out of her pocket and covering her mouth.

A buggy driver was offering rides for a city tour. Grant turned to Samantha. She nodded and Grant spoke with driver. The buggy was conveniently stopped next to a cast-iron two-step mounting block, in decorative filigree, used for ascending and descending buggies and carriages. Samantha held her hand up, and Grant took it, supporting her as she stepped onto the mounting block and into the buggy.

She sat down. Then Grant climbed in and sat on the same seat next to Samantha. He said, "I am surprised to see you here. London of all places."

"Are you disappointed?"

"No. No. You show up so unexpectedly, conveniently. As if I do not have a choice in the matter."

Grant's perception was curious; he had an inkling Samantha's company was providential. The buggy was now moving. And Samantha said nothing.

He said, "I do not know why I ask, 'What are you doing here?' How do I know your answers are not contrived?"

"My, we are curious today. Are you not happy to see me?"

"Yes," Grant replied.

Samantha perceived that Grant was a henpecked husband. So she too could manipulate the situation to her benefit. "And I am delighted to be in your company. Let's not ask the 'why' question. Let's enjoy the sights."

Sam Time

He complied.

They rode by the Tower of London, which was still used as a prison.

"That's a wretched place."

Grant agreed. They both had done their homework before visiting London: studying the history and sites for a more enriching experience. They talked of what they knew. In her best imitation of a British accent, Samantha described what she knew about the Tower of London. "There is a legend that ravens live in the tower, and if they should ever leave, the Crown will fall with the tower."

Grant interrupted, "How do you do that?"

"What do you mean?"

"You said you arrived yesterday, but your British accent is polished."

Samantha could not say she'd watched all six seasons of *Downton Abbey* and a hundred hours of BritBox.

She cringed. "Our import-export fabric business is with British merchants who visit New York often."

She then turned the other way to view the city she had visited as a child with her parents and sister. Now the city was obviously smaller. The Tower Bridge had not yet been built. Although the main roads were cobblestone, there were many buildings she had seen before: Buckingham Palace, Westminster Abbey, the British Museum, Big Ben, and the Palace of Westminster. Samantha was fascinated by the passing horse-drawn carriages, buggies, and their occupants.

Then Grant said, "I hope the people receive me well here."

Samantha turned to Grant and said firmly, "Well, they should. We were there when they needed us."

Grant furrowed his eyebrows as if to ask, "Why?"

Samantha slipped, again, forgetting the time period she was in. World War II hadn't happened yet. Her best recovery was, "I am referring to trade. America imports so much from England, the country has prospered because of business with us. Besides, if they do not like you, you can call them sore losers."

Samantha blurted "sore loser" and then thought, Is this term in use yet? Grant smiled, meaning he understood it.

"You are meeting the Queen?"

"Yes. I told the driver to take us to St. James's Park."

"Splendid."

The buggy stopped at the entrance to the enormous park. Grant descended out of the buggy. Samantha stood, stretched out her arms, and put her hands on Grant's shoulders while he put his hands under her elbows, lifting her out of the buggy. She noticed Grant was wearing shoes instead of boots. Once Samantha was firmly on the ground she said to Grant, "You are most kind."

He said, "If I may say, the years look good on you."

"You saw me last year."

"Yes, at the centennial. But I thought then, as I do now, I am the one who has changed," he said, placing his hand on his round stomach. "Have you found the Fountain of Youth?"

"A lady does not reveal her secret." And this was a big secret.

They walked the grounds, passing by other couples, many women in lovely linen walking dresses and bonnets. Some men were now sporting the sack coat, a hip-length jacket, resembling the predecessor of the present-day suit jacket.

"So, do tell me about the last eight years. I saw you twice, but it was short. I would like to hear your thoughts."

Sam Time

"I never wanted to be president. They nominated me. I accepted and won."

"You must feel vindicated after many hard years; you achieved the highest office in the land."

"It came with unrelenting burdens. I had little time to enjoy it."

"What was the best part of being president?"

"Julia was delighted. To her, it was a dream. I am glad one of us enjoyed those eight years. I am happy it is over."

They strolled and he said, "While in the White House, I often left the office in the afternoon. Walked for four or five miles."

"If you are saying that you desire a long walk today, I can do it. I wear sensible shoes. They are not pretty, but no one sees them. I enjoy a long promenade too," she said.

"Do you mind if I smoke?"

The general could not manage an hour or two without smoking a cigar. If Samantha wanted to spend time with him, learn some history firsthand, she would have to tolerate the cigar smoke. They were outside, which helped. "No, I do not mind if you have a cigar."

Grant's presidency was plagued with scandals. Samantha wasn't going to act like a twenty-first-century got-you journalist. Grant was her friend. He virtually said so and made time to see her. She would push only so far. But she did try. "I would like to know more of the details of the Black Hills matter."

Grant said nothing.

Black Hills in South Dakota was the home of the Sioux Native Americans. When gold was discovered on the land, the Grant administration tried to broker an agreement with the Sioux to relocate, which they refused. A military conflict ensued, and ultimately the federal government took possession of the land.

Samantha reiterated, "Black Hills?"

He shot her a disapproving look, firmly showing he didn't want to talk about it. She was taken aback and pulled out her handkerchief to cover her mouth. Samantha was speechless, which was rare. Thoughts raced through her head. When she was with Grant she ought not to be the history professor searching for a fresh angle on history. Instead, if she wanted to be in his company, she was to play the role of Miss Samantha. That's what he wanted.

Granted inhaled his cigar. They walked side by side, not saying anything. The gravel crunched with their footsteps.

She thought, Silence is good, silence can cure. The day was so wonderful and I spoiled it.

Crunch, crunch of the gravel beneath their footsteps.

Then Samantha did what came naturally. "We were having such a nice day, and I made a royal mess of it. Courting disaster. Call me the queen of trouble. My crowning achievement is making you cross with me."

It was corny, but it was the best she could do. She glanced to her side to see his reaction. He was holding this cigar in his hand and smiling.

She continued, "You should rein me in because I lost my head."

He roared, laughing. When he stopped, he said, "You once said to me I was never a general to you. Well, I am not a president to you either."

It was an elegant way of saying he didn't want to talk about the last eight years. Despite Samantha's desire to hear Grant's thoughts on his presidency, he was paying her a compliment that being with her was sufficient.

"As you wish," she said.

Sam Time

They strolled the grounds, content in silence. No passersby recognized the former American president. Several large white pelicans roamed the grounds, amusing Grant and Samantha.

Then she said, "It appears the centennial was uplifting. And the mood has lingered." This was the main premise of her dissertation. She was pleased when Grant talked uninterrupted for a while about her favorite topic—and one of his. He had become her de facto doctorial advisor. Her near-complete written paper needed polish, and Grant unwittingly was providing Samantha embellishments for the final copy.

When a few raindrops fell, they sheltered under a large tree. Samantha said, "This tree will keep us dry, but Benjamin Franklin would caution lightning could strike."

"It's only rain."

They stood close to the thick trunk of the tree. Samantha said, "It would be a shame if your suit got wet. This beautiful fabric is like silk," she said, touching the lapels of his frock coat.

She looked up at Grant, and he was staring at her. "Think of the people who wove this exquisite fabric, and the tailors who made this lovely garment. You would not want the rain to ruin it."

She noticed ashes from his cigar rested on the shoulders and lapels of his coat. And Grant's light-blue eyes were still staring at her. She sensed he wasn't even listening to what she was saying. So she tested her theory. "Perhaps it is best for our country to split into two, North and South. Since George Washington started the tradition against holding office for a third presidential term, you could run for president in the new Confederate South."

He had no reaction to this absurd comment because he wasn't listening. Samantha was flattered. She turned to one side then the other to see if they were alone. They were. She placed her hand on his chest. "Oh, Ulysses, I am so very fond of you."

"And I of you."

His sentiment warmed her heart. She would never forget it.

She rested her head on his chest, and he wrapped his arms around her. She could hear his heart beat. The heartbeat of Ulysses S. Grant. She closed her eyes.

She tried to enjoy the moment without thinking she would have to air her dress outside for a day to remove the cigar smell. That her hair would smell like cigar, and when she laid her head on her pillow, it too would smell like cigar.

After a few minutes, Samantha lifted her head. "I think the rain has stopped." She stepped away and stretched out her arms. Her shoes and the hem of her dress were wet. "It is safe. Your lovely suit will not be ruined, but the grass is wet." She took his hand and let go of it once they were beyond the tree. They walked to the gravel path saying nothing.

"I would like to call again. After your foreign travel, when you return to the States."

"Please do," Grant replied.

Samantha was pleased to have an open invitation. "Our home is in Atlantic Highlands; it is a one-hour buggy ride to Long Branch."

"Yes. We have a cottage on the beach. You may call with an escort and come to the beach."

Samantha smirked. "The folks, like my family, who live there year-round call it the Jersey Shore."

He repeated, "The Jersey Shore."

"Yes," Samantha said, then thought, And if that's not what they call it now, they will in a hundred years.

Sam Time

Samantha heard a rustle and turned around. Someone was close by. A man came closer, and she noticed he was carrying a small box. Then she realized what it was and said, "This chap has a camera."

In this era cameras were owned only by professionals. They were square, boxlike, too large to hold with your hands while taking a photo. This photographer had come with a tripod.

She said, "You have been recognized. I should go."

How to say goodbye and make this departure memorable? London was formal, so Samantha raised her right hand for Grant to kiss it. He obliged, taking her hand and smiling at her. Then he bent over and kissed her hand.

"Good day, Miss Samantha."

"Good day, General."

They walked away in opposite directions. Samantha looked back at Grant. He pulled a cigar out of his pocket and lit it up.

The city streets were wet and empty. Samantha easily found an isolated spot, exiting the past with the magic pose.

She returned back on the chaise lounge in Philip's office, pleased the time-travel gods approved of her new launching spot. Having packed her laptop, she opened it and typed notes based on Grant's monologue. Then she took off her dress, changed into her casual clothes, and turned on her cellphone. All was quiet at 1:31 a.m. There were no messages from Aaron or Grace. She collected her things and called security to escort her out of the building. Then they escorted Samantha to her car.

She thought, That went well; I'll do it again next week.

Donna Balon

Summer 1881
Long Branch, New Jersey

Samantha covered her face with her hands. She had been writing her dissertation for several days. She thought, That's enough for today. I can't do anymore. I need a break.

She sat at her desk, staring at the wall. Her mind wandered, recalling her time-travel trips: Eureka, New York City, Galena, Fort Henry, Vicksburg... Her mind jumped; she had now traveled from 1854 to 1873 wearing dresses made with 1882 fabric. In an aha moment, she realized: I'm supposed to ultimately go to the 1880s. That's my final time-travel destination.

She grabbed her history book, flipped through, and then paper-clipped the page. Tonight she would travel to her home state and she would launch again from Philip's office. Her preparations included carrying her powder-blue dress in an extra-large beach tote bag with a zipper closure, along with the braided halo hat, mini drawstring change purse, handkerchief, history book, and laptop.

Sam Time

As usual, she styled her hair in the double-braided crown. After gathering everything she needed, she called Aaron.

"Hi, sweetie."

"Hi, still working. It's going to be a late night."

"Well, I'm going to the library."

"Tonight? Why?"

"I find I need a change of venue to promote ideas. I get stuck when I'm in one place. I went to the library the other day and got some fresh ideas."

"But at this time? At night?"

"I'm still wide awake, and I think going to the library will be productive."

"Go tomorrow during the day. It's safer than walking around campus in the dark. Really, I'd feel better if you stayed home."

Samantha changed the subject. "How are things there?"

"Today it's personnel problems. I won't bother you with it. Anyway, someone is calling me. Talk to you tomorrow. Love you."

"Love you too." They hung up.

Then Samantha texted Grace: *Hi. What's up?*

Grace texted: *Out with friends. Leaving restaurant soon. Everything okay?*

Samantha texted: *Yes. Just wanted to say hi. Still working on dissertation.*

Grace texted: *Call you tomorrow. Got to go. Bye.*

Having reached out to Aaron and Grace, Samantha felt confident she could time travel from Philip's office without incident. She drove to the university and walked through the library to his office. Then she put on her pink dress, lay on the chaise lounge, snuggled under the afghan, and fell asleep.

SHE ARRIVED in an isolated, narrow, white-painted corridor and could hear the hum of people talking. Following the sound, she walked into a cavernous foyer where people were milling around. A sign above the door entrance read "West End Hotel." Samantha had descended in Long Branch, New Jersey, a coastal town where the Grants summered.

She admired the people in their Victorian attire: ladies in cotton and linen dresses and cute bonnets, some sporting a nautical look in blue-and-white-striped dresses; many men wearing sack coats in dark colors, tans and cream colors with matching waistcoats and pants. Straw boat hats for men were now in style.

"Samantha? Samantha Hunter," a man's voice said. And it wasn't Grant's.

She was startled someone would know her in this busy place over 130 years from her present day. She turned toward the sound of the voice. Ten feet away was a bearded, mustached man wearing a black top hat, a dark-colored linen sack coat, matching pants, and a waistcoat over a white shirt with a thin black bow tie. Who was this man with squirrely eyebrows, green eyes, and a brown beard that extended to the base of his neck?

The man sensed Samantha didn't recognize him. "Miss Samantha Hunter."

Who is he? she thought. How could someone know me here?

The man was now only several feet from her, but she still did not recognize him.

He said, "Captain Carter."

She put her hand on her chest. "I did not recognize you. You are not in uniform. And I did not think you remembered me."

"You are unforgettable."

Sam Time

As pleasant as the compliment was, Samantha was incredulous. "On several previous occasions, I tried to engage in polite conversation without success."

"I was in service for the general. There was no time for banter."

"Well, it is a pleasure to see you, Captain."

He asked, "What brings you here?" As if he didn't know it was Grant.

"Our family residence is ten miles north in Atlantic Highlands. I like taking a buggy ride here, then strolling. Even though I'm breaking protocols without an escort. The day is so lovely. My beau does not return until evening. I must fill my day somehow. And this hotel is magnificent. And you? What brings you to Long Branch?"

"I have an invitation from the general."

They both knew what would transpire, but they had to play it out.

"My son was to join me, but he had another engagement. The Grants are expecting me with a guest. Would you like to accompany me? The general would be happy to see you."

"Well, this *is* a happy coincidence. I should not refuse fate."

She didn't know what time of day it was and didn't know how long the visit would be. She said, "I do have only a few hours. Then I must return. Mr. Parker will be disappointed if I am not home when he arrives. I do not want to obligate you to escort me back. I know the way."

The Captain nodded, then extended his elbow. Samantha smiled and placed her hand on his elbow. They walked outside. The West End Hotel was a large, wooden, three-story structure, with one-hundred-plus rooms and windows every few feet. Many other shoreline hotels had two-story balconies.

The day was a traveler's dream, cloudless blue sunny skies on the Jersey Shore. Long Branch was the place to be on a warm summer day.

They walked along Ocean Avenue. Even today this road runs parallel to the coast for miles. In this era, however, the hard, sandy road traveled by horse carriages and buggies was a novel sight for Samantha. So too was the bluff overlooking the ocean. She felt the need to explain the contradiction that she knew the area well while curiously looking around. "I am always amazed at the scenery and sights here."

During their stroll, Samantha learned that Captain Carter had a first name, Daniel. His wife had died after giving birth to their second child, a baby boy, who died a month later.

After they spoke for a while Samantha asked what she had wondered: "Captain, did you think I was a Rebel spy?"

The captain smiled.

"Your smile tells me your answer is yes."

"The general is a loyal man. If you have his confidence, he cannot see guile in a friend or acquaintance. We were protecting him."

"I am not offended. Only curious," Samantha replied.

The captain said, "And to be frank, your timing was always impeccable. I could not comprehend how you did it. If you were a spy, you would have resources to know where and when to conveniently see the general."

Samantha stared straight ahead, self-conscious, not knowing how to defend the obvious. "I was never a spy."

Sensing Samantha's discomfort, the captain dropped the subject. Then he said, "It is a short walk to the Grant cottage. I should have asked before we left the hotel. Do you mind?"

Sam Time

"I prefer walking."

The "Grant cottage" wasn't a cottage and wasn't Grant's. The house was a three-story stick-style design with a veranda and second-floor balcony, both of which wrapped around two sides of the house. A porte cochere with a circular gravel driveway faced the road. On the beach side of the house, accessed from the veranda and upper balcony, was a hexagon-shaped, two-story solarium. A friend and donor allowed the Grant family free use of this fully furnished home.

Grant greeted them at the door. Four years had lapsed since Grant had seen Samantha in London. He was age fifty-nine. "This is a pleasant surprise." Then he said to the captain, "I wager she popped out of nowhere."

The captain said, "It did seem like that."

Samantha straightened her shoulders for perfect posture and said defensively, "I gather you are both happy to see me, no matter the manner of my arrival."

Julia appeared and Grant turned to her. "Our guests have arrived." Turning back toward Samantha and the captain, he explained, "Our children and grandchildren are in New York; usually the house is full. They return tomorrow."

The women exchanged pleasantries. Then the Grants led their guests onto the veranda.

The captain took off his top hat and sack coat. Grant wasn't wearing a coat either. Apparently, "casual" for Grant at the beach was a long-sleeve white button-down shirt with a thin bow tie, covered by a vest and trousers in a dark fabric.

Samantha waited for instruction on where to sit. Happily, she was given an ocean-view seat. The men sat across from each other, as did the women.

This would be Samantha's first meal in the past. Unsure of Victorian table manners, she would observe and follow. Then she thought: The Edwardian customs I've seen on *Downton Abbey* should suffice in place of Victorian customs.

The sun was high in the sky, so she guessed this meal was likely lunch, in the early afternoon. The food was local: steamed clams, biscuits with gravy, boiled potatoes, and baked fish. Hot tea was served. Freshly cut peaches followed for dessert.

The men talked politics and current events. There was much talk about James Garfield, who had been sworn in as president in March 1881. On July 2, Garfield was shot in a Washington, D.C., train station. Doctors probed the president's body with unsanitary fingers and instruments to locate the bullet, causing infection. Garfield would die in September.

During a lull in the conversation, Samantha said, "I read about this inventor, Thomas Edison. He is here in Menlo Park, New Jersey. Has anyone heard about his latest invention? Something called an incandescent light bulb?"

Grant and the captain read the newspapers and did hear about some laboratory work, but Edison's revolutionary discovery was still in its infancy.

After Grant's two-term presidency, he and Julia went on a two-year world tour of Europe, the Middle East, and Asia. On returning to the United States, they traveled from the West to the East Coast, then to Mexico and Cuba. He was well received everywhere, now internationally famous and admired.

Samantha asked, "How was your world tour?"

Grant said, "You can talk with Julia later. She will be most happy to tell you all about it."

Sam Time

Samantha replied, wanting to hear Grant's comments about the trip, "What were some highlights? And what didn't you like?"

"It was over two years. And there were so many wonderful moments," Julia said.

"That is the challenge. To succinctly talk of the highest and lowest moments," Samantha said. "So who goes first? Mrs. Grant, highlights, low moments?"

Julia said, "We had some bad weather when we were at sea. It violently rocked the ship. The best? Well, I shivered at Napoleon's tomb. His sarcophagus . . ."

Samantha asked Grant, "What did you think?"

"I did not go. He was a military genius, but he was a cruel, selfish man. I did not want to go to his tomb. The whole trip was a splendid education. We saw many cultures and learned much. I had long conversations with Bismarck, which I enjoyed. Japan, the country and people, are beautiful."

"And your worst? Mrs. Grant has answered."

Grant said, "All the banquets. Too many of them."

Julia said, "We took a tour of the mine shaft in Virginia City, Nevada. We descended on the platform to a depth of one thousand, seven hundred feet."

"You are braver than I. No one could have persuaded me to go down a mining shaft," Samantha said.

"Oh, it was fun," Julia said.

"Fun?" Samantha was incredulous. She had to suppress her urge to say, "It's not an amusement park ride!"

Julia explained, "The general thought I would not go. I was pleased to show him I had the courage."

Samantha asked, "And, General, what did you think of the mine?"

"I was curious to see the operations. I always knew it was hard work. I wanted to see it myself." Grant said.

Samantha wanted to mention meeting Peter Hunter during the carriage ride with the Grants and that he worked in the Virginia City mines. But when dessert was served, the conversation lightened to the discussion of the delicious food and beautiful weather.

After dessert the men and women separated. Grant and the captain sat on two wicker chairs at one end of the veranda and lit cigars. Julia and Samantha sat at the other end of the veranda. Although Samantha wanted to hear and join the men's conversation, she was obligated to sit with the hostess.

Julia delighted in having an audience. Samantha was bored and strained to hear what the men were discussing. As Julia droned on about "her" years in the Executive Mansion and grand world tour, Samantha smiled obligatorily and gently nodded her head, giving the impression she was intently listening.

Meanwhile Samantha was thinking: I knew Long Branch was a family affair. Fortunately, Grant's unremarkable offspring are away. I was too optimistic in hoping for a few hours alone with Grant, walking on the beach or sitting on a bench in the summer sun. But in the company of Julia, I ask myself, what am I doing here? She's talking of cute little teacups she desired on her trip abroad. And of foreign souvenirs that were lost in U.S. Customs. Of what use is this to me? I came here for insight, to be enlightened by history, and I'm stuck here listening to this drone. I need to extricate myself. But how to do so gracefully?

Julia is a plain-looking woman, Samantha thought. But she presents herself well in that lovely cream-color linen dress. I do feel self-conscious. My dress is pretty, but its medium-weight cotton

Sam Time

fabric is unsuitable for a summer day. Julia notices this. Thank goodness for the gentle breeze; I'd be sweating otherwise. To be fair, she is so well mannered she hides her contempt for me. And she is an adoring wife and mother, running a happy household that includes grandchildren.

Then the servant Betty approached Julia about a matter. She excused herself and went inside the house. Samantha sighed in relief. She could hear Betty and her young daughter talking. The little girl wanted to wade her feet in the ocean, and Betty said she was busy with guests.

Samantha turned to them and said to the little girl, "What is your name?"

"Violet."

"Violet, what a lovely name. I like to wet my feet too." Samantha said to Betty, "On a nice day like this one, the ocean water at your feet is refreshing."

Julia returned to the veranda, startling Samantha. Fraternizing with the help, a woman of color, was inappropriate behavior for a houseguest. To cover her misstep, she turned to Julia. "I heard the little girl say she wanted to wet her feet. I enjoy walking on the beach." Then to distract and embellish she said, "Sometimes I tack my skirt hem, raising it to dip my feet in the water."

"The captain will escort you to the water's edge. And Betty will fetch you a needle, thread, and scissors. Please come inside," Julia said.

"Splendid idea!"

They went inside the house. Betty handed Samantha a spool of white thread, a needle, and scissors. Samantha had trouble threading the needle, taking several tries while squinting her eyes before succeeding. She pinched the front right side of the fabric and the petticoat about a foot from the hem and lifted them up higher on the dress skirt. Then she tacked the fabric and petticoat in place with the sewing thread and knotted the thread ends together. She did this on the left front side and the back, the same as the front—all in fifteen minutes.

Although the threads were visible close up, from only a few feet away, the thread blended with the fabric, and the four swags were flattering. The hem rose several inches above her ankles. Samantha removed her socks and shoes.

Having temporarily altered her dress in private, Samantha walked back out onto the veranda. Julia had retrieved the captain, who had taken off his socks and shoes and rolled up his pant legs. Samantha smiled and took his arm, walking to the water's edge.

The captain was a good sport, spending time with Samantha. Like her, he would have preferred sitting next to and talking with the general. Samantha turned around and looked back at the veranda. Julia was sitting at her husband's side. They were holding hands.

Samantha thought, She's a smart lady. Arrange for the guests to walk along the beach, making solitary time with her beloved husband.

The sun was strong, and Samantha was glad her moisturizer contained sunscreen. Wading her ankles in the water, she seized the opportunity to ask the captain about historic events he had witnessed.

"I met the general when he was stationed at Fort Humboldt. During the gold rush, my family bought some mining claims. Then we returned home, here in New Jersey. But on occasion, we traveled for business. If I knew the general was in town, I would call. The general and I have had an ongoing discussion about our young nation. Well, we're over one hundred years old now. We talk about what keeps our country united and, most recently, the ways in which the centennial united us.

"Like the general, you have witnessed historic events. What would you say to the historians of the future about today's sentiments regarding our nation's unity? Or lack thereof? And what is the written trail, if any?"

The captain obliged with much knowledge and opinion. She smiled when he described in detail his travels throughout the country, events, and resources. These would be nuggets, finishing touches to her dissertation. She listened keenly, so she could recall everything he said once she returned to her present.

They lingered for a while at the water's edge. She lost track of time, then walked with the captain back to the house.

Betty was on the veranda, holding a towel for Samantha to clean her feet. Then Betty escorted Samantha into the house, where she slipped on her socks and shoes and then cut the threads on her modified dress so it fell to its intended length.

Back on the veranda, Samantha walked to the nearest high-back wicker chair and sat. The men were on the other side of the veranda talking, and Julia was inside the house.

New Jersey was her home state, and Samantha knew Long Branch well. Seeing the pristine, near-deserted beach was magnificent. But there was no boardwalk. No lemon ice stand. And no Aaron.

In the warm air, she leaned back in the chair, closed her eyes, and then opened them when she felt herself falling asleep.

Samantha thought, As long as people are around, if I fall asleep, I won't disappear.

She closed her eyes and drifted into a dream in which Aaron was worried and searching for her. She woke up feeling uneasy, but no one had noticed she'd dozed for a few minutes. The dream, however, was so unsettling, she wanted to go home.

Before leaving she needed to use the water closet and approached Betty, who showed her into the house to a small room on the first floor. Afterward, Samantha spied a mirror to catch a glimpse of herself. She gasped, shocked at what she saw.

She was older. If Grant had aged thirty years since she first met him, she was looking at a sixtyish version of herself: crow's-feet at the corners of her eyes, wrinkles under her eyes, thin skin having lost collagen, jowls around her mouth, and white streaks in her hair.

Even though she felt well, she did have trouble threading the needle, indicating her eyesight had diminished. And what secrets were hiding under her dress? Moles? Skin tags? Or evidence of something worse?

She recalled what Grant had said to her in London. "The years look good on you. Have you found the Fountain of Youth?" She assumed she'd never aged. But his compliment implied "for your age."

Then in Central City, Colorado, when she met Peter Hunter and washed her hands, she saw her reflection in the mirror. She thought she was tired, but she was actually viewing her forty-nine-year-old reflection.

Shocked, she looked again into the mirror and thought, Damn, those time-travel gods aged me.

Time travel had consequences. She wanted to leave quickly and return to her present.

Sam Time

She walked back onto the veranda and told Grant and the captain she hadn't realized it was so late, and she needed to go. The men stood and she bid them goodbye.

"General, it is always a pleasure," she said to Grant, who bowed his head, returning the sentiment.

"And so delighted, Captain, to make your acquaintance again," she said to the captain, who bowed his head as well.

Grant insisted his butler escort Samantha back to the hotel. She waved goodbye to Violet and Betty. Before leaving, Samantha stopped to speak with Julia. "I am honored to be invited into your lovely home and appreciate your fine hospitality. The general appears relaxed and happy. I see your hand in this fine household. There is much to be admired. It has been a wonderful and memorable day."

Samantha wasn't faking it; she meant every word. Julia smiled, accepting Samantha's sincerity.

The butler escorted Samantha from the house, assisting her into the buggy, and drove her to the hotel. She thanked him and, in haste, gathered the skirt of her dress and jumped off the buggy, landing two feet solidly on the ground. She hurried into the hotel, to an isolated corner, struck the magic pose, took a deep breath, and returned to the present.

Donna Balon

The Fallout

Samantha awoke on the sofa in Philip's office. She flipped on the light switch, grabbed her tote bag, rummaged through it, and pulled out her handheld mirror.

Looking at herself, she thought, Thank goodness, I'm still young.

Then she retrieved her laptop and typed notes, recalling the entire conversation with Captain Carter, which was rich with novel insights. She reread her notes, then whispered, "Good trip, after all. Good trip."

She slipped out of her dress and into casual clothes. Then she turned on her cellphone. The home screen showed the time was 1:32 a.m.

Not too late, she thought.

Samantha's serenity evaporated when she checked her messages.

Aaron: *Call me as soon as you get this. Did you turn off your phone?*

John: *Are you home? I knocked and tried to open the door, but*

Sam Time

the key doesn't work.

Aaron: *Still waiting to hear from you. It's been hours. John went to the house and couldn't get in. They found your car in the library parking deck. Concerned. Hope you're okay.*

Aaron: *Where the hell are you?*

She was alarmed. Something was wrong. There were no messages from Grace. Had something happened to Grace? Her pregnancy was in the second trimester. Were Grace and the baby okay?

She called Aaron, who was still out of state on business. As she was waiting for him to answer the call, she looked out the window. Campus security vehicles were flashing their lights.

Samantha thought, Oh, this isn't good.

"Aaron, it's me."

"Oh, Sam, I'm so glad to hear from you. Are you okay?"

"Yes. I'm fine," she said emphatically.

"Where have you been? I've been worried."

"On campus. Anyway, what's the matter?"

"Grace was in an accident. She's in the hospital. She's okay, the baby's okay, but she's staying overnight for observation. We've been trying to find you."

"I'm in Professor Philip's office. Remember him? I ran into him the other day and told him I work late sometimes on my dissertation. He lent me a key to his office. He has a sofa."

"Your car is in the library parking deck."

"Yes, I told you I was going to the library. I was there and I was on a roll when they were closing, so I came up here to continue. Then I fell asleep."

"Well, you scared the hell out of us—again."

"I'm sorry, sweetie."

"Did you turn off your cellphone?"

"I guess I did by accident."

"Why don't you mute it or put it on airplane mode? At least I could track you in an emergency."

"I'm sorry. I was making progress and didn't want to stop. So what happened to Grace?"

"She was with her friends, coming back from a restaurant—"

"I knew she was out because I texted her."

"A guy ran a red light. She was in the back seat and wearing a seat belt, so she's okay."

"Is everyone else okay?"

"I think so. It was a residential street, so he wasn't going too fast. But there was an ambulance and the whole thing."

"I'll go to the hospital."

"Yes, John is there; Grace is asking for you."

Samantha cried, knowing Grace was asking for her sister.

"Sam, we have to talk later. I mean, this is crazy. When I couldn't get a hold of you, I asked John to go to our house. Then I thought maybe you went to the library, so I called campus security. Then they called me, and said they found your car in the parking deck. We've been looking for you for three hours. Worried sick!"

"I'm so sorry, sweetie. I was just so focused on my immersive research. This evening I came on some novel insights."

"Sam, this is not about your research. You know I support your work. But this is the second time you've disappeared. In the middle of the night. Your phone is off. And I don't know what to think."

"I'm sorry, sweetie, things have been erratic. But it's going to get better. Anyway, it may take me a while to get out of here. If I open the exterior doors, it will set off the alarm."

"That's just great." Aaron was annoyed. "Just get to the hospital as fast as you can. I'll call John, tell him you're on your way. He needs to get home. He has court in the morning."

"Okay. I have the phone number to the security guard station."

"We'll talk in the morning."

"Love you," Samantha said, but Aaron had already hung up.

Samantha called the security desk and explained the situation. She quickly rolled up her dress and packed it in her large tote. As she hustled to the front door and waited for security, she took the pins out of her hair, removed her hat, undid her braids, and then tied her hair into a ponytail. Security arrived, disabled the alarm, opened the doors, let Samantha out of the building, and then escorted her to the library parking deck. She apologized for the commotion. Ironically, the night crew seemed energized with something to do on an otherwise boring night.

WHEN SAMANTHA REACHED the hospital, she texted John: *I'm here. Can I see Grace?*

John texted: *Only 1 family member allowed. I'll come down.*

Samantha was standing in the hospital waiting room. John motioned for Samantha to come out to the parking lot.

They walked to several rows of empty parking spaces, where they could talk privately. "How is she?" Samantha asked.

"She's fine. She's sleeping. But she was asking for you."

"I was in the library, then went to a colleague's office—"

"I know. Aaron told me. Sam, I've been lying to Grace. I didn't want to upset her, not knowing where you were."

"I'm so sorry." Samantha had never seen John like this. She was upset both Aaron and John were angry with her.

"And Aaron calls and wants me to look for you. I leave my wife in the hospital to find you, and the key to your house doesn't work. Do you know we actually talked about me breaking a window to get into your house?"

"No, Aaron didn't tell me that."

"I checked your neighbor's pool, and you weren't there. Then Aaron remembered you said something about going to the library. So he called campus security. I guess you know the rest."

"I'll get you a new house key."

"Did you give us a bum key?"

"How could you say that?" She thought, I can't believe he figured it out.

"Because you play games, Sam. It's always fun and good. But this. I just have a sense—"

"Like a sixth sense."

"Whatever. I sense something is not right. We're family. We're friends." John moved his hand back and forth between Samantha and him. "So I care."

The streetlights in the parking lot cast their shadows. John's towered over Samantha's.

She defended herself. "Well, Aaron is away—"

John didn't let up. "Don't blame this on Aaron. He's really worried. I've never seen him like this."

"If I knew this was going to happen, I wouldn't have gone—"

"Sam, this is serious. Aaron's my friend. My best friend. And I look out for my friends. Aaron was really upset tonight. You need to know that."

Samantha knew he was right.

"Whatever you're doing, you have to stop."

"I'm working. Working on my doctorate. Nothing more. There's nothing else. Aaron's the one—"

"That's your answer, it's the doctorate."

"John, am I on the witness stand? But yes, I've worked hard on this dissertation. Day and night. And tonight was very productive."

Samantha paced. "Apparently tonight, I've gotten everyone upset." Then she raised one hand and said, "You know, the bad guy here is the guy who ran the red light, not me!"

John said, "I have to go. I have court tomorrow morning. Maybe my second chair can cover for me. I want to be here to take Grace home."

"I can do it, if you can't. I'll go up and be with Grace. Go home and get some sleep. I'll be with her. What's the room number?"

"Three thirty-five."

"Oh, did you call our parents?"

"No."

"Good, I'll speak with Grace. They don't need to know anything; it would only worry them."

John turned around and walked to his car. Samantha followed. "John," she called out to him. His stride was so long, she had run to keep up with him. Her ponytail swung back and forth as she ran. "John." He came to the car door and opened it. Samantha held the door open.

She said, "You're a good friend to Aaron. I'm glad you told me this, even if it hurts. You know I love Aaron. I would never want to hurt him."

"Well, he's hurting tonight."

Samantha took her hand off the car door. John shook his head, then got into the car, and slammed the door shut.

She stepped back and he drove away. A couple of streetlights placed several parking spaces apart cast two shadows of Samantha's body at right angles. Samantha looked down at the two opposing shadows and thought, I have to end my double life.

Grace was asleep when Samantha entered the room. She sat in the chair next to the bed.

She texted Aaron: *With Grace. She's sleeping. John left to get some sleep. I'll be here until he returns in the morning. I guess I really messed up tonight. Please forgive me. So sorry. Speak to you in morning. Love you.*

Aaron texted: *Let's talk early tomorrow.*

Samantha was too upset and didn't get much sleep sitting in the chair next to Grace's bed.

WHEN GRACE AWOKE in the early morning, she was happy to see Samantha. That the baby was unharmed was a relief to the expecting mother. Grace was the only one not angry with Samantha, who forced herself to act as if nothing was wrong. They chatted about fun things, the baby's room, the wedding.

When John arrived, he was cool to Samantha, and apparently, Grace didn't notice the tension between them. Samantha left the hospital and returned home. Then she gave Aaron a call.

"Hi, it's me. Is this a good time to talk?" Samantha began.

"Yes, I'm still at the condo, haven't left for the client's office yet."

"Sweetie, I'm so sorry about last night."

"Listen, Sam, I don't know."

"You don't know what? You're scaring me."

"Well, how does it feel?" Aaron snapped.

"I guess I deserve that. What do you mean, 'I don't know'?"

"It's been a roller coaster with you lately."

"But that's going away. You'll be back from this client assignment—"

"So it's my fault?"

"No, sweetie. I miss you. I love you. We're getting married in a couple of months."

Aaron was silent.

"Aaron, we're getting married in a couple of months." Samantha panicked.

He said, "I love you, I'm in love with you, and I want to marry you—"

"But, there's a 'but,'" Samantha said.

"But here we go again. And I know I'm at fault too, because of what I did when we were first together."

"Aaron, I told you, you're forgiven. It's buried. In the past."

"And why are you so magnanimous about that? It's as if, I messed up, now you can mess up. Because you sure did last night."

"No. I want to move forward and not look back."

"'Don't look back,' says the history professor!"

Samantha had no reply. There was silence; then she said, "I'm not keeping score. How many times do I have to say it. I love you and I'm so sorry."

"I wonder if you are keeping score. Like when I bought the coin set I wanted. You agreed to it, because you said someday you would want something. Is this how our relationship is going to be? I mess up, so this means you can mess up? That's not love."

Again, Samantha had no retort.

Aaron said, "You can say all you want, but it's your actions.

Last night you said you were thinking of going to the library. And I said I didn't like you going out to the campus that late. And you went anyway. Hey, you can do what you want, but you didn't consider how I felt. And then look at what happened. It's like you disappeared into thin air. How am I supposed to take that?"

"I promise you, it won't happen again. What do I have to do? Tell me. What do I have to do?"

"Maybe we should speak with a therapist at the clinic."

"We don't need to speak with anyone." Samantha thought, Oh God, not Dr. Nancy.

"See, see. You want me to marry you, but twice you've scared the hell out of me, not to mention you not telling me about your hand injury. You don't leave your cellphone on, so I don't know where you are. The wedding is a couple months away and I'm saying, 'What am I getting myself into?'"

Full-on panic consumed Samantha. "Okay, you want us to meet with a counselor or therapist, we will. But I think we can work this out on our own. When you come home tomorrow, we'll go to bed early—"

"Why do you always do that?"

"What?"

"Think that sex is the cure for everything."

"Because it works." Samantha answered.

"Not this time. You've always been this cute younger sister who can smile and charm her way out of things. Well, you can't rhyme your way out of this. Not this time. This is what I mean about the up-and-down roller coaster, the sweet cute Sam and then the disappearing, I-don't-know-where-she-is Sam."

"I thought you liked my resiliency."

Sam Time

"Of course I do. But this is too big of a low for you to rebound to where we were without something, some reassurance that—"

"That I'm not crazy," Samantha completed the sentence. Aaron was smart and Samantha had been asking herself the same question since she began time traveling.

Then Aaron said what Samantha feared: "Maybe we did rush into everything. Our relationship moved too fast."

Samantha teared up. "Don't say that."

She took a deep breath to compose herself. "Things did happen quickly because it was right; we're right together. I don't have any doubts."

There was silence. Aaron was having doubts.

Samantha said softly, "Listen, when you get home tomorrow, let's just reset. Pick up from here and I'll be good. We'll have a nice weekend together."

"Well, I've decided I'm going to work through the weekend."

"You're coming home, though. You'll work from home."

"No. No. I'm staying here and plow through all this work here."

Samantha was hysterical. "But if we have a problem, we should be together and work it out."

"I think it's better if I throw myself into this work. I'm upset. Angry. Disappointed. I need time to let some of this emotion pass. Then we can talk."

"But it will be twelve days without seeing you."

"You can work on your doctorate."

"Please, please come home. I want to fix this now. What about Sam time? Don't you want Sam time?"

"Sam, it's one weekend," Aaron countered.

"But you're going to marry me in two months. Say you're going to marry me in two months." She cried.

"I said, I'm angry and disappointed."

She suppressed the urge to beg, knowing she would look unattractive. Best she hold herself together and be strong. Resiliency, that's what he liked about her.

"Okay. Will you text me, like when you're leaving, when you're back at the condo? Things like that?"

"Sure."

"Okay. I'll do the same, so you know I'm here."

"Listen, I gotta go."

"Love you."

Aaron hung up without saying the same.

Samantha was distraught and replayed the conversation in her head over and over. She was most shaken Aaron wouldn't say he was marrying her. He said he was angry and disappointed. He'd have to get past that before affirming their matrimony.

She went out for a run, hoping the endorphins would alleviate her emotional pain. When she returned home, she wandered around the house aimlessly. Walking into her home office, she saw the history book on the desk. Aaron would be away this weekend. It would be convenient to time travel. She paced and contemplated her theory that the 1880 decade would be her final destination. Although her visit to Long Branch in 1881 was productive, she was still looking for another ghost, a third ghost. So despite her promises to Aaron, tonight she would make one last trip. Samantha was breaking bad.

Sam Time

July 1885
Saying Goodbye

This would be her final time-travel trip. But would the time-travel gods allow this visit? The dress fabric was labeled 1882 but Samantha desired to travel to 1885. She thought, There's one way to find out.

She opened her history book to July 1885, Saratoga County, New York, slipped on her powder-blue dress, and climbed into bed and fell asleep.

SAMANTHA AWOKE, having arrived in a narrow empty hall of the Balmoral Hotel, a three-story building with a first-floor wraparound porch and second-floor wraparound balcony. The hotel was full of people interested in seeing the famous resident down the road in Mount McGregor, New York. Grant had recently settled in the furnished home, which was owned by a friend who offered the Grant family free use of the house during the summer.

Since Samantha had last seen Grant four years ago, he'd had a reversal of fortune. Having invested all his money in a partnership that failed in what Samantha's contemporaries would recognize as a Ponzi scheme, the humiliated former president was virtually penniless and sustained living expenses through loans and charity of wealthy friends. He embarked on writing his memoirs, the sale of which would ultimately support his family. While writing feverishly, at age sixty-three, he was suffering from terminal throat cancer, which caused him fits of uncontrollable coughing and gagging.

This visit would be a delicate encounter. Most of his family was at the residence, so finding a moment alone would be tentative. Samantha didn't want to do anything that could trigger a choking episode. Although she wanted to see Grant, Samantha was sympathetic to Julia, the doting wife, who was screening all visitors to maintain the family's tranquility.

Samantha was nervous searching for a coach. She had enough money but would have to share a ride. A coach had just stopped, and the driver climbed down to assist ladies out of the carriage. Although deep in concentration, Samantha noticed the women walking away from the coach seemed to be looking at her and giggling.

After the driver helped the last lady descend from the coach, Samantha approached him. "I am Miss Samantha and would like to make a call at the Grant residence. I have this for the cost of the trip." Samantha held up a quarter.

"I am going past there. I have another stop. Then I'm going back to the carriage house in town."

"That would be convenient. The first stop at the Grant residence, then second stop in town at the carriage house. What's your name?"

Sam Time

"Matthew. Matthew Reilly."

Samantha gave Matthew the quarter, and he held her hand as she stepped onto the crate and into the coach.

Three ladies were sitting forward in the coach. Samantha sat in the empty seat facing the back.

As the coach drove away, Samantha stared out the window, contemplating how she would handle a potential awkward situation at the Grant house. She was distracted by the giggles of the three ladies sitting forward. What was so funny?

Samantha then noticed the fabric on the inside of the door. And the fabric on the inside walls and seats of the coach. It was her powder-blue dress fabric!

She looked down at her dress that blended in with the coach seat, exactly matching the coach interior. How embarrassing, Samantha thought. This would be hysterical if I weren't the one wearing the dress made of upholstery fabric.

Her embarrassment was short-lived. The three giggling ladies exited the coach only a short ride down the road. After they got out, Samantha moved to the forward-facing seat. She noticed a small plaque on the door: "Edgar and Son Carriage Company."

The coach stopped at the driveway of the Grant house. Matthew climbed down from the driver's box and assisted Samantha out of the carriage.

"Matthew, I will return in a few minutes."

"I'll be right here, Miss Samantha."

She made her way through groups of people staring at the house, and at Grant, who was sitting on the porch in a wicker chair, wearing a dark overcoat and suit, a white shirt with a thin black bow tie, and a silk top hat. The former president and revered general gained near-constant attention of photo journalists and well-wishers, so perhaps this was one reason for his wardrobe choice. Also, because of his illness, he had lost weight; the clothing hid his emaciated frame. The throat cancer manifested in an orange-sized tumor at the base of this neck, so he covered it with a dark scarf. He was alone on the porch, but when the coach pulled up to the house, Julia came out the front door.

Samantha walked quickly up the driveway, approached the porch, and appealed to Julia. "Mrs. Grant. I am Miss Samantha. You and the general were so kind to invite me to your Long Branch home. I would like only a few minutes with the general to bid my farewell, if you would be so kind."

Before Julia could reply—likely the answer would have been no—Grant moved the chair next to him, making a sound so the two women looked in his direction. He raised his arm and motioned with his hand to come and then placed his hand on the arm of the chair, signaling Samantha to come and sit.

Sitting with his legs crossed, Grant had been reading the newspaper. He took off his black-trimmed round glasses. His sideburns were untrimmed and fuller—perhaps to give the impression his face was not as gaunt as it was.

Samantha magnanimously said to Julia, "Thank you, Mrs. Grant. I will be only a few minutes."

She climbed the steps and walked toward Grant. His hand was still on the arm of the chair. There was a cane on the chair seat, and Samantha noticed Grant was wearing slippers. She assumed he shuffled onto the porch and into his chair unassisted. Samantha took the cane off the seat and leaned it against the front of the chair. Then she sat and turned toward Grant. Julia would still hear anything Samantha said. She placed her left hand on top of Grant's.

She said, "I know you're in pain and you cannot speak." Samantha's voice cracked. She tried to remain composed while looking into his blue eyes.

"I came to say it has been an honor knowing you."

He grabbed both of her hands. His fingers revealed how fragile he was. But he held Samantha's firmly.

"An honor." Then she mouthed, "Honor."

Tears fells down his cheeks, and he tightened his grip on her hands the best he could. She nodded, understanding what he was conveying.

"Godspeed," she whispered, tears falling from her eyes.

He let go of her hands and lifted his top hat off his head.

Samantha stood and walked quickly to Julia. "My prayers to you and your family." She wanted to run down the driveway, but it wouldn't have been proper. She looked back. Grant motioned for Julia to sit next to him. She did, and he held her hand while she sat sadly but contentedly next to the love of her life.

Matthew was waiting for Samantha. "As I said, Miss Samantha, I'll be goin' back to the carriage house. I'll stop and let you out before I pull in."

Samantha nodded, too distraught to say anything. Matthew held her hand as she stepped onto the crate and then into the carriage. The coach pulled away, and Samantha cried, looking out the window.

Matthew did as he said, and he helped Samantha out of the carriage.

"You have been so kind, Matthew. Have a good day."

"Good day to you, Miss Samantha." Matthew guided the horses and the carriage into the barnlike structure.

Samantha walked toward the small rural town center. A man came toward her, who was scowling and pointing at her. He resembled the Monopoly game board mascot. Short, round face, white mustache, black top hat, and a white vest covering his round belly.

"That's my fabric. That's mine. I had that special ordered," Mr. Monopoly said.

Samantha tried to ignore him.

"I had that special ordered for my carriages. The inside of my coaches. The fabric rolls where stolen from my stable."

"I bought this fabric from a reputable seller, and a dressmaker sewed this dress for me. I know nothing of what you say."

She lengthened her stride and noticed another short, young fellow walking quickly behind Mr. Monopoly. Young fellow pointed at Samantha. "She is a thief. She is the one who stole the fabric rolls."

From his appearance, Samantha thought this little teenage fellow was the "and Son" of the "Edgar and Son Carriage Company." Mr. Monopoly was Edgar.

"This is preposterous. This is my dress. I had it made and paid for it."

"Thief! Take her to the constable!" Young Fellow said.

They moved quickly toward Samantha to grab her. She picked up the dress skirt and made a dash for it, running as fast as she could.

With adrenalin pumping, she could outrun Mr. Monopoly and Little Fellow—if she were wearing running sneakers. But she was wearing her flat leather-laced shoes and could feel the laces becoming loose, having forgotten to double-tie them. Also time travel had advanced her age to sixty-plus. She was no longer the fit thirty-one-year-old who had the endurance to run five miles.

Her fear was intense and her heart was beating fast. She gained enough distance that she stopped and tied both her shoes in double knots and started running again.

She passed a few buildings and found an alley. She struck what she hoped was the magic pose.

It worked. She was back in her bed. Samantha's heart was still pounding. She took off the dress and hung it deep in the closet next to the other two. She vowed she could never wear the dresses or time travel again. Samantha loved Aaron and loved the twenty-first century.

Donna Balon

Third Ghost

Samantha awoke and texted Aaron: *Up, making coffee.* No return text from him.

While sipping coffee, she thought about the events of last night. She no longer liked her dresses, knowing the intended use was for horse-drawn coach interiors. And she didn't like Edgar and Son after they accused her of being a thief. But was this another piece of this time-traveling puzzle? It gnawed at her. Not merely curious, she needed to investigate.

The fabric is a key element to this mystery, Samantha thought. Call Mary Sanchez, the dressmaker.

Samantha asked Mary about the origin of the fabric. The dressmaker reiterated: the fabric was discovered during a neighbor's house renovation.

"You know I love the gowns. But I also like history. I'm a history professor, so I'm very curious about this fabric. I think it's fascinating that it is so well preserved for its age. It's a mystery. Would you check to see if there are any markings or labels that can tell us more about the fabric?"

"I'll check," Mary said.

"If you do find a label, would you take a picture and text it to me?"

"Yes, Miss Sam."

After ten minutes, Mary returned, saying she did find labels, previously not seen, on the inside cardboard rolls. "I'll take pictures and send them you."

"Thank you, Mary," Samantha said before disconnecting.

The photos showed the labels, "For Edgar and Son Carriage Company."

Samantha searched the Internet for newspapers in Saratoga County, the location of the carriage house. Perhaps there were articles in the 1880s about a theft of fabric rolls from the Edgar and Son Carriage Company.

The Internet archives of local New York newspapers, however, were sporadic because this supposed theft took place in a rural part of the state over one hundred years ago. Over several hours, Samantha placed many calls, believing there had to be a local historical society, a seasoned librarian, or a regional history buff who knew something. There was.

Walter Thompson, a regional historian, knew about the Edger and Son Carriage Company case. After several texts, Samantha and Walter arranged a time for a call.

Samantha told Walter she was a history professor, working on a doctorate, and she'd stumbled on this intriguing case.

Walter said, "That was a big case for the area, because the man accused of theft and his family were adamant he was innocent."

"What happened?"

"This carriage company had special fabric manufactured for the coach interiors."

Samantha was anxious listening to the story. The limited details she knew were consistent with Walter's version.

"There was a jury trial. The prosecutor claimed the defendant stole and then sold the fabric rolls. The evidence at the trial was the money found in the floorboards of this man's boardinghouse. They said the wages of this man were too meager compared to the large amount money in the floorboards."

"So what was the defense? Where did this floorboard money come from?" Samantha asked.

"The family said it was planted."

"Did they ever find the fabric rolls?"

"No."

"How could they convict on such little evidence?"

"Well the accused was a Black man, and the jury was all White."

Samantha asked, "So to make sure we're talking about the right case, this is the Edgar and Son Carriage Company, right?"

"Yes. That sounds familiar. And I remember the defendant's name: Matthew Reilly."

The story was even worse than Samantha imagined. It stung. The nice coach driver she met was convicted of this crime.

"Do the local papers ever revisit yesteryear stories? If there was new evidence found?" Samantha said.

"New evidence? It's been over a hundred years!"

"Yes, I know it sounds strange. But in my research, I discovered these fabric rolls labeled for that same carriage company. The fabric is well preserved, as are the labels. Do you know any reporters who may want to investigate this story?"

Sam Time

Walter called a good friend, a blogger, who was interested in writing a feature story. The blogger called and spoke with Samantha but never asked how she discovered the fabric rolls were stolen. Samantha had two requests: she remain anonymous, and the blogger email her when the story was published.

Donna Balon

Purgatory

Two days passed. Aaron had not called and spoken with Samantha. He sent only obligatory texts: one in the morning and one at night. But he hadn't called Samantha. She thought about texting him a limerick and multiple puns, but Aaron was clear she could not charm her way out of this. So she sent only several texts of her daily routines.

She was out-of-her-mind worried he would end their relationship. Although time travel and meeting Grant were extraordinary, it was the past. Aaron was her future.

Samantha texted Aaron: *It's been 2 days. Would love to hear your voice. Do you have time for a quick call?*

Within a half hour, her phone rang with Aaron's unique ring tone. Samantha grabbed the phone and said, "I want to hear your voice. Say something."

Aaron said, "I'd like a large pizza with pepperoni and sausage."

"Oh, please tell me you didn't dial the wrong number and wanted pizza instead of me."

Sam Time

"I'm teasing," he said.

"Well, in that case, it's funny. How are you?"

"Busy. Inundated."

"It would be nice if you called once a day. I miss you."

"Sam, I said to give me some space. I'm calling you now."

Samantha was crushed to hear this but tried to recover. "And I'm delighted to hear your voice. Everything is fine here. No news. Just holding down the fort. My written dissertation is almost complete. I've been reviewing it over and over. And I'm preparing for my orals."

"I'm glad to hear that. You've been working hard on it."

Then there was silence, so Samantha asked, "Is anyone in the room?"

"No, it's just me right now."

"Well, do you want me to do anything for you here? I'd like to do something for you. Is there anything you need or want?"

"No, I can't think of anything."

There was more silence; then she asked, "How long are you going to keep me in purgatory?"

"I want an explanation."

"I told you."

"I want a full explanation. We're not going to do it on the phone. We'll talk when I get home."

"Is your flight booked for Friday yet?"

"Yes. The flight lands around eleven p.m. They arranged a car service to pick me up. I won't be home until just before midnight."

"Why so late?"

"I want to work a full day here. Make sure I get everything done."

She felt like crying, but she tried her best to sound upbeat. "Well, I'll be in bed. Maybe even asleep. I'll leave some low dimmer lights on in the house, so you're not walking into things."

"Thanks."

Samantha said, "I'm wearing your green Henley."

"The olive one?"

"Yes."

"Sam, that's my favorite shirt. Can't you wear something else of mine that I don't like as much?"

"I'm holding it hostage. If you don't call me every day, you'll never see Henley again."

Aaron laughed. "You are cute. But it's not enough. After the other night, I'm just—uncertain."

"Don't say that."

"Your jokes still amuse me, but we're not going to skip over what happened the other night. It's unfair to me. I need to know what's going on with you. But we'll talk about it when I come home. All right?"

"Okay."

"So I'll call you every day. And talk to you tomorrow. Hey, no coffee stains on the shirt," Aaron said.

"I'll be careful. Love you."

"Love you too."

Samantha dissected the call. He said he loves me. Uncertain. He said he was uncertain. That could mean he loves me but can't live with me—won't marry me.

Although he joked a little, he was businesslike. Maybe that was because he was in a client's office. In general, there was little thawing in his demeanor. But he did call.

Sam Time

Samantha stared into space. He said he wanted a full explanation. If she told him everything, he might cancel the wedding.

How would she feel if Aaron was living a double life? If he said it was over, she would still marry him because she was so in love with him. Samantha could only hope he felt the same.

She played other scenarios in her head. She may have to confess to something, give some ground.

Aaron was right. Samantha should work on her doctorate, rather than waste the week. But she had trouble concentrating, recalling the happenings since Aaron began his out-of-state assignment. Visiting the mid-nineteenth century had given her perspective. Even with present-day struggles, her life seemed infinitely easier. Hadn't anyone noticed she had changed? She felt as if she had grown, matured. There would be no more tantrums, anticipating loneliness or loss. Because she could recognize and manage them. She had choices. Options. Today's option: speak with Philip.

She texted Philip: *Are you in your office? If so, may I stop by for a few minutes?*

Philip texted: *Sure. Here for a few hours.*

SAMANTHA ARRIVED at his office. "Is now a good time?"

"Sure. Sit down. Close the door."

"I'm giving back your key because my time traveling is over. I went back to New York State in 1885 and had another upsetting experience there."

Philip said, "Wait a second. Didn't you say the dress fabric was from 1882?"

"Yes."

"That doesn't make sense."

Samantha was firm. "I know time travel doesn't make sense. And I don't know why I was allowed to go to 1885. But it happened. And if you're trying to catch me in a lie to prove I'm making this up—I don't know what to say. You're the one who told me we can never know the ways of the universe. Anyway, I'm not in a good frame of mind now to go into everything."

"Is everything okay?"

"No. Thank you again for the key. It did work. They don't know about my disappearing act, but they couldn't find me. And I'm in the doghouse."

"I thought that only happened to men."

"Aaron is very upset with me. Painfully so. And my brother-in-law, who is Aaron's best friend, thinks I'm having an affair. It's a mess."

"What now?" Philip asked.

"Well, before I debrief with you, which I want to do, I have to sort things out with Aaron. But he's not back until this weekend.

"I gathered from these sessions that if this were some psychosomatic fantasy, as long as it didn't hurt anyone, maybe it was okay. But I think this was real, very real, and it is hurting my relationships. I was so concerned with the 'why' of time traveling, and the purpose. I didn't think it would interfere with my present-day life.

"I wanted it both ways. Past and present. And time traveling happened at night. Can I have some peace at night? Well, I did travel a lot. I was caught only twice, but it was enough to raise suspicion. I was living two lives, really. And everything was fine, but the other night, some idiot runs a red light, and hits a car my sister is in, and then they were looking for me."

Sam Time

"Is your sister okay?"

"Thank God, yes. She was in the back seat; she was wearing a safety belt; it was a secondary road; he wasn't speeding; he ran the light; and he hit the car on the opposite side of where Grace was sitting. She's pregnant, but she and the baby are okay. Grace doesn't know I was AWOL for a few hours; my brother-in-law was covering for me."

Samantha put her head in her hands. "I'm very scared Aaron is going to leave me. It's bad."

He then said, "I have to ask. Are you okay? I mean, do you have any thoughts about hurting yourself?"

"Philip, no. No!"

"I have to ask. You've come in here with these fanciful stories and you're down. You're handing in the key."

"Like I said, I went back to 1885. When I returned home, I tore off the dress I was wearing and stuck it in the back of the closet, thinking, I'll never wear it again. But then, the next night, I thought I'd try to go back, as a test. I've tried twice, and the dresses don't work anymore. Two nights I've gone to bed wearing one of the dresses, and I sleep through the night. And I'm glad it's over. So I don't need the key. But I'm not saying goodbye for good."

Philip persisted. "I've accommodated you. No notes, no discussions with colleagues about your case, a pledge that I would never write about it."

Samantha added, "And a key to your office."

"And a key to my office. These are red flags."

Now crying, Samantha picked up her tote bag off the floor and placed it on her lap. She took out a tissue and wiped her tears. She kept the tote bag on her lap and wrapped her arms around it. "I would never hurt myself. I have too much to live for. There's Grace, my parents, my grandparents, my friend Deanna. Deanna was my sorority sister, and I was boarding in her house when Aaron and I first met. And Aaron, even if he dumped me, he would be devastated."

"When is Aaron coming home?"

"Friday night, late."

"Well, you still have several days when you're alone, and I want to know if you have thoughts about hurting yourself."

Samantha cried, "My only thought is that Aaron is going to cancel the wedding and leave me. I'm really scared. I'm crazy in love with him."

She stopped, and then said, "Bad pun. But I'm not crazy enough to even think about ending—"

"Okay. But I want you to text me every day. Morning and night. No specific time. Just a short text."

Samantha held her tote bag tighter.

Philip added, "But if I don't hear from you, I will text you. And if you don't reply, I'm calling social services and I'm calling 911."

Samantha cried. "Okay. I'll text you every morning and night. But if I forget and you text me, give me time to get back to you. Just in case I'm in the shower or something. I don't want Aaron to come home and find out his fiancée is in a locked psych ward."

"Okay. If I haven't heard from you, I'll call. And if you want to talk at any time, call me. And here." He slid a business card across his desk to her.

She picked it up. The bold print displayed a suicide hotline phone number. She took a tissue to wipe her eyes and nose and held up the business card. "This is not me."

Sam Time

She sniffled and said, "But I understand your point. I'll text you twice a day, early and late. Through the weekend?"

"Through Sunday. Let me know how things are going with Aaron."

"Okay."

Samantha left Philip's office. She walked out of the building and flipped the business card into the first trash can she saw.

Donna Balon

Homecoming

Samantha dutifully texted Philip, as he'd requested. She toyed with the idea of joking: *Still here, haven't found any bridges high enough.* Philip, however, lacked any sense of humor and might misinterpret her jest. So she sent only bland texts, saying all was well. The night Aaron was flying home, Samantha sent a nighttime message to Philip: *Spoke to Aaron. He's at the Denver airport. So excited he's coming home. Good night.* She went to bed and fell asleep.

She awoke and looked at the clock on her nightstand: 11:57 p.m. She heard Aaron brushing his teeth. So happy her Aaron was home, she wanted to leap out of bed and hug him. To kiss him. But she had caused a rupture in their relationship, and she needed to temper her actions. She rolled over on her back with the blanket and sheets up to her neck. And she watched his shadow.

When Aaron came into the bedroom, he saw Samantha was awake. "I was trying to be quiet. I didn't mean to wake you."

"That's okay."

He turned off the light and climbed into bed onto his side facing Samantha, who rolled over to face Aaron. He kissed her forehead. "It was a long week. I'm exhausted." He closed his eyes and fell asleep.

Samantha lay on her side and stared at Aaron, taking pleasure in being near him and listening to him breathe. She fell asleep an hour later.

WHEN THEY AWOKE, daylight was streaming through the blinds. Samantha slipped out of bed, went to the bathroom, and returned to the bedroom naked, having taken off her T-shirt. Aaron watched as she slipped under the covers and rolled on her side to face him. Then he got up, went to the bathroom, and returned to the bedroom having shed his clothes.

He climbed into the bed under the covers, and Samantha didn't hesitate. This was the longest gap since they'd made love. It was quick and intense.

Afterward they lay face-to-face, still not having uttered any words. Why say anything when the day was beginning so well? Aaron stroked her thigh.

Then Samantha said, "Do you want waffles?"

"That sounds good."

She suggested, "Do you want to run first?"

"Yes. Run, then breakfast."

They dressed quietly in their running clothes. Samantha took her cellphone, and sent Philip a brief text: *Delighted Aaron is home. Things are normal, but haven't really talked yet.*

When they returned from running, Samantha made coffee

and waffles. They ate breakfast in silence, not talking but reading their electronic devices. When they were finished eating breakfast, Samantha closed her Kindle and closed Aaron's laptop.

"What?" Aaron asked.

With her hand still on his laptop she said, "What do I have to do? What do I have to do to win you back?"

Aaron took her by the hand, and led her to the sofa, where they sat facing each other. He then held both her wrists and said, "I want you to stop lying to me."

Samantha was stunned. Tears rolled down her face.

"There's a bunch of crazy stuff that's been going on with you, and it's weird; it doesn't make sense. And I can tell when you're not truthful. Your fingers flare out like a fan. You spread them as if you're tense. I noticed that in the grocery store when you were telling me about your hand injury and the night walking to George's pool. I dismissed it at first, but I know you, and you've been lying to me."

Apparently, Aaron knew the tell signs that Samantha observed in others.

Samantha shook her head and cried. "I want you to marry me. I can't. You won't want to marry me."

"Try me."

"Let's just go forward. I promise you I'll always keep my phone on. You can always reach me. There will be no mystery."

"Sam, that's not good enough. I need an explanation of what has been going on. We can't go forward unless you tell me the truth."

Samantha closed her eyes and cried harder. She had no choice. "There was this nice man."

With that, Aaron's eyes filled with tears.

"When John told us about the resort trip, and we agreed to go horseback riding, I went to this stable. And I met him there."

"Where?"

"There's lots of places here." Still mixing lies with the truth.

"And I hurt my hand that first day. He was nice, but we were friends, only friends."

Her fingers fanned out with tension. It was her tell. Aaron let go of her wrists and waited for Samantha to tell the truth. She looked down at her fanned-out fingers, now realizing why Aaron wanted to discuss this with her in person. He wanted to see her tell. And now he knew she was lying.

Samantha sobbed. "I went back to the stable one more time. It was only once."

"Once?"

"Once." She grabbed a nearby box of tissues, took one, and blew her nose.

"Oh, Sam." Aaron made a quarter turn on the sofa, so his side was facing her. He put his head in his hands. It was a crushing tell. His body language was moving away from Samantha.

Samantha took another tissue, wiping her face. "Just before our HIV tests. I was at the university, and some women wanted to take me for one last fling before the wedding. To go to the bar that had male strippers on Wednesday night. That planted something in my head, and I didn't go out. But at the horse stable, the second time I saw him, it happened." She sobbed and covered her face with her hands.

Aaron stood and was pacing back and forth. "So that's why you were so upset about our HIV scare. You thought you may have passed it to him."

Samantha didn't say anything, affirming Aaron was right.

He paced and shook his head. "I was home every weekend, and we made love every weekend. That was not enough?"

"I said I was tempted, and it was this bachelorette thing."

"Do you regret it?"

"I do now." She was stunned at her own veracity. "He was nice, sex is nice. You want me to be honest. But I always thought of you, every day when you were away. I always loved when you came back home. You're the one. It was one time. After that he left. He's gone. Gone." She waived her hand.

"The other night I was at the library—by myself. I was in Philip's office—by myself. That time when you came home a day early, I was at George's pool—by myself. I've been guilt ridden and have had trouble sleeping, so I work at night or, on some warm nights, I swim. That's the truth." She made sure to keep her hands in a fist, so a tell would not reveal her lies.

"So if he was still here?"

"We would just be friends. Friends."

"What's his name?"

"I'm not going there. I never asked you about your liaison woman. It's not going to do any good. I've confessed. That's hard enough. And it's never going to happen again."

She took another tissue, making an unladylike honk in blowing her nose. "I tell you, I promise you, it's done. Over. Never again. I can't lose you. You know how to make me laugh."

They sat for a while in silence, and then Aaron said, "This week while I was away, I was bracing myself for the news you just told me. It seemed like the only explanation. But to hear it is—" He didn't complete his sentence, but he didn't have to.

Samantha stopped crying. "So you expected what I would say.

Sam Time

This morning we made love, ran, had breakfast, and read the news. We weren't talking but we were doing normal things. You didn't even bring it up. I brought it up. You wanted everything to get back to normal. So you do want to marry me."

"Well, I don't know now."

Samantha became emboldened. "It hurts. I'm so sorry. But are you really going to throw away this great thing we have because of one incident?"

"It's a pretty big one."

"Let me remind you of your liaison."

"Oh, here we go. Now we're even. I remind you that my one-night fling was two months after we met. I'm finding this out two months before our wedding. Not a good start."

"You know me, Aaron. I'm still the same person you fell in love with. Are you really going to end this? That—would be nuts."

Aaron flopped back down on the sofa a couple feet away from Samantha. He lifted his feet onto the ottoman, laid his head back, and stared at the ceiling.

Samantha pleaded, "We bought this house together. Our life has already begun. Our families are wonderful, Grace and John are around the corner. We can still have a great life together. Have kids, live happily. I'm so sorry about this. I know you have to process all this. But forgive me. Please forgive me. I promise you, you'll have no regrets. I promise I will give you no reason to doubt me ever again."

Neither said anything for a few minutes. She let Aaron absorb what she had said. Then she made one final pitch. "I want to use my Monopoly card. My one get-out-of-jail-free card. I'll call it my Monogamy card. This was one time only. I promise."

Still staring at the ceiling, Aaron said, "I was scared you were going to tell me what you did—or at least some version of it. The short of it is, I love you too much not to forgive you."

Samantha sighed in relief, moved closer to Aaron on the sofa, and rested her head on the top of the back cushion. They let the silence linger.

Aaron said, "On the flight home, I knew whatever you were going to tell me, I wanted us to be together. But I wanted you to be honest with me."

Samantha placed her hand on his. He didn't move his away.

"Please marry me," Samantha said.

"Sam, I want to marry you."

"You're going to marry me?"

"I'm going to marry you."

Samantha snuggled against Aaron and sighed in relief. "I love you. I love you, Aaron."

"I love you too. It's not good for us to be apart. I worked straight through this past week, so I'm done. I don't have to go back to Denver."

"You should have led with that. My Aaron is home for good."

"Also, a client here in Austin called me. They're looking for a CFO. I'm going to interview for the job. That would mean no traveling, or very little, if I'm working for a company here. No long lonely stints."

"That would make me happy."

They embraced for a while. Then Aaron said, "I got something for you."

"You did?"

"Stay here. I'll be back."

When Aaron returned, he handed Samantha a picture book of

Sam Time

horses, which included the history of horses. As Samantha paged through the book, Aaron said, "It was twelve long days without you. I missed you. I missed us. One day, I took a break, and there was this street fair. I saw this book and thought of you. It reminded me of that day at the resort, when you stunned us with your horseback riding. You were so happy—and hot!"

They laughed.

Aaron said, "Remember when I first told you about the Denver assignment? I said maybe we should get a pet."

"Yes, but Mom is allergic, and I want my parents to stay with us when they visit."

"Sam, if we did have a dog or a cat, you probably would not have gone to the library that night. You would have had company. Anyway, toward the back of the book, there's a chapter about how animals help with the loneliness of their human companions. And horseback riding is therapeutic."

Samantha hugged the book.

"When I bought the book, I thought you should find a stable, group, or club. If we can't have a house pet, it may help, if you continued to ride. I'll learn to horseback ride too. At a different stable than the one—"

"Aaron, it's over. I'll never see that man again. I love the book. I love that you thought of how to ease my loneliness. I love that you want to learn to ride. Then we can ride together."

They kissed. Then Samantha said, "I have a few chores to do."

"Yes, I want to see John."

"About John."

"What?"

Samantha said, "He's not happy with me. That night when

Grace was in the hospital, we met in the parking lot and he spoke frankly. He said you were upset and that made him upset. Basically, he said I needed to get my act together. I don't blame him. He's a good friend to you—and me. I'm not angry with him. But you'll need to say we're okay, and he'll warm up to me again."

"Okay."

"And the key we gave them to the house no longer works. So we need to give them a new one. I'll go to the hardware store, have a few keys made. You can check emails and take a shower. I'll take one now. Will you text John?"

"Yes."

When Samantha was at the hardware store, she texted Philip: *Aaron and I fought, then made up. Wedding in 2 months. Would like to meet this coming week. Do you have 1 hour on Monday?*

Philip texted her a time on Monday for them to meet.

LATER SAMANTHA AND AARON walked to Grace and John's house. The expecting couple was excited about becoming parents and showed Samantha and Aaron the baby's finished room. Then the guys went outside while the sisters stayed inside.

Grace showed Samantha the tailored matron of honor gown, then asked, "So is your bridal gown ready?"

"No."

"Sam, the wedding is in two months!"

"I know, but the dressmaker, Mary, says I have plenty of time. She said often brides-to-be want their gowns completed months before the wedding. The brides either gain or lose weight, and she needs to alter the gowns."

"Mary the sage."

Sam Time

Samantha asked, "What do you mean, 'the sage'?"

"Mary has this sixth sense. My friends who go to her shop all have stories. For a long time, I thought they were exaggerating, but then it happened to me."

Samantha looked quizzically at her sister.

"Early in the fall, I bought this dress. Thought it would be nice for John's firm's Christmas party. So I went to Mary to have it hemmed and taken in at the waist. And she says to me, 'I see you have happy news.' I didn't know what she meant, so I just smiled. Then she says I shouldn't have the sides taken in. I was insulted. But a week later, I went to the doctor and found out I was pregnant. Sam, she knew about my pregnancy before I did! And by Christmastime, I was showing, and the dress fit perfectly."

"Grace, that's a one-off story. A lucky guess."

"No, Sam. There are others. Like I said. My friends have stories too. Karen said she went to Mary's shop to pick up an ensemble. She was in a hurry to leave, but Mary insisted Karen try on the outfit. Well, there was a bad car accident a few miles away. Karen says had she left the shop without trying on the outfit, she would have been in the accident. Then Lisa said she had a dress altered by Mary. The first time she wore the dress, she met her husband. There's more, but I can't think of them right now.

"I spoke with Elizabeth; she's been here in Austin all of her life. She said Mary's husband is Mexican. But Mary's family is Native American and her family are descendants of a well-respected chief."

Samantha thought, Is this another piece to the puzzle?

Then she said, "I thought I knew what I wanted for a bridal gown—altering Mom's gown for me. But Mary made the matron of honor gown first. It's as if she knew. Then she made the two other gowns—I didn't want you to think I was crazy—but I wore those dresses while I was at home researching and it was illuminating. Now my dissertation is done. And over the past several months, my thoughts about the bridal gown and the veil have evolved. I no longer want a period piece or Victorian-style gown. I want to stay strictly in the present; I want a contemporary gown."

She covered her mouth with her hand, thinking everything she had heard in the last few minutes. There were so many mysteries. One that had nagged at Samantha was the fabric weight; the dress was made of upholstery fabric. Mary knew fabrics and must have known the fabric weight was suitable for furniture. But she made the gowns anyway. The dresses were pretty, and the fabric with the lining was comfortable. So if Mary had some sixth sense—well, it worked, and Samantha time-traveled.

She shook her head to snap out of her pensiveness and said, "That reminds me, I need to text Mary for an appointment on Monday to finish the bridal gown alterations."

Samantha fell silent again. The near-fracture in her relationship with Aaron weighed on her. She forced a smile, while pretending to listen to everything her sister was saying. Grace insisted Samantha touch her stomach to feel the baby kick.

Looking out the window, Samantha could see Aaron and John. If only she knew how to lip-read. Perhaps she was better off not knowing. Then she assumed what was being said. John's suspicion of Samantha's infidelity was confirmed. But Aaron also admitted to his cheating early in his relationship with Samantha. They were, however, a committed couple soon to marry.

When the guys came back in, they sat next to their mates on the sectional sofa. Samantha and Aaron held hands.

Sam Time

Grace said, "I heard the guy who ran the light and hit us had a a heart attack. He's a middle-aged man. He's fine. The prosecutor isn't going to press any charges."

John mercifully changed the subject, while Samantha's mind wandered. *That's just great. This guy has a medical problem based on a lifetime of bad choices or a congenital defect. And it manifests in a heart attack at the exact same time the car my sister is in crosses the intersection. Now I'm in this hot mess, and Philip has me on virtual suicide watch. Philip is right, of course. I'll never understand the ways of the universe.*

Grace interrupted Samantha's thoughts. "Sam, you're so quiet."

"In eight weeks, I'm going to marry this wonderful man" was Samantha's non sequitur. She was humiliated the guys knew the real reason for her silence. She looked down, not making eye contact with anyone.

Grace said, "What's the matter, Sam? No rhymes?"

Samantha replied, "I'm rhymed out."

Grace persisted. "It's unusual for you to be this quiet."

Aaron and John weren't going to rescue Samantha with a diversion from her sister's queries. How should Samantha respond? If she made something up, Aaron and John would know it was a lie, and she would lose her fragile credibility. She couldn't make a joke of things; the guys would find it disingenuous. And no one wanted to upset pregnant Grace with the news of Samantha's infidelity.

Samantha surrendered. "I'm remorseful. We had our first fight. It was my fault."

She paused and punctuated, "All. My. Fault."

She took a deep breath, tilted her head on Aaron's shoulder, and said, "But he's such a great guy, he still likes me."

Aaron kissed Samantha on the forehead. She asked him, "Are you ready?"

As they were leaving, Samantha and John hugged awkwardly. While Samantha and Aaron held hands walking home, she said, "I'm sorry if I cut our stay short. Did you want to stay longer?"

"I have a bunch of work emails. Also John had work too. He was taking a break. Besides it will be nice to spend a quiet day at home."

"I wasn't going to be good company. I'm still shaken by this past week and this morning."

"I know. Me too."

Together they unclasped their hands and walked arm in arm.

THE REST OF THE AFTERNOON and evening was subdued. That night, when they went to bed, Samantha lay on her side facing the edge of the mattress. Aaron put his hands on her waist and slid her along the sheets close to him. She giggled, adjusting her pillow under her head. Aaron laid his arm over hers and they clasped hands. Samantha thought, There's no place like home—in Aaron's arms.

ON SUNDAY MORNING Aaron walked into Samantha's home office and asked, "Do you want to go to New York City?

"Why would I want to go to New York?" Samantha countered while still looking at her computer screen.

"Because I'm going."

She turned around. "Why?"

"The deal is pricing this week. The company is launching its IPO on Wednesday on the stock exchange in New York. And I'm invited to the after-party, with the partner, and our spouses are also invited."

"They would pay for my flight too?"

"Yes, it's been a long haul, and our firm knows we've been away from our families. They'll pay for our flights and the hotel. We would leave on Tuesday. Have dinner with the partner and his wife in the evening. Probably at a nice restaurant in the city. The next day, I'll have meetings; you could tour. At night there's a party; you can come. And we leave on Thursday."

"It's so soon. But I could swing it. Maybe I can ask Deanna to meet me in the city."

"Come with me, Sam. We'll be in the same bed. It will be a little business, a little pleasure. It would be good for us."

Samantha stood, wrapped her arms around Aaron's neck, kissed him, and said, "Grace is very pregnant now. I'm sure she'll let me borrow some nice outfits for the evenings."

Moments later Samantha called Grace and told her the news. Grace was delighted to hear her sister in good spirits again and told Samantha to come over to borrow clothes for the trip.

ON MONDAY Samantha met with Philip in his office as they'd agreed. Unlike her last visit, she entered in a cheery mood. Then she summarized her final time-travel trips and weekend.

Philip raised his eyebrows as she talked about the Edgar and Son Carriage Company case. She concluded, "I kept wondering why I was time traveling. Maybe this is another reason."

Samantha shook her head. "It's certainly a circuitous route to get there. But I have a trilogy: your relative, my parental great-great-great-grandfather, and Matthew Reilly. And Grant's whereabouts triangulated these discoveries. And my dissertation is complete.

"I am glad this whole time-traveling thing is over. It was

fascinating but disruptive. I'll stop by to say hi. But say goodbye to my case. And close the book on it."

He had no comment and remained silent.

"Philip, say something. Please say something."

"I'm pleased your relationship with Aaron is intact, and your situation has stabilized. I'm still here if you ever need to talk."

"And about my case?"

"It has been the most intriguing case I've never had. I'll leave it at that."

Although she was grateful for their sessions together, Samantha was disappointed, but not surprised, she had not convinced Philip her story was real. She thought, He still thinks I'm a loony who conjured up this fantasy to cope with my loneliness.

When she returned home, she placed the three Victorian dresses in long zippered garment bags. Then she hung them deep in the guest room closet. She wasn't even sure why she was keeping them. Should she give them away? Would their once-magic powers be transferred to another owner? Rather than contemplating the answers, she shoved them in the back of the closet. She'd keep them hidden, as her secret.

Sam Time

New York Resolution

Despite the hassles of flying, Samantha and Aaron enjoyed being together on the flight to New York City. After checking into a Manhattan hotel, they dined with another couple. Then they returned to the hotel, christened the sheets, and watched free hotel streaming into the early morning.

The next day Aaron attended meetings, while Samantha met Deanna to see some city sights. Samantha dressed in a V-neck lavender-colored T-shirt, jeans, and lace-up shoes with a travel cross-body handbag. She borrowed Grace's black leather car coat. As usual, she styled her hair in a single, centered, back-of-the-head French braid.

Although it is not a popular tourist attraction, Samantha wanted to visit Grant's Tomb on Riverside Drive. Deanna agreed it would be their first stop. A wide stone path led to the stairs of the granite and marble-stone square building topped with a round dome.

Deanna remained on the main level with a tour guide, who referred to the site under its official name, the General Grant

National Memorial. Meanwhile Samantha scurried to the lower level to view close-up the tombs of Ulysses and Julia. After making sure she was alone, she said, "Good day, General Grant. It's Miss Samantha. The real Samantha Hunter."

She felt self-conscious. "I'm in New York with Aaron Parker, my fiancé. We'll marry in a couple of months. So I'm not a lost cause.

"I'm sorry for all the lies, the deception. But if I wanted to seize the opportunity, it was the only way. I hope you understand. Please forgive me. I've been saying that a lot lately."

She turned to both sides to make sure no one was watching her. She could hear the tour guide on the upper level.

"I loved you, my friend. But I guess you know that. If what Professor Philip says is true, death is total knowledge. So the irony is, now you know more than me.

"My dissertation is complete, with your help. Thank you for all the knowledge you imparted. I so enjoyed our conversations. I hope you did too."

She took a deep breath. "As I said to you when I saw you last, in your final days, it was so wonderful, such an honor to have met you. Thank you again for letting me into your world."

Closing her eyes, she whispered, "And maybe if it is true, if there *is* something else, we will meet again."

She walked away, ascended the stairs and met Deanna on the main level. Once outside, they sat on the mosaic benches.

Samantha said, "I researched Grant a lot. I think I know him. This resting place is over-the-top and conflicts with his modest Methodist sensibilities.

"The interior of this memorial is a smaller version of Napoleon's mausoleum at Les Invalides in Paris. Grant disliked Napoleon and refused to visit his tomb when Grant was in Paris. I believe Grant coveted being a father, a husband, and a general. And he wanted to be buried at West Point, but the academy wouldn't allow his wife to lie next to him on her death.

"This is what Grant's family and fellow citizens wanted for him. It was the Gilded Age, and the fashion was to go big and bold."

Samantha looked at Deanna and said, "Sorry, I'm going on."

Deanna replied, "No. I'm fascinated at your depth of knowledge. You're so passionate. Coming here and listening to you, I feel as if I'm transported back in time."

THAT EVENING, Samantha dressed in an above-the-knee, black V-neck knit dress topped with Grace's leather coat. She wore two-inch wedge heels with ankle-strap shoes, and a mini cross-body handbag hung on her shoulder. Her thick wavy, hair fell down to the middle of her back, and she styled a lace braid from her side part to the opposite ear to keep her long bangs secured and out of her face. Aaron wore a navy sports jacket over a light-blue long-sleeve button-down shirt with khaki pants and laced black shoes.

Samantha was at Aaron's side the entire evening. Much of the conversation was business related. Samantha understood little of what was being said, but she enjoyed watching her fiancé converse with others.

At one point during the evening, he put his palm on her back and said, "Are you okay?"

She replied, "I'm with you. I'm great."

Aaron rubbed her back and smiled.

After a few hours, they left the party to roam the city streets.

Samantha said, "I've been so consumed with my immersive research of the nineteenth century for my dissertation, I feel as if I've been living it. Let's go to Times Square. I know it's crowded, tacky, and loud. It's far away from the Victorian life I've been consumed with while writing my dissertation. I want to bathe in twenty-first-century LED lights."

They walked arm in arm under the flashing signs and billboards. Samantha looked up at the white, blue, red, and green lighting flashing on her—symbolically washing away her life in the distant past.

A month after Samantha first contacted a blogger to investigate the theft of the fabric rolls from the carriage company, an article was published in a local paper and then syndicated throughout the country.

> *Saratoga County, N.Y. Matthew Reilly was convicted of theft in a jury trial and sentenced to seven years in prison. Three months into his sentence, Matthew died of an untreated illness. His family and ancestors mourned his death. After over 150 years, his ancestors are searching for justice.*
>
> *In 1882 the Edgar and Son Carriage Company sought to distinguish itself from other companies with its custom fabric coach interiors. Oliver Edgar and his son, Nathan, sought a trademark look by designing fabrics the customers would fancy during coach rides.*
>
> *Large quantities of yardage were ordered and*

manufactured in a mill outside of Atlanta, Georgia. Cotton fabric was used for the walls and the seating interior.

In 1885 three fabric rolls disappeared from the stable office. A year later Matthew Reilly, a coach driver, was accused of the theft. The fabric rolls were never found, but over $200 was found under the floorboards of the Reilly residence. The amount was a large sum for a coach driver on a salary of $5/week.

Nathan Edgar was one of two witnesses the prosecution called to the witness stand. He testified Reilly had access to the office, that he saw him enter the office, then leave on his wagon, which was filled with something that looked bulky and covered with a large burlap cloth.

The constable was the other prosecution witness, who testified to finding the money in Reilly's home.

Reilly took the stand in his own defense, but the jury convicted after one hour of deliberation. The defendant was a Black man, and all the jurors were White men.

The Reilly family said the conviction was a gross injustice. During the selection of the jury, four Black men were eliminated from jury selection at the request of the prosecution. The judge was a cousin of Oliver Edgar and should have recused himself. In addition, the judge ruled exculpatory evidence was not allowed: the Reilly family did not have a wagon or access to a wagon. Reilly's case was on appeal when he died in prison.

Reilly predeceased his wife, Evelyn, and their four children. The pain of his conviction and death was felt throughout succeeding generations. New evidence has now emerged giving the Reilly descendants consolation.

Over 1,800 miles away in a suburb of Austin, Texas, Mary Sanchez, a dressmaker, unwittingly discovered the missing fabric rolls.

"My neighbor was renovating her house. When they knocked down a thick interior plaster wall, three fabric rolls were discovered that were covered in burlap. The fabric was this beautiful cotton in three colors. They knew I was a dressmaker, so they sold the fabric rolls to me.

"The tags attached to each roll, which were clearly visible, showed the year 1882. We were surprised it was in such good condition.

"A customer was looking for bridesmaids dresses, so I made three gowns for her, one from each of the fabric rolls."

The customer is a high school history teacher who was curious about the origin of the fabric. After asking questions, Mary discovered inside labels showing "Edgar and Son Carriage Company." The history teacher searched the Internet for Saratoga historical societies, making the connection between this fabric and the Matthew Reilly case.

This investigative journalist dug further into the property records of the Austin house and ancestors of the Edgars. The discovery was stunning.

Milton Edgar, a great-great-great-grandson of Nathan Edgar, lives in Danbury, Connecticut, and tells a family secret. Nathan Edgar, who testified in the Reilly trial, died in 1953. Knowing of his imminent demise, he made a deathbed confession.

Nathan Edgar's scheme was to take the fabric rolls and sell them for his own profit, so he could quit the family business and move out West. He had been pilfering other items from the Edgar family home. The fabric rolls were in storage for a while, and there were multiple rolls of the same design and colors. So Nathan thought his father would not notice three fabric rolls were missing, like so many other items in the house.

When the father, Oliver, discovered the fabric rolls were missing, Nathan spun a tale about the coach driver Matthew Reilly. On his deathbed, however, Nathan admitted to lying during his testimony and completely fabricating the story of Matthew stealing the fabric rolls. Nathan stole money from the company safe and planted it under the floorboards of the Reilly house.

Nathan did quit the business and moved to a suburb of Austin. He held on to the fabric rolls with the intention of selling them as originally planned. But the Reilly family kept the story of the unjust conviction alive for many years. Nathan was haunted that if he sold the fabric rolls, he would be caught.

In hiding the fabric in an interior wall, Nathan consulted with a museum curator to learn the best way to protect the fabric, in case he ever had the courage to sell the fabric rolls. After many years, the hidden fabric was forgotten, and the house was later sold.

Milton Edgar said his great-great-great-grandfather wanted the family to keep his confession secret. Milton feels it's time the truth be known.

Tammy Smith, the great-great-great-granddaughter of Matthew Reilly, sought remediation for the injustice of her beloved ancestor. But the statute of limitations barred restitution. In a GoFundMe campaign, however, family friends raised over $500,000 for Ms. Smith and her heirs.

Samantha's secret remained safe; she was referred to as "a high school history teacher"—not as a history professor. Moreover, the Reilly story gave resolution to the purpose of her time travel.

Sam Time

Time Passes

The weekday morning was typical. Samantha dressed in a short khaki-colored double-breasted jacket with a matching above-the-knee-length skort. As the coffee was brewing, she placed on the table a bowl of fresh blueberries, a pitcher of milk, four bowls of cereal with spoons, and two plastic cups filled cranberry juice. Then she hustled eight-year-old Alex and six-year-old Jill out of bed and into their school clothes.

One-by-one the family took their places at the kitchen table. The table seating arrangements had been fixed since the kids were born. Samantha and Aaron sat across from each other so both children were in arm's reach should a necessity arise. Neither parent noticed Jill had placed her juice cup near the table's edge.

Samantha stood to get more coffee at the same time Jill swung her arm hitting her cup propelling it off the table. The cup hit Samantha's midriff, splattering cranberry juice, leaving a large Rorschach inkblot on her jacket.

Samantha gasped. Jill froze in fear she was in trouble, while

Alex snickered with his father.

Samantha padded her daughter's arm. "Sweetie, it's okay. It was an accident. It's okay." She grabbed a sponge and paper towels to clean up the little bit of red juice that had not splashed on her clothes. Then she filled Jill's plastic cup with more cranberry juice. Placing the cup away from the table's edge, she said, "You still need to drink your juice." Then she looked at Aaron. "Watch so nothing else becomes a projectile. I need to change." She unbuttoned her soiled jacket and walked out of the kitchen.

Alex asked his father, "What's a projectile?"

"Something that flies through the air."

"Cool."

Aaron tousled Alex's hair.

When Samantha returned to the kitchen, she was wearing her white terry cloth bathrobe with the waist belt tied. The kids had finished their cereal. Samantha took the bowls off the table. Jill's cup was still full of juice.

"Jill, drink your juice."

Samantha turned around to rinse off the dishes. While she wasn't looking, Aaron picked up Jill's cup of juice, took a few gulps and then placed the empty cup in front of her. Alex snickered.

After putting the dishes in the dishwasher, Samantha saw Jill's cup was empty.

"Jill, show me your tongue."

Too young to know why, Jill complied.

It isn't stained red, Samantha thought.

"Aaron, show me your tongue," Samantha demanded.

"No!"

Alex giggled.

Sam Time

"Guilty," Samantha said, pointing to Aaron.

"Okay, Alex and Jill, brush your teeth." The kids left the table and headed for the bathroom.

Samantha said to Aaron, "You said you had an early meeting, but can you take the kids to school?"

"Yes, I can push back the meeting. I don't mind taking the kids. You always want to do it."

"I know. Not today. I have a few things to do before I leave, and I need to find something to wear. Some of my good clothes are at the drycleaners. Mary Sanchez is altering a few new ensembles. I don't see anything I like in my closet for today's lecture. American History 101 with eighty students. Most are freshman. My lectures are performances. I need to entertain them to keep their attention."

"Sam, I'll drive the kids to school. No problem."

"Maybe there's something in the off-season closets." Samantha walked into the guest room and opened the closet doors thinking, Mary Sanchez, performance.

Aaron and the kids, with their backpacks, were assembled in the kitchen, ready to leave. Samantha came into the kitchen, and Jill was the first to notice her mother. "Mommy, you look so pretty."

Aaron said, "What's this? Halloween?"

Samantha was wearing the powder-blue Victorian dress. Even after having two children, Samantha maintained her svelte figure and still fit into it. She styled her hair in a double-braided crown, topping it with the braided halo hat.

"Today's lecture is about the Civil War. Pretty serious stuff. Maybe I can entertain with this period-piece dress.

"Little Lady, come to Mommy." Samantha opened her arms to her daughter, who was still tearful over the juice-cup accident.

"Sweetie, Mommy loves you. It was an accident." She hugged Jill. "When you come home this afternoon, I want to know what you learned in school today." Then she turned to Alex and hugged him. "Okay, little guy. And I want to know what you learn today."

He said, "I learned what a projectile is. Best breakfast ever!"

Samantha looked at Aaron, then back at Alex. "Well, I'm glad you were entertained—at my expense."

She kissed Aaron on the lips. They walked into the garage. Samantha helped the kids into the back seat of the car and made sure they were buckled in safely.

Aaron reversed the car out into the street. The kids waved at their mother, who waved back. A next-door neighbor was outside and looked at Samantha as if to say, "What's with the Victorian dress?" Self-conscious and not wanting to give an elaborate explanation, Samantha said, "Auditioning for community theater. *Annie Get Your Gun.*"

SAMANTHA ARRIVED in the university lecture hall at the start of class. The students giggled when they saw their professor wearing a Victorian dress. Samantha grabbed the mini microphone, clipped it onto the bodice of the dress, and slipped the receiver into one of the deep dress pockets.

She turned on the microphone and stood in front of the podium, waiting for absolute silence. "Do you ever have one of those days when you search your closet and you have nothing to wear?"

The students laughed.

"So in my walk-in closet, the oldest clothes are in the back. And I thought, maybe there was something I hadn't worn in ten, fifteen years that I could wear today. Apparently, my closet is deeper than

I thought, because this dress is a hundred and fifty years old. How fitting." She paused to emphasize the pun. "Because today's lecture talk is about the Civil War."

A few students sniggered, but she had everyone's attention. She began the lecture and felt in character, speaking as both a professor and someone who had been there. The dress brought out her passion for that period of history, and it seemed to resonate with the students. At the end of the class the students applauded. And Samantha bowed.

THAT NIGHT Samantha and Aaron snuggled together in bed, turning on their sides face-to-face in the center of the mattress. His bare feet touched her socked cat feet. As parents, they didn't have much time to talk during the day. Many nights, they caught up on the day's events at bedtime.

Stroking Samantha's arm, Aaron asked, "How was your lecture?"

"I think it went well. No one fell asleep. Not many students looking at their cellphones. They asked questions, more than usual. I think they liked the dress. When class was over, they applauded."

She sighed then said, "I had forgotten about those dresses. After class when I came home, I left a message with the community theater. They got back to me, and they'll take the dresses."

She paused then said, "It brought back memories. Wearing the dress. The time we had that big fight before our wedding."

Aaron stopped stroking her arm and put his hand on her shoulder.

She continued, "I begged you to forgive me. And I promised you I wouldn't give you any reason to doubt me."

If she had something more to say, Aaron had heard enough and said, "Samantha was better than her word. She did it all, and infinitely more."

Samantha smiled. "You're quoting Charles Dickens from *A Christmas Carol* and attributing it to me."

He whispered, "Yes, I know you like that story. I know it well too. And it fits. We're coming up on our ten-year wedding anniversary. Since then, you're family-centric. You're a nurturing mother. You keep me happy—and satisfied."

They laughed.

"You're still spunky and fun. You look great. You even still fit into that dress. The years together have been fantastic."

Samantha turned around so they were spooning. Aaron's arm was around her waist, and she laid her hand on his.

"I love you, Aaron."

"Love you too."

Aaron said, "Will you promise me something?"

"For you, Aaron, anything."

"Promise me you'll never mention that fight again. Keep it buried in the past."

"I promise, happily."

THE YEAR OF THEIR tenth wedding anniversary, Samantha and Aaron vacationed with their children in New Jersey. It was economical, because Samantha's friend Deanna invited them to stay at her house in Atlantic Highlands.

The last day of their vacation, Samantha received a text from a colleague. That morning Philip Hastings had passed away in his sleep. Although shocked and saddened, Samantha determined she

Sam Time

would enjoy the rest of the family vacation and grieve when they returned home to Austin.

The family went to Long Branch wearing T-shirts and long shorts. Hats for all, baseball caps for the boys, a straw wide-brim hat for Samantha, and a white cloth hat for Jill. Samantha and Aaron also wore sunglasses.

The warm, sunny day was a few days before Memorial Day weekend, the official start of the summer season when the beaches would open with lifeguards and charge admission. This weekday before the summer crowds, Samantha, Aaron, and the kids took off their shoes and walked onto the beach sand and to the water's edge.

Since the children were born, Samantha and Aaron had not been as touchy, because they were typically holding a baby, the hand of a toddler, or now a grade-school child. But today, as the kids ran around up to their ankles in the swash, Aaron stood behind Samantha and wrapped his arms around her, kissing her neck.

In her joy, Samantha's mind wandered to the last time she was in Long Branch. It was 1881, and she waded in the water up to her ankles.

The Grant house, which was built in 1866, stood for nearly a century before it was demolished. A local historical society was unsuccessful in raising federal funds to preserve the failing structure. The oceanfront property remained poignantly empty.

All the hotels Samantha had seen in 1881 were gone. Many were destroyed in fires or nor'easter storms. And there was no longer a bluff overlooking the ocean.

In the afternoon, they walked around in the nearby town of Freehold in the historic district. On a lonely side street, Aaron spotted a storefront promoting Civil War and industrial era illustrations and photos. "Hey, Sam, don't you think you'd be interested in this?"

"I didn't see it," Samantha replied.

The family of four entered the crammed store. There was a plethora of illustrations and photos. The box camera of that era would take only one black-and-white photo at a time. The pictures were small, typically six by four inches. Now, however, the photos could be carefully scanned, digitized, and colorized—then downloaded for purchase.

Samantha looked with interest. Some illustrations and photos she had seen on the Internet. But many she had not seen before. None, however, were worth the price the store was asking for a piece of history.

The family browsed and the store owner watched. Samantha said to the owner, "I'm a history professor and find many photos here I haven't seen on the Internet."

The store owner said, "Most of these images are from estate sales. People build a collection, then pass away, and the families want to sell the collection for the money, not knowing the importance or value. I've bought images never seen before, even some from foreign countries."

Samantha realized the owner was passionate about his business and relished speaking with someone in person.

He wanted to chat. "I do have a website and get a lot of traffic and orders, but this store surprisingly gets people wandering in and often buying something. I need a location, and the rent is cheap on this side street. Now with NFTs, business has picked up."

"NFTs?" Samantha asked.

"It's a non-fungible token. Many of these illustrations and

photos can be sold as an NFT, which means the buyer has a one-and-only authenticated image."

The family was ready to leave the store when Jill said, "Mommy, this looks like you wearing that long pretty dress. And the pretty angel halo."

Samantha walked to where Jill was standing and viewed the photo—of Samantha wearing her Victorian dress, the double-braided hair crown with the braided halo hat. The time-travel gods had aged her a quarter century when the shot was taken. Jill didn't recognize the man in the photo wearing a top hat and holding Samantha's hand before he kissed it.

That day in London, after the short rain shower, Samantha had noticed a photographer with a box camera. Unbeknownst to her, he had snapped a shot of the special moment. Samantha and Grant had earlier shared their fondness for each other.

The caption of the photo read "London, June 1877. General Grant greets an admirer during the first leg of his world tour."

Samantha was stunned and excited. Aaron was perplexed. "This is eerie. There's a strong resemblance, the dress, the hair, although she looks older than you. If this weren't an 1877 photo, I'd say that was you."

Only before they were married when she was time traveling had Samantha lied to Aaron. Now she had this perfect life and didn't want to spoil it with an out-of-this-world discovery.

Not wanting the store owner to hear, Samantha whispered, "I have seen this picture before." It was a lie.

"I loved the dress and the fabric. So I made a sketch of the dress and gave it to Mary Sanchez, the dressmaker. She had this fabulous fabric, which was similar. Then I copied the hairstyle and the braided halo hat."

Aaron nodded his head, convinced by Samantha's explanation. She was relieved and didn't want to lie ever again to him.

She wanted the photo. "Aaron, remember the time when you wanted to expand your coin collection?"

"I do remember, and I know what you're going to say. You want me to agree to this purchase because you agreed to mine. Do you want to make the photo your display background on your computer?"

"Maybe if it's not too grainy. But I want it. Please, Aaron. I'm so happy to find this photo—again." All was true except the last word.

The price was more than Samantha would ever pay for something she wanted. This was, however, a one-off and worth it.

She said, "And my little lady, Jill, found it. You made me so happy." Jill smiled.

Aaron said, "You finish here. I'll take the kids up the street. I saw a park with benches. We'll be there."

"Thanks, sweetie."

Aaron and the kids left the cramped store.

Samantha asked the owner, "Aren't old images in the public domain no longer protected under copyright?"

"You're asking why some of these images are so expensive when you can download them for free on the Internet?"

"I've never done this before, and I want to know the process."

"Images dated prior to 1923 are in the public domain. We have some here, but we sell high-resolution images. Colorized versions of former black-and-white photos. So the quality of our photos is significantly better than downloaded photos from the Internet."

While pointing to the photo of Grant and Samantha in London, the owner said, "This photo is more complicated. There is no doubt it was created before 1923, but it has not been published. This was in an attic trunk somewhere in London. I bought this a few weeks ago. So because the photo was not published before 1923, the copyright hasn't run out. Which is good for you as the buyer. You will not only own the photo but the copyright, which is good for at least seventy years. I have the copyright law on my website if you care to review it."

This was too complicated for Samantha to understand on the first pass. She was also focusing on the news the photo had lain in a trunk.

Good, she thought. Aaron didn't hear this, because Samantha's explanation was that she had previously seen the photo and copied the woman's look.

Moreover, what would Philip say about this photo? His typical refrain was that Samantha's memory recalled something she had previously done or seen, and she was constructing a dream based upon it. But this image was newly discovered. So this was evidence—in favor of Samantha's belief she time traveled.

Samantha was still absorbing this happy treasure as the owner explained, "Good that this photo was in this sealed trunk; this original is in fairly good condition considering its age. So what you're getting for this price, along with the copyright, is the original image in this vacuum-sealed case, the high-resolution black-and-white digital image, the colorized digital image, and the NFT, the digital authentication. So you'll have everything, and no one else will."

She handed him her credit card. After walking out of the store, Samantha didn't have time to reflect more on the photo.

THE NEXT MORNING the Parker family flew back home. On the flight, Alex sat in the window seat, Jill in the middle, Samantha in the aisle seat, and Aaron in the aisle seat across from Samantha. The kids were watching a movie, and Aaron was sleeping.

Now, at thirty thousand feet, Samantha contemplated the discovery of the photo: We wanted to take the kids on our ten-year wedding anniversary trip. Aaron noticed the store, I didn't. Jill found the photo. And the only reason she recognized the dress is that she spilled cranberry juice on my outfit, and I changed into the dress for a Civil War lecture that day. A confluence of events, all aligning to this happy discovery.

And Philip died the morning of my discovery of this photo. Coincidence? Is he now in some afterlife dimension enjoying full knowledge? What would he say?

It was as if she could hear his voice "Do not to try to understand the ways of the universe."

Samantha rested her head back and stared into space. She smirked and then thought:

> *There was a woman in her prime,*
> *Who could impress all with a rhyme,*
> *She traveled to the past,*
> *Found the best proof at last,*
> *That she and Grant enjoyed Sam time.*

Dear Happy Reader

Now that you've finished *Sam Time*, I would like to hear from you. If you enjoyed the book, please leave a review. You can trust I will read your comments. I am grateful and thank you for taking the time to share your thoughts. Also, other happy readers will be pleased if you click the "Helpful" button on their upbeat reviews.

Best regards,
Donna Balon
Author, *Sam Time*

About the Author

Sam Time is the debut novel for the author Donna Balon. Raised in New Jersey, she graduated from Rutgers University. She practiced as a certified public accountant and tax attorney before retiring. Donna resides in Las Vegas, Nevada, with her husband.

Acknowledgments

After researching over two dozen books in crafting this story, I sought the expert consultation of Victorian customs from Sarah A. Chrisman and her husband, Gabriel Chrisman. Sarah is the author of *Victorian Secrets* and *This Victorian Life* (Skyhorse Publishing) and the book series *The Tales of Chetzemoka*. I am grateful to Sarah and Gabriel for the specificity of period-piece advice and their sharp editorial suggestions.

A team of skilled professionals collaborated in producing this book. As the assessment editor, Laurie Chittenden counseled me on driving the narrative and bridging transitions between the present and past chapters for a more engaging read. Copyeditor Jennie Cohen expertly combed through this manuscript. Sara Walker masterly proofread producing this clean copy. The talented Laura Duffy designed an enticing, nothing-like-it book cover. I am delighted this experienced group joined in this project.

My good fortune is having smart people contributing their time to my endeavor. Abby Smith, author of *Pettikin*, provided critical insights; I rewrote chapters based on her comments. My husband, Gregg Evans, reviewed the first drafts and tolerated months of updates on the book, the book.

Made in United States
Orlando, FL
18 February 2025